FIRST FICTIONS

Christine Harwll

Oct '92

FIRST FICTIONS

Introduction 11

faber and faber

LONDON · BOSTON

First published in 1992
by Faber and Faber Limited
3 Queen Square London WC1N 3AU

Phototypeset by Wilmaset Ltd, Wirral
Printed in England by
Clays Ltd, St Ives plc

'Flashing Tin Foil' by Sophie Frank first published by
Overland Extra, University of Melbourne, Australia, December 1989
Extract on p. 108 from 'Cascando' by Samuel Beckett from *Collected Poems
1930–1989* published by Calder Publications Ltd, London.
Copyright © Samuel Beckett 1936, 1984, 1986. Reproduced
by permission of The Beckett Estate and Calder Publications
Limited, London
'A Modest Apocalypse' by Anthony McCarten first published in
Vital Writing, Godwit Press Limited, Auckland, New Zealand,
1991. All three stories by Anthony McCarten also appear in
the collection *A Modest Apocalypse*, Godwit Press Limited, Auckland,
New Zealand, 1991
'In Milwaukee' by Denise Neuhaus first published by *Stand* magazine,
Autumn 1990

A CIP record for this book is
available from the British Library

ISBN 0–571–16704–7

CONTENTS

v

CONTENTS

Publisher's Note

In this collection, the eleventh to appear in the prose *Introduction* series, it is our aim once again to bring new writers to the attention of a wider reading public. None of the contributors has had their fiction published in book form in the UK before. As always, the number of writers is restricted, to give each the advantage of presenting a substantial amount of work.

The *Introduction* series has seen the first publication of several successful authors. They include Ted Hughes, Julian Mitchell, Tom Stoppard, Christopher Hampton, Kazuo Ishiguro, Anne Devlin, Deirdre Madden and Hugo Hamilton.

Biographical Notes

————

Rukun Advani was born in 1955 in Lucknow, India. He was educated at St Stephen's College, Delhi. His Cambridge PhD appeared as a book, *E. M. Forster as Critic*, in 1985. He works in the editorial department of Oxford University Press, New Delhi.

Lynne Bryan was born in England in 1961. She moved to Glasgow four years ago, after completing the MA in Creative Writing at the University of East Anglia. She works for a women's support project, and is a member of a co-operative hoping to launch a new feminist magazine for Scottish women in 1992. She writes in her spare time, and is working on a collection of short stories.

Sophie Frank was born in Manchester in 1961. Her first story 'Birth', was published in Heinemann's Best Short Story Collection 1988. Since then her work has appeared in the British journals *Ambit* and *The Fred*, and in the Australian *Overland* and *Scarp*. Over the last ten years she has lived in both Sydney and London.

Kirsty Gunn was born in New Zealand and educated at Victoria University and Oxford. She has had a number of jobs including coat check in Manhattan and reporting on weddings for *Brides* magazine. She now writes leaflets for Pedigree Chum Tender Bites and Select Cats, and lives in London.

Jonathan Holland was born in Macclesfield, Cheshire, in 1961 and educated at the Universities of London and East Anglia. From 1985–9 he taught in the south of Italy. He now lives in Madrid.

Philip MacCann was born in 1966. A graduate of Trinity College, he lives and works in Dublin.

Anthony McCarten was born in New Plymouth, New Zealand, in 1961. After leaving school, he worked as a journalist for two years before enrolling for a BA degree at Victoria University Wellington. He now lives in Wellington and works as a full-time writer. He has written seven plays, including *Ladies' Night* (with Stephen Sinclair), which has been translated into six languages and toured internationally, and *Via Satellite*. *A Modest Apocalypse*, his first volume of fiction, was shortlisted in the 1990 Heinemann Reed Fiction Award, judged by Angela Carter.

Denise Neuhaus was born near Woodbridge in Suffolk and raised in Houston, Texas. She received an MA in Creative Writing from the University of East Anglia in 1989. She has lived in London for the past seven years.

RUKUN ADVANI

———

The Othello Complex

---

for Kéya

It is a truth fortunately rare that a woman in possession of just one husband should produce two unlike sons, one resembling a Greek god and the other a skunk.

It is a tragedy unforgivably singular if you, looking in daily disgust at the mirror on the wall and framing the same nauseating question, are repeatedly informed that your brother looks considerably more desirable than you.

My brother looked even better than Apollo, who we'd seen in our *Illustrated Myths*. For one thing, my brother's eyebrows were nothing like the sun god's. They were a lot heavier, a lot more desirable. You wouldn't have thought it then, when we listened to the sound of a piano by our river which filtered its slow way through the shadows of fading palaces, that my brother's eyebrows would grow to constitute his centre of attraction. But they did. As he grew to manhood I saw them fiercely shade his eyes, giving him that devastating Spartan look. Later, it made the women come in droves to nuzzle up. I closed my eyes and saw them all move their lips, one by one, along the lines of my brother's eyebrows. It was disgusting.

I looked vainly in the mirror for my own resemblance to Apollo, for the women who would come in quietly like ballerinas on tiptoe from the distance behind to soothe my brows. But I seemed specially chosen to resemble one of the higher rodents. On my better days I could have passed off as a rat; when times were hard I barely made it to a racoon.

On one occasion I nearly convinced myself it wasn't true, that only thinking made it so bad. That was when I grew my hair, eked out a stubble, put a Swedish headband round my forehead, clutched a tennis racket and looked in the mirror for Bjorn Borg. He was there. I rushed away to share this triumph with anyone dear who might be near, but only caught my mother at a bad moment. She was weeping silently over half-cut onions on a chopping board. When she saw Bjorn Borg approach she wiped her eyes, a bit carelessly I thought, to check she wasn't halluci-nating. This only seemed to make her more lachrymose and considerably dimmed her view of things. She was looking sneezy and reddish, going on purple, and the movement of my neurons told me the colour purple signified maternal instability. Discretion suggested I either take up the onions on her behalf or escape *molto pronto*; instinct directed me, with customary wisdom, straight to the door. At least, I thought, my physiology was finely tuned and functional.

My failure to look good drove me to a daily bath, so I'd at least smell good. It helped for a few days, till the dog, who I loathed, came up sniffing and gave me a friendly lick. That drove me to poetry. Our mother, who was well-read and sensed the con-tortions in my psyche, said I was old enough to have a go at Philip Larkin, but the understated global despair which bathed all his nail-on-the-head observations only reminded me of the wonkiness in my own *Weltanschauung* and made my misery deepen like a coastal shelf; I got out of him as early as I could. In the end, a last, careful, forlorn look in the mirror matured me to a sardonic reconciliation. I wasn't Bjorn Borg, nor Clint Eastwood, not even Charles Bronson. My closest famous lookalike was E. M. Forster. There was no more to be said. I had no option except to cultivate the ironic mode and keep the sublimity that swelled up down to a minor key. My self-image was right.

I shrugged what little there was of my shoulders, grimaced in the way that Bjorn Eastwood might after losing a Wimbledon final played out in the Wild West, and retired, like my tennis hero, into a helpless watchfulness. The women would lie in my brother's world; mine lay only inside my head and got mixed up with all sorts of stray images and tunes, the odds and ends that shored me against my racoonic ruin. I resolved upon acquiring the epistemology of a skunk by nosing my way through the world, supplementing this with the ontology of a dachshund by scurrying here and there after my brother. I gave up looking at my brother and myself, and, after an epic inner struggle which got me confused about which bit of me came out victorious, I stopped stroking my eyebrows to thicken their appeal. There were better things to massage in my imagination.

In one of the two houses next door, by the banks of our river, a young Austrian woman, golf-widowed, attempted the 'Apassionata' on an ill-tempered clavier. Her keyboard was an antediluvian Steinway which had soaked in a large portion of the Ganges coming upstream from Calcutta to our city. It sounded bass during the monsoons and treble in the dry season. She, nostalgic for a world that lay beyond ours, played it every evening all year round, sometimes in concert with the pianists on her long-playing records. At first the melodies seemed alien to us. Then we got used to them and they filtered their way into our circulation, making us whistle in instinctive accompaniment to all her favourite pieces.

She was called Felicia Blumenthal: I should say 'spelt' rather than 'called' because she wrote her name so littered with diacritical marks it required a pronunciation table alongside to make her out. Her speech was similarly accented. She was emphatic about her foreignness, her difference and distance from things Indian. Not that she needed to stress her outlandishness. Her music, the pallor of her skin, and the pastel loveliness of her home amid the garish constructions and the mud huts of our city – all these made her uniqueness palpitatingly clear to my brother and myself.

The simple obsession of our lives in those days was to get as voyeuristically close as possible to Felicia. Most evenings we managed to watch her unobserved from the shores of the river, where we'd stroll down to feast our eyes on the coolness of the water and the heat halo that radiated out of her bosom and legs. Her Mikimoto pearls swung gently over ebony as she hunched spectacularly over that temperamental Steinway. Her playing soothed our innards, like the mellow movement of yoghurt down the oesophagus; it temporarily enriched our lust with a supplementary feeling which my brother said must be Romantic Love.

Ludwig van Beethoven frowned down at Felicia from where she'd hung him up above her instrument, his chest riddled with the notes of the 'Waldstein' sonata. She liked to infect the unwary with her worship of him, and once showed us nineteen versions of the 'Emperor' concerto out of her large record collection. She knew we liked her tunes and played that particular concerto for us several times. I found the music suited my biorhythms. It began with a very passionate bang which got me all a-tingle, then it interspersed lots of other impassioned bangs with soothing and fluid melodies. The records had seductively beautiful covers which made me want to look at them, hold them. They went with how I felt about Felicia. I smiled sheepishly in uncomprehending sympathy when she said, once, that her own genealogy only stretched back to Liszt who, she said, gave her great-grandmother music lessons in return for her body. But that wondrous mix of aural and physiological contact seemed only to have been transmitted down the ages as a genetic code which ended up with Felicia like the Lady of Shallott, forlorn and palely tinkling.

We were in our early teens then, and Felicia Blumenthal's fingers seemed to strum at the chords that lay deep within us. Our bodies were on the rise and she, with her impressive and alien pallor, her collection of Emperors and her elegantly stroking fingers, was all we desired. She belonged to a world of music and softness that we craved, mostly because we wanted her so much, but partly I reckoned because she aroused, even within the consuming hardness of our adolescence, a sublimer softness which we inherited from our mother. Music and desire together thickened our blood.

Felicia was married to a Dravidian golfball. He was globular, dark and uniformly pock-marked, and, like all male South

Indians, he went by the generic name of Subbu. My brother said he had been a Siberian crane in his previous life, he was so seldom seen. We decided he slept with his putter on a green and expended his nocturnal desires upon the eighteenth hole, looking at pictures of Arnold Palmer and Jack Nicklaus. He was affable enough on the rare occasions we met him, but most days we only woke to the sound of his car disappearing towards the golf-course. We couldn't fathom his devotion to golf with Venus herself consenting to share his abode, though his lack of interest in her was some consolation against our own distance from her body. We asked our mother about their marriage.

'Felicia suffers from the Othello complex,' said Amma, adding reflectively, 'He loved her for the music that she played, and she loved him that he did listen.' My mother was always adapting Shakespeare to suit her own needs. She had Europe in her bones.

We had to concede the golfball some credit for having discovered that the way to Felicia's heart was up her fingers, but it cheered me when our mother reminded us that Othello came to a grisly end. It got me anticipating the time when Subbu would be brained by a flying Aryan golfball, leaving the coast clear for me to marry Felicia and live happily ever after. But there was a huge spoke in my wheel. He lived next door too.

He was called Laurence Corbett and he had no diacritics to his credit. Corbett lived on the other side from Felicia. Like her, he was in his late twenties, but unlike her handicapped husband he was tall, dark and passing handsome. Every time I saw him the same unfailing Americanism came to mind: 'Drat.' Of course I never spoke it out. Amma had a Beethoven frown reserved for everything American except Marlon Brando.

Corbett was about the last Anglo-Indian in India, the others all having become brown with us natives or having escaped, after powdering themselves white, to their utopias in Australia and Canada. We asked our mother how he got so singularly left behind and she said the visa queues to the white world didn't move for dark people.

'There's no need to feel sorry for him though,' she said. 'He's inherited the Corbett money.'

We didn't feel in the least bit sorry for Laurence. He was merely a male and so would normally have been of no more consequence to us than an insect, except for several things – his disgustingly muscular and dusky physiognomy, his potential as a thorn on account of Felicia's Othello complex, his presence as our hated sports teacher in school, and his descent from the writer we most admired, Jim Corbett.

That name, Corbett, had about the same currency in our world as Gandhi and Nehru. At the time that Gandhi and Nehru were shooing out the colonials, Jim Corbett was shooting his way through the country's tiger population, claiming the beasts were all man-eaters. He was Anglo-Indian and had retired from the railways, following up his shunting and hooting years with years of hunting and shooting. It's a fair bet he went about giving the tigers a bad name so he could kill them all for fun, but whatever the truth, he wrote up very many hair-raising man-eater stories that got gobbled up by the million and made him a man of much property. His sole surviving descendant, our neighbour, inherited his ancestor's mantle and his arsenal, in addition to that considerable and undeserved fortune. But he wasn't content to rest, as any sane man would, on his ancestor's laurels. He harried unwilling schoolchildren like us into boxing-rings and made extra money over school holidays by taking foreign tourists on shooting expeditions, using his filthy lucre to beget more filthy lucre. His ambition, by rumour, was to bag a tiger of his own.

Laurence Corbett belonged to the world of hardness we feared and hated. He plagued our blissfully inert lives with compulsory physical activity and dampened our emotional aspirations with the dark and indubitable fact that he existed. I feared and hated him a lot more fiercely than my brother, but I always smiled unctuously at him out of congenital cowardice. Being petrified of even the most minor forms of physical injury, I had no desire to displease Laurence lest he do me bodily harm.

The activity of my imagination assuaged the frequent dullness of my days. I used the weapons of the weak against Corbett and got even with him in my mind. My favourite nocturnal fantasy which didn't feature Felicia was the one in which I commanded Laurence to accompany me as my coolie on a tiger-shoot. I sauntered calmly ahead, he followed gasping, too terrified of me to curse the overload on his head and shoulders. As Amma once said in a more sympathetic context, in India the white man's burden had to be borne by the Anglo-Indian.

When we reached the forests where Hunter dispatches Fearful Symmetry back to the blacksmith who forged him for the pleasure of the hunt, I discovered I'd forgotten to bring the goat which would serve as bait to lure in our man-eating tiger. I blamed this on Laurence, of course, cursing his stupidity and giving him a few kicks for good measure, making him cower where all self-respecting coolies cower: in the background. Naturally the hunt, being an activity divinely ordained, could not be abandoned for mere lack of a goat: the Anglo-Indian would have to serve instead. As my mother might have said, adapting some irrelevant poet or other to present exigency, they also serve who only lie as bait.

I trussed up the last surviving descendant of Jim Corbett like a spring chicken, then scattered a whole lot of spring onions all over him to make it a salad day for the incoming tiger.

'This way the tiger will know he has to spring on you, Laurence,' I said with a wicked chuckle, carefully inserting a couple of spring onions into his nostrils.

Laurence did not seem in the least bit amused. He snorted, dislodging one of my spring onions. It emerged with a bit of goo, so I had to replace it rather gingerly, without soiling my fingers. His initial grovelling had degenerated into a most unaesthetic variety of abuse in Hindi, which unnecessarily brought my mother and non-existent sister into the picture – the dominance of the mother figure in our country is prone to make the Indian male Oedipally complexed, as seemed manifest from Laurence's very un-Anglo-Indian vocabularly. To quieten him down, I was forced to place my last spring onion within his mouth, so that he might lie in wait for the tiger feeling bitterly supine.

I myself shinnied up, much like Tarzan, to the extemporé tree-house I had so skilfully constructed, following Laurence's forefather, who had the good sense to shoot all his tigers sitting safely cocooned in a *machaan*, several feet beyond the mightiest leap ever recorded for a tiger. I fell asleep in that dark and womb-like enclosure: it made me feel handsome and secure, and safe from the travails to which sensitive people like us are so subject in this mighty universe of ours. I woke briefly to the sound of a man-eater scrunching his way through spring onion and bone. I snuggled deeper into my pillow, smiling with cathartic satisfaction at the poetic justice, late achieved, of feeding the last Corbett to a man-eater.

The trouble was really that, as Hamlet said to Horatius while defending the bridge, there were more things between heaven and earth than could be made to perish by one's philosophy, the chiefest among these being El Corbett. Laurence Corbett's existence was as inescapable and real as my resemblance to Clint Eastwood was not, and his proximity made me quiver with a feeling of profound physical vulnerability. So did Felicia. The difference was that Laurence Corbett was all I did not desire.

One day Felicia came by to borrow some tomatoes and was speaking to our mother in that voice straight out of Lauren Bacall's stomach. We hung about to sneak in some soulful looks at her legs, and at whatever else might become visible if by some miracle she had to bend. Our tactility was very alight, making us all soft and speechless. Our mother made up for us. She had once sung in the Amen Chorus of Handel's *Messiah* and studied English Literature, so Felicia considered her a soul-mate in the great heart of darkness which was our city, and bared her life in the spasms of neighbourliness that are aroused when you come to borrow tomatoes.

They were chattering happily when our pet lapdog nosed his way into the kitchen and gave Felicia's leg a lick, making her bend to pick him up and pat him fondly. Every dog has his day, said our fluttering hearts, after the paroxysms ceased.

Felicia's affection for dogs gave me an idea.

'Why don't we take the dog to her place sometime?' I suggested to my brother. 'She'll want to stroke him.'

'What's the good of that?' asked my brother. 'He'll have all the fun and won't know it. How 'bout getting her to stroke *us* instead?'

'That's the general idea ya,' I said. 'You wait and see.'

My brother shrugged his muscular shoulders. I twitched mine in painful imitation. But for a change I was going to hold the leash.

All pet dogs in India in those days were called either Tiger or Caesar, regardless of sex. Their function in life was sensibly dogly – to guard houses night and day, preferably on no food at all, so that their bark and bite might achieve an equal ferocity. Our dog was different. He was a runt of a Pekinese with little bark and no bite who'd been spoilt by affection. Our mother fed him a *haute cuisine* which weighed twice as many milligrams as he did, and, on account of her perverse immersion in things theatrical, she named him after a villain in Shakespeare. My passionate feelings of sibling rivalry, laid latent against my brother after much inner strife, got directed against Iago every time my mother fed him a cheese soufflé or a chocolate mousse. There, into that overgrown earthworm, I thought, goes my food again and again. It was revolting.

I tried to think up a plan that would kill two birds with one stone, getting a feel of Felicia and getting cathartically even with the dog. My brother, all benign and rippling, was sceptical and content to do the watching.

So, the next evening, hearing Amma safely crooning her base version of Schubert's 'Ave Maria' under the shower, I borrowed a bone from the fridge and went off to lie in wait by the river. For a change I wasn't idly hoping Iago would drown: suddenly even he had a use. I tantalized him with the bone till he was in a state of high frenzy, then soothed him into thinking he was about to get the bone, then tantalized him again into a slavering hysteria for the meat. This sort of torture requires much intellectual precision. You have to know exactly how far you can play Tantalus-cum-Torquemada without letting the dog get depressed into losing faith in his own ability *vis-à-vis* the bone. You can more or less gauge a dog's IQ by how long he takes to lose interest in a hunk of meat cooingly offered and then systematically denied. Paradoxically, the stupider the dog the longer he exercises himself in the manner of female Romanian gymnasts on a balancing beam, jumping endlessly towards the impossible. I was the world expert on this variety of Pavlovian torture and could keep Iago going like a yo-yo almost endlessly: you could see that from the expression of disgust on my brother's face and the snarl on the dog's.

All this stopped when I heard Felicia cease hammering her clavier: her post-hammerclavier period was always a gentle stroll in the garden, which sloped down to the river.

I gave Iago one last sniff at the bone and threw it carefully in the direction Felicia was likely to take. Iago rushed off after the bone; I rushed off after Iago with feigned fury, as though trying strenuously to prevent him violating the boundaries of her house, all the while composing my features to give out a red-skinned mixture of apology, outrage and helplessness in the face of canine lunacy.

Sure enough, Felicia was astroll in a gratifyingly mini sort of outfit which gave away her legs and some other good bits above the belt. Iago appeared with his bone safely in his mouth. I envied him his meat.

'Terribly sorry Felicia,' I said, 'the dog seems to have spotted something in your garden and got away before I could stop him.'

I grinned cravenly by way of a neighbourly apology, picking up Iago with a rough sort of lunge to indicate masterly annoyance.

'Oh,' said Felicia, 'I thought you were making him chase his bones towards my garden.'

Her Austrian pedigree gave an interesting turn to her English syntax, and another sort to my stomach. I was wondering how to frame a reply that would create subtle confusion, enabling a change of topic, but to my relief Felicia wasn't being at all accusatory. She smiled benignly and I smiled back nervously, petting and smacking Iago to indicate a transition to fond annoyance, getting in a couple of hasty looks at her cleavage in the process. Sufficient unto the day was the joy thereof. It was a lot better than my brother'd ever managed.

I was emboldened. She was so near, and yet, as my mother would have said, a man's reach exceeds his grasp – which inane bit of poetic sagacity would have meant just the same to me if it had been framed the other way round.

'Nice evening though', I said, venturing a *non sequitur* that might give me another few seconds of stolen glimpse.

'Oh yes,' she said, 'November is my most favourite season.'

'So's mine,' I said. 'November is definitely my most favourite season too.'

'You see,' I added, blundering on joyously and with light-headed anarchism, 'I was born in November, and ever since then it has been my most favourite season.'

'Ah,' said Felicia, looking a bit mystified.

I knew there was something wrong in what I'd said the moment after I'd said it, as frequently happens when Man is confronted with Woman, but the blunder wasn't of the insuperable sort. In fact, I thought, a little confusion was just right. It allowed me to hang on a further few seconds, and, if I didn't overstep my tongue, it might even miraculously lead on to the bower of wedded bliss. I was already seeing this as our First Real Meeting.

'December's not bad either,' I said, 'though it's a bit cold for us.'

'Hm.'

'You see,' I said more confidentially, 'as Indians we aren't really used to the cold. But you as an Austrian must be used to the cold.'

'Hm.'

Two 'hms' are just about companionable; a third might have made me feel crowded out.

'It must be quite cold in Austria,' I added quickly, frantically searching my surcharged cells for further information on Austria. They sent me back the Blue Danube.

'The Danube,' I said with a slow reflectiveness which I hoped she'd recognize as profundity, 'must certainly turn blue with the cold.'

She laughed most prettily at that, making me feel uneasily triumphant at having parried away another 'hm', and at getting time to switch off the weather. My neurons had just about compiled a hasty list of composers for me to start blabbing about, beginning with Allegri and ending in Weber, when she began slowly strolling, as if to say she'd see me down to the river. I followed a step behind, in the manner of a dutiful Hindu wife, though for better reason – it gave a good view from the rear.

'Oh,' she said, after two steps (which let me see both her two legs), 'I forgot to take off this necklace. I wear it for my piano-playing only.' She raised her arms to undo her pearls and got me nearly into a swoon at the sight of her armpits. In my delirious haze I saw a lucky Jesus swinging dangerously down her neck at the bottom of a slim golden chain.

'Oh,' she said again, 'the clasp of this stupid necklace has got stuck.'

I swallowed hard as a preliminary to digesting this gift from God.

Now, I ask you, lives there a man, *any* man, who calls himself man, who has not dreamed this most innermost of all dreams, where his Immortal Beloved comes into the garden, strolls awhile apace with him, stops with a feminine start, says she must unclasp herself, fails prettily after exposing armpits, and, after a final and most becoming hesitation, asks him to undo her, with a blush?

I don't remember how I unclasped that clasp, my fingers were trembling so bad, but I remember it involved, first, dropping Iago with a thud, second, touching Felicia's neck for at least two seconds, and third, hearing something that sounded like an epileptic fit from the direction where I reckoned my brother was stationed.

'Thank you,' she said, laughing most becomingly, just like the One in my dreams. My index, middle and ring fingers got a one-point-five-second touch as I handed over the goods. Felicia dripped the necklace into a mini-pocket.

'Iago likes November too,' I said, trying a new line to stave off the Death of Parting. 'He hates the summer and the monsoon because of the ticks. I'm sure he'd be happy in your country. There couldn't be too many ticks there, are there?'

She laughed and looked at the dog, but didn't bend to pet him. I wasn't desperately disappointed. After the unclasping, my feelings had been transformed from lust to love, and once the soul comes into the picture, one does not mind quite as much if the object of one's desire fails to reveal herself instantly and continuously.

This was the right time for the master plan. I picked up Iago with a nonchalant sort of swoop, scratching around his ticks to keep him soothed and unstruggling.

'He's quite a friendly dog really and doesn't mind being petted by anyone,' I said, letting out the hint.

'Not like other dogs,' I said, by way of reinforcing the suggestion.

'Oh yes,' she said, looking affectionately at the villain. That was good enough to bring the second stage into play.

I moved my left hand towards Iago's throat and let my right take his hindermost, stroking him kindly with the fingers of both and throttling him now and then, until he dropped the bone from his mouth in disgust. I smiled and smiled to offset Iago's expression, remembering with some discomfort the bardic view that one may smile and smile and be a very villain.

'Here Felicia, you can stroke him a bit if you like,' I said.

That sentence was constructed along a careful syntax. It had to sound, for authenticity, as though I was doing her the favour, that she couldn't stroke my dog as long as she liked, but only as long as I was pleased to let her. By this time my facial muscles, all eager to please, were working overtime towards that primal, dedicated stare by which the natural hero deposits his soul into the beloved; regrettably the outcome, on that occasion, was something akin to a hideous grin, because Felicia merely smiled palely and stroked the dog under his chin.

This was a momentary blow, but unmomentous for one who knew not vanquishment or defeat. I edged my left hand imperceptibly forward and stroked Iago too, pretending to keep my fingers carefully distant from her area of the dog but actually letting them stray cautiously into her territory. It worked pretty well and our fingers touched casually several times, slightly diluting my love back towards lust, but without seriously impairing either emotion.

It was going well for me thus, and who knows how many more seconds it might thus have gone on going well for me, had there not been a loud 'Hullo' heard from the other side, where Laurence Corbett lived. That was probably the first time in my life I actually uttered the word 'drat': Laurence Corbett had clambered over the low wall and was sauntering over towards the Happy Couple and Dog, not so much with neighbourly bonhomie and good will as with an aura of masculine assurance, the way I knew Man must walk when approaching Woman.

The absolute philosophical disjunction between my dream world, where Corbett had been consumed by a man-eater, and reality, where he approached with fearful symmetry to eat into my own flesh and blood, felt like a hit below the belt. To my depair, Felicia looked all aflutter and reciprocal. She stopped fondling Iago and forgot about me. Her skin took on a different glow. She undripped the pearls from her pocket and, with the skill of practised fingers, hooked them gracefully round her neck again, suppressing Jesus once more.

That simple gesture made me feel as inconsequential as an insect. It made me want to go rushing back to my mother, to my brother, to a hole in the ground where I might crawl in and die. It spoke out a whole world of feeling, undoing all the constructions of my mind, all the tremble that my fingers had felt, all the love and lust I ever felt for anything. The music and desire that mingled in my own being for her were now reflected outwards from her body, at the intruder who strode so casually and confidently towards the regions of my happiness. In all the years that I had lived, in all the time I had spent cultivating the ironic mode to keep my features safely distant from my emotional life, I had never before felt so completely helpless.

Felicia's eyes gleamed a welcome to Corbett and I knew, looking at the exalted sort of radiance she gave out, what my mother meant when she said that Felicia suffered from the Othello complex. It was one of life's great mysteries to me that she, who belonged to the world of softness and music and could distinguish between nineteen versions of the 'Emperor' concerto, could suffer so badly from a biological pull which allowed Laurence Corbett into her world with such carefree and naked ease, so completely without strategy and master plan. It was the first time Reality kicked me as hard as that, making me understand the value of a life free of vulnerability and dreams.

I dropped Iago with a thud. He hadn't a chance in life. Nor, I thought, had Subbu; it made me less sceptical about his fondness for living out his life in bunkers. Watching Corbett and Felicia that day, and sensing the clicking of chemistry between brown muscle and white skin, my premonition was that the future lay in wait only for my brother.

Corbett and Felicia had reached the low boundary which scarcely separated them from each other. My house lay in the opposite direction. I walked towards it and away from Felicia, towards my brother and my world, where affection and the cultivation of an ironic selfhood shored me against my romantic, racoonic ruin.

It was, on the surface, a peaceful and undramatic evening, with a gentle breeze ruffling the water, when my brother sat by our river as it filtered a slow path through the shadows of fading palaces, watching in suppressed silence as I tried out my hand in a world that lay so near and yet so remote from our own.

As for me, I had come as close as I ever would to immortal bliss. It was time for me to get back to being my brother's keeper.

The Secret Life of Mikhail Gorbachov

_____

for S.K. and M.M.

When my brother, who looked like Zeus, had his third emotional crisis, I saw the pattern in his life and rang up Gorbachov. Raisa picked up and said Gorby was on the pot, struggling with a recalcitrant flush-chain. They don't make them like they used to any more, she said. It's all rusted up and clogged and nothing's going out.

Oh, I said, thinking of my brother.

I've phoned Chancellor Kohl, she said. He's sending a plumber and a single-lever mixer. Isn't it exciting?

Yes, I said. Very.

My mind was on my brother. He had thick eyebrows and a handsome, hooded look. Once, when we were growing up together on the vulnerable Achilles, he told me, looking at a map in our Homer, that Sparta was located in a province called Laconia. Those names and the words that sprang out of them stuck in my mind, and an image of my brother, Spartan and silent, took root inside me, being modified only a little as the years passed.

How're you, Doc? Is it urgent? Raisa asked, returning to me. Shall I call Gorby out?

I debated for five seconds and thought I'd try pulling the flush on my brother by myself. He needed badly to be dowsed in water to clear his head and feel undrowned by his third emotional crisis.

No it's OK, I said to Raisa. I'll call again if I need old Gorby's powerful mind.

Raisa laughed affectionately. Yes, she said. It was OK while he

19

was into crumbling walls but he better get our flush in order or I'll crumble him.

She sounded affectionate, and was, but I couldn't get away from feeling the low current of power and threat that often flowed just beneath so many of the things she said. I recalled the Raisa and Gorby I had known in New Delhi all those years ago, within the walls of the Lodi Gardens, by the flower-beds where they first met each other, and saw it was still the same between them. She was never in awe of him, not when they began, not now after he'd been king of all Europe. That felt nice. It made me feel people didn't fundamentally change with power, that relationships might, occasionally and unaccountably, transcend politics, that at least Gorby and she had managed to keep his politics out of their personal lives. I wondered if her mind, like Gorby's or mine, forged mysterious links between the old and ruined walls in Delhi by which we once walked and which never sealed their dead kings against the common touch, with others more unyielding, in Berlin and China, that her husband had helped to crumble.

I thought then of my brother, who resembled Zeus, suffering his third emotional crisis, and the implications of the pattern in his life for all the people who cared for him.

Our first single-lever mixer, said Raisa.

She was often generous and concerned, but her own interests came first. An old feeling about her, a kind of emotional knowledge long lost, floated back inside me, reminding me that her personal excitements always swamped other considerations.

What? I asked, having briefly forgotten her single-lever mixer.

You better come over and see all the new stuff Gorby and I are getting in from Europe, Doc.

Yes, yes, I said. But I'm really ringing about my brother.

What? she asked, focusing on to me again. You mean Jehova? What's up Doc?

I knew Raisa would perk up and focus when I mentioned my brother. She lived a full life and was slow at focusing on things that didn't directly connect with her immediate needs. But affection lay dormant inside her. And besides, she was my brother's first emotional crisis and only collared Gorby on the rebound while he was licking her wounds. She always called my brother Jehova because he fitted better with her own image of outward sternness, which was only a veneer.

My brother only looked full of foreboding. It brought the women towards him in flocks. Inside he was silent and soft, and he suffered from short spells of intense sentimentality. Whenever he felt his life lacked grandeur, which was frequently, he worked himself up into a state of acute morbidness by reading *Hamlet*. That made him feel depressed and grand. He wallowed and revelled in tragedy. Outwardly he was always calm and taught history with the correct degree of passion, though he said his discipline was only a jumble of contending perspectives and had nothing to do with the truth. From our early years we'd both got accustomed to believing in fiction. Once, when someone asked my brother what he was made of, he said formally, as though he'd thought it through carefully, that his insides consisted entirely of milk, water and gelatine. If you move me, he said, the jelly quivers and makes me emotional.

The usual thing, I said to Raisa. Just another woman he's got hooked up with and doesn't know how to disconnect. He says it'll pass.

Oh hell, not again, said Raisa. How old is Jehova now? Stop pulling that blessed chain for a minute Gorbs, she yelled.

Even her brief distraction on the line gave me a little time to myself, and I felt distant from the telephone, from her voice, from the universe. I took myself off to a satellite in the sky that made slow, Sisyphian circles round the world. I was its lonely, spaced-out occupant. I wore a tracksuit and jogged in circles inside my satellite. I felt free of people. An amnesiac moon on its own circular trip showed me the Great Wall of China, reminding me of our vulnerable Achilles. But this wall stood firm. It didn't look vulnerable. It didn't look as though Gorby or anyone else was about to make it hit the sack.

Jehova? I asked Raisa feebly.

I felt and sounded absentminded on the phone line. There was an international resonance on account of my voice having to travel to Raisa by satellite. It delayed my voice and gave it an echo that made me feel hollow. In my mind I had moved on to Alexandria, where the early church fathers developed out of Jehova. An early father there, Origen, though inclined in his philosophy towards the sublime, castrated himself to staunch the flow of passion. I saw him climb a Platonic ladder to a *barsati** from where he saw the rainy Pleiades vex a dim sea, shining out without ambiguity in the night sky.

What's up with you and Jehova, Doc? I heard Raisa ask. You know I mean *my* Jehova, don't you? The first one in my bloodstream, Doc. First one in your bloodstream is the worst, she added with what I recalled as her rare, caring Russian laugh. Very difficult to get the first one out of your system, Doc. Maybe that's why our flush systems are all clogged, she added, chuckling impulsively with the thought.

I was getting impatient. The phone meter was drilling a hole through my pocket and she was still trying out tentative conversational profundities.

Is it bad again? she asked more urgently, perhaps sensing the impatience in my silence. My brother was the first one in her bloodstream and her residual feeling for him was a certain indication she still hadn't been able to flush him out of her system.

Well he's hitting his mid thirties, I said, and says it'll pass. But it doesn't look that great to me.

Oh hell, she said, confirming what I felt. Who's the girl? Never mind. Hey Gorbs, she yelled in Russian, and came back to me. I better tell Gorbs to meet Jehova soon, she said. He's great at pulling people out of these stupid messes. Hang on a minute. I'm sure he'll love going back to Delhi to see you both.

I hung on for a minute and visualized her going off to tell Gorby about my brother, her first lover, and thought of her days

* Hindi for 'rooftop flat'.

with my Greek-god brother, who she called Jehova, and of how he slowly fell out of love with her while she clung to him, a remote and adjudicating deity.

Mikhail Gorbachov chanced upon her in the Lodi Gardens one winter day. She was sitting under a tenebrous tree, smoking a Marlboro Mild. He was out for a walk with his two pet monkeys, Lenin and Trotsky, one on each shoulder. He'd trained them to put lice into his thinning hair. He would make them leave the lice to wander off and hide in his scalp, after which the monkeys would pick them out and eat them up, their hands moving from scalp to mouth with an urgent indifference. His strong sense of the bizarre made him irreverent and very good at rescuing lost souls. It seemed consistent with his own sense of the absurd that he, a man born never to rule, should have been driven by Raisa, once she'd collared him in the Lodi Gardens, to acquire in their later years an authority that he only wanted everyone to flout. By temperament he was a breaker of rules and she their maker.

He saw her in the shadow of the dead kings that lay in the Lodi Gardens and knew she was a lost soul, suffering cosmic gloom on a park bench. She told me later, sitting on my brother's lap in his Defence Colony *barsati*, that Gorby looked a three-headed Hanuman, appearing like that with Lenin and Trotsky. It was her farewell session with my brother: there was only affection between them once she knew she'd got Gorby on her leash. The monkey god saved her from Jehova and she carried him off to make him King of Russia. She was much more into power than he ever was, and she settled for what seemed a regal possibility when she found her deity, my brother, shaking free. I was glad for my brother, and he was too, for himself and for me. Raisa could be wrathful, like Kali. She mostly got what she wanted to get, and, after the initial surge of blinding emotion had passed, my brother was afraid she wanted him.

Of course all this was a long time ago in a garden where the dead were nicely hidden by domes and flowers, and to be fair to her she didn't know then that she and Gorby would become king and queen. I sensed her motivations, the subdued affection and the impulse, but can't say I really knew what stirred her jelly. Like everyone, she had a complicated inside. She genuinely cared for people she could mould. The small circle of dystopian aesthetes in which I moved with my brother was more sure about her than I was. They knew she had Europe in her bones, and that Gorby was doomed to get her all she wanted. After she stopped wanting my brother and had run through Gorby, she wanted Europe. There was no way, then, that he was going to carry on wandering the Delhi parks, with Lenin and Trotsky on his shoulders, for to get her Europe he had to get a move on in life and be King of Russia. His nomadic life was done when Raisa decided on him. Our small circle foresaw him being somewhat smothered by her, but we had Europe in our bones too and were not unsympathetic to Raisa. Something of her was in all of us. We lusted madly after Europe, where the streets were often free of people, sipping Old Monk in our *barsatis* at the margins of our city, falling in love now and again with each other and feeling depressed by the shortage of space around our lives.

That was many years ago, before things really began to crumble, inside people and all around them.

Raisa was back on the line. If it's serious Gorby'll fly over to Delhi tomorrow, she said.

Thanks, I said. It was nice to know he hadn't changed with power. I recalled his Forsterian heart; if he had to choose between saving his country and saving his friend, he wouldn't think twice. In his personal life, which came first, he behaved as though the soul of a man he knew came before the soul of the country where he had been king. His politics seemed to flow out of a quiet vision.

How're Lenin and Trotsky? I asked Raisa. Can Gorby bring them along?

Gorby's magic with people always worked better when the monkeys were with him, as it had with Raisa all those years ago in the Lodi Gardens. It was as though his deeply emotional ability to communicate depended in some obscure way upon the weight of the two monkeys on his shoulders.

Yes, she said, they're older and not so playful now but they're still clinging to him. I'll tell him to take them along. I don't really get along with them on their own anyway. Remember to carry peanuts and bananas to the airport, Doc, or they'll drive you nuts, she said, chuckling again, this time invitingly, at her small joke. She was always fishing for admiration, but I wasn't in a very obliging mood.

Yes OK, I said tonelessly, then felt a flash of guilt. How's Wanda? I asked by way of compensation.

That was the name of her new goldfish and I knew she felt personally wanted if people asked after its general health. It seemed in character for her to offset Lenin and Trotsky with Wanda. Gorby couldn't feel for fish and so had merely an aesthetic interest in them, but I thought he probably approved of Wanda as a concept. I had realized soon after I got to know him that, in fact, he didn't merely approve of the irreverent and the bizarre but was frequently moved by it. The idea of a fish called Wanda in such tranquil and domestic proximity with Lenin and Trotsky seemed a notion in harmony with his general way of thinking. It was also in keeping with their relationship, their way of undercutting each other while staying close. Raisa got a real kick out of gazing for hours at something that didn't drown in water. It made her nicely different from Gorby, who saw sense in monkeys, dogs and horses, none in frogs and fish.

But my mind was on my brother. He was different from them both. My brother's mind was flooded with drowned sailors.

I tried a mind-over-matter job with my bladder, clogging up my pipe by shifting in spasms from one leg to another, while Raisa told me about the particular yellowness of her goldfish. I imagined prizing open Wanda's mouth, unzipping, shoving myself carefully in, feeling the relief as the yellowness left me and bloated Wanda, watching the fish balloon from gold to jaundice yellow before exploding into crumbs that looked like bits of the Berlin Wall.

Can you hear me? Raisa asked urgently from Russia.

Yes, that's wonderful, I said, clutching my crotch and shifting weight. She'd been going on about the virtues of the new fishfood she'd got from Margaret Thatcher.

I've heard about Horizon Fishcrumbs too, I said. It's drowning out our TV with its ads about having all the hormones that open up gills and let the fish breathe easily.

Yes, Doc, she said. Cuts out the aquamarine claustrophobia, they say.

That sounded too nice a phrase to have been spontaneous. She must have got it from some ad I'd missed. She really hadn't changed at all, I thought. There seemed still the same interest in variety and new words. I flashed to a scene from an old film we once saw together, in which Dirk Bogarde asked his secretary if she approved of violence. No, said the secretary. Neither do I, said Bogarde. It reeks of spontaneity.

Shall I send you a packet of Horizon Fishcrumbs through Gorbs? Raisa asked considerately.

I don't have a fish, I said, and I've got to piss.

What? She asked with some incredulity. She probably thought she misheard me. Doubts were too minor to clog her mind, and she just went on in her mildly frenetic way. Then get one, Doc, she said. They're very soothing. Why don't you get one for Jehova? Get him a, what's it called, pomfret? It'll soothe him down and if he doesn't like watching it swim he can eat it.

She was distracted and unfocused again. Her immediate concerns were still switching her off the inner life. Still, I was glad her years with Gorby had infected her with his affection for the grotesque. I was also very full of fluid and she wasn't letting me off the hook. She was bad at that. If she felt someone going without feeling she was letting them go, she felt they'd beaten her. I suppose some people feel like that on account of their mothers having taken away the nipples too early from their mouths. It was the opposite with my brother, though, and helped him become a homeopathic gynaecologist and gave him that suckling tenderness with womankind.

Come Mr Talleyrand, tally me banana. Belafonte had arrived in my stereo. I twiddled his knob and he piped down. His sentence circled in my mind and summoned up Gorby's arrival in Delhi, with Lenin and Trotsky eating bananas and lice off his shoulders. I sucked in my stomach and pressed my crotch. There was a mirror by the phone. I looked past it to a door that gave to an empty pot. I knew if I pulled the chain above it the waters would gush out obligingly, cleaning out all the yellowness I might put in. I remembered Gorby saying, once, that life's most overrated pleasure was a good screw, its most underrated a good shit. My brother's life looked immersed in it, and it required a fine flushing system inside his bloodstream to stop him clogging. Gorby, I knew, was more than a passable plumber.

I'll pick Gorby up from the airport tomorrow, I said to Raisa. Tell him to look out for the bearded guy with the banana in his hands.

She laughed at that. You don't have to do that, Doc, she said. He'll probably pick you out from the airplane.

We made pecking noises on the phone by way of fond farewells. I remembered, illogically, Richard Burton gasping all over Elizabeth Taylor.

Below my brother's *barsati* the daily queues of women were forming. When he was not a historian, my brother was a homeopathic gynaecologist. He was greatly into healing biodegradable women non-invasively. In my mind I saw the forms of other queues near Raisa's house, blanched and snaking slowly towards Lenin's tomb, of couples newly married. They looked happy in the cold, awaiting patiently the impending benediction from the tomb of a king whose bones were fast crumbling. I saw in my mind a half skeleton grinning liplessly at the women in white, carrying flowers. His sockets gazed blindly at pearls that were once his eyes, now on the necks of women in white. My brother didn't look anything like that, of course. He was handsome and tall and wholesome and strong, and tender with the women who waited in queues to be seen by him. Sometimes there were only Rajasthani women, many in vermilion, with the thirst of the deserted around their eyes. A cluster of them once sat gracefully by the sidelane below the *barsati*, scattering their red smocks around them, looking like upturned poppies. I imagined the sibilant hiss of piss that only comes out of women. It gave me a momentary flutter of joy and stirred the little one sleeping in my crotch. I shifted weight in the correct way and he went back to sleep. The women rose gracefully, stepping aside from their little puddles. The queue moved forward slowly, half a shuffle at a time. A brown dog with furrowed eyes sat close by, her legs crossed over with a protective daintiness. She seemed to watch the ritual unmovingly.

Once I asked one of the women in the queue, who was a regular, what she got out of seeing my brother. I never asked my brother how he went about healing the women who queued up for him, or what exactly homeopathic gynaecology involved. It always sounded to me like a sort of euphemism for something better, not a profession. But I kept my wickeder thoughts to myself, for though we were brothers, we liked savouring the deliciousness of the unsaid. It would have broken a low wall between us that we both cherished if I'd asked him a personal question. I didn't need to anyway. But it felt nice to ask a woman who queued up for him what it was all about. I could tell just by looking at her that she'd suffered through English Honours at some posh college and taken to men. I thought she might have lots of literary lines stuffed inside her jelly, but she was simpler.

It's because we're all pretty fucked up, I suppose, she said, except when we're with someone special like him. It's a kind of fix. Very healing. Doesn't everyone need a fix? What's yours?

She was into American quickness and repartee, and I wasn't sure I wanted further elucidation about her life, or about my brother's as a homeopathic gynaecologist. I remembered instead the slow and gentle eyes of elephants, and retreated.

It sounded pretentious to reply Beethoven.

Music, I said.

My brother's second emotional crisis was the least serious. Her breasts were like the Spiral Nebulae but she was like clingfilm, and at first my brother didn't realize he was only lusting after her. All the usual tenderness had welled up in him and blinded him to the truth that beneath it all he didn't care a fuck about her. Later he felt very guilty about it all. It made him introspective for a few days and got him hooked on Thomas Hardy for a short while, till his emotional need for wallowing in the tragic destinies of beautiful women greatly wronged had been satisfied. But he always knew women would smother him and that the second one was no better in that respect. He felt guilty about her, as he did about his indifference for our mother, but he disentangled himself gently, trying all the time not to hurt her.

After that, until his third crisis, my brother ran through the daily queues of women that were constituted for him with the silence of a knife. The women stepped down from his Defence Colony *barsati* one at a time, some slowly, others quickly on account of departing buses, flicking their sarees to get in one final touch of order, looking contented, sometimes checking the colour of their hairlines, the vermilion scattered around them.

My brother's third emotional crisis slowed him down. It made him look and feel older, his face looked heavier in the mirror. I would have said 'fuller' were I not so vicarously narcissistic, always imagining myself as him and feeling inhibited about admitting the truth. I felt helpless, as on the earlier two occasions, because I couldn't get personal with my godlike brother or ask him about the latest girl. It would pass, but he needed flushing out then, to make it pass. I phoned Gorby and Raisa because they were distant, powerful, and cared about him. He looked like Zeus and was made of some special jelly which must have gone into him on account of our mother always letting herself into his mouth and denying me. Later, when she died slowly, he behaved like the dispassionate historian he never was. I did the nursing and felt drained.

I met Gorbachov, Lenin and Trotsky off the Aeroflot flight. Lenin grabbed the bananas, Trotsky took the peanuts. Gorby had a sack slung over his shoulder. We got in the car after bear hugs.

You look bushed, I said, having rehearsed the joke several times over since the phone call. We held hands in the car. We were old comrades and went back a long time, since our days together in the Lodi Gardens, where the dead kings stored their bones, from before the time he saved Jehova from Kali, looking a triadic Hanuman and getting collared into being King of Russia by a woman on a park bench smoking a Marlboro Mild.

What's in the sack, I asked.

I call it my Cul-de-Sac, he said, laughing hugely and drawing me in.

He was like that, very infectious. He could crumble things or mend them, or do it the other way round, just as he liked. I never saw anyone as good as Gorby with people. Being with him was like being with my brother.

It's got bits of the Berlin Wall in it, he said. Want a piece? It's sort of symbolic of the times, Doc. Keep a bit. I've been handing it out to anyone who wants a souvenir.

OK, I said, and dipped into the sack. Lenin and Trotsky were looking at me. They were trained to observe the ritual.

What's up with Jehova? Gorby asked.

Our hands were firmly cemented with a fast balm which thence did spring. The waters flew out from under the head of a virgin, raped and dead and wearing white, in the Bergman movie. There's only truth in fiction, I thought. I thought of my brother, who looked like Zeus but was vulnerable like Achilles, and of Gorby's days with Raisa that had made him succumb to thinking of my brother as a lesser deity.

It's his third crisis and he's getting old, I said. He needs some of your healing touch and your monkey tricks.

My brother and I and Gorbachov felt like the eternal triangle, sitting together in the Defence Colony barsati. My brother was silent early in the evening. The evil hormones had been flooding his bones. He was thinking about Phlebas the drowned Phoenician and the undersea currents picking his bones in whispers. There were lots of stray literary lines mixed up with the jelly inside him. I was thinking about Brigid Bardot playing the part of a hypotenuse. Lenin and Trotsky were doing their tricks and going at the Old Monk. Belafonte was singing the Jamaica Farewell in the stereo. Rum is fine any time a year.

Gorby knew when to relax and when to talk. He sat with us in that small room in a warm and peaceful silence. For all his liveliness and levity, he possessed the gift of silence. Quietness never embarrassed him. He could be strong and silent or weak and voluble, as the occasion required. That evening he let Lenin and Trotsky get sozzled on the Old Monk and slowly nursed his own Bloody Mary. Though he'd taught them their tricks, he shared our mirth. Lenin dressed up as Al Capone, smoked a cigar and quoted from Kissinger's Memoirs. Trotsky did a difficult Reagan imitation: he had to sit still for a whole minute, looking dumb and grinning sheepishly from ear to ear.

I could never tell Lenin from Trotsky. The years and continuous proximity had made them look even more like each other than they once did, as happens to husbands and wives who start off looking only like themselves and end up looking like brother and sister. But my brother, who knew history and was passionate about animals, could always distinguish Lenin from Trotsky. He tickled their chins and chattered away with them in different directions that led nowhere. I disappeared for a space into Dostoevsky, to where Ivan Karamazov saw Turkish soldiers throw infants into the air, catching them on bayonets as they fell. Later, when Lenin and Trotsky had passed into a stupefied sleep, cuddled up with my brother under his blankets, Gorby and I talked about many things, about Raisa's latest passion for fish and the latest in sanitary ware. The Russian cold still froze the taps and he said it was a good thing she was badgering Kohl for new pipes that never clogged. We recalled the ruin of kings and the beds of flowers along the walls where we had walked, and of the many things that would not yield. He made politics sound as though it had something to do with human beings.

On the main road in the distance a traffic jam was building up. Through the distant horns of motorcars Gorby worked the Hippocratic oath. I twiddled the TV to check on the daily cabinet reshuffle, then realized Gorby needed a holiday from all quests for power. I electrocuted the latest cabinet by twiddling another knob and saw, in the shade of the television's goodbye flash, an instant of pleasure on Gorby's tired face.

It's so democratic to finish with politics like that, he said.

I saw the emotional fatigue, the toll of falling walls. He needed a break just as much as my brother, and I was glad Raisa and I had haphazardly, through our telephone talk, organized one for them together.

I rang Raisa the next morning to tell her Gorby'd arrived safely and that things seemed OK for my brother with him around. But she wasn't about to give me a chance to start.

Chancellor Kohl's sent the single-lever mixer and the plumber's fixed it up, she said. It feels just like Europe. Come over, Doc. Give Gorby the phone. Tell him to bring Jehova and you back on the return flight. You've got to see this tap flow.

OK OK, I said, feeling something start up inside me. Maybe nipple-denial got me so my kidneys get going just when someone's on the line. I looked at the mirror near the phone and saw in it the image of my brother.

Gorby's just taken Jehova off to the hills for a few days, I said. The change should do him good.

Great, she said. I'm glad they've gone into the country. Gorby needs the change too, Doc. He needs to get way from all these city walls. How's he doing, Doc? she wanted to know.

Fine, I said. They'll both be fine I think.

They both needed more space and clean air to flush out the pollution, I thought, and Raisa seemed to think so too. I wondered if Raisa had ever felt anything else for me on the occasions we'd been together all those years ago, during moments when our feelings and thoughts had seemed to coincide. But she was with my brother then, and later with Gorby, and my stray thought soon faded out like the slow dissipation of an image in an old movie, leading to other images, another story.

I thought instead of the Phoenician sailor, of the aesthetic satisfaction in my bowels after a morning clearance, of the absence of traffic on a broad road, of Dick Francis trampled untimely on a race track, of the many days I spent with Commander Dalgleish plotting the poisoning of P. D. James and her convulsive, deserved death, of our mother awash in a well-wrought urn, and of the relief one feels after taking a leak.

How's your flush system doing? I asked Raisa.

But our connection failed just at that moment, and, though I strained my ears to keep our link, I only managed to hear Raisa's reply being drowned by the unchained roar of cascading water.

Incident by the Pangong Lake

for C.V. and R.W.

My brother, who resembled Zeus, was once sitting by the Pangong Lake in eastern Ladakh, quietly breathing in the scant and icy air at fourteen thousand feet. He watched a black dot which was really a yak disappear through an afternoon into a cream-coloured hill that froze over a navy-blue lake which stretched itself out all the way to Tibet, and he wondered with slow thought, as people sometimes do, why it seemed so aesthetically pleasing to him to be sitting there all alone, just watching the water.

There wasn't much to do except just silently gaze at the water and feel heroic. He watched the water with slit Clint Eastwood eyes and imagined his heroic face with its desirable stubble, and his slim, long figure, all being watched with a mixture of tenderness and unadmitted desire by Shabana Azmi, the always unreachable movie heroine of his frequent mental wanderlust. He looked at the lake and she, the forever lovely Grecian-Urn beloved of his mind, watched him. Once or twice he made her sigh quietly with desire. It amused him that he could in his own mind revel in a power play which so fluently allowed a complete reversal of their real-life positions. The knowledge that he had a permanent inner capacity to make himself her hero provided him with a deep and wholesome satisfaction. It gave him a strong sense of his own being, and because he had the intelligence to recognize this power as an aspect of narcissism he cherished, he could control or restrain it at will, or alternatively allow it to swamp his insides with all the hormones of lust.

He chuckled sweetly to himself at the attractiveness of the

34

scenario his mind had constructed, felt vaguely sorry once more that there was no one to thank for an imagination that bestowed him with images that came like sudden, unexpected gifts, and smiled at the thought of a safely distant feminist circle which frowned in conjunction at the hideous maleness of all the operations of his mind. He tried to focus on specific faces within his feminist circle, looking for something undogmatic and physically desirable behind the cigarette smoke of hardening expressions. There were possibilities, but by that navy-blue lake, at that moment, it seemed too tiring to pursue this train of thought towards a passionate conclusion. It took only a split second to file away his feminist circle. It felt nice to know his mind filed faster than his personal computer as he switched, he thought, to another software.

The world looked good, and nothing bothered him there, by that lake. The sounds of horns and motorcars belonged to another universe as he let the alchemy of silence and spectacle slowly flood his veins towards the experience of a harmony that, elsewhere, within the cities of noise where he was often forced to make a living, came to him with the power of a narcotic through certain slow movements in old symphonies. There was an eternal tranquillity to the lake and the colours around my brother were more bizarre and compelling than any to be seen in Dali. It required no exceptional imagination – merely the barest topographical realism in fact – for a writer to paint with words a world as extraordinary as any to be found in Màrquez. The hills slanted sharply up in spasms of strange colour, cream and black and green, and the maroon of garnets lay muffled in their stones. They formed a new conjunction with the full moon which was nearly as lucid as a sun that dipped on the opposite hill and coloured the lake towards a lighter shade of grey. The slow meanderings of my brother's mind as he watched this scene were an analogue of his unencumbered travels through the valleys and passes of Manali, Lahul and Spiti, to the point where he sat upon garnet stones by the Pangong Lake, constructing in his mind the pleasing images of an impossible relationship.

It was here that, stirred by the sweep of the Pangong Lake, a new run of images began to gel in my brother's mind. He tried to sort out these images towards a narrative which would convey with some exactness the circumstances that culminated in his being there, by the purple beach, but he discovered, even as he thought, that there were many alternative histories inside him which concluded in his position by that lake-water lapping with low sounds upon a high and remote shore. There was at one level a dull and circumstantial history, the shallow rehearsal of recent physical activities: the coughing back-kick of a cold motorcycle flinching to the downward arc of a feeble and wind-bitten leg, the dry lips and the dark glasses below a warm helmet, the donning of gloves and the revving sounds which soothed his heartbeat, the drooping yellow of willow trees that hid the pale blue flow of the Indus near Leh, the clicked gears and the passing blackness of a bare road which snaked its way through deserted mountains and the tongues of glaciers towards the lake.

This seemed one way of telling the truth about how he got to that altitude of colours: he had evidence and no doubt. But there seemed an infinity of other narratives which served as interesting preludes to his view upon that chromatic afternoon of a disappearing yak, images to be tracked along unexpected contours, all waiting to be ordered by a distinctive and personal logic into a history which defined only his own soul. The water reminded him, as he kick-started a mental motorbike, of the colour of his old school blazer and a day, twenty years earlier, when his blazer accidentally tore upon a nail and was freed by a boy who, some days later, ran away from the school. It took him to his own construction of that boy, Vincente de Rozio, who, dislodging his blazer from a nail, asked him on that day, all those many years in the past, 'Hey men, you ever seen the Pangong Lake?'

Our horizons were small in those days. Our school lay by a beautiful ox-bow lake, cut off before our time from a river that flowed dimly in the distance, and we had seen the bigger lakes of Nainital, Bhimtal and Srinagar when our parents herded us there to save our skins the annual baking that began in earnest after the first week of May. There were other lakes, much larger, Chilka, Titicaca, Michigan, that filled our minds with the notion of an enormous tranquillity. Even the smaller stretches of water we encountered in our city – the mud-brown ponds circumscribed by mud huts where buffaloes sank with the barest trace of their nostrils, and the river that swayed every evening with the shadows of decaying palaces – even these seemed havens of rest, cool islands of refuge from the blaze of bicycle traffic and horns that pursued us through every street of our city. Though we did not know it then, my brother said later he realized most fully, sitting by the Pangong Lake, how deep the feeling for a bounded expanse of water had sunk into our minds. The calmness and colour of that water belonged to a better world than ours. Or perhaps I should say, more truthfully, that they belonged to a better world than mine, for my brother was less held up by the routine pleasures of family and friends, and he was able to travel and live in worlds that I could only strain to imagine.

To de Rozio my brother said, twenty years before his reconstruction of that event – no, he hadn't heard of this lake, what was this Pangong Lake? He remembered the quirky comparison Vincente made when he said the lake was bloody large and looked like it was all made of blazer cloth. He said it was half in Ladakh and half in Tibet. His father's regiment, said Vincente, was posted at Tankse, an army outpost not far from the lake, and he'd seen it floating about amid the colour of the mountains after a five-hour ride through yak-dotted terrain which seemed to have been specially set apart from human beings.

A few days later Vincente de Rozio ran away from the school, and for many years out of my brother's life, until he found him coming alive in his mind because of a torn blazer and the purple of the Pangong Lake. He thought back to the time when de Rozio fled the school and recalled it as an incident which, like the tranquillity and colour of the lake that lay before him, liberated his mind from the certitudes on which we were all being fed, on all the home truths which made the majority of us, in our adult lives, captives to office and a pressure-cooker domesticity. It was one of the things, he said, that made him a traveller. I think he meant by this that it made him emotionally and intellectually restless, for he didn't physically travel until quite long after our years in school and much after the de Rozio incident. But the incident freed him somehow. It informed him, in the odd and obscure way in which these things inform the subconscious and only later assume the shape of links within a pattern, that he didn't have to receive the truths on which we were being educated. The possibility of dissent, the possibility that we were being schooled on lies or values that weren't universal truths, the possibility of a spectacular and radical denial of authority – these seemed all to coalesce in his recollection of de Rozio and the circumstances in which he fled the school. It was an image he couldn't dissociate, within the convolutions of his mind, from the fact that he himself had become restless and a traveller.

We were both sceptical about what constituted truth and reality and value: they seemed to shift so much from day to day, depending on the weather, the topography and the temperature of our bodies, that we had become attuned to believing in the more acceptably uncertain virtues and disappointments we encountered in friendship, fiction and music. My brother went much further in this direction than I. He moved around the world with such dogged restlessness and with such little interest in material ambition that the worldly-wise knew him only as a shiftless tramp. His whole life seemed a negation of all that they had been taught to valorize – consistency, purposiveness, possessions, an ordered life in a safe city which assured a position, a pension, a provident fund. My brother would have none of these. He liked looking at lakes and the water of different countries. He loved women all over the world for the short periods of time he stayed with them, then moved on and loved other people, other sights, picking up the threads easily from just where he'd left them every time he circumnavigated his way back to an old haunt or a far-flung friend. He valorized movements, newness, change, a purposiveness without purpose which I could only envy. He sought out lakes and the stretches of water on which his eyes could feast and rest, but even here his mind was mostly on the move, travelling backwards and forwards on a train of images, some recollected, others constructed, all equally real because they appeared gathered together into an experience of immediate and transient value, to be cherished because they could not recur in the same shape, near the same expanse of water, at that precise temperature and altitude. So my brother didn't know, nor much cared, how that important little incident of his past *really* happened. But this is how I think he made history happen inside himself, sitting by the Pangong Lake.

Late on an October night towards the close of the 1960s, in the biggish city of Lucknow upon the Gangetic plain of north India, Vincente de Rozio, fourteen years old and an obscure descendant of certain Portuguese merchants who once lived in Goa, made his escape down a drainpipe from a school that had quartered him for much of his life. His heart raced in his ears as he made his tentative way down the rough edges of a rusting pipe towards the ground, where three cast-iron cannons, fired once by Lord Cornwallis against Tipu Sultan, now pointed the direction to a triangular ox-bow lake in which seven crocodiles had made their home, being shot and logged one at a time over seven mythical years by Major Townsend, the old school warden with the bandmaster moustache. Fearing detection and inching quietly down the thirty feet, Vincente de Rozio did not notice – as my brother did then, creating the scene – the fading moon, slit here and there by arrow clouds and shining upon the ox-bow lake a hundred yards away. It only took Vincente de Rozio five minutes of ear-ache and sore thighs to feel his black Bata pointed shoes touch ground. He looked up and sideways to make sure he was alone and safe before beginning his walk over the low school gate, over the culvert that ran over an arm of the lake, over the fifth hole of the golf course, across Fairy Dale and towards the limp flag of the third hole, on to the Dilkusha Gardens, and finally beyond the big city towards the Civil Lines.

Questions about where de Rozio went from there and what ultimately became of him were asked every day for several months, by all the schoolboys, soon after the news got around that he had run away. No one could recollect an instance of such spectacular rebellion. If you couldn't answer the questions that were asked in class, it was logical to expect a beating to follow. Some beatings were merely savager than others – it depended partly on the master whose questions you blanked out on. If it was history, you had no time. The history master looked black as a panther, weighed more than Muhammad Ali, had a nasty temper, a pencil moustache that went too far in both directions before dipping menacingly, a wife with whom his relations were rapidly souring, and an unending sequence of children who all said Daddy Daddy with gratuitous regularity and without adequate cause. Given this, it was unlikely to benefit your scholarly destiny if you were prone to confusing, as de Rozio was, the Chandlers of Bundlecund with the Rohillers of Rohill-cund. An exact scene grew within my brother's mind as he gazed towards Tibet, vaguely connecting the silence there with the one into which de Rozio had disappeared. It began with the period bell which rang out the time for history to start, followed by the arrival into the class of the Black Panther, his moustache twitching, his mouth in a shape which gave out the unfilial echoes of Daddy Daddy, his face with an expression that suggested considerable marital deterioration since the last lesson, in his hand a cane which he placed on the desk in front of him.

'Wake up ya buggers.'

That sounded quite normal to the class: it was the Panther's favoured way of combining a greeting with a warning and seemed to call for no special wariness.

'Albert ya bugger.'

'Yessir,' said Albert Joel Kumar Menezes.

'Your bloody dad is in the bloody army, ya bugger, and I have

40

to buy rum in the bloody market. How d'you think you're going to pass in history, Albert? No rum, no marks, heh heh heh. Just tell your dad to send his batman to the canteen and get me some rum ya bugger. *Hum bloody paisa dega man, but tum bloody rum kab bring karega?'*

'I'll bring by Monday sir, *pukka* sir.'

'You heard that, bloody Vincente de Rozio? You're another useless worthless bugger I say. Do you bloody know what bloody Portugal is most famous for? Port, ya bugger, port. Not bloody port like bloody Bombay and Madras and all men, port inside bottles. Port-oo-bloody-gull. And have you ever had the basic decency to get me a bloody bottle from your bloody native land? My birthday's coming up next month, ya buggers, and you know how I like to celebrate, heh heh heh. Look sharp bloody de Rozio, I don't want any of your bloody Latin looks or I'll give you such a bloody kick you'll land in bloody Lisbon with your grand-daddies.'

It was suddenly hot. The boys in the class shifted uneasily in their chairs and glanced from de Rozio to the Panther. It was incredible for de Rozio to have looked anything but placating: there was no precedent for sullenness and rebellion in history until then, my brother said. The world did not exist outside the class, the violence of its atmosphere holding everyone tightly captive. A strangulating blackness which struck deeper than fear had closed every mind against the worlds which lay outside, where there was movement and the calmness of lakes. The Panther's mood was unmistakable and my brother knew, with the certitude of the habitually defeated, that success in history only meant humouring a regularly dangerous animal. Later, when he came across Carlyle's remark that the only thing man ever learnt from history was that man never learnt anything from history, my brother thought it applied very ironically to de Rozio who, on that day, seemed to think of the history period as one in which we were meant to learn history. Perhaps de Rozio had suddenly and unaccountably developed more expectations of education than the rest of us; or perhaps the intellectual sickness which was as characteristic of our school as its physical charm struck him suddenly on that day, so many years before my brother and I were able to see it that way; or perhaps he was better equipped than we had guessed with the special thickness of mind and skin that served well as a strategy for survival in our school; or perhaps he just had less to lose by being defiant. Whatever it was, no one who was present in that class ever forgot what followed. The Panther said the topic for the day was . . .

'Aurangzeb the bugger. I'll give you his story in the form of a . . .'

'Skeleton, sir,' said the boys dutifully.

'And you will go back home and fill in the. . .'

'Flesh, sir,' said the boys dutifully.

Vincente de Rozio's voice was not heard in the chorus. He was looking straight at the Panther.

'One of Aurangzeb the bugger's problems was transport,' said the Panther. 'No bloody motorcars and all men, only bloody horses. Big buggers. Huge buggers. Big huge bloody horses. By the time Aurangzeb the bugger put on his armour and sword and shield and all, his bloody horse was ready to sit down. So Aurangzeb couldn't bloody move, ya buggers. Besides it was too hot for the bugger. Bloody Mughals had come straight from Summercund, I say, nonstop kitapit kitapit kitapit kitapit on their horses. Everyone told the buggers India was the land of bloody milk and honey. No one told the buggers about our bloody milkmen I say. Bloody Arjun Kumar I thought your dad was going to send us fresh milk from last week on men, what happened eh? You want to bloody fail in history just like bloody Albert or what men? Just remember. So what was I saying, yes, by the time it was bloody Aurang's turn to be Emperor, his blood ran dry with the heat I say. Look up Summercund in your maps for the next class, ya buggers, that's the hideout from which all those chinky-eyed cut-cocks came, from Genghis Khan to Tamer bloody Lane to our own haircutting Babur heh heh heh. Straight line of descent to Aurang bloody zeb. So what was I saying? Yeah, Aurangzeb the bugger. Everything was hot and heavy I say. Bugger must have cursed bloody Babur for bloody leaving Summercund and landing him in this land of bloody milk and water. Bloody Arjun Singh I hope my gentle hints heh heh are not lost inside your thick skull. Yes, so Aurang bloody zeb. His cannons were heavy, all full of balls and all men. Everything was heavy ya buggers. Bloody Mughals had got used to booze and dames by the time they got to Aurang I say. Even their horses men, heh heh heh. Empire was bloody decaying. When you feel like lying around with some booze and your horse doesn't feel like bloody moving either, what can you do, I say. What d'you think about all these things Albert ma boy? You don't think, Albert ma boy. That's the trouble with you, Albert ma boy. I'll tell you what Aurangzeb did, Albie ma boy. He just said bye bye to his empire, just bye bye, *khatam*, finish. That's the story of the decline of the bloody Mughals, I say. All their enemies had bloody *tatoos* which went kitapit kitapit kitapit kitapit faster than they could think. So Aurangzeb the bugger just gave up the chase and said bloody *jané do yaar*. And that, ma boys, is how the Mughal empire ended. You buggers can flesh out all the precise historical details in your homework books. I've given you the skeleton, you give me the flesh. Now it's time for some questions. Aurangzeb the bugger's biggest problem was, do you know who?'

'Sir sir sir sir sir sir sir sir.'

Three hands were up in the air. The brighter boys always waved their hands frantically, wanting to answer the Panther's early questions so as to be just that little bit distant from a beating if they later failed to answer a more difficult question.

The Panther allowed Raj Kumar Kripal to answer.

'Transport sir.'

A hysterical giggle was suppressed into a quickly vanishing grin by my brother. Kripal's answer was logical enough as a sequel to the Panther's account of Mughal decline, but everyone knew immediately it was the wrong answer simply because the Panther didn't look amused. Or perhaps it was the right answer; it was merely not the answer the Panther had in mind.

'Heh heh heh, bloody transport eh? Come here men. *Hamara nageechoo bloody ao*. Always in a bloody hurry to answer questions ya bugger? You think transport is a *who*? Bloody transport eh? Next time listen carefully to the question.'

One sadistic, stinging blow later, R. K. Kripal was a red-faced boy on his chair; there were no waving hands in the air.

'You ya bugger de Rozio, useless worthless bugger I say. If you can't get me port I hope you can at least tell me who was Aurangzeb the bugger's biggest problem, heh heh heh.'

The Panther was on the prowl for his next victim, and we knew de Rozio was in for it. My brother recollected the current of common apprehension that flowed through everyone in the class that day, bonding them within a petrified silence through the agony of the passing seconds that lay between de Rozio and the Panther's powerful hands. This was a feeling with which everyone in the class was familiar. It happened regularly; in our school we were resigned to the fact that history repeated itself in this way and that no one could ever escape it. De Rozio had never been one of the hand-waving boys who succeeded in answering the Panther's questions. Aurangzeb had obviously had problems with his weighed-down war-horse, but it seemed reasonably clear that the right answer for the end of empire wasn't the name of that horse. My brother didn't know who else had plagued Aurangzeb, nor did anyone else in the class. Aurangzeb was likely to have had several dozen enemies up his sleeve, and it seemed, on balance, more dangerous to try your luck with a name than to just lie low. The thing to do was to look humble, mentally prepare your skin for pain, try and calm your racing mind, and cling with desperation to the knowledge that the present would fade into a past, taking history and the Panther away with it.

But de Rozio didn't seem to be doing any of these things. He seemed in possession of some peculiar knowledge which gave him the power to look with defiant clarity at the Panther. It made my brother's class frightened and uncomfortable and unsettled. History was not following its expected course and my brother's

44

mind, Richter-scaled to register even the silences that preceded seismic echoes, tried desperately to stem the tremors that gathered like waves towards an apocalypse.

But the age of miracles had not passed. My brother recalled the incredible collective astonishment of everyone in the class when de Rozio, against every odd, came out with the answer which was in the Panther's mind.

'Shivaji the Maratha,' said de Rozio.

My brother remembered the precise clarity and the exact tone of voice with which de Rozio said those words, just as, sitting by the Pangong Lake, he remembered de Rozio's strange remark that the lake looked like it was all made of blazer cloth. He remembered de Rozio saying 'Shivaji the Maratha' without adding the customary 'sir' at the end of that incredible piece of correct information. The precision with which de Rozio uttered those three words and the careful absence of the vital honorific at the end of them made him sound grown-up; almost, said my brother, as though de Rozio thought he was Shivaji himself, facing Aurangzeb as an equal.

It was clear from the moment's silence that followed de Rozio's answer, and from the Panther's infuriated scowl, that his victim had scrambled up a tree he couldn't climb. He would have to ask another question which would bring de Rozio down and within reach. We all knew this; we knew that it would happen; it was, for us, the lesson of history. Until that day de Rozio had offered not the remotest indication of possessing the enormous conceptual resources required to cut loose from the vice-like hegemony in which our lives were held for almost all our years in that school. Dissent was unthinkable, and even by the Pangong Lake, so many years later, my brother was unable to fully account for the way in which de Rozio so simply turned the tables on the Panther, and his own mental world upside down.

De Rozio did not wait for the next question. He knew it would be beyond his ken and that it would make him, in some sense, legitimately accessible to the Panther. He got up from his chair and my brother saw him walk in a determined way straight up to the desk behind which the Panther sat. Then, he said – and this was something we always found both difficult to believe and wonderful to hear – then, he said, he saw de Rozio pick up the cane which lay on the Panther's desk. He saw de Rozio pick up the cane and he saw the swift, stinging, whip-like movement with which de Rozio brought the cane crashing down upon the Panther's pencil moustache and teeth. My brother saw the Panther's dark pencil moustache crumple and twist into blood, and he saw the reflex movement of the Panther's hands as they rushed to rescue his mouth. He saw de Rozio run out of the class but remembered the ensuing pandemonium only dimly because after this his mind went blank with the event. Someone ran out in the direction in which de Rozio had gone, others pelted frantically towards the principal's office, some helped the Panther limp into the infirmary. De Rozio was caught hiding by the oxbow lake and shut into a high room until the principal, as bewildered as the rest of the school, had measured out meet punishment for a crime that defied conception. The period bell rang out indifferently, signalling the end of that period of history. Everyone was aghast with excitement and awaited the next momentous event – a public thrashing, disgrace, expulsion, something only fractionally short of a grotesque and mangled death. But all this was never to be; that night de Rozio made his escape down a rusting drainpipe and disappeared for ever from the school, leaving my brother with the complicated business of rearranging his whole way of thinking about life.

Although he did not see de Rozio after he escaped our school, an image of de Rozio stayed dormant in my brother's mind and he never ceased wondering what happened to him. I think de Rozio became for my brother a concept he could chase in several directions within his own mind. What *really* became of de Rozio didn't bother him terribly; de Rozio was never in the news, nor became the chief minister of Goa, nor, like many of the people of his community, did he ever become Robert the Second Sidekick to Jaykay the Arch-villain in every Hindi movie. He was not to be found playing 'Come September' on the electric guitar, wearing drainpipes and an oily Elvis Presley puff in the Royal Café band, nor 'Oh Bloody Oh Bloodah' in the sleazier cafes by the sluggish river where men with silver rings on all their fingers and one long painted red nail drank Black Knights and lurched in surreptitious Fiats towards their uncertain nightly orgasms. He was never seen by my brother in all the private schools he visited for three years as a travelling salesman, persuading impecunious and corrupted schoolteachers to prescribe the books his organization published, wondering if one day he might hear news of the long vanished de Rozio, or see him suddenly as the inevitable schoolteacher saying, 'Men Men C'mon Men,' his pink acne guarded by sideburns or a stubble, his familiar black drainpipes and pointed black Bata shoes complemented now by a slackening necktie and a thickening chin. He was never a roadside mechanic affably guarding from his customers a mind fine-tuned to the exact degree they could be overcharged, nor was he ever any of those that screamed for a spanner or a screwdriver at emaciated and blackened little boys who washed motorcycle carburettors with old saris and the darkening petrol that dripped from their hands into the rusting hub-caps of Ambassadors. Vincente de Rozio disappeared into a silence as profound as the one that lay over the Pangong Lake, an aesthetic oblivion, and to my brother it did not really matter, beyond the immense curiosity of his imagination, that he was never able to find him and place him and fix him to one particular spot. What *really* happened to Vincente de Rozio after he ran away from the school seemed almost, in retrospect, a tiresome question. It was the sort of question asked by empiricist historians, or by people systematically conditioned to seek a banal satisfaction in the meaninglessness of ordinary events, never in the imaginative construction of possible stories and multiple endings that might prove more interesting, much more real, and infinitely more wonderful on account of their remoteness from the predictability of objective truths. But this valorization of fiction, this boredom with the truth, it turned out, also had its ironic aspect, for when I think about what *really* happened to my brother in connection with de Rozio, it seems to me that the truth can occasionally be more satisfying than fiction.

After he quit his job as a travelling salesman of textbooks, my brother wandered off to make love to Scandinavian women and look at fjords in Norway. That done, he left for the lochs of Scotland, and, having trekked through the Highlands towards Loch Lomond, he reached Glasgow. Here he stayed with a Sindhi chemist called Bhagwan Brahmani who manufactured test-tube babies.

My brother told me later how test-tube babies were done, and it sounded quite simple really, just like many of the other things that made up life. The Sindhi chemist would take an egg, extracted by a gynaecologist from the insides of a woman. He would put this egg into a special soup which kept it fresh and preserved. Next, he would take a phial of frozen sperm from his deep-freeze, unfreeze it, and empty its contents into the soup. Millions of sperm would immediately begin thrashing each other and their tails in a frantic clamber to mate with the egg. My brother saw them all through a microscope, swimming desperately within their soup, a purple-coloured lake, towards an island which falsely beckoned as refuge. None of them seemed to know or care that they were all doomed, except for one. The egg towards which they were flagellating themselves was physiologically monogamous. It protected itself from multiple entry by a circular ring which allowed only one sperm to break through into its nucleic paradise. The very moment of life at which that one lucky sperm made it across the lake was the exact moment of death for the million others who, oblivious of their destiny, continued in helpless, restive travel to the end. The egg was Shabana Azmi, said my brother, the sperms thrashing about looked like the rest of the world swimming to its doom upon the Pangong Lake.

It seems the Glasgow clinic in which this Bhagwan Brahmani made his test-tube babies was flooded with customers from the Orient. Women came to it from the Middle East, where they were hungry for sperm that would make them socially productive, and from the Indian subcontinent, where rich Hindu women in Hawaii slippers and nylon-georgette saris searched for the sperm of tall, fair-skinned vegetarian Hindus, caste no bar. My brother's chemist friend bought and sold sperm by the gram, for it was in demand in many of the test-tube baby clinics of the West and fetched a reasonable living. Being of Indian origin, and with the success of Sindhi enterprise in his genes, he'd decided to specialize in Third World sperm, and this had paid off. His sperm bank was a deep-freeze full of phials. He showed these to my brother, rubbing his paunch.

My brother, as I said, got on well with all sorts of people. They showed him the most odd and amazing things in all the different parts of the world where he travelled. This paunch-rubbing crotch-scratching Sindhi chemist, for instance, who made his living by freezing and unfreezing the stuff of life – I doubt that he would have let *me* into his world in the casual and disarming way in which he let in my brother. People never needed to be guarded or defensive or closed up with my brother; he was a traveller, and this was an aura within his personality that Sindhi businessmen too could sense. They knew he wasn't ever going to compete with them, that he would move on and look at other things, that his interest in their world lacked purpose in their sense of that word.

And so my brother saw Bhagwan Brahmani's fridgeful of tubes, with several billion possible lives frozen inside, all awaiting a solution. One tube was labelled: 'Sunni Muslim, non-vegetarian, brown skin, hair curly black, 5ft 8in'; another read: 'Hindu, vegetarian, fair skin, hair straight, 5ft 10in'; and so on. The sperm donors had to be at least 5 feet 8 inches tall and capable of a thick ejaculation, else the creative potential within the fluid fell to below the desired level and the sperm count was too low for it to be commercially viable. It wouldn't do if you were short, because women almost invariably wanted tall off-spring. Brahmani's phials were mainly full of potential Hindus, Muslims, Buddhists, and Sikhs, but his collection was also known for its variety and elaborate subdivisions. He'd collected fluid from Hindu Jats, Haryanvi Sikhs, Bengali Muslims, Syrian Christian Keralites and Telugu Brahmins. One of the numerous greatgrandsons of Mahatma Gandhi – medical ethics forbade him saying which – had filled one of his phials, and my brother saw this tube, a billion possible Gandhis awaiting their thaw within a purple solution. There were also three test-tubes called Tamil Tigers; Bhagwan Brahmani said these were part of his belief in forward trading, an investment in a future when women from Sri Lanka started coming into money and ran short of men.

The going rate for ten grams of sperm was quite a lot in those early days, when people were always mildly inhibited or embarrassed or alarmed at being asked to spout into a phial. My brother merely needed the fifty pounds on offer and was amused at the thought of his fluid travelling pellmell over a purple lake to fulfil the needs of unknown women. A couplet from Dryden floated in and floated out, when man on many multiplied his kind, ere one to one was cursedly confined. The chemist showed him into a room plastered with posters of women in the nude, posing seductively to tease out the desired flow. An Air India calendar made up of Mughal miniature paintings hung incongruously amid the posters: it said March 1988, but the picture on it was not calculated to arouse. It showed what looked like a Mughal court scene, with the Emperor Aurangzeb gazing at his retinue of courtiers, and then helplessly beyond that towards the succulent delights on offer upon the next poster. My brother thought back to Aurangzeb and the rebellions of Vincente de Rozio and Shivaji the Maratha as he slowly felt himself coming to the end of the Mughals in a mix of memory and desire.

As he put my brother's tube into his freezer, Bhagwan Brahmani said it looked rich enough for ten women. 'Ideal for Goans, Anglo-Indians and fairer-skinned subcontinentals generally,' he said with a satisfied look at the colloid. 'Many of them aren't fussy about its religious composition if I tell them it's unusually potent,' he said. At a hundred pounds a head, he winked, he was going to make a killing in the market.

*

The Zoji La, a mountain pass which leads from Kashmir into Ladakh, usually thaws to the annual flow of traffic and travel in July. A day's hard drive takes the traveller to Kargil, halfway to Leh. Another nine hours through spectacular but infertile terrain dominated by the ascetic heights of Buddhist monasteries ends by the pale blue flow of the Indus at Leh. My brother crossed Zoji La in the August of 1989. He was heading for the Pangong Lake, so he did not stop for long in Leh. He passed Tankse on his way and remembered it as a familiar name, connecting it with de Rozio only five hours later, by the lake. He sat upon the garnet stones near the lake all through that afternoon, until a yak disappeared entirely into a cream-coloured hill. Then he made his way back to Tankse, where he hoped to scrounge out a night's halt in an army barrack.

Four army officers stood talking in a group, and my brother, ever anxious to establish contact with people who might command and bestow shelter, stopped his motorcycle by them. Introducing himself, he asked if he could hole out for the night in one of their encampments. One of the officers looked at him intently and seemed to listen carefully to his voice.

'Are you from Lucknow?' he asked finally, after a few sentences of conversation.

'Yes', said my brother, seeing the marks of acne on the man's face.

'Vincente de Rozio's the name,' he heard the man say. 'Remember me?'

My brother said Vincente and he caught up with each other that night and exchanged their life histories, from the time de Rozio fled the school to the time his own regiment, like his father's, got posted to Tankse, near the Pangong Lake. It seems nothing very spectacular ever happened to de Rozio after he got away from the school. I think my brother found this fairly disappointing, having stored him up in his mind as a symbol of the most consummate and successful rebellion he'd ever experienced. But

51

we believed in fiction, and things that seemed disappointing about real-life characters didn't bother us excessively, because we knew there was always more to people than met the eye. And as it turned out my brother was able, in the end, to retain his image of de Rozio as a character whose life was tied by some strange destiny to his own.

De Rozio told my brother he'd run off to railway relatives and finished school privately, then joined the army, and now spent most of his time skiing and playing golf. My brother saw no sign of the extraordinary in his eyes; a Spartacus once, he seemed now to have become like the rest of us, a father and a friend. He had married five years earlier and said with predictable, commonplace pride that he had a daughter; she was just over a year old. 'Must tell you the extraordinary way in which we got her, men,' he added.

There was no stopping people once they started confiding in my brother. The travel aura around him said very clearly he wasn't competing, that he could be trusted with things that were intimate and needed guarding against other people, that he would be moving on to look at other things. It made the women let their hair down and open up with him in ways they just wouldn't with me. It made de Rozio comfortable and relaxed enough to want to part with something personal, almost as though he needed to share something that belonged only to him with my brother.

'To tell you the truth,' he said, a minute or so before my brother left that part of the world, 'she's not my daughter at all, strictly speaking, but just keep this to yourself, men. Thing is we tried for three years to get a child but it just wouldn't work, y'know. Anyway, an old pal of mine in the II Sikh Rifles suggested this place called Third World Clinic in Scotland, and so off we went to one of these sperm merchant fellahs they have there, some Sindhi chappie called Brahmani or something li' that. I say, men, these Sindhis will sell you just about anything.'

He laughed, and my brother forced out a smile. 'Anyway,' said

Vincente, 'long and short of it is that now we have a bonny little lass. Must show you her picture some day.'

My brother swung to the correct position on his motorcycle, flexing himself to begin the next leg of his travels. He felt the cold air of Ladakh on his hands. He saw his past swim volitionless over purple-blue water into a future de Rozio, and, as he adjusted his dark glasses, the colour of the Pangong Lake came into his eyes.

'Yes', he said vacantly. 'Yes, you really must,' he said.

LYNNE BRYAN

Better Than Beer and Skittles

———

Frank drops me off outside the sisters' flat. He waves goodbye in that leather-clad way of his before accelerating down the road. I watch a while, seeing how his bike's suspension copes with the potholes and uneven tarmac. Then I remove my helmet and shake my hair, which is a silly move because I've very little hair to shake. I had it cut a couple of days ago by my brother's girlfriend Geena. She smokes as she cuts and I half expected to have the singed look, but she's done a good job. She's clipped it up the back, but kept the fringe long. This is fine by me. I have this habit of pushing my fringe off my face when I talk, so I would miss it if it got the chop. Frank says, 'You doing that so I can read your lips?' I don't take offence. The sisters confide that before I visit they always turn their hearing aids up a notch – 'to catch your dulcet tones'.

Frank and I are going through a rough patch. It's all to do with my visits here: every Tuesday night I come, regular as clockwork, and at first he accepted it. But now the work's beer and skittles has been moved to a Tuesday, and he's pissed off that I'd sooner be with the sisters than with workmates. I tell him the sisters' is like a breath of fresh air; that I don't want to spend my evenings with the same people I stand next to during the day. It's hard enough as it is to last my forty-hour week cooped up with Marjorie and Sheila and the rest packing those sausage rolls, six rolls to a box, every roll three inch by one inch, every box red and orange striped: 'Authentic English Pork'. I dream about sausage rolls. I dream that Marjorie and Sheila and the rest push the rolls one after the other down my throat until I gag and balloon and finally burst – my insides, my brain, my heart, nothing but sausage roll. Frank says I'm too sensitive and swears he'll run off with Louise, the mini-skirted dwarf from Quality Control. But I know he won't. We have something, Frank and I. When we get together, it's fireworks. Yes.

'Hello, love,' says Helen, tapping me on the shoulder as I stroll up the entry.

'Hiya,' I say. 'Is he out there again tonight?'

'I'm afraid so,' says Helen. 'I've pleaded with him, but he says he's doing no harm; just checking his wife's up to nothing immoral.'

'Immoral,' I say. 'Big word.' I look past Helen's shoulder and can just make out the front end of a blue Cortina. Inside, I know, sits her husband Derek, a fat man with no taste. He wears bright orange and red lumberjack shirts, shiny tracksuit bottoms, and shoes with Cuban heels. He's about fifty and believes the sisters' is a knocking shop. Ever since Helen's first visit six months ago he's parked his car and, fingers drumming against the dashboard, has waited to catch her at it. A diseased mind. He must know by now that only women visit the sisters'. Perhaps he thinks we're porno dykes and our sewing boxes hide kinky sex aids: strap-on willies, massage oils, a whip, a chain, a crutchless panty, and a peek-a-boo bra. I doubt though that he'd be able to think of such things. He's the type of man whose mind can only cope with the missionary position; the dainty woman lying back and thinking of England, the bulldog pumping her from above. Do I sound bitter? Mmm, perhaps I had too many of those nights myself, before I met Frank and his amazing bag of tricks.

'Rose phoned the other day,' says Helen, slipping the key into the sisters' front-door lock. 'Asked me to bring some Fishermen's Friends. Apparently Ivy has a summer cold. She's been in bed on and off the past week.'

'Got to be careful at her age,' I say, pushing open the door.

We step into the flat. I love this flat. The sisters haven't changed a thing for years. The wallpaper is old, creamy, and covered in pink roses. The carpets are worn thin and have lost a lot of their colour. Everywhere smells fusty, like the insides of my nephew's duffel-bag, the one he uses for PE.

Rose has come out of the Quilting Room to greet us. 'Did you manage to get the Fishermen's Friends?' she asks. Helen nods and fumbles in her dress pocket for them.

'For fuck's sake,' shouts Jean, her voice husky from fags, reaching us from the room. 'Grab her before she collapses. Eighty-eight is not the age to go chasing Fishermen's Friends.'

'I've always liked a sailor,' jokes Rose. She's wearing her green dress again, which suits her. It is very low at the front and reveals her thin breasts. She always dangles a necklace between her breasts. Today it's her fruit and nut necklace, made from varnished hazelnuts and wood cut to look like a slice of pear or peach or apple. She must have been a real goer when young. Don't know why she never married, probably had more sense.

I follow Rose and Helen into the Quilting Room. Jean gives us a queenly wave of welcome, while Ivy smiles. Two years older than Rose, Ivy looks like she's at death's door. Her hair is very white, though she wears it down in a girlie way, with clips holding it from her eyes. Jean bought her the clips for her last birthday. One is a luminous orange that glows in the dark, the other is pink with gold glitter sprinkled on it. She also has a lime-green headband which is dotted with huge cream daisies, but she only wears this when she feels like partying. The horrible thing about Ivy is her skin. It is very wrinkled and covered in large brown blotches. It hangs off her like she's lost a lot of weight. Poor Ivy. She looks flushed. It must be her cold, or perhaps it's the sunlight shining through the window. It glows around her head like a halo.

'Come and sit down,' says Jean, sewing to the left of Ivy. Jean is the one who got me into this . She's a funny woman: funny ha ha and funny peculiar. She gets obsessions.

She was first married to Lyle, still alive, a good-looking bloke who runs the local pop round. Jean talks of him fondly. 'The first you marry for love, the second for money,' she says. Lyle was a real love. When Jean gets on the vodkas and limes she tells of how Lyle makes her heart beat. She remembers hot, exciting nights. Lyle is no missionary position man. He's inventive. But Jean is into status. She couldn't live for long with a man whose sole income comes from selling lemonade. So she ran off with George. George is the opposite of Lyle. He's short for a start, but he's also rich. He owns a chain of discount stores; those shops where you can get sanitary towels made from shredded cardboard for 20p a dozen. The type of shop that is doing our Ozone. His hairsprays are lethal. Geena uses them on the blue rinse OAPs, those that like their hair to be as stiff as a corpse. She warns them though not to stand too close to a fire or to her fag or else they'll end up the corpse. But George is not all bad. He bought Jean her patchwork and quilting shop; something she'd been hankering after for ages. She loves her business. She claims that patchwork is an important art form, that it speaks volumes about women. She goes on about this, strutting around her shop like the original burn your bra. Silly cow. I say to Jean that she's not liberated, that she's owned by George. But she won't have it. 'I chose him,' she says. 'I'm in control.' And that was how I first met her, doing her 'I'm in control' bit, when I went to Mother Goose to buy some cottons. She seized me by the shoulders and pointed out a notice.

'*Help!*' it said, in scrawly spider hand. '*We are two ancient ladies trying to achieve the impossible. Fifteen years ago we set ourselves the task of sewing quilts for all our nephews and nieces. We have managed to sew a quilt a year so far, but we still have four quilts to go. As our eyesight and everything else is failing we would appreciate a hand with these remaining quilts. Once a week will do. Tuesdays at 7.00 p.m. Come to Lower Flat, 20 Kennedar Drive. Tea and biscuits served. Mind next-door's Alsatian.*'

'I think,' said Jean, 'that we ought to attend this, you and I. I can see you're the type who's looking for something extra. Be a change, get you away from chasing the men, hey?'

Frank told me to steer clear, but there's something about Jean that's very persuasive. She has this face that dares you. She's pulling it now, because I'm refusing to settle. It takes me a while to start my sewing. I like to wander, to look at my friends, to chat. I'm like a bee droning about every place but on the flower where I should be, sucking up my honey.

'Samantha, you got ants in your pants?' says Jean.

'She's just admiring the decor,' smiles Ivy, who knows the way I go about things.

'It's nice,' I say. 'I know what to expect when I come here.'

'A tip,' chuckles Rose, passing the packet of Fishermen's Friends to her elder sister. Ivy opens the packet. She pulls out a sweet and drops it into her skinny mouth.

'Yuk,' she says.

When Jean and I first turned up at the sisters' we had a bit of a shock. They are not your normal everyday old ladies; not at all like Granny, stuck as she is in the past with nothing in her head but death. No, Rose and Ivy have spunk, ambition. They began their quilting marathon when Rose turned seventy, Ivy seventy-two. They pooled their savings to buy a huge quilting frame, which they assembled from kit form in their living-room, now called the Quilting Room. In their hurry, they didn't clear the room to make a real space for the frame, but they pushed every piece of furniture outwards. Even now their sofa, telly, radio, bookcase, drinks bar, and aquarium line the walls of the room like they are second-hand goods waiting the rag-and-bone man.

The aquarium is best. It stands on the sofa and the fish swim back and forth against a backdrop of cream and brown stripes. Jean, when she first saw this, thought of contacting the sea-creatures' branch of the RSPCA, but changed her mind. The fish look healthy. There are always six of them and they always shine golden, not white like they are sickening. OAP fishes. Perhaps they live off the dust that hangs like curtains in this topsy-turvy room. 'The Twilight Zone,' says Frank, when I talk about it. 'Strange things happen to those who enter the Twilight Zone. Little old ladies turn into willy weirdo witches. Watch out.

They'll strap you to their frame one of these days, and will suck you of your youth and beauty.' Beauty! I often tell Frank that he should write, such a vivid imagination he's got. But he says he has no time, that he's devoted to becoming a world-class beer and skittles man. Could be Jean's right: 'The first you marry for love, the second for money.'

Today Jean is dressed in her Spanish costa packet outfit. A bolero trouser suit made out of red felt-like fabric and fringed with black tassels. She looks a bugger, but somehow carries it off. Confidence, I suppose. Helen, who has taken my place beside Jean, is a different kind of woman. She's into British Home Store Specials. Make her look kind of dowdy, but no doubt her husband wouldn't want her to dress in anything more appealing.

Helen joined us ladies off her own bat. She heard about Ivy and Rose through the neighbourhood grapevine. She loves sewing, wanted to be a needlework teacher once, and so defied her husband for the very first time and came here. She reminds Ivy of her and Rose's mother: a small sweet person who was married to a drayman. His first love was beer, the second horses. Women weren't noticed until they didn't get the dinner on time. Same with Helen's husband. He didn't take much notice of her until she started trekking out on Tuesday nights. Then he started playing the Grand Old Man Possessive. Sometimes Helen mentions how she makes him a treat steak and kidney to butter him up, mostly though she keeps her mouth shut. She pushes him to one side like he's a nasty mess that needs seeing to, but not before she has had her fun. Her sewing box is neat and tidy, a real tool of pleasure. The quilting cottons are arranged in colour order; the needles stuck in straight lines in the padded lid of the box; her thimble, which she slips on to her finger now, has a special resting place wrapped in a lace hanky. 'Touch the quilt, Samantha,' says Helen to me, looking at it like a lover.

'Beautiful,' I say, running my hand, which I've checked to see is clean, over the ivory and cream silk and the teeny-weeny quilting stitches. The quilt is the sisters' last, their nineteenth. It's for their great-great-great-niece who is ten years old. All the quilts that the sisters have sewn take away the breath, but this one can't be beat.

Ivy and Rose have quilted from the year dot. They made quilts for their mother from scraps. The quilts were usually used for bedding, though Ivy has told us how her mother once persuaded their landlord to take a crazy quilt in exchange for a fortnight's free rent. Jean thinks this is a wonderful story and has added it to her patchwork museum that she's set up above her shop. She got Ivy to write it out, and has stuck it with a picture of a crazy quilt on a display board under the heading: 'Quilts vs homelessness. Women do it again!' A lovely image I say, but I bet many landlords, even in the old days, would sooner have had a bit of the other. I know my landlord, when I'm behind with the readies, wants payment with some up and under. But I'm not having it: once they're in your pants, they're hard to get out. Got to be careful in this twentieth century. One man, a heavy-duty rubber, and a closed back passage. Simple pleasures.

'This seat taken?' I ask Rose, plonking myself down on the only free chair in the room. A wonky chair, it rocks in time to your sewing arm.

'It's yours, no strings,' says Rose, smiling.

'Why thanks.' I rest my sewing box on my knee. I click it open, and rummage through my jumble of cottons and pins and needles and templates. 'Do you think this is going to wash all right?' I mutter for the sake of muttering.

'The quilt?' asks Helen.

'Mmm.' I find a decent needle and thread it through my jumper so I can't lose it.

'Don't see why not,' says Jean.

'Well those dresses were never meant for washing. You're only supposed to wear them once.'

'Nothing to worry about, I washed them when we got them home, and they were OK,' says Ivy, looking as if she couldn't wash a pair of pants, let alone four wedding dresses. 'We always do this for every quilt. You should know, Samantha.'

'Sorry, I forgot,' I say, remembering quick, for the sisters still use what they learnt when small. For a start they never buy new fabrics. They use old fabrics, like used clothes or curtains. They wash them, then play around with them, matching this and that, before cutting them up and sewing them into quilts. Making something new and different from something else. The sisters say that by reusing fabrics they add a little extra to the quilts. I agree. I watched a programme once where this woman, whose daughter had died, made a quilt from out of the daughter's summer dresses, so that when she slept beneath the quilt she felt her daughter was still alive in some way, close to her. 'Spooky,' said Frank, bullied into watching. 'Too arty-farty for her own good.' But Frank has no idea: he can't get his head round this nineteenth quilt at all, made as it is from wedding dresses.

Jean helped the sisters get the dresses. She took them out to Bridal Delight, which is on the verge of bankruptcy – too many youngsters living in the big S for Sin – and they bought them at the cheapest of prices. The sisters wanted wedding dresses because they want this quilt to say something about being pure. I say a wedding dress in this modern world is more than a sure sign that the bride's been tried and tested. Second-hand goods, but clean second-hand goods – if you get my drift – is all that's wanted now. A disease-free bride. But Rose and Ivy won't have it. They believe their dresses speak of innocent things like the Virgin Mary; like their old age without sex; like their little niece who is still before sex. Frank tells me that this last part is crap, loads of his friends reckon they know ten year olds who are dying for it. I say it's wishful thinking. Men like to believe there are nympho ten year olds walking the streets, when really little girls have nothing more on their minds than hamburgers and soap stars. Perhaps when they reach twelve it's different. Twelve is when your breasts begin to show. Twelve is when John across the road touched me up in his den. My first.

I take my quilting needle from my jumper. I hold it high so the summer sunlight shines through the eye, making it easier for me to know exactly where to stick my cotton, and I thread it. The funny thing about John is he's only supposed to have one ball, that's what Louise, the mini-skirted dwarf from Quality Control tells me, but I can't remember.

'Day-dreamer, wake up!' says Jean. She gives me a look with her hard face, before bending over the quilt again, her black back-combed hair making an ugly spider shadow upon the silk. Perhaps I ought to introduce her to Geena and her magic scissors, but then Jean's hair is like Buckingham Palace, a national monument. It would go against God, England, and Margaret Thatcher to touch it.

I sew a stitch. 'Are you watching, Jean?' I ask.

'And about time too,' she smiles, not one to hold a grudge for long. 'We've got a lot to do on this.'

Too true. The quilt is just a plain strip quilt which suits the silk, but it's covered in real difficult stitching. Ivy and Rose don't go in for this usually: they tend to go for a tidy running-stitch which follows the outline of the patchwork shapes such as SHOO-FLY or THE GRANDMOTHER'S FAN. But for this quilt they have pricked out a design of CABLE and FEATHER WREATH. It's not quite like embroidering the whole quilt, but it's close. Time consuming. We've been at it for nine months. The sisters joke they've made this last piece so fiddly to delay things. They're afraid, as we all are, about what's going to happen once this last quilt is sewn.

Jean has pressed for the sisters to hold an exhibition of all nineteen quilts, once the nineteenth is finished, in her museum. A good idea for her business, certainly draw in the crowds, but, as she admitted to Helen on the quiet, it would give the sisters something to look forward to. The sisters said no. They're unsure if all nephews and nieces have kept their quilts, whether all would be returned, whether they'd look as clean and as good as when they were first made. They told Jean that they'd be upset to see tea stains or egg stains or sick or sex upon their handiwork. So they turned down the offer, as usual not mincing their words.

'You're beginning to fill out, Samantha,' says Rose, stitching expert and fast, proving my point.

'Tell me about it,' I mutter. Frank has been saying the same thing, says my breasts are getting heavier and my belly more rounded. He wants a kid so he's hoping that's the reason. I'm hoping it's age creeping on. Once you hit twenty-five they do say that the body goes. I don't want my body to go, but I'd sooner that than a kiddy. I can't face the thought of squeezing one out: the pain. I don't like pain. And what happens when it gets to be a teenager? Teenagers treat mothers like shit. I threw a can of tomato soup at my mother when she wouldn't allow me at fifteen to go to the Free and Easy Singles Disco down Canal Street. It hit her on the thigh: I was aiming for her heart.

'Oh, but I think it suits you,' says Ivy. 'Bonny. You can be too thin, you know.' She snuffles and rummages in her pocket for a Fishermen's Friend.

'Thinness equals meanness of spirit. Look at me!' laughs Rose.

'Your spirit is far from mean,' says Helen quietly.

But I can't be bothered with this, I'm rattled. 'Well, I'm not pregnant, if that's what you're getting at,' I nip. 'Precaution is the name of the game with me.' I stitch the curve of a Cable badly, and tutting begin to unpick the thread.

'There's nothing wrong with being pregnant,' says Jean. She's speaking with her head bent more so over the quilt. 'I loved it.'

'You pregnant!' What a revelation. I thought Jean was the original Ms Contraception. I stop my sewing.

'Mmm,' says Jean. 'Didn't last long. Lyle got me humping round his crates of pop. I lost it. Just sat down on the toilet and there it went. Whoosh. Like a big period.'

'But that's awful,' I say. Jean has never opened up like this before. Usually she is jokey or all strident new woman. Perhaps I should hug her or something, but she doesn't look huggable in that bull-fighter's outfit. I can see Helen and Rose and Ivy are thinking the same. So awkward. Ivy is losing herself in her hanky, while Rose touches her necklace like she has prayer beads in her hands. Helen just looks shocked, doubly-shocked, because suddenly there he is pressing his outsized nose against the window pane.

'I know you're in there,' shouts Helen's husband. 'I know

what you're doing. You bitch. Has he got it up you yet? You're breaking my heart.' He raises a hand to shade his eyes, trying to see into the room. Jean is first off the mark. She helps Ivy from her chair. 'Better move back, just in case,' she says.

'Yes' I whisper, watching the orange and red lumberjack shirt as it sways backwards, forwards. It blocks out the usual view of the sisters' flower boxes, stray dogs, kids and council flats. I begin to wish next-door's Alsatian, which used to cause us so much trouble, hadn't died. It would've sunk its teeth into Derek for sure.

'Getting enough are you? Enjoying yourself?' the bully shouts. 'I can see you. I can see you.' He bangs his fists hard against the glass. Thump. Thump. Thump. Thump. Bloody big fists like flesh-covered boxing gloves. I wonder whether he uses them on Helen: she's never actually said.

'I'll go out to him,' she murmurs. She looks afraid, shrunk into her flowery dress.

'No don't,' says Rose, 'that's what he's wanting.'

'Too right,' says Jean, stepping up to the window.

'For fuck's sake,' I say, pushing my fringe off my face. Old habits die hard even in troubled times. 'What are you playing at?'

Jean flaps a hand, 'I'm going to teach this bastard a lesson.'

She pulls back her bolero jacket to undo the blouse beneath. One by one the buttons slip from their holes. Easy. 'George likes this outfit,' she smiles. 'It's husband-friendly.'

Ivy, Rose, Helen and me: we are quiet. Can't say a word. There is Jean and she looks magnificient. The blouse has fallen open and there shines her body – brown, healthy, and perfect. Her breasts are much better than mine. They are big, motherly, but they don't sag. They are powerful. A black tassel fringing her bolero rests just above the left nipple; it's a finishing touch. She looks like a painting hung on the wrong wall, because all the while, behind her, stands this pathetic angry man.

Jean turns to face him. 'Watch my technique, girls,' she says. She begins to rub herself against the pane, up and down, up and down. I can only see her back, but it's enough for me. I squeal, excited: my head full of lovely tits pressing fat and warm upon the icy glass.

'Ooohh,' I squeal. 'Ooohh.'

'Shh, Samantha, shh,' whispers Helen, her eyes brighter, no longer frightened. 'You'll spoil her concentration.'

'You know,' says Rose, huddling up, 'that kind of wiggle takes years of practice. I myself have never mastered the art.'

'Monroe,' says Ivy, 'she had it.'

'Oh quiet,' says Helen. 'Jean's having problems, can't you see? I reckon Derek needs glasses.'

And true, it looks like Jean's show is wasted. Helen's husband peers through the window, blind as a bat to her gorgeous flesh. Till she stretches up, pretending to kiss him. Then it registers, and it's like he's witnessed death. His face turns a ghastly white, and he begins to back from the window, his arms held out, sweat patches darkening his lumberjack shirt. 'That's it, boy,' shouts Jean, triumphant. 'You've no idea, have you?' She works her body wilder now, like an upmarket belly-dancer.

'Never,' says Ivy, 'have I seen anything so. . .'

'Marvellous,' laughs Rose. 'And look at Derek. What a Derek! He's been hit between the eyes!'

'Enough,' shouts Jean. She spins round and with a final nifty move draws the Quilting Room curtains on the man.

'Wonderful,' I say. 'Bloody wonderful.' I imagine Derek stumbling to his Cortina, see him tripping over his own feet – so confused is he, so winded.

I reach for the lamp, which stands on top of the sisters' drinks bar, and I switch it on. The lamp has an orange glass shade and the light that shines through it makes the room glow magical. The quilt shimmers. The water in the aquarium appears a dark blue like the deepest blue of the sea where whales and sting rays swim. I feel very safe, and I can see that Helen and Rose and Ivy and Jean, who has buttoned her blouse, feel very safe too. There's a Famous Five feeling. Yes.

'I believe there are a few old bottles of rum and gin and perhaps sherry in that bar,' says Rose.

'And glasses,' adds Ivy. 'Nice ones too. If I remember rightly they have a pattern of gold crisscrosses around the brims.'

'I could do with a drink,' admits Helen. 'Make mine a large one.'

I sit with Rose and Ivy and Helen and Jean around the quilting frame. We slug our glasses of booze, making sure not a drop spills upon the quilt, but going for it all the same. 'You know,' I say, 'Frank's been trying to get me to jack this in. Wants me to go to the works' beer and skittles night instead.'

'But this is much better than beer and skittles,' says Ivy, poking around in her Fishermen's Friends packet for another sweet.

'I know,' I smile. 'And what's more I don't think you should be mixing cough stuff with the strong stuff.'

'You tell her,' laughs Jean, trying to run her hand through her black back-combed hair, but getting her fingers stuck half-way.

A Regular Thing

I'm confused. For years I hoped Emily would stop charging me. Now she has I find I don't want it. I feel the bottom has dropped out of my life. I feel threatened, insecure.

I'm thirty-six. I first met Emily when I was twenty-nine. At my work in Astley Central Library.

I started in the library at sixteen. A natural step: I've always been fond of books and during school days was nicknamed 'Boff'. But I'm not intellectual. Most books are beyond me. Like the books Emily reads on advanced economics.

I'm just comforted by books. Well thumbed books with cheesy pages and broken spines. Like the paperbacks in the Romance section. At sixteen I kept away from Romance, thought it sissy. Now I'm section head.

I met Emily two months into my promotion. I was rummaging behind the loans counter for the most recent edition of the *Romance Writers' Quarterly* when I heard coughing. The coughing was accompanied by a voice. Such a voice, husky but efficient. 'Excuse me,' it said, 'but I'm in a rush. Can you stamp my books now?'

Used to disappointments I expected the voice to belong to an elderly spinster with a smoker's throat. So I was abrupt. 'Sorry,' I said, 'I don't work the loans counter. I'll get Miss Pedi to deal with you. *Miss Pedi!*'

Then I saw Emily. My eyes worked upwards from her girlie breasts, to her face with its cold eyes, its bob of oily hair. My heart somersaulted, and my penis began to stiffen. I rubbed it casually against the loans counter. 'Hello,' said Emily. 'I'm called Emily.'

'Steven,' I replied.

'Steven,' she said. 'Nice name. Before Miss Pedi comes can I ask a question?'

I nodded, flushed. Something told me the question wouldn't be about books.

I'm not usually daring. I tend to stand back, watch others walk into the lions' den. But Emily bewitched me. She has tremendous power. She knows how to make a coward brave.

When we met at the fountain she looked like a lonely man's dream: tight black jumper, skirt, and those little lace-up booties with pointy heels made from shiny plastic. I felt ill-equipped. 'I haven't much money,' I said. I clutched my thin wallet; even as section head I make less money than my father who sweeps for Astley Precision Tools. 'I can stretch to a Chinese and a couple of beers.'

Emily smiled, an amazing smile, the lips pulling back to show the fleshy pink underside. 'What do we want with a Chinese?' she said. 'Let's make our own entertainment.'

Emily took me to her home, a flat above a babywear shop. A small flat with one main room painted white. Two archways led from this room. Through one archway was a kitchen; through the other, the bathroom. Swinging bead curtains hung from each archway. They were identical, depicting an American usherette wearing a Stars and Stripes bunny outfit. Around the usherette's neck hung a tray. The tray rested on her large breasts. She smiled a big smile, and a bubble led from the smile. 'Peanuts, sir?' she asked.

I didn't really know what to make of the flat. It was so sparse. The bead curtains provided the only real decoration, and they seemed to be deliberately over the top. Like they'd been chosen as a statement. But I couldn't work out the statement. They hung there, shimmering, threatening. And instead of asking Emily about them, J turned to her bookcase.

The bookcase ran between the curtains. It was huge. Filled

with books. For a while, I examined the books. They were all on finance. 'What's wrong, Steven?' asked Emily. She slid a thin arm round my shoulders.

'There's not a novel in sight,' I said.

'Or a book about women's troubles,' she laughed. 'I'm a practical girl, into what makes the world go round.'

'Money,' I said.

'And sex.' She took my hand and led me to the only other piece of furniture in the room – her bed.

I'd dated before Emily. Mostly nice girls with soft bodies and big eyes. Willing girls. But unadventurous. No costumes. No games. No dirty talk. No slapping, kicking, punching, or spitting. That first time with Emily showed what I'd been missing. She made me feel like a king, a conqueror. 'Emily,' I said, 'that was wonderful.'

I was unprepared for what followed. I thought we'd have a drink, swap stories, relax with each other, feel our way. But no. Emily sat astride me, bending her arms behind her back, making her small breasts point forward like individual jellies, and made plain what was going to happen.

'This one's for free,' she said. 'Charging first time is counter-productive. You'll not come back for more. Not unless you're desperate. And I don't want you if you're desperate.'

I don't think myself an idiot. But perhaps I am. Perhaps Emily saw me coming. Sometimes I check myself in the mirror, to see if it's written over my face. But there are no clues. Only my spectacles, my thin mouth, my blondish hair, my bad skin stare back.

'But Emily,' I protested. She placed a finger upon my lips and hushed me.

'Don't knock it,' she said, 'it's a good deal.'

My body was hungry for Emily so I began to see her on a regular basis, once a week, twenty pounds a time. But I wasn't swept along. Mentally I kept distant, tried to sort out the situation. I took to spying on her.

Early mornings, library lunchtimes, dinnertimes and most

evenings I waited outside her flat to catch her at it. But no men in dirty raincoats, no young boys anxious to lose their virginity, only a small woman dressed in a suit and carrying a briefcase.

'So Emily, you're not a prostitute?' I asked, casually as I could. She lay on her bed, looking wonderful: her top half naked, her legs covered with a wrap of black silk.

'No,' she said in her husky voice. 'I'm your lover.'

'But then why do you charge me?'

Emily explained. She said men had treated her badly. They had taken her love and used it against her. So now she charged. Because charging meant she was in control, charging meant she was safe. She spoke matter-of-factly, like she was reading a shopping list. But I believed her. It made sense to me.

The confession strengthened our relationship. We began to see more of each other, took the test, and stopped using condoms, and though Emily continued to ask for money I felt encouraged, hopeful. I imagined a day when we'd be like any normal couple, exchanging our love freely.

After a year we bought a flat together, and I took Emily to meet my parents. They hated her. On sight. They wouldn't admit to it. They were polite. They talked to her about her job, gave her ham and boiled beef sandwiches, iced fancies and a cup of weak tea. But you could see it in their eyes. My mother looked Emily up and down. As she took in Emily's thigh-boots, hotpants and lycra top, her face was blank, her pupils marked with distaste. She actually said, 'A word in your ear, Steven. Is this the right kind of girl for you? Isn't she a bit unclean?'

I replied, 'I love her, Mother. We get on well together.'

Then I began to feel less positive. There were days when I'd look at our relationship, and see nothing. Emily and I would meet after work, go out for a meal or to the pictures, return home, and yet still seem separate. I knew it wasn't my fault. I offered myself; told her my history, my likes and dislikes, my longings. But Emily was so closed, only gave out at night when we touched. And she spoilt that by charging.

At one point I nearly cracked. Her charges rose above the rate of inflation. They began to cripple me. And I had to take an extra job, collecting pools monies from Astley's nastiest estate – Craigheath. It wasn't a pleasant job. I had a couple of dangerous customers who once got me in a back alley. They beat me. They took off my glasses, stood me against a wall, and pushed ring-covered hands into my face. 'Poor poor Steven,' cooed Emily when I returned home.

'You could stop it, you know,' I said to her as she dabbed a cotton-wool ball over my cheeks, nose, ears. The ball was soaked in Dettol. It stung. To take my mind off the pain I concentrated on Emily's breasts which moved across my chest, tickling.

'How can I stop it?' she asked, innocent. 'Should I take up karate, go out for revenge?'

I squeezed her hand. The Dettol trickled brown down her skinny wrist. 'Getting ready to thump me now, are you?' she said. Her eyes were strangely bright.

I went to the doctor. I told Emily it was because my wounds were infected. It wasn't a total untruth. Blue-green pus lined the cut which ran across my cheek.

I chose a locum. I didn't want to confess to my regular, who'd seen me grow, who'd watched my testicles drop. The locum traced her gentle finger along the cut, then asked me what I'd really come for. 'Sexual problems?' she asked.

'Sort of,' I confided.

The locum listened carefully. She nodded her head, made notes. 'I think you should approach the mother,' she advised. 'You shouldn't blame the mother, mothers get blamed for too many things. But I think you should have a chat. Mothers can be very helpful.'

Emily's mother dresses like a man. She favours double-breasted suits made from merino. Beneath which she wears a white shirt, and a yellow or black tie. She sports cufflinks, Argyle socks, and brogues. Her hair is cut to the scalp; her face free of make-up.

Emily introduced us at the flat-warming. I recognized her

immediately. 'You used to visit Emily at her old place,' I said. 'Tuesdays and Thursdays. I saw you.'

'Yes,' said Emily's mother, 'I know all about your spying.'

I hated her then. Now not at all. She speaks her mind, and, beneath the macho stuff, has a heart. Emily loves her too. The flat seems to lighten when her mother's around. There's more laughter, and Emily opens up, tells stories I've never heard before.

It took me a while to confide in Emily's mother. I was reticent because I suspected she wasn't straight. I imagined her as a lover of women similar to herself – all short hair and men's suits. Of course I couldn't ignore the evidence. But somehow I thought of Emily as a one-night stand: Emily's mother lying back and taking it because she wanted a child. But no.

Emily's mother loves men. My boss, Mr Brudly, confided in me. 'She's a real fire-cracker,' he said. 'A rare and dangerous woman. Our affair lasted five months.'

'Yes,' said Emily's mother when I faced her. 'It ended badly. I told him it was over while waiting my turn at the outpatients.'

Then I learnt that Emily's mother knew about her daughter. About how she charged me. 'Emily has told me all,' she said. 'But there's little I can do. My daughter's headstrong, opinionated. She'll always approach life her own way. You could try to make her jealous. But that's a crude device. I suggest if you love her, then just persevere.'

'But,' I said, lifting my head off her fly-buttoned lap. 'But I don't even know if she cares for me. She's so controlled.'

Six months ago, Emily made the spare room into an office. She left her job as financial advisor for Dryson, Dryson and Sons to go it alone. I was worried. For a while I thought it'd cost me more for sex. Extra revenue to cover loss of earnings, or to fund the computer, desk, headed notepaper, filing cabinets, photocopier, and electronic pencil sharpener. But she didn't seem to need it. Emily poached clients from her old firm. She ran an advertising campaign which promised personal service; a promise headlining beneath a profile shot of Emily looking her best. Soon her desk diary was full and she was having to turn away clients.

She now has a host of regulars. Mostly men, though some are women. The women power-dress and carry briefcases. They snub me. The men wink.

I was jealous of the men. I took a fortnight off work to check Emily was giving them financial advice and nothing else. One evening she came to me and said, 'This business is kosher, Steven. I only want to sleep with you.'

That night Emily and I had our first real row. From opposite sides of the bedroom we slung insults, grievances. Emily said I was a typical chauvinist. I told her she was a typical whore. We made our demands: Emily wanting to be loved for herself, me wanting free sex.

That argument may have been behind Emily's change of mind. That and my decision to become celibate. Though I still desired her, I turned my back on her.

Eventually she confronted me; complained that her incomings from our sex were at an all-time low. 'Why, Steven?' she asked.

She looked confused when I explained. 'This isn't normal, Emily,' I said. 'My paying you has to stop. It puts a barrier between us. I've lived with you for years and still I don't know what you're thinking. Since I've met you I've been on an emotional roller-coaster. I'm tired out.'

She watched me closely. Her cold blue eyes, unsympathetic, searching. I began to cry. I lifted my hand to my face, and that was when she changed. The eyes stayed the same cold blue, but her chin, her cheeks, her mouth lost their hard edge. She wasn't my Emily.

A week later she handed me a letter to read on my way to work. I slid it in my jacket pocket, fearful of the white envelope, the bold 'STEVEN' on the front. I entered Elder Park, found a bench by the pond. The sun shone, gardeners raked stray twigs and Coke cans from the murky water, the boat-keeper untied the paddle boats. I listened to the sound of rope dragging across wood. Then I opened the letter. At first I couldn't read the

writing. It seemed to blur, and inside I felt sick, imagined Emily
was saying goodbye. When I could focus I was surprised to see
her words stretched across the page gigantic, urgent, saying
something very different. *'Dear Steven, I've decided to stop charging
you. It doesn't make sense. We've been together for so long. Let's start
afresh. Emily.'*

I read the letter three times. Each time I felt more elated, felt
my future advancing – hopeful, warm, blessed.

Now I'm not so sure.

Emily hasn't charged me for a while. In the early days it was
glorious. Real pleasure. I found my wallet growing fat. I treated
myself to new clothes, bought Emily finance books and sexy
underwear. We made love whenever and wherever. The fore-
play was gentle. Our caresses not governed by how much I could
afford. And after sex we would open up, reveal our fears,
desires. Emily had some terrible tales to tell. A man had once
tried to set fire to her, threw a lighted box of matches into her
hair. Another man had kept her locked in his room, fed her on
chocolate and Sweetheart Stout. I would hug her as she spoke of
these things. And she was generous. When I spoke of my past,
and my petty difficulties with girls who'd behaved too nicely, she
never condemned, never claimed her experiences more important, more painful. Then she flipped.

I should've seen it coming. Emily is a professional. If she
chooses to do something she does it right. She does not skip
corners. She began to borrow books from my section of the
library. She would devour the slim pink volumes, jot down
endless notes on Romance. She would take these notes everywhere with her, consult them when washing, eating.

She wears rose print dresses now. Puts a large silk ribbon in
her hair to soften it. She's talking of selling her business. She
wants me to be the breadwinner, while she stays at home. She
wants to get married. She wants to have children. She's become
submissive; her conversation punctuated with phrases like
'Whatever you think, darling', her love-making conventional.
She's lost her cold cold gaze.

Last night, I telephoned her mother. 'Please do something.' I begged. 'I can't stand this. It's torture.'

Emily's mother laughed. 'I've told you before, Steven, I have no control over my daughter. She's stubborn. Besides, why are you complaining? Isn't she giving you what you've always wanted?'

I was silent.

'Well, isn't she?' pushed Emily's mother.

'I suppose,' I replied. 'I really don't know.'

This morning I wake, raise myself on an elbow, watch Emily as she sleeps. She is very beautiful. Despite the little girl ribbon. Despite the flannelette nightie. I touch her upon the shoulder, brush a hair from her mouth. I am so confused. I wonder whether I should've let things be, not forced her to change. I have no answer. I feel like the floor has been taken from under me. That I have nothing solid to stand on. I feel desperate.

Hair So Black

———

I check myself in the bathroom mirror. My fine, grey hair is scraped into a bun. My face free of make-up. I look naked, old, as if I've been pickled. My only concession to ornamentation is a pair of earrings: silver drops like solidified tears.

This is a bad day for me: the day my friend and neighbour, Daphne Carter, is to be buried.

I was with Daphne when she died. We were sitting side by side on her sofa watching a wildlife programme. She reached across my lap for her knitting. She was knitting some awful multi-coloured coat. And she collapsed. Her head falling heavy upon my stomach.

'Daphne!' I cried. 'What are you playing at!'

When she said nothing, I began to stroke her hair. I ran my fingers through the glorious curls. I cooed gently. My actions surprised me. I lost control later that afternoon.

During my primary school years a boy locked me in a shed. The shed was a damp wooden construction planted in the middle of some waste ground. As soon as he pushed me inside and turned the key, I began to panic. I didn't scream. I was unable to scream. I just gulped, large gulps of air, one after the other, fast. It was like I was trying to gather in as much breath as possible to preserve myself. It sent me dizzy. I blacked out, fell to the grassy floor. I did the same four hours after Daphne's death. My doctor, a large useless man, tried to comfort me. He told me it was natural, said it was nothing to worry about. 'Like an exorcism,' he explained. 'You'll feel much better for it.'

*

He was wrong. The days between Daphne's death and her burial have been terrible. Her departure has carved a hole inside me. Like my innards have been scooped. She was only fifty-six. Her going has made me more aware of my own mortality. But worse. It has left me exposed. Suddenly I have nothing. No friend. No one to turn to. No one to chat with about the past. I flounder, only able to decide on one thing. I cannot attend the funeral.

I place my basket of provisions on Daphne's back doorstep. I feel in my cardigan pocket for the doorkey, insert it in the lock, turn it slowly. I shiver, not knowing what to expect.

The door swings open, revealing Daphne's kitchen. It is a small kitchen. The floor is covered with red and white lino. The fridge is white, the cooker brown. The units are old, not fitted. Daphne hated her kitchen, thought it shabby. But she'd never done anything about it, preferring to concentrate her energies on her vegetable patch.

I pick up my basket, step into the kitchen. I know I am being foolish, but the sameness of everything makes me wait for Daphne. I look at the door leading to the hall and anticipate her welcoming smile, hear her golden voice, 'Come in, Audrey. Tell us all about it.'

I wait a good five minutes, trapped in past time. Until I see it. The house is empty. Unfleshed air surrounds me.

Fretfully, I unload my basket; place a carton of crackers, slab of cheese, tin of cocktail sausages, tin of pineapple, box of cocktail sticks, home-made prawn and egg quiche, and a plate of peanut cookies on to a worktop.

I run a hand along the worktop. It's been scrubbed. Jeff's doing. A faint smell of lemon cleanser colours the air.

Jeff is Daphne's son. He is thirty-five years old. He has olive skin and hair so black it looks dyed. He resembles Elvis, the plump version.

Jeff is spoilt. Daphne mothered him till he was unable to think for himself. Then she began to resent his clinging. She tried to pass him on to me. But I said no, which led to an argument.

I had to to tell Jeff about his mother, and I expected tears, panic. I expected him to ask, 'Well, what is going to happen to me? Who's going to look after me?' But his fleshy face never altered. And unlike me he feels able to attend the funeral. He seems quite cold. I guess he's not losing sleep; I guess he's not dreaming my dream.

The past few evenings I have dreamt of being an astronaut, abandoned by ship and colleagues. There I am floating aimlessly among the unreal stars, arms and legs akimbo, eyes petrified.

Jeff promised to leave me a note. I glance round the kitchen and find one attached to the fridge door, held in place by a magnetic figure. The figure is of a jolly snowman, with orange nose and little black eyes. I pull the note from under him, hating his idiotic smile. 'So good of you to offer to do this,' I read. 'The extra salad stuff, marg and cheese are in the fridge. There's a box of other foodstuffs in the unit by the backdoor. Can understand why you want to give the funeral a miss. Hope you feel able, though, to welcome us back about 2. Looking forward to your lovely tea. Mum always admired your cooking. Jeff.'

I stare at the round childish handwriting, tuck the note into my cardigan pocket. I'm finding it hard. Yes, Daphne always admired my cooking, and I shall miss her appreciation, the look of pleasure. She liked sweet things. She liked my trifles, and the little sponge cakes I make set into chocolate cases.

I place the last doily on the last plate, and load the plate with sausage rolls. I place this plate next to the others. I'm unsure how many will be returning for the tea, but I've made enough for a bus-load. Daphne has always attracted a crowd.

I have done a good job. My night-school in food presentation has paid off. Daphne laughed when I registered for the class. She wanted me to do something practical like car maintenance. But I wanted something soothing. Food presentation taught me how to make mouse-shaped jellies, how to turn a simple sandwich into a bread painting. Of course, I haven't used the more frivolous techniques for this tea; just a few touches to make it special. It's my offering to Daphne. A sort of private joke and a farewell gift.

I take the trays and plates of food into Daphne's living-room. At the far end of the room lies a big table. I recognize the table. It belongs to one of Daphne's admirers, her old boss. Bill, the local pharmacist, employed Daphne from the early days of her widowhood until the day she died. He is a generous man, warm, but too fat. Daphne always used to refer to him as 'too fat'. She used to flirt with him, but had no serious intentions. Bill was useful to her. He fixed her central heating.

I place the food on the table. The table has been covered with one of Daphne's Spanish tablecloths. The cloth is white, decorated with tiny red flowers, green ivy shaped leaves. The tablecloths used to hold bad memories for me. But not now. The passing years have removed their edge.

I went to Spain with Daphne shortly after my husband left me. Daphne thought the trip would be therapeutic; believed it would ease my pain. It also gave her an excuse to escape from Jeff. But it was a disaster. I was in no mood for the beach, the country, the charming waiters. Daphne was frustrated, only perked up when she saw the tablecloths. She bought ten. She liked their rustic charm.

I have no idea why my husband left. We'd been married for twenty years. It had been an uneventful marriage, no children, no pets, no rows. But it had been pleasant, almost happy. There were days when I was quite thankful for it. At least I wasn't beaten about the head, made to wear kinky costumes, told how to act, speak, think. At least I wasn't classed freakish like Daphne was: a single woman spending her prime alone.

Not that it was Daphne's fault. Fate dealt her a rough hand. Her husband died young, when she was twenty-one, him twenty-three. An outrageous bloke. Always flirting. Always laughing. His death was pathetic. For a time Daphne wanted to dress it up, to make-believe he died heroically. But she found his death was common property; not hers to tamper with.

He died at his workplace, Billingston Laundry. He used to put washed and crumbled overalls on to a rack that shunted its way in and out of a steam press. A hot and boring job. But not especially dangerous. 'A freak accident', the bosses called it, which was fine by Daphne. She never wanted to know how he came to be beneath the mountain of hospital pyjamas, delivered twice weekly from the Southern and General. She used to joke that he crawled under there to escape married life. Mickey had been good at Romance, but not the everyday.

The pyjamas suffocated him. He went to his grave marked with impressions of pyjama-top buttons.

Daphne was seven months pregnant when Mickey's coffin was lowered. Her mother-in-law thought it obscene, Daphne standing there with her big belly and rosy glow. She said Daphne could've chopped her hair, looked more distraught. 'Not on your Nelly,' replied Daphne, suspecting her motives. Daphne's hair was her best feature. It reached close to her buttocks and was as black as black. Many a man wanted to wrap himself in that hair, including Mickey's father.

Daphne turned to me after the death. She stopped behaving like a polite next-door neighbour, and opened up. I welcomed her friendship. I realize now it would never have happened if Mickey had stayed alive. Daphne, despite her independence and strength, was a man's woman, preferred male company. But it was difficult to pursue that interest as a widow. People liked to talk, to cast the first stone. And she had no wish to marry again. 'Marriage is not for me,' she used to say.

The friendship was a good one. Though it got talked about in the early years. Gossips claimed Daphne was using me. For baby-sitting services mostly. But my womb was a mess, had to be removed. There was no way I could have children. So Daphne loaned Jeff to me. It was never spoken about, but I know Daphne had no need to spend every Sunday at the pictures. She was doing it out of kindness. She was doing it out of love.

I feel a real warmth when I remember those days. My husband doted on Jeff. We would venture out like a proper family, taking trips to the seaside, visiting the bats at the local zoo. Daphne would sometimes join us. Then it was even more fun. Daphne added excitement, a certain glamour. It never rained when Daphne came along.

As Jeff grew older, grew more pleasing, things changed. Daphne became overly protective, hid the boy away. I pined, and so did my husband. My husband would try to catch Jeff on his way to and from school. I hung over the garden fence desperate to touch the boy's hair, to see his smile. Daphne never revealed why she became so possessive. She said it was one of those things.

The friendship suffered then. It only picked up when my husband went. After the trip to Spain, we would not go a day without seeing each other. We rarely shared intimacies. We just pottered about, watched the television, cooked each other meals, visited the local antiques and crafts fairs. We argued twice.

Daphne complained that I was too reticent; I countered she was too loud. And then there was her daft suggestion that I should take Jeff as a lover. As if she couldn't remember the past. As if it didn't count.

But it was a special friendship, like having a close and forgiving relative. I will miss her. My life extends empty. Perhaps I should fill it by joining one of those over-fifty clubs, arrange to go on holiday with a coachload of strangers. But I know I'd be seated next to a woman with broad hips and a perspiration problem or, worse, a man picked to woo me. I have been on one blind date, in the early days after my husband left, before I had more sense. 'The man,' I'd been told, 'is your type.' He turned out to be an immigrant from Estonia, with very poor English. He could only talk fluently about his egg farm; a small holding crammed between a row of council houses and Billingston's Methodist chapel. Instead of a rose, he handed me a brown bag crammed with bad lays. I flushed the eggs, some no bigger than strawberries, down my toilet.

I look at my watch: forty-five minutes to go. I push the food plates around, till they look appealing. Polish the wine glasses. Dust the tea cups and coffee cups and place them in rows upon the broad mantelpiece. I am disturbed, unsure whether to stay, to welcome people to the funeral tea, or to leave. I sit upon Daphne's floral sofa, try to reach a decision.

I'd like to avoid the tea. I'm not in the mood to share memories about Daphne, to swap anecdotes. Neither do I want to counter those who'll go on about Daphne's bizarre dress sense, her loud voice and crazy behaviour. But I ought to stay, for Jeff, and because I need to get it into my head that Daphne has really gone.

Feeling dizzy again, I kick off my shoes, and curl my legs upon the sofa. I move a cushion, to place it behind my back. A small brown envelope falls from the cushion cover. The envelope is marked '1962' and is unsealed. I can see a wad of photographs crammed inside. I'm not the nosy type. Daphne always used to say, 'Audrey respects others too much.' The reticence is more to do with cowardice, though: I've always been afraid of what may be uncovered. But today I need to keep my mind occupied. I prise the photographs from the envelope.

The photographs are black and white. Some are square, most of them a peculiar oblong shape. I haven't see these photographs before, which is surprising. Daphne was fond of taking pictures, and fond of showing the results. I've spent many evenings in Daphne's front room flicking through her albums, laughing at the images. Daphne arranged her albums according to subject. There was the Daphne Album, the Jeff Album, the Daphne and Mickey Album, the Men Before Mickey Album, the Holiday Album, the Daphne and Audrey Album.

The first few photographs are of a seaside town. I recognize the town, but am unable to put a name to it. It is a seedy place. Litter blows down the promenade. Beach umbrellas lie upon the sand, half unfurled. One photo is of a Jack Russell peeing up a rusted lamp-post. The photographs have a strange haunted quality. They are very familiar. But clouded over, obscured. I take my time, examining the photographs, turning them this way, holding them upside down. I wonder if they belong to Jeff. I wonder if I should mention them when he returns from the funeral.

I decide not to. Half-way down the pack, people start to appear. A group of women, hunched together, laughing, pointing at the camera. A single shot of a small boy. The boy is Jeff. He's wearing his primary shorts, his sweater with the too long sleeves. Carefully I place Jeff to the side. And there it is. Daphne and me standing arms linked, smiles wide and happy upon our faces.

My husband had taken the photograph. I remember now. It was on a day trip to Cromer. And for a while Daphne and I lost Jeff and my husband. I don't know how it happened. It wasn't planned. Neither was the salty kiss. We were just walking along the beach, arm in arm. The wind was cold. There was the sickening smell of fried breakfasts. I turned to Daphne to say something about my sandals letting in the wet, when our bodies seemed to meet. The kiss was long. I could taste the sea on Daphne's lips, feel a desperation in the open mouth, the thick front teeth. 'What is it, Daphne?' I whispered. She never said, just pulled away from me, switching on her bright, bright smile as she pointed to my husband and Jeff paddling in the sea.

'Let's ask your old man for a photo,' she said. 'A nice one of you and me. A buddy shot.'

I wake. It is still night. I've been having my dream again. The same dream I've had since Daphne died. I roll back my duvet, allowing the chilly air to creep across my body. I look at my thickening thighs, run my hands over the rounded shape of my stomach. I never used to be so plump.

I find it strange that my dream hasn't changed. I expected it to. Because, on waking, my mind is still coloured by the kiss. To this day I do not know what Daphne was asking of me. We never spoke about it, and obviously Daphne wanted to hide it away, not put it in the photograph albums as an official part of her life. And me? What did I think about the touch? I remember confusion. I remember sensing need. I remember how lovely her teeth felt. I remember wanting more.

I turn on to my side, check my alarm clock. It is set for eight. The little red hand points conscientiously to the big brown eight. And I laugh. I have no idea why. But suspect it's something to do with embarrassment. And loss. The laugh is loud. Hysterical. Gulping. It cripples me and I curl with the stitch. When the stitch subsides I feel so hot I have to pull off my nightie. Then I comfort myself. I'm clumsy at first. But soon I have the rhythm. I sink into it, and try to forget. For a while.

SOPHIE FRANK

———

Flashing Tin Foil

I was standing at the side of the road under the big blue sky at the time. It had been a long day of painting night skies for a horror movie and now I needed rest. No one gets buses in this town but I was waiting for one. I wanted an experience, not a cab. I was thinking – I can't keep this up – fantasy sucking it out of me. I was thinking – I want something to come real. Then it happened. Suddenly, like flashing tin foil, fiction into fact.

A car – green, metallic, chunky – pulled up at the lights. Inside was a girl – dark-haired, wearing shades and a rose-printed dress. She wound down her window. 'Want a ride to the desert?' I thought she might have a gun. Women do – this is Los Angeles. 'The desert?' She nodded slowly, as if she was already bored. 'You heard me . . . the desert.' She spoke with an English accent. So do I. I was waiting for a sea change. I'd go.

I opened the passenger door, jumped in, slammed the door shut. It fell off its hinges. She leant across my groin and pulled it back into place. 'My name's Cathy,' she said, half-way across me, pushing the words out as if she was blowing gum. 'What's yours?' 'Jack.' She said she'd figured, by the wilted look of me, that I could do with a blast of desert air and she asked me to choose some music. I scratched around on the floor of the car, thick with cigarette ends and empty cans and found a tape of Spain – flamenco. There's two types of music – good or bad – and she had all good.

She told me that she came from Liverpool and she'd been in tinseltown a year now painting people's faces and egos (she was a make-up artist). She lived in Hollywood alone. There had been someone who came over with her but he had gone. I make it sound as if she was all tough, all hard, but she wasn't. I liked her instantly. She'd taken blows – I could see the scars – and she knew how to hit back.

It was five in the evening and the freeways were blocked up. The car got hotter and hotter and for an hour we hardly moved, just listened to the music crackling, shifting from one broken speaker to the other. Suddenly all the cars fell away – like specks of dry sand falling on dry concrete – and the road opened out and slid under use like a ribbon in the wind. We turned up the proud music and laughed at the sound of the alien music in an alien landscape. 'Let's stop,' I said, 'I need a drink.' We pulled up at a shabby Seven Eleven and I went in, shirt sticking to my back, and bought Coke and beer and crisps, and all of it was giant size.

When I got back to the car she had taken off her glasses and her eyes were soft and round as marshmallows, big enough to get lost in. Everything was blown up, under a magnifying glass. It does that to you, this city, makes you feel you can do it better than anyone else.

'We'll go to the end,' she insisted.

Open road, music. Gradually on either side of us the small squat houses, nestling in rows of regimented dusty trees got fewer and fewer, the ground redder and redder and the vegetation more and more spartan. Even the sky was optimistic – blue all over – happy as a giant cone of ice-cream.

After a while we pulled off up a side-road towards a sign that said 'Indian Reserve'. There was no reserve – only dark faces working petrol pumps in gas stations that no one ever made it to. We'd either taken the wrong route or this was propaganda. The road petered out and became a bumpy dust-track. We drove past a thin, sad string of bungalows, built cheap as garages, and stopped dead where the road did, in front of a huge rock-face. The car hiccupped and sprang to a halt.

'We're here!' She flung open the door and put on her shoes – black, spiky heels, all come-on – and got out. The silence was vast and still – like being inside a huge underground cave or down a well. A dry wind hit our faces like the breath of a hairdryer. She climbed up on to the bonnet of the car, lit a cigarette, lay back. I handed her a can of beer. 'We can drink now,' I said, 'now we're off the road.' They're hot on that here, hotter on that than on guns. We drank, smoked long cigarettes and stared at the sky and at the rock-face as it changed colours and moved, like an ocean, reflecting and soaking up the last of the sunlight. Underneath us the car swayed to the music. In the distance a full moon was growing darker until it became mauve then purple and ended up a midnight blue and all that was left was a full fat moon and a fistful of stars. Our hands crept under one another's clothes like melting wax. 'Ever used a gun?' she asked. I told her I hadn't. 'D'you like it here?' she asked. She had a direct way of speaking. I said I felt it was make-believe. She went quiet – retracting into herself as if she was hurt. Then she said softly, 'Me – make-believe?' 'Not you, make-believe, the whole thing. This city, America.' She understood. That's what she liked about it, the fact that anything was possible, anything might happen and all you've got to do is ride with it. That's what I liked about it too. You don't get that back home, possibility. You get caution.

After three hours it was getting cold and we thought we ought to find a motel to stay in. We got inside the car. That's when we noticed the two front tyres were flat. Coffee arms and coffee legs, a voice that was lush, that's what I'll call her from now on, not by a name but by a voice that was soft as she was in her rose-printed dress and hard leather jacket. 'What are we going to do?' 'Who cares?'

Vaguely she pointed out a row of houses – squat bungalows with cosy windows and glimmering electric bulbs. 'That's America', she said, giggling. 'We'll go there tomorrow. They'll help us.'

At eight the next morning some kind of life started moving in the bungalows. A net curtain began to twitch, cars came and went and an old man came out into his garden, pulling a garden hose behind him.

He began to water the desert plants, juicy flowering cacti.

We watched him, peeping over the top of the back seat. Another old person came out of another bungalow and started watering her garden. Sky and rock, I thought. Sky and rock – some kind of a place to retire to. It might drive a man mad, all this nothing.

We pulled on our clothes and chose the old man's house only because of the red flower in the garden that she had fallen in love with. He came to the door in candy-striped pyjamas and slippers holding a Bible in one hand and a bacon sandwich in the other.

'Yeah,' he growled, eyes scanning the scriptures. 'Whadd'ya want?' He spoke like a cowboy.

She explained – all we needed was a phone.

'Today's my wedding anniversary. D'ya know that?'

Thin, mean lips. When he smiled he looked like a skinned rabbit. I smiled back. 'Well it is.' Tight shiny skin pulled across a bony face.

I looked around the room, which was tidy and neat – like a train compartment after the night-cleaners have swept through it. 'It's in there, the phone.' He pointed to the hallway. Lush walked through. He plumped down on the sofa and turned on the TV.

A news item came on, something about a local competition for oversized cacti that followed mention of a mass supermarket killing back-to-back with the President at the summit.

'D'you know of any garages around here?' Lush shouted out.

He didn't.

We found a directory and started calling numbers. One garage said they'd come.

'D'you read the Bible?'

I said No.

'We love reading it. We love America. We love the President and he loves God.'

I nodded.

'D'you love America?'

I didn't want any trouble. Here was a big man. 'Well – *do* you?'

I nodded. Another smile.

'Wipe that flaming grin off your face, young man,' he lashed out. Then he stood up, jerking hip and shoulder together as if he was drawing six guns, hammily. 'Don't you ever come round here again. Understand?'

A sheep wandered out from behind the G-Plan sofa. It had wool on its back and blue eyes, pale pale blue, like washed-out marbles. President Reagan came back on TV. The old man waved his arms around. 'And this here's my wife,' he roared and he chuckled, taking hold of the animal by the horns.

I looked at Lush. 'Let's go,' her big brown eyes were saying in morse.

I muttered thanks, and we began to move fast to the door. But he wasn't having it – wouldn't let us go as easily as that. He stood in the doorway – arms spread out like a scaffold.

I didn't want to try force. Once you get started on that game you don't stop – there's only a winner or a loser. I retreated – Lush standing behind me. She began to talk – polite English, reasoned sense. 'Thanks for letting us use the telephone. Now – can we get past, please?'

No response. 'Well, if we can't get by that way, we'll have to try the other door.'

She began to walk through to the kitchen.

'*Gotcha!*'

At that point, out of nowhere, he produced a gun.

We stood rigid. He flopped back into the sofa, relieved he'd got so far, and he pointed a silver revolver straight at me.

'This is what I want to tell you. I want to tell you. . .'

He paused, taking a huge breath. 'I want to show you – someone, anyone – that I, John Turner from Idaho, call the shots.'

The sheep bleated.

I asked him what he wanted from *us*, what was the deal. He either didn't hear or he didn't understand or, most likely, the word 'deal' involved a logic that was beyond reach. Deadlock.

Lush said one word, reading my thoughts: 'Mechanic.'

A few seconds later there was a knock at the door. The old man swung round and off went the gun, accidentally. A bullet raced through the window and somehow the glass exploded into a million pieces outside the house. John looked shaken.

The knocking at the door stopped.

Then we waited, us standing, him sitting just stroking the sheep whose eyes were swollen with fear. An hour went past, slow as a dripping tap.

Finally we heard sirens and the screams of cars. Within seconds, at each window, we saw the face of safety – waxy faces, guns and sideburns. 'Don't move!' one face said.

John Smith was still sat on the sofa, still sat with the gun held out in front of him. He swivelled. He took a shot. Straight at the TV set.

Someone took another shot. Straight at him.

The police didn't want to know much, they weren't bothered. They took our names, addresses and that was that. An old man had died in the desert and no one had listened.

After it was over the mechanic towed the car up to a garage on the highway and fixed us up with new tyres. We sat on the garage steps, watching the cars soar past, taking stock, numb, dazed.

'Where will we go?' Lush asked.

It wasn't a question of us separating. We were here now, thrown on a wheel, holding hands, playing it for all it was worth.

'Dunno – where?'

'How about it?' She pointed to a road-sign. Fifty yards ahead, that said 'LAS VEGAS 200 M.' 'And then?' I asked, meaning the future.

She shrugged her shoulders and we laughed – same thoughts,

same time. How it could only happen here, chance tossing you up – all of you – like a pancake in the air. The old man, flip side to the same coin, product of a place where anything might happen, anything goes and no one gives a damn.

Home News

Barbara wore a kruggerand round her black neck and once she had a lump on her breast. She can't remember if the lump was malignant or benign. She had a knack of erasing whatever hurt too much to hold on to. 'They're not all racist in South Africa,' she told Liz, her fellow receptionist. 'And besides, gold is gold. Gold is gold the world over.'

The switchboard lights began to flash. Barbara picked up the receiver and put on her sing-song voice, the one that sounded the same for everyone. 'Good afternoon. Dunne's brewery. Can I help you?' The accent was hard to place, a mixture of Moss Side and Kingston. Hard to say if it was five years Kingston and twenty years Manchester or vice versa.

'They're not all racist in South Africa,' she said when Liz had questioned her about her dubious medallion. 'Mmm,' Liz had replied. 'What's on TV tonight?' Barbara had asked, painting her nails and blowing on them gently, a light caress over those red talons.

Commercials.

The dream comes out of the television set. This is the dream. It is manufactured by a group of men and women who sit round a black table-top on top of a white carpet in an office, usually in London. The dream is to have a perfect family. The dream is to have a white face. The dream is to live happily ever after. The dream has very little to do with Barbara or her friends' lives.

When Barbara goes home from work she kicks off her high-heeled shoes and puts on the TV. When the commercials come on, instead of turning down the volume and making herself a cup of coffee she finds herself locked in to the thirty-second fantasies, and she is sucked in, unable to switch off. When she goes to sleep at night it is these images that she dreams and when she wakes she holds these images, this fairy-tale, in her heart. She uses this tall story as a yardstick. Something to measure up to, and to judge by.

In late June 1988 Liz Howell took a receptionist's job in a brewery on the outskirts of Manchester to tide her over for a while. Though the job was as menial as could be, she had to lie to land it. She had to say that she would stay for ever – or at least indefinitely. She had to look enthusiastic about pension schemes. When Mandy Davis, the personnel officer, had offered her the position Liz had gone out for a walk over the dimpled Cheshire fields to mull over the proposition. She didn't want the job at all but *voilà*, employment, it's what we all need and it's what, here in Moss Side, people were fighting to get hold of. So she had accepted, rang back, and got through to Mandy's effervescent voice. Liz had played the game and had sounded every bit as bubbly as Mandy.

The riots, June '81, when the sky was red with flames and Manchester looked like a war zone, a blitz city, the air full of screams and sirens and shattering glass. Something was coming together then and what it was didn't have an exact name, nor an exact cause. Like a low-lying virus, it was infuriatingly unquantifiable. It had been building up and like a boil it had to burst.

That afternoon Liz had taken the slow bus home instead of catching the train. The drive out into the suburbs was pleasant and still. It seemed a summer night like any other, only it was hotter than it had been for a few weeks. The air didn't want to move; it hung heavy like a velvet curtain.

Liz had cooked dinner and they had gone to bed early. They

were making love when the news came on. Liz and Sri's black and white limbs were entwined under a TV screen showing blacks fighting white, showing whites fighting whites, showing anyone with any grievance destroying anything that they could. Sri's hospital bleeper had gone off. It gave him a cue to come, which he did instantly. Then he got up and rushed out of the house.

Over in Wythenshawe Barbara had turned on the TV and had spent the evening sucked in. Her husband, Bill, was on a late shift. When the news had come on Barbara had turned it off in favour of a long hot wallow in a foam bath. Then she had gone to bed. As she fell asleep she heard noises outside but it had seemed ordinary, just lads who had had a good night out and were on their way home, smashing up what they could, for the hell of it.

Sri didn't come home for three days. He was working in casualty as an SHO and there was too much for him to do even to take an hour's rest. He didn't get any sleep for forty-eight hours and when he did come home, finally, in a taxi (he was too tired even to drive), all he could do was fall into bed and sleep.

Liz had spent the weekend reading and quietly cooking, intermittently poking her nose through the bedroom door to look at the sleeping Sri. I hope the child will be strong and resilient, like a nettle growing out of asphalt, she thought.

Barbara's husband, Bill, had come off all right in the riots. Returning home at dawn, hunched over the formica kitchen table-top, eating fried eggs and tomatoes and marmalade and toast, he had told Barbara that the riot shields were strong guards and that any man worth his salt knew – instinctively – how to duck a flying brick or a bottle. Only the easy targets, the soft ones, got hit. Bill reckoned that the colour of his face had kept him out of trouble. The rioters didn't know what they were getting. The stereotypes had been thrown and Bill was free to walk the burning streets, a brave man in a uniform, the protector and the protected: a hero.

Like a goat, Barbara swallowed everything that was thrown at her. She soaked up the slogans and opinions and most of the time carried them around with her, inside her head, a large reference library of angles and ideas. When she first heard them they sounded strong and viable. Afterwards they didn't seem to hang together cohesively, not at all.

Bill had listened to Anderton on the radio and Barbara had heard the transmission too.

'We believe that a kind of military strategy was used, with look-outs and the use of Citizen Band radios to pass on messages.'

The morning after the Anderton interview, Barbara came into work with an argument she stuck to – a razor-sharp line. It had been black versus blacks. It was blacks stepping out of line. She wouldn't be a part of it. She made a phone-call to the hairdressers to have her hair straightened. She and Bill were getting out: somewhere they belonged, somewhere hot, somewhere she could have her dream home which included a kitchen and a microwave.

Liz wasn't particularly surprised at Barbara's stance. In other circumstances it might have laid dormant, slumbering for a lifetime, rumbling like a troubled appendix or a troublesome wisdom tooth. She didn't say anything. She kept quiet. She knew it would be futile to speak, or to try and convince otherwise. She couldn't force her politics on anyone else: it didn't work.

There was an irony involved. Though black, Barbara was whiter than white and Liz, though white, was, often, along with her friends, blacker than black. What the hell did that make Sri, her Asian lover? Liz closed her eyes and faced towards the window, out and up at the sun. Through the membranes of her eyelids she saw just one colour: red, the warmest colour on earth.

*

Liz had told Sri a night or two later. They were in Manchester for a meal and it was the first time they'd been together, quietly, for a week. 'I'm having a baby,' she had said, feeling she was dealing with an absolute and she might as well be saying, 'I'm going to die.' Sri had smiled, calmly.

'Well. Do you want a child?' she asked.

He had shrugged his shoulders. 'There's no one I'd prefer to have one with.'

'You're not answering my question, Sri.'

He didn't answer. He had asked for the bill and had mumbled that he had thought she was pregnant some weeks ago. He was a doctor, after all.

Liz felt she was living in a world full of zombies. She was living with a man who seemed increasingly robotic (the more months he spent at the hospital saw to that), and she was working beside a woman who seemed exempt from any sense of heritage. If Barbara was an airhead, then Sri was an airheart. And Liz was somewhere in between: level, like the low line of the horizon. She had a voice. She spoke words but until now that was all that they were – words. Not solutions, only stirrers.

A week later Barbara had dropped the bomb, though she didn't see it that way. She saw it as good tidings. She had come into work late, some excuse about a doctor or a dentist, and had sat down, opened her bottle of nail-varnish and had said two words to Liz: 'South' and 'Africa'.

She elaborated during the lunch-hour. They sat beside a fountain in the Arndale Centre, where youths hung around hoping for something to happen, like love or revolution. She gave her view on moving to South Africa.

'This is the way I look at it. We all want to have the same thing, right? We all want to have it easy. Right? Bill wants the same. Money. A nice house.'

'You think you'll get that there?' By now Liz actually felt nauseous. She kept swallowing – it should keep it down.

Barbara had nodded enthusiastically. 'The British police force trains you for all eventualities. The world is Bill's oyster. He can be a security guard. He could join the military police out there. There's tons of work, and it's hot.'

Suddenly she turned her gaze away from the twinkling five pence coins that lay in the fountain's basin. 'What about you? What are you going to do?' She asked her question with an intensity quite out of character.

Liz felt the child kick inside her stomach wall. 'I'll just carry on. Be here.'

She watched a dog sniff round the base of a plastic palm tree and finally lift its leg. She reviewed her life so far. She thought of the jobs she had had and had held – the politically sound advice centre work, the housing for the homeless work and she thought of Sri. A belief, something far harder than a feeling, kept returning to her like a rubber ball off a wall. Politics start in the home. Best still, in the gut. This is the way to change things.

Barbara had rambled on, impervious to Liz's silence.

'People say it'll be bad out there, you know, all the unrest and so on. But I say, you shouldn't believe all you see on television. They just want a story. And besides, bad is what you carry round in your head. It won't be bad out there.'

'CRAP!' Liz had gone. 'Crap. You're talking SHIT.'

She spoke slowly and evenly, with regular beats between the words. She had spoken softly. Barbara froze.

Liz bought three cans of lager and she had walked home which was a distance of over seven miles. When she reached the house she sunk down in the sofa and watched TV.

I will sit here and wait.

Kit was born in December, a cold blue day, two days after Christmas. A week later Sri had gone to a football match with his old college friend Matt and the crowd had suddenly turned, picking him out, one of the few Asian faces in the stands. He lost consciousness instantly. He died a few days later. No one could say what exactly it was that he died from. There wasn't any specific injury. His whole body was bruised. It had given up and like an apple left too long in a fruit bowl, it had collapsed within its own skin.

Far away, in Johannesburg, in a hot African summer, a black woman and a black man spend their days guarding a white man's house and picking leaves and dead insects from the top of his swimming-pool. In Manchester a woman takes her caramel-coloured child to the playground. 'All blood is red,' the mother tells the boy.

The riots came and went and someone swept the streets very neatly when they were gone.

Heart Too Full for Words

Why can't I say it, 'I love you,' when I love him, Hazel thought. What *is* wrong? There was plenty that was wrong with her: friends said she was barking mad, but Hazel knew it wasn't true. She just saw the world clearer than most people, and from odd viewpoints that no one else dared climb to.

I love you, she wanted to say to him at the bus stop, in the bath, watching television, on the underground. I love you. I love you. I love you. In the swimming-pool. At the Wimpy. I love you. I love you at the seaside, in the off-licence, at the fairground. I love you at the bank. In the supermarket. She wanted the words to spin out of her mouth and tumble over his body like kisses from her lips.

But whenever Hazel tried to say the words her mouth went dry and she couldn't speak.

She went round to an ex-lover – someone who, on the Richter scale of love, had reached a mere three (Nick a grand nine), someone she cared for like a brother. She told him the problem. He looked at her; her mad hair, her lunatic appearance, her handbag full of oddments (a knife, a fork, a spoon, make-up, letters, a diaphragm, a loaf of bread, spermicide, bubble-gum, receipts, photographs) and had thought just how impossible, and disorganized, she was. 'Just say the words, Haze,' Justin had said, finally losing patience after an hour of getting nowhere.

Hazel had sighed and had started to cry. 'I can't talk to him any longer,' she blurted out. 'The more I feel the less I can say.' And Justin, who knew this conversation would be a record stuck in a groove unless he took matters into his own workmanlike hands (he was a carpenter), had said, simply, 'Leave it to me,' and Hazel had sobbed some more then, all of a sudden, had forgotten her deep sadness and was back to her old self telling filthy jokes and laughing so loud that she filled up the room with her mood.

Nick was in the bath when the phone rang, dreaming of Hazel's huge breasts and tiny waist and all the imaginative things that she got up to. He was moving up and down under the water trying to keep warm on a cold January day in London when he heard the phone ring and he'd moved slowly – swearing – out of the bath to answer it. Nick never ran for anything.

'Yeah?'

'Hello. You don't know me.'

Nick ran the paranoid possibilities – clinics, debt collectors, double-glazing salesmen who never go away – through his mind, like water through a hose.

'Yeah.'

'I'm a friend of Hazel's.'

Hell, what had she done now?

'She loves you. You should know it. She lives with you after all.'

The caller hung up.

Nick had got back into the bath and had wallowed for another half an hour until his fingers, then chest, then heart felt warm again. Hazel. What was he going to do? Go? Stay? They had reached an impasse: they weren't moving on, or anywhere. And the more he tried to open things up, in an American kind of way, the more she retreated, clamming up completely. He went under the water again and closed his eyes and tried to forget her and consider, instead, relevant issues such as red reminders. The only conclusion he could come up with was that it was a crazy world and women like Hazel throw themselves into it and everyone like a swimming-pool, and that was that. He was underwater when a strange sound crept through the waves. It sounded like music. It was in fact Hazel herself.

'HELLO!' she yelled, coming through, banging the delicate glass door open like a bulldozer might. 'I'm pissed off. Everything pisses me off. I've bought you these because you piss me off too.'

She revealed a bunch of red roses and threw the flowers one at a time, into the bath, wrapped her arms around Nick's neck, kissed his dark wet hair, sucked a bit of water out of a strand or two, and sat down on the loo, crashing down on it as if it were a soft armchair, forgetting its plastic surround. '*Ow.*'

'Did Justin call?'

'Someone did.'

'What did he say?'

Nick had the same problem. He too couldn't say the word. He'd just ask.

'Do you?'

'Some days,' she replied, pulling up her jeans. Then, catching his eyes in the mirror she threw back a question, a big one, possibly the biggest. 'Do you?'

'Some days.'

'So?'

So, they both agreed, there was no problem and that was the end of the day although it was only lunchtime and the rain seeped in through the roof and gathered in a green outsized bucket beside the bed and it should be fixed, shoes should be mended, dental cavities filled and life, all of it, addressed.

They were lying in bed, talking about nothing, slipping in and out of sentences and each other now and again. Suddenly Hazel sat bolt upright, swung her legs over the side of the bed and started to get dressed. 'I know what I'll do,' she said, rolling on her stockings and picking her clothes up from a huge pile on the floor. Nick was pissed off. Just when sentences were beginning to be formed, she was moving off. She started applying heavy lashings of red lipstick, then put on her coat; and all of this took only three minutes flat.

'I'll be back in two and a quarter hours. I promise. I will.'

Nick groaned and rolled over and rolled another joint. There was no point in trying to ask why or where: clearly something was on her mind and she had to exorcize the demon. He turned on TV and spent three hours doing the things he enjoyed doing when she wasn't there: watching TV (anything, everything), turning up the stereo full blast, all at the same time, and taking the phone off the hook.

Hazel in the meantime leapt on a bus and went to the biggest and worst bookshop in London. She had once read a poem, penned by one Samuel Buckett, and she had to find it again. She asked a wan, skinny, poetic sales assistant for help. He had smirked, called her Modom, and had returned with the book (which looked to Hazel like a giant sandwich) in his hand.

'I think this is who you mean,' he had said, purposefully not referring to Hazel's *faux pas*, but brandishing the book as hard as he could, with the author's name in bold capitals in front of her face. Hazel had opened the volume, rooted around and, among the French lines and words, had found the poem she wanted.

On the bus home she had copied the words on to purple notepaper in thick black gothic script.

> the churn of stale words in the heart again
> love love love thud of the old plunger
> pestling and unalterable
> whey of words
>
> terrified again
> of not loving
> of loving and not you
> of being loved and not by you.

They weren't her words. They seemed to say it all. Everything she had wanted to say to Nick that morning but couldn't.

He had switched channels and was watching the soccer results when she finally reappeared.

'This is it!' she had said, taking the book carefully out of her handbag as if it were precious, the only remaining copy of the Bible in the world. 'It's a present and I want you to turn to page fifty-eight.' She sat down on the bed beside him. He read the poem.

'You're mad,' he had said, laughing, and that was it, another day gone completely nowhere.

The next morning Hazel had had to get up early to visit her great-aunt in hospital who was having her cataracts removed and Nick had the whole day to fill up. He could have asked some friends over. Or he could have gone into the studio and painted a masterpiece, but what he did instead was search in the same book Hazel had given him for a reply.

He soon came up with one. 'I could have done with other loves perhaps but there it is. You either love or you don't.'

That's how he felt about her exactly. He spent the day remembering other loves and how they didn't compare.

He whispered the lines to her later that night just after they had made love. 'I could have done with other loves but there it is you either love or you don't.' Hazel was not amused. The lines, taken the way she took them, reduced her to nothing. No sooner had they been said than she felt the old feeling, that of retreating into herself and locking the door, take place. She froze. She didn't open her mouth – except to remind him to pay the rent – for twenty-four hours. 'What have I done?' Nick kept asking, shrugging his shoulders. 'I didn't mean. . .' Hazel swept past regally, ignoring him.

When she did finally open her mouth, it was to Justin, and it wasn't a wise move.

'Shit, Justin, how come?' she had said after it was over and they were lying on the floor and they were both thinking that this is nothing more than drafty and dusty.

'A moment of ecstasy, a couple of shudders, a tidal wave. The same old story. That's how.' Justin paused for a few seconds. 'Tell him you love him, Hazel.'

'Tell her you love her.' Hazel had replied, nodding to the photograph beside the bed.

'It's true!' they had both then said, in unison.

Afterwards they drank mug after mug of tea and wrestled internally with their perceptions of each other, struggling to push one another back into a role – friendship – that they had spent two years trying to establish brick by brick. Nothing was said, and the music was turned up loud.

'Promise me you'll say the words? Promise?'

He picked a couple of dark hairs off her red jumper as she stood in the doorway.

Hazel let herself out, and jumped back on to her bike, feeling entirely separate, suddenly, from what had happened. 'I love you, Nick, I love you, Nick,' she repeated to herself on every sixth rotation of the bike's front wheel as it splashed through the potholes.

She finally arrived home and struggled with her bike up the narrow staircase to the apartment door. There was a loud sound coming out of the flat. In addition to listening to music and watching TV, Nick was typing up a short article for the local paper, something about tendon strain in greyhounds aged two-and-a-half years and over. Hazel put the key in the lock, turned it and stood, dripping wet, in the doorway.

'I LOVE YOU!' she bawled, at top volume, over and above everything else.

Nick jumped out of his skin. Three words and five years to get there.

'I LOVE YOU TOO!' he bellowed back and before he made it over to where she was standing she had passed clean out.

'Where have I been?' she asked, when she came round, not recognizing that she was in the same place as before only all was different.

KIRSTY GUNN

The Swimming-Pool

_____

You could hear the kids yelling in the pool. Through the hot air, you could hear them, the sound of them playing in that blue swimming-pool water. They'd be tossing up water and throwing it around so it made silvery strings against the dark blue sky. They sounded far away, those kids, but they were only up the road, in the park where the pool was. They were like a crowd cheering, happy for something.

And the silvery strings, your arms tossing up the bright water, a million glittery bits . . . Remember how it felt?

We weren't doing anything much, just sitting on the front steps, and Billy was burning up ants with a magnifying glass.

'Zap!'

It's not cruel. The ants don't know it's happening because it's instant death. They simply feel a heat on their heads, like the sun only hotter, then – pop!

'Incineration!'

Kitty says it's quite humane, the speed of it. 'It's probably the best way to die. . .'

Is humane the same as human?

'There's no pain, you see,' says Kitty. 'They don't feel a thing.'

I was watching them, those little lines of ants. They were running along the side of a crack, then down into a hole where it was cool and dark. I could imagine them running along their corridors, in and out of their tiny doors, running through their ant rooms. They were so busy they wouldn't be checking up on their friends. There were so many of them, how could they know who was missing?

What happened was that Billy chose one ant and followed him with the magnifying glass, holding it over his head so it cast a wide circle of light around him. It could have been the ant's own little circus ring lit up with floodlights, getting hotter and hotter and –

'Got him!'

Billy had one pile of sugar for bait and another pile of deads. They're so teeny weeny when they're dead, just a crumb or a bit of dust. Like a fairy's raisin, that's how small.

Billy was counting the pile. 'Twenty down,' he says. 'Twenty trillion to go!'

Lots of kids play this game, not only us. And we weren't particularly playing it, it was just a thing to do. It was pretty hot, that day, the concrete on the front steps was baking. I could feel it through my dress, which was my best dress. Queer, to be in best clothes in the middle of the week. Church, when it wasn't a Sunday. I could feel how crammed up my feet were from having to wear shoes and socks. And up the road you could hear all those kids in the pool. Jumping around in the water, sliding around in it like we used to.

No one was stopping us swimming, it wasn't a rule. It was just that we . . .

Maybe it was something to do with having the pool so close, that we didn't feel grateful enough for it. Maybe that's why we don't go any more.

It's not that the pool isn't good, you see, because it is. Other kids go to it all the time. From far away even, they come especially, on the train, just to swim in it. You can see them, from my bedroom window, walking up our road. Their towels are rolled into sausages under their arms and their togs mashed inside. Some of the girls have proper beach bags to carry various things: e.g. suntan lotion. Kitty has a bag like that, with a special compartment that zips and with little loops for lip salve and, I suppose, lipstick.

'Promise you won't tell!'

She's not allowed to wear make-up, Dad says so.

'But I do promise!'

'Swear!'

Another thing I would never tell on is the kids who smoke. Mostly train kids, and they do it in the changing sheds so no one can see and report them. I bet half of them just come to the pool so they can be away from their parents and the girls can wear bikinis and not feel ashamed.

So many kids come down our road. They all know each other, that's how they act, like they're all each other's friends and in a group. In the morning the sun makes prints on the footpath and the sky is pale blue and fresh, it reminds me of a flower. Then at evening, when the pool's closed, those kids come back down our road. Golden, from the way the sun is setting, the sun low over the bush, last slivers of it over the edge of the hills.

Then those kids go home, only then. When everyone's tired from the sun and the water. They've got ice blocks and sweets from the swimming-pool shop, the coloured packets they leave in the gutter of our road. They drag their feet along the footpath, or play granny steps and walking backwards. They have iceblock fights and some boys flick some girls with their towels – for instance, the girls who walk home with their bikinis on. Or just a towel wrapped around but leaving the top bare . . .

'Martin Thomas, I'm going to get you!'

'That really hurt . . .'

'You're in for it!'

You can hear them laughing, those girls aren't really mad. You can hear everything they say from my bedroom window.

'Sally Davies is in lu-u-u-rve!'

And someone whistling at her.

They don't have to be at home at a certain time, those particular kids. They're more teenagers, anyhow. They don't even have to wear shoes, not even sandals. Sometimes, at school, they don't wear shoes. My mother said it was because they were poor.

'If you have an extra piece of fruit at lunchtime, you ought to give it to those poor little train children . . .' That's what she said then.

But they weren't even little!

'They don't get the opportunities with fruit that you children get.'

Like they were orphans! Or out of some sad book! When we knew the truth which was that they did things like smoke and kiss with tongues.

If my mother had known what they were really like, if we had told her, would she still have said those kind words?

But my brother Billy loved the train kids. When he used to go to the pool, before he stopped going to the pool, he used to go with this gang who came from six stops away on the train. From those funny houses that were all stuck together and faced the station and didn't even have gardens. My mother didn't know anything that went on between those kids and my brother. But Billy did get up to real live stuff with the Parsons boys. It wasn't just talk.

I never told on him though, I wouldn't have.

'Billy's been jumping over the swimming-pool fence and not paying!' – this was a sentence, for instance, that I would never have told my mother. Or, 'Billy's been hanging around with the Parsons boys at the pool and nicking change from the custodian's office. . .'

I didn't tell on him to my mother because that kind of information would have made her even more sad. When she couldn't bear some particular piece of information, there was this one sentence she used:

'You children are going to make me very ill.'

She became so sad and tired then, her prettiness torn up with crying.

'Do you want to put me back in hospital?'

These were the kinds of thoughts going on that afternoon, sitting on the hot steps. But trying not to think them too, humming some dumb tune.

It was so still with the heat. Like sitting in a painted garden, being on a stage with the bright lights turned way up. Because everyone had been looking at us, all day, because of what had happened. Starting with us having to walk in separately and sit right in the front of the church. Only now no one was looking any more, it was only us, and Billy doing this thing to the ants.

'Whoosh!'

Another ant made a little pop – and died.

'Oh, man.' That's Kitty. Oldest and all the time acting like she's so cool. Like this day for instance, the day that I'm talking about, she was wearing blue eyeshadow. Acting so neat and tidy with her little blue eyelids going flippety-flip. Still, I knew that if I told her that the eyeshadow looked dumb she would have started to cry. Acting so neat and tidy but easily tears could have come bursting out. Just one little word is all it would have taken.

It was that sort of day when any dumb thing could have happened. Like when Billy killed the first ant I laughed so hard I was sick. A combination of the ant and all the chocolate people had been shoving at us all day. Why do people only give you fancy chocolates as a sly thing? Why is it always that they only give you chocolates when some bloody old horrible thing happens?

That word bloody.

Swearing too used to make my mother mad. Bloody this, bloody that. It was another bad habit Billy caught from the Parsons kids. Once, in the hospital, he screamed bloody-bloody-bloody all the way down the corridor. Who knows why. Perhaps because those corridors always made you think they were the only things left. Like there was nothing else in your life except walking down those stinking corridors, going for miles and miles down them, until you got to the right door.

Bloody-bloody-bloody.

Like they were the only things, stinking bloody stupid cor-ridors, like hospital was the only thing in our lives. Like it wasn't even summer because there wasn't the feeling of being on holidays. It was always instead being inside, the same smell, the same stupid sicky green colour on the walls and on the floor and everywhere. The hospital smell and that sicky old colour. Like the kind of puke you might have if you were taking bloody old pills and having some machine . . .

When Billy got to her room he said, 'I bloody hate you,' to my mother and she didn't even tell him off. She just let him put his head on her lap, even though we weren't really supposed to touch her, just put his head on her lap and she patted his hair.

For example, that's the sort of thing I meant before about not knowing what emotion could happen next.

Like how weird it was that it was summer and we hadn't been going up to the pool any more. All those kids were up there yelling, you could hear them having fun. Ducking each other and dive-bombing off the high dive – although I'm frightened of doing that . . . Still, a lot of kids think it's fun. Hitting off the high dive – wham! Straight on to the blue water.

I did it once. That minute, that tiny second when you hit the water flat on, you lose your breath. All the air flattens out of you – like going flat out on concrete. Then the next second you're sliding through, sliding and sinking slowly to the bottom of the pool. You touch the bottom, you bounce once there gently like an astronaut. And you feel the bottom of the pool against the soles of your feet and that's queer – but not queer, because you're the same person, aren't you? Just in another place that's all, you've still got the same body there. You look around, in that blue time, in that deep place. You look around with the same eyes, at the milky chlorine blue, and you have so much time there. Deep in the water with your same body, but everything's different, everything's better.

I'm never coming up again.

I wave my arms, so white and fishy down there, my arms like some old squid, wavering like a beautiful flower, my fingertips could be tentacles, sucking, sucking – softly little noises . . .

there, do you hear them? Under here where it's nice? Those quiet little tentacle sounds? And there too, you hear the beating of your own blood, the air in your own head – it's you, wanting to come back to yourself, wanting to float back up to the top and breathe a mouthful again.

'Once upon a time. . .' You know those stories you have when you're a kid? And your mother makes up the stories and you yourself are always in them? Like, for example, you are the sort of hero who rescues a person when they fall off a cliff. You put their bones into the right sort of bandage so that the wound will heal and not cause so much pain for the injured person. And you make a stretcher from driftwood and things you find on the beach – a fishing net, say, and an old bit of rope to tie it on to the twigs with. And all this happens near to where the person's body is lying. So you put that sick person on the stretcher and carry it all the way up to the cliff yourself, up some narrow little rocky path – once, you nearly fall yourself! But there, you're safe, and you're going across the paddock to . . . look! A little house in the distance! And you make it across the paddock to that house and you ask if you can use the phone and the people let you, and you call the ambulance, and the ambulance people come and you know what they say. They say, 'You saved that person's life!' You! You saved it! You managed to do that even though that person seemed almost dead and not the person you knew at all. So the story ends happy ever after. Ever, ever, ever.

I used to have a bunch of friends myself. And then we did used to go swimming together up at the pool. I mean, I went with them to the pool and we had some fun there, making up ideas about how to swim, and doing things based on the Olympic Games.

Thinking, I was thinking there as I sat on the steps that day: I'll bet those same people are up at the pool right now, running around the edge of it and then – tipping over in: Man Overboard! The favourite drowning game. Overboard into where it's pale blue and quiet. So gentle there with your fishy arms. And strings of water like necklaces hanging from you. You would think the fun feeling of that game was a feeling you could rely on. Wouldn't you think that? But no, because now swimming gives me no pleasure. You can hear the kids at the pool, the same kids, but even though it's the middle of summer you're not going up there. Even with it being so hot that the dog's stretched out like a rug on the steps, just the little corner of his tongue showing, sleeping like he's never going to wake.

'Zap!' Another one.

Billy's magnifying glass came out of a set that one of the aunts gave him in the morning, after we'd all come back from the church. It was one of those days for presents. Like the fancy chocolates that come in big boxes with ribbons that are so pretty you could use them in your hair. Those fancy presents, and all the dumb flowers.

'Twenty-one and counting . . .'

My father was inside the dark house, perhaps sleeping. Perhaps listening for the telephone.

'Zap him!' Billy was laughing, then it was quiet again. The quiet shadow of the magnifying glass, casting its eye upon the concrete – the worst kind of sun for ants.

And far away – can you hear it? The noise of the others? Those little voices from miles and miles away, nowhere near you?

It's all kid's stuff, putting ribbons in your hair. Having people around you like it's supposed to be fun. Kitty's got that blue slick on her eyes and it's the only thing left of the swimming-pool she's taking with her.

'We've got to go on.' That's what my father said.

Kitty's got that glinty blue eyeshadow on because she thinks the next best thing to going on is growing up. The colour dribbles down her cheeks, like little bits of the pool. That dumb swimming-pool is where all those other kids will be going to for the rest of their lives. You could tell, just by listening to them, they were all there that day.

The Hook

———

Billy. Beautiful, late.

Three months I lived with him, his parents' flat – you could hardly call it an affair. But he had the knack of touch, little gestures. It was that kind of tenderness.

Waiting for him was a special feature of our life together. A test, he said, those hours spent watching for him in the wind, wet shoes from puddles. Time should mean nothing to young lovers. They stand on street corners in the rain, their faces scribbled with anxiety. They . . . attend.

'You waited and you proved your love . . .' Billy cupped my chin in his hand and his eyes searched mine. It was the *Brief Encounter* scene with Trevor Howard and that actress clutching a little bag. Like her I was always hanging around in railway stations, bus stations, terminals. Anywhere the puddles were mucky, any bit of muck for the hole in your shoe.

'Will you come home with me now?' says Trevor Howard.

'Oh yes, yes,' says the actress.

I saw Billy last Christmas in a crowded street dotted in with everybody else. He was doing last-minute Christmas shopping like we did that time. With a rush in the street, the memory of him took body. Same jacket, same face. . .

Oh, Billy.

The second you plucked a piece of fluff from my dress I laid down my nets for you, you lover. I remember how your face was intent with love or desire or something you'd practised from a film. 'Let's be very, *very* happy. . .'

*

We had those three months in a swaying flat at the top of the Shakespeare Tower. It was a place his parents had chosen, with all of London spread out below but nothing for miles. No supermarkets, no shops for food. Instead we got used to having the Royal Shakespeare Company stamped on everything we ate – on the packets of sandwiches, on the gilded tubs of ice cream – like we were part of an institution. The players were clawing and prancing in The Pit while, twenty storeys above, we watched TV or slept.

Billy was a clever boy, with his poems and notebooks. He kept talking about his dear neat mother and, stuck for words, I took it as my cue to clean. Spent hours over the kitchen surfaces with the little lost crumbs. Swept strands of water back off the stainless steel . . . Still now in my head I hear me say: Anything else? Is there something I've missed?

Funny, I thought I was OK. I seemed happy there with my damp cloth and my part. With the packets of ham sandwiches and bottles of screwtop wine in the fridge . . . it was practically a fairy-tale for me. But Billy wanted real life, and besides he loved his parents. So they visited in the weekends and while I was in the kitchen they murmured in low voices from the next room:

'Billy, we can't *talk* to your little friend . . .'

'Can she be good for you, darling?'

She had a kind of suntan, his mother, his father was something in Cork Street. Once I mentioned a painter to him, our only conversation, and he answered, but looking away.

'The way he paints hands . . .' he said, and his voice had a yawn in it. 'You may admire him but he's not up to much at all.'

I'd clattered the tea tray and sugar all over the floor, was fumbling amongst sugar and broken china.

'Smudged hands,' said father.

So it went, weekends of it. The awful awareness of limbs. My moist handshakes, my great jerking elbows. I became aware of the placements of legs and arms about the sofa, of my silences. Three or four times in the course of an afternoon I could make tea – escape at last to the kitchen and stand and breathe. Over the kettle, for slow long minutes, I could hear the low voices coming from the other room.

When Christmas came the three months were up. Billy went Christmas shopping for big, expensive presents, gift-wrapped by Harrods. It was the same day the Sussex homecoming was due. 'But Billy, *darling*. You've brought your friend . . .' After the turkey, after the pincered silence of church, the tiny sherries taken by the tree . . . The scene in the toilet, after hearing what they said. That was me, doing those things. That was my little opera.

Anyway, who cares, he was only a boyfriend, there was nothing really to finish. But as mothers will tell their daughters – first boyfriends are always the worst. They feed the bait out on to the still water and wait for their love to catch. First boyfriends and their old girlfriends and the old girlfriends' abortions . . . you feel yourself jagging on the end of the line. Without warning, at night maybe, when some guy's got you parked up after a party or after a bar . . . that's when you might feel it. You're in a car with a stranger or twisted in his bed but what's real is the watery dawn. There's a sly, clever little boat, like a thumbnail, in the distance – and all at once you know that something you thought was removed entirely has actually caught there, that it's with you still.

Grass, Leaves

Nan reckons rain. Feels the big, sticky clouds, she says, pumpkin-yellow and mean as a man's eye, piling up over the far mountains. In her mind's eye she sees it, the storm. Brewing to pour and the air aching for it. The poor ground's dusty mouth gaping for water.

In the paddocks across the road, cows doze and the sheep pick at yellow grasses. The land behind them goes barren and lost all the way to the sky. It's our view, it's safe. I could dream all day up here with Nan, sitting on her front veranda. The things she says turn into pictures in my own mind, things happen there.

Peas in a pod.

Drops of water like flowers.

Nothing could be more lovely to me than sitting here with Nan, Little Si playing beside. The three of us alone and nobody else to worry for.

The hot wind shudders through the pines, stops. Makes me think what the rain will feel like after all these weeks of dry. Will it be a refreshment? Perhaps a sign? When Jesus died, the storm clouds opened and it rained for three days before Mary could gather up his ghost and fly with him to heaven. Rain can be important to a person who waits for signs. It could mean summer's ending and everything will change.

Little Si thinks about none of these things. He runs around with the hose, filling up his paddling pool. Backwards and forwards to the tap, a little cut-out boy, just his underpants on, a leaf.

'Look at me, Nan! Look!'

He swings the pipe so the water flicks a necklace against the blue sky. He dances through it and the plastic tube flicks and turns. The water an arch for him, a circle, a window.

'I'm magicking! I'm magicking!'

He waves his arms and leaps through the water again.

'I'm swimming around the world, Nanny-Nan! Look at me!'

Nan shakes her head, she smiles. She reaches for the bowl of peas to start shelling. She could eat that child on toast, that's what she says.

Little Pixie Darling.

Little Pea.

When she cuddles him, she kisses his face all over, she nibbles at his ear like an old fish. She could bite his head clean off.

Little Si is her own favourite boy, my own brother. Perhaps this will be the holiday that we'll be able to stay here for ever with Nan and be our own complete family, just the three of us like in the Bible. A sign may never come that says we have to go home and we could stay here instead, quite safely, with Nan. The bowl of peas there for us to shell and no storm for trouble.

Last night in bed, that's what she talked about, about keeping us with her. How we could go to a little country school, if we liked. Have a lunch packed, with sandwiches and a piece of fruit and a cake to finish off with.

'Would you like that, honey? Come home here for your tea every day?'

I couldn't speak at first, it was so like a miracle. I'd been praying to God: Why should our mother want us back when the bad sickness is over? Wouldn't she like it more if she could be on her own? And us not there to bother her and make her ill?

'Nan said, 'Stay up here always, how would that be?'

And as I held her in bed, my arms tight around her body said *Yes*. I wanted that wish so bad I could have broken with it. And if Little Si was older I know he would have wished for it too. *Please, please*. Let us stay. Change our names and be Nan's children. *Please, please*. Make the wish come true in heaven.

In my mind's eye I saw all the white angels gathered with our bleeding Lord, but even then I couldn't stop the creeping spider thought: Does Nan mean it this time? Because why had she said it before, said we could live with her always, when it didn't come true? Why had she let us go home in the end?

I'm evil in that way, not believing hard enough for my prayers to come true. A person without sin knows that to truly believe, you must put yourself square in God's eye. Have Him see you and notice your wish. It's not enough just to pray for miracles, you must prove your love to have them come true. You must stretch the boy's throat back on the altar, your own son. Or perhaps it is an animal that must be killed . . . But always, in the Bible, it's the murders that make the wishes come true.

If you're stained and contain demons, it's not easy to try for miracles. When I clean up afterwards, I know it's my fault that our mother gets ill – she never wanted that baby. How can I pray when I spoiled her life? Her dances and balls and all her boyfriends? How can I pray now, torn out of her wedlock? When I'm the reason she's sick now, and frightening?

Nan says to give up on praying because it's all rot. She used to, she's stopped. She gave birth in a thunderstorm, a man she hated for a husband and a daughter man-sick . . . All these things come out in the songs she sings instead of hymns.

My roof's got a hole in it and I might drown.

There's whiskey in the jar.

Nobody knows the trouble I've seen.

All the songs have people hanging, wading in water, birds drowning. What do these signs mean? How much of these songs are true? Maybe there's a jump in the song, a joyful note. Nan might whistle the songs instead of sing them, but even then the pictures they contain are full of sadness. The earth crying, a baby born naked somewhere and left that way.

She sings these songs to us in bed at night, she never leaves us in the dark. Tonight, when the sky splits into rain and wind ghosts through the skinny old pines so their barks creak and moan, we'll be safe. We'll be inside the lemon bedroom with the roses on the wallpaper that look like little faces in the dark, with eyes and mouths, but kind. Nan will cuddle us up at her front and back, the blankets folded over and all the soft sheets. Little Si held in her lap like a cat or a plate of cakes or something else that you carry with gentleness . . .

Peas in a pod, sad babies.

Drops of water, grey goose-down but nowhere to sleep.

In bed, I pray hard to Heaven that we can stay here in the room with the lemon roses. Pray that everything Nan says will come true and that all the songs will have simple pictures with happy endings and no one killing the bird or causing that boy to hang. And we'd never go back, because from now on Nan would decide things, not our mother.

Pray, pray. Make her die, Jesus Christ. Snatch her to Heaven. Don't let her come for us, like when she came the last time and took us away.

'Darling. Look how *tall* you are. How you've *grown*. How I've *missed* you looking after me . . .'

She wore red lipstick gashed across her mouth, and high pointy shoes. The tips of them went click-click as she walked across the floor.

'And my little boy, let me kiss him . . .'

Little Si was on Nan's lap, tucked under her cardigan. His face was hidden in her shoulder.

'We don't have to go back with you,' his voice was muffled from hiding. 'Nan says we don't have to.'

My mother looked at Nan then, her eyes had a glint. 'What have you been saying to them?' She took a step forwards with her bent body, on her pointy high-heeled shoes. 'What lies?'

At first Nan didn't say anything, she was stroking the hairs at Little Si's neck, that tender part. She was stroking.

Then she made her reply.

She said, 'No lies.'

She said it was just a story.

She said it was nothing that was ever meant to come true.

How my mother's red lips parted then. She smiled, she was so glamorous. She took my hand in her cool hand.

'I have presents,' she said, 'for my own two darlings. For being so good and staying with their old grandmother while Mummy was sick.'

Her bracelets jangled as she searched in her bag amongst her cigarettes and the little bottle hiding there. She picked out two packets with papers that were bright and tinselly. Little Si peeped out of the cardigan, seeing the present that was to be his own. His hand reached out.

'But only if you kiss me first,' she said, she was walking towards him. 'Only presents when you kiss . . .'

Click, click. She was coming closer. Her hand containing the tinsel and bright paper, and Little Si still reaching. Later, his face would be smeared from chocolate and from crying, but for now he stretched out his hand towards her.

'My darling boy . . .'

She was using all her special loving words, all her jewellery was shining.

'My precious darling boy . . .'

There was nothing Nan could do to protect us.

But why am I thinking about these mean things now? When the blue sky's an apron? When Little Si is a boy carved out of a nut, running freely in the sunlight and his own paddling pool there for him?

'Watch me swim?'

He runs over to his pool, jumps in, thrashes there like a caught fish. His smile and shriek and the trinkets of water all little hooks to keep us, caught and safe on God's line.

Nan looks up from the dish of peas, plucking out the peas from their neat homes and letting them drop. 'I'm watching, honey . . .'

She splits a pea like a trick, pops the pod into her mouth and swallows it whole.

'Just think,' she says to me. 'All this will pass. Grass, leaves.

Our little piles of twigs . . . How they will wither. Everything to dust . . .'

She looks around herself, at all the bright day.

'We can't change things, you and I. We sit up here all day, under a bad sun, but we can't stop the weather turning. We make our piles of earth and they become graves around us. Nothing's as important as it seems.'

Across the garden, the hosepipe spins crazy water on the green grass. The glitter from the little pool could hurt your eyes. The red flowers lining Nan's paths and borders could hurt your eyes. Little Si's voice, calling out, calling to her, that could hurt you.

'Watch me swim, Nanny-Nan! Watch *me!*'

Nan loves Little Si because he's easy, just a stick. He's always been her own little boy, she's kept him safe and he's never had to pray to an angel or cut for blood to say sorry to Jesus. The red petals are thick on the path from where I picked them – but they wither under God's eye.

The world turns to dust, dust in the paddocks rising. Even the wet little boy out swimming had better cuddle up quick, he's another fish caught, safe but dying. Nan says she'll keep Si little for ever but one day he'll realize thoughts poke in.

The shelled peas are filling the bowl. Nan whistles the song about the poor Irish boy hung; she huddles against the weather turning. But now she can't always decide things and have them come true. She may know the storm will come for us tonight, banging on the roof, the wind hungry, but she can't know it all, only God, and He won't come back again unless I cut. In the darkness tonight I will reach for them.

I love you.

I love you.

Nobody will ever see us in the lemon bedroom.

Nobody need ever learn who I am.

JONATHAN HOLLAND

———

An Afternoon in America

McBride wandered into the building society the other day, thin, pointy-faced McBride, downtrodden and hunched up and wearing sunglasses in February. It was like they were all that was left of the old McBride.

'McBride,' I said through the grille. 'Thought you'd be in California by now.' This I meant kindly.

'Aah,' he said. 'Fuck off.' Still a bit of twang to his voice, too.

I hadn't spoken to the bloke for five years. I wasn't going to ask how he'd been keeping, not after that. He looked as if he'd been locked up, and if he hadn't, then he looked as if he ought to be. The worst thing was that, despite the swearing, I don't think he recognized me.

'Funny,' I said. 'School. Seemed bad at the time. I feel quite fond about it now.'

McBride took the ten pound note I'd given him and held it up to the light. Squinted up and through it. Didn't speak, though. It was slightly sad not to hear him speak.

He just hurried away. Well, it wasn't clever, what I'd said.

It was after the Easter holidays. The academic lives of about a hundred sixteen-year-olds were drawing to a close. Our English teacher was a pony-tailed admirer of Michael Foot and a strong contrast to the pig-eyed spite engines that made up most of the staff. 'Hi,' Mike Curry would say at the start of lessons, rubbing his hands together, hopping from one foot to the other.

'OK,' he said. 'Your stories. You kick off today, McBride.'

I was right behind McBride, dreading my turn. I had spent

three hours the previous evening in Bollington Library, copying out a story by Henry Somebody which I hoped Mike Curry had never come across. I didn't concentrate on McBride, merely made some last-minute adjustments to *The Real Thing*. As I tinkered, I realized that the coughing and shuffling which formed the natural background to lessons had ceased.

I looked up at Slash Hyde. Even Slash Hyde was all ears.

'From New York,' McBride read out, 'we headed on up to Buffalo. We worked our way round the Great Lakes and crossed the border into Canada for a rendezvous with Janine's cousin Taco Paco, a Mexican smuggler gone north to turn over a new life. Spent a little time at Thunder Bay, crashed out under the arcing, starlike glimpses of a new future. Going, we were moving. Then it was down through Duluth to Minneapolis and due south through Des Moines to Kansas City, bright nightwind in our hair, the smell of burning oil, burning rubber, our feet jammed hardflat down on the running boards, rushing fearless into the oncoming lights. Me and Janine.

'We hugged the Gulf of Mexico as far as Houston, Texas, and lifted the jewels off the neck of the faceless daughter of a dollar billionaire. Diamonds in the dust of America, falling, a cascade of release in the shadows and sweat and sun of America: Charlie Parker on the radio.

'In California we held hands, Me and Janine. Filled with the charge and the burning we lay in the hot sand and we sang and we sang, and then we leaped overtumblingover, devilsdice, into the bluedeep Pacific, and when we came up, we looked at each other and laughed without control and our noses were dripping and O her lips and in our faces we saw all the Whys we'd never known, and we kissed while the beaten white sun lowered its shy face behind the Californian mountains, kissed for love and for fear, victims of our love, Me and Janine for ever.'

McBride stopped.

Silence. There'd been nothing like it since Slash Hyde let off a stink-bomb in Divinity.

'Mmm,' said Mike Curry. 'Really good, McBride. Really

atmospheric. Any American blood in your family, as a matter of interest?'

'No, sir.'

'Well, just one tiny thing, then. It sounds rather as though the punctuation could do with brushing up.'

Slash Hyde stood.

'Excuse me, sir,' he said, a small miracle in itself. 'I don't think it matters, like, the punctuation.'

'Well, Hyde, it does, you know. If McBride really wants to communicate –'

Greatorex stood up to interrupt. The class idiot, an albino.

'That were a great story,' he declared. 'Nothing wrong with that story, sir.'

Two or three others murmured their approval, and then somebody at the back, probably Nuts O'Brien, started to bang his desk lid. In ten seconds, chaos: shouting, clapping hands, whistling. McBride stood and looked about him, wiping his hands on his trousers and blinking, a silly grin on his face.

Mike Curry was grinning, too.

'OK,' he said loudly. 'That's enough. Good one, McBride.'

When it had died down, he pointed at me.

'Sir. When the porter's wife,' I started up, 'who used to answer the house-bell, announced, "A gentleman and a lady, sir," I had, as I often had in those days – the wish being father to the thought –'

'Oh, shut it, Pownall,' shouted Slash Hyde. 'That's crap.'

'Not only that,' said Mike Curry. 'It's stolen crap.'

But there was chaos again, and nobody else heard him.

The Central School was small and news-hungry enough for the reputation of McBride to become legend in a short time. He breathed the air of triumph for three days, and it brought with it a change in his bearing. Previously silent and forgettable, McBride took to acknowledging the people who greeted him with a nod, a wink and the word 'hi', not unlike Mike Curry. He was seen with Debbie Hough herself in Water Street, waiting for the last bus to

Congleton and, Tone Willis reported, 'wearing a bloody bootlace tie'. In lessons, McBride took to stretching himself out, his fingers crossed behind his head, with the serenity and aloofness of one bathing in hard won applause. But the school's public memory was shorter than McBride believed. There was too much else, in the way of events, vying for space.

In the changing rooms after football, I caught him standing and chewing gum in front of a mirror, backcombing his hair and murmuring to someone under the gurgling cisterns. I concealed myself behind a pillar. A glance round the side showed that the someone was himself.

'You know something?' McBride said to his reflection, his eyebrows high on his forehead as slowly he nodded. 'You're a fucking cool guy. Don't you worry 'bout a thing.' McBride winked at himself and smiled. 'Hey,' he said. 'Shit.'

'McBride!' I called out. I had to break this. 'Give us some of your gum.'

McBride wheeled about.

'I've not got any.'

'What you're chewing. Well, not that actual gum.'

'No,' he said, and opened his mouth. I wasn't about to start exploring McBride's mouth, but it did look as though there was nothing there.

'What you up to, McBride?' I asked, keeping my distance.

'What?'

'Talking to yourself. You want to watch it.'

Suddenly, McBride altered. His face twisted itself into a sneering smile and his jaw grew busy again as he looked at me sideways.

'Hey,' he said. He drew the sound right out. 'Shit.'

I couldn't handle that. I turned and went.

McBride's condition became steadily worse. He was obliged to continue wearing the school uniform, but sticking out from beneath his trousers there was now a pair of white, spurred boots. From being twitchy and agitated like the rest of us,

McBride fostered a languidness which brought him into lessons long after the bell, with the excuse, for example, that he'd had a little business to attend to back there. To accompany this, there was an accent which at first sounded merely outlandish but which soon became identifiable as that of a youthful John Wayne. Rumours circulated, unconnected with McBride's new Americanness but made plausible by its oddity. McBride was a poofter. McBride had sex with his mother.

Any affection Slash Hyde might have felt for McBride quickly evaporated. Slash Hyde came to believe that McBride needed the shit hammering out of him, and so it was that McBride found himself being cornered after school one day, behind the changing-hut down by the running track. I went along with Slash Hyde and Nuts O'Brien to see what would happen.

'Get that fuckin' cigar out your mouth,' was Slash Hyde's first request. 'And take those sunspecs off. Listen, McBride. You're nobody's friend. You fuck your mum.'

McBride stood up. He was chewing gum again and today had gel in his hair. He pushed the sunglasses up with his forefinger and smiled. Chuckling and nodding as if he knew precisely where Slash Hyde was coming from and envisaged no problems in dealing with Slash Hyde, he took the cigar from his mouth and studied it.

'Hey,' he drawled. 'Slash. It's OK, man.'

'What's *Oah Kie*, McBride?'

'Hey, Slash,' repeated McBride. 'The *shit*. The *shit's* OK. Say, I got a little something here might interest you guys.'

He lowered his sunglasses. His hand moved to his pocket.

'He's got a fuckin' gun, Slash,' muttered Nuts O'Brien, which could easily have been true.

Instead, McBride drew from his blazer pocket something which looked like a massive cigarette. Not taking his eyes off Slash Hyde's, McBride placed the massive cigarette between his lips. He took a light from his cigar, which he then tossed over his shoulder into the long-jump pit.

*

I don't recall much of the next two hours apart from their excitement. It was like Mike Curry's lesson again, except that this time it lasted longer and we were in the sun and free to really laugh and swear. We sat or squatted in the long-jump pit and brought our attention to bear on McBride, who every so often drew out another massive cigarette. The effect of these made McBride expansive and us reflective.

'Look around you,' McBride invited us. We saw an old man struggling to get his lawnmower started. We saw a mongrel cocking its leg against the fence.

'Small lives, in a small town, in a small country,' breathed McBride, smoke jetting thickly from his nostrils. 'There has to be more to life than this.' He juxtaposed local and American place names to make his point. Matlock and Mississippi, Pott's Pool and Thunder Bay, Littleworth and Los Angeles.

'Here, he's right,' croaked Slash Hyde, now on his back. 'He's fuckin' right. I know what he's on about.'

'That story I read,' said McBride, 'that story was my life in exactly three years from now.' He explained to us a thing called the American Dream, which he had got from books. I wondered at the courage of McBride in mentioning books to Slash Hyde, but Slash was just spread out there in the sand with his mouth open, laughing occasionally, sometimes when nothing funny had been said. The American Dream, McBride told us, was just a fabulous thing. Who, he asked, had ever heard of the English Dream?

'Not me,' said Nuts O'Brien. 'Fucking *hell*.'

'It's the land of youth and of possibility,' McBride told us earnestly. 'Now listen. Dickens, Smollett, Milton. OK? Now. Hemingway. Kerouac. Capote.' We listened to the sounds of these words and muttered our agreement that there was something more exciting about the second group, although we couldn't put our fingers on it.

'"Michael McBride",' said McBride. 'Who wants to be called "Michael McBride"? I'm "Dean Columbus".' That was true, too.

Who wanted to be called 'Brian Pownall'? I didn't even have a nickname. McBride was coming out with all this stuff.

'Why "Columbus"?' asked Slash Hyde.

'You could do worse than read a little history, Slash,' said McBride, and didn't get hit.

'Here, read your story again,' said Nuts O'Brien. 'OK, Slash?'

McBride read and we all lay on our stomachs in the long jump pit. Before too long the long-jump pit had turned into Long Beach. The lawnmower likewise became a Harley Davison: the dog ceased to figure. The story of McBride and Janine was the story of a journey across America. The journey, McBride explained, was more important than the arrival. In our minds, we tasted the dust and sweat of America. We drank bourbon in its roadside bars and rode at a hundred-and-twenty miles per hour down its desert highways. We met prostitutes in motels (I think McBride must have left this part out with Mike Curry) and we listened to lonely saxophones in tenement blocks. Finally we plunged into the blue Pacific, all of us there with McBride and his Janine, with whom I found I too was slightly in love.

I felt shattered when McBride had finished reading, and thought I was going to be sick.

'You been out there, McBride?' asked Nuts O'Brien with nonchalance.

'Only in here,' McBride said, tapping his temple with his forefinger. 'But I'm getting out, guys. Soonest.'

'Ow,' said Slash Hyde. 'I feel fuckin' terrible. What was that stuff, McBride?'

'Mary Warner,' said McBride.

'Ow.' Slash Hyde pulled himself to his feet. 'Fucking hell. You trying to poison me, McBride?'

'Hey, Slash.'

'Make me feel better, McBride. Go on. Ow, my fucking *head*.' He plucked the sunglasses from McBride's nose and sort of folded them in half.

'Cool it, Slash.'

But Slash was not to be cooled. 'You cunt,' he said. He took a fistful of McBride's hair and pulled McBride's head down on to his knee, which he simultaneously jerked upwards. 'You bastard,' he said. Twice he stamped on McBride's groin as McBride lay there, his mouth half full of sand, trying to sing something.

'Sweet American dreams, McBride,' said Slash Hyde as he staggered away through the lengthening shadows.

Nuts O'Brien followed. I felt I should stay to help McBride to his feet. But I didn't want the hassle of being linked to McBride. It was safer being linked to Slash.

McBride's chance to 'get out' came sooner than he thought. The following day Mrs Hyde rang the headmaster and McBride was expelled that afternoon. Slash Hyde, Nuts O'Brien and myself were put on report for the term. I heard later of legal proceedings, but never got the details.

'Off he goes,' Nuts O'Brien said, at the school gates at the end of McBride's last day. 'Riding off into the fuckin' sunset.'

Slash Hyde's vow was that he'd wrap McBride's head round a lamp-post if he ever saw him again, but privately I disagreed. Life at school was dull, after all, and it was only someone with a Slash Hyde mentality who could fail to see that our afternoon in America with McBride was something to be cherished and perhaps even worth being punished for. I went back to the library and found out that Hemingway was a writer and not, in fact, a place, and that he wrote little stories about big men which didn't taken long to read and weren't hard to understand. My own vow was that I would never again copy out a story for Mike Curry, but would try to write my own.

An odd vow, really, I realized later. Because McBride's story was as far from being his own as a story can be.

His absence led to the growth of a new interest in him on my part and raised questions which you didn't normally ask about your schoolmates. Did he have sex with his mother? Where did he live?

I found out and called round at his house.

'Hey,' he said. 'Good to see you.'

The surprise must have showed on my face, because McBride then told me that getting out of that school was the best goddamn thing that ever happened to him and that in two weeks he was leaving the country.

McBride's bedroom was a different world. It was badly lit, and since McBride wore a new pair of sunglasses, I was surprised he could make out anything at all. The room was covered, ceiling included, with posters of American film stars of the 1950s, and smelt strongly of the stuff we had smoked in the long-jump pit. No Snoopy posters for McBride. No *Star Wars*. His shelves contained about ten books, not one of which was connected to his formal education – not even an atlas, which was how I'd guessed he'd written his story. McBride put on some music which he told me was called 'bebop' and took from his wardrobe a bottle of Jack Daniels.

'Hey, Ma,' he called down the stairs. 'Two glasses and some ice for my friend here and I promise not to break anything.'

'I've got an interview,' I told him. 'At the Halifax.'

McBride smiled in such a way as to equate the prestige of a job in a building society with that of piles. 'Must be very nice for you,' he said.

His mother came in with two glasses, a meagre, tired woman who didn't return my greetings. I knew then, seeing her in the flesh, that I'd never be able to ask if she had had sex with her son. As for asking McBride, I wouldn't have trusted his answer anyway.

'What you going to do in America?' I asked him.

'Well,' said McBride. 'There's the chance of a little script-writing.'

The term was unfamiliar to me.

'You know,' said McBride. 'Hollywood.' He raised his glass, squinted up and through it. 'To Hollywood,' he said.

'To Hollywood,' I heard myself saying.

'Then a bit of travelling,' mused McBride. 'Me and Janine.

Janine's an ex-whore from the Southside. Waiting on me in New York.'

'Sure.' I'd never said 'sure' in my life, and it was somehow fun.

'Yeah, best thing I ever did,' said McBride, 'getting out of that goddamn school. Try these.'

He handed me the sunglasses.

'See how good it all is?' McBride said. 'How dark?'

Oh, he was mad. His way of looking at the world was all his own. But it was fun, in an odd way, there in his room. I had McBride under my skin. I couldn't forget how right I thought he'd been.

The next thing, six weeks later, was when the end of school was days away.

JOYRIDE GOES HAYWIRE

Dean Columbus, sixteen, of Paradise Street, last week crashed a 1956 Ford Mustang stolen from the house of Mr Norman Allan, second-hand car dealer of Lake Drive, Prestbury. The alcohol in Columbus's blood was found to be more than twice the legal limit. In addition, police found five grammes of cannabis. Columbus, a former student of the Central School, was treated for minor injuries before being taken into police custody.

My first thought was an odd one – that they had arrested the wrong person, that they were faced with the problem of charging Dean Columbus but releasing McBride.

I sat in our front room and imagined McBride careering squealing-tyred through the Lancashire countryside, making up the words to go with Charlie Parker, his fingers round the neck of a bottle of Jack Daniels, his arm round the shoulders of his imaginary Janine: seeing Los Angeles for Littleworth, dusty highways for winding lanes, tenement blocks for oak trees – seeing a big, dark mysterious world for a small, too-clear one. I imagined him feeling really, really good, laughing and singing away, and not giving a damn if the feeling didn't last. It made me feel slightly envious, that feeling.

I thought it would all make a good idea for a story. I wrote the story in the style of Hemingway and was all set to put it in for Mike Curry's end-of-term competition. But I got nervous about it and tore it up. I mean, people would only have laughed.

The Ugly Woman's Finger

Just as there is no need for a bible in a bank, so there was no need for Mr Morcillo as Mapas Mundo. The company had been founded, in a different era, by Mr Morcillo's uncle on his father's side. But computer graphics could do it all now, certainly with greater precision, and arguably with as much beauty. Thus Mr Morcillo, who for several reasons had never been offered promotion, had been offered instead a tiny department which consisted of himself and no one else. Mapas Artísticos. The Director, valuing Mr Morcillo's craftsmanship, had perceived a huge market in Spain for antique maps – maps of regions as they had been a long time ago, before Franco, before industry – maps which charted nothing but the progress of their owners' nostalgia. The most expensive of these, and deservedly so, each came with a small strapwork cartouche in the lower right-hand corner, containing the words 'B. Chaparro Morcillo' in flamboyant swash lettering.

Mr Morcillo had loved maps since his childhood, when he had caused his mother to fret over his sexuality and his father over his eyes. His first pride and joy, a gift from his uncle, had been a large wall-map of the world, taken from Mercator's late six-teenth-century *Atlas sive cosmographicae meditationes de fabrica mundi et fabricata figura*, which had been over Mr Morcillo's bed for most of his life and which had survived the death of his grandparents, his father, his sisters and his fiancée. If Mr Morcillo at age ten was to be found tracing the coastlines and rivers of the old world with a chubby, unsullied finger, it was not, as his mother fondly hoped, that he was preparing for a life as the new Amerigo Vespucci or Cristobal Colón. As his father pointed out, the boy couldn't see three metres in front of him. He was not imagining the charted land and seascapes: he was not reading. Mr Morcillo was merely taking pleasure, dangerous pleasure, in the map's colour and calligraphy, and in the precision of its engraving, its forms and contours, which had struck him, then as now, as more marvellous and complex than anything El Greco or Velázquez had to offer.

Mr Morcillo's apprenticeship had thus been a question of guiding him away from the contemplation of beauty and towards reality, towards an understanding of the cartographer, in his uncle's phrase, as 'the historian of geography'. Of Mr Morcillo's craftsmanship there had never been any doubt: at age eighteen he had, by way of thanks, presented his uncle's family with a map of the mainland. His aunt had proclaimed it the most beautiful object she had ever seen, and it had entered her coffin with her.

Sometimes Mr Morcillo would think about that map, wondering whether it was in better repair than his aunt would now be.

So Mapas Artísticos was a second childhood for Mr Morcillo. The rigours of accuracy again took second place in his mind to the free play of his artistry. It was with excitement that he again chose his own legends and colours. On occasion, Mr Morcillo would, like the medieval map-makers, set East rather than North at the top, in deference to the holy places of the East. He would include two linear scales, English miles as well as kilometres. Had it been possible to include heraldic shields, Mr Morcillo would have done this also, but here the director drew the line.

It was satisfying to sit back and contemplate the finished product, which was not only a representation of topographical reality but also a representation of Mr Morcillo himself – in short, a work of art.

One day in September, two column-inches on page six of the national *Diario 16* were devoted to the event of a young couple, Eduardo Morales-Tenorio and his wife Angela, having walked off a cliff on a small island off Galicia. Police, the article quaintly claimed, were 'uncertain' as to whether they should open a murder inquiry.

Among objects found near the site was a Mapas Mundo map.

In his office, the Director was grave:

'I spoke to the young man's father. He tells me their map was cartouched.'

Mr Morcillo's hands remained on his knees. His pale eyes struggled behind his bifocals.

'Now, I'm not suggesting –'

'Yes, you are,' Mr Morcillo said. 'That I made an error.' He touched his lower lip and examined his finger, as if for blood. 'This is the first time I have been accused of a cartographical error.'

'I understand, Mr Morcillo. They were silly to have used –'

'The first time, Director.'

'I assured the father that I would rebuke the person or persons responsible. There will be no ugly consequences.' Apart, thought the Director, from a short-term decline in sales; but he did not wish to trouble Mr Morcillo with this. 'There is always the escape clause.'

'The escape clause,' echoed Mr Morcillo quietly. 'Does the paper not say there was the possibility of murder?'

'That will never be believed. There was no motive. The risk would be enormous on an island like that.'

Mr Morcillo looked at the Director and saw a man fifteen years younger than himself, but with at least fifteen years' worth more experience of life. He reflected briefly on how he could never have uttered three brusque sentences like that, one after the other, to dismiss a possibility. Never could he have sat where the Director was sitting, in a leather chair, with a computer blinking intelligently at him. Mr Morcillo felt the slight sadness which came to him often, but which never came when he was working. Whenever he was not over his maps, the sadness was free to intrude.

'I should like to be assured,' he said, 'that the young couple was murdered.'

'I beg your pardon?'

'I have difficulty sleeping, Director. This will not aid my condition.'

Since Mr Morcillo did not continue, the Director said,

'It's *possible* they were murdered, of course. Although I personally would prefer that this were not the case.'

'People do strange things, do they not?' asked Mr Morcillo, removing a grubby handkerchief and dabbing at his brow.

The Director did not recall ever having conversed at such length with Mr Morcillo. He did not understand why Mr Morcillo, who was now suggesting that the couple must have committed suicide, should wish to represent in the darkest possible terms an event that had surely been a simple accident. It had been easier consoling the young man's father.

'I do have the greatest difficulty sleeping,' went on Mr Morcillo. 'I wet my bed, Director.'

The Director squirmed. 'It might be a good idea if you returned to your desk now,' he said. 'Good man.'

Mr Morcillo struck the desk with the flat of his hand and stood up. A golfing trophy, awarded to the Director in Salamanca the previous year, fell to the carpet. 'To whom can I appeal,' cried Mr Morcillo, 'if not to you?'

'Mr Morcillo, there is liquid coming from your nostrils. Now, why not –'

'You do not understand.' Mr Morcillo was trembling. Rapidly he blew his nose. 'The fact is, Director, that I cannot pick up another pen until I feel sure that this was murder.'

For all these years, thought the Director, I thought I had a diligent craftsman on my hands. Now I find he is a prima donna. A neurotic artist. Quickly he sized up the situation.

'September,' he murmured. 'A nice time for a holiday.'

'I can't.'

'Don't use that. Not on your eyes. Here.' The Director handed

Mr Morcillo a tissue. 'Now, whoever heard of a man who couldn't take a holiday?'

'I am that man.'

'What you are saying is that you can't work and you can't take a holiday. Which is awkward, because everyone on the blessed planet must be doing one or the other.' The Director felt pleased with this insight. Insights occurred to him every so often. He reported them to his wife. The Director went on, firmly telling Mr Morcillo that he had a choice between paid work and paid holiday. He knew, he said, which he would choose.

'Can't I sit on my stool and not do anything?' whimpered Mr Morcillo.

'Bernardo,' said the Director, feeling able to, 'you have more than two years' paid holiday owing. Why not take some of that now?'

Four days later, Mr Morcillo stood inside Chamartín railway station, trying to keep his suitcase under control. It had been a long while since he had stood still anywhere apart from home or office, paused to absorb the noises, the colours, the activity of this hard world. Doing so brought the taste of his mother's *callos* to his gullet.

She had been angry in her wheelchair when, between forkfuls, he had blurted out that he was going away. He had known she would be, and when, after fifty-seven years together in the same cramped flat, she had called him a fly-by-night and said that she would definitely be dead on his return, Mr Morcillo had almost relented. 'What will you do?' she had muttered with scorn. 'What will you do, on this "holiday"?' He would rest, he had explained, unsure of what that entailed. 'You are unfit to lie on a beach,' his mother had replied. 'Look at you. You are old. *Viejo*. Women will laugh at your breasts and point their fingers.' All this was true; and Mr Morcillo, realizing that he would have to *do* something, had that night decided what it was that he would do.

The suitcase was very heavy.

The train moved out of Madrid as rapidly as escape, passing

through ugly, concretized suburbs which Mr Morcillo had never visited. All his life, he reflected without contentedness or regret, he had lived on the second floor of an eighteenth-century building in Embajadores. He mentally designed a map to chart the progress of the train as it passed through a landscape which appeared almost featureless, an undisturbed expanse of hot earth, irregularly punctuated by villages like shanty-towns. He had at one time charted these, engraved their names with love. He was glad now not to have visited them.

At Santiago, Mr Morcillo, following the Director's careful instructions, waited, changed trains, opened a too-warm bottle of Mahou and unwrapped a *bocadillo*. The taste of his mother's hands on them was a comfort.

He did not like being here. He felt got at, worried, by what he saw through the greasy windows: the activity, the mutability of what was out there was an irritation to one whose vocation was fixing things. There were huge black wooden bulls on the tops of hills, advertising wine; forests razed by fire. On the maps of Mr Morcillo, no bulls, no fire: to chart *this* world, you would need a new map every week. Every second. And the lapping of waves, he imagined, and a falling leaf: how could you chart those? The arm of a child, waving at a train?

Mr Morcillo slept.

The train was late in arriving at Vigo. He awoke in his carriage and looked at his watch and at his timetable, and he panicked. He had informed the hotel that he would arrive at nine o'clock, and now it was a quarter past. In a town as full of movement as this, it was certain that the hotel would already have booked another person into his place. Mr Morcillo began to sweat and moan, and had to be reminded by a woman that perhaps he should alight.

The street-map of Vigo with which he had been supplied was not pleasant on the eye. It contained only three colours and far too many sharp angles. It was also inconveniently designed, the railway station at Vigo being neatly divided in two by a fold. Mr

Morcillo doubted even whether it was to scale. On his return to Madrid he would find out who was responsible.

He emerged from the station and followed the map rigorously, gripping it with his right hand while with his left he trundled along his suitcase, which had wheels. He scarcely raised his eyes, for fear of losing his position. For fifty-five minutes Mr Morcillo proceeded in this way, aware only of the map and, more vaguely, of the high, salty odour of the sea and of the warm breeze which carried it. After a further half an hour, Mr Morcillo screwed up the map with a cry of 'useless' and threw it from him. He was in the docks: ahead of him, ships' bows rose heavy and awesome from the water. They cast huge shadows, from which a man emerged.

'You shouldn't be here,' said the man loudly. 'Can't you read?'

'I'm tired,' replied Mr Morcillo. The man came up close and Mr Morcillo shrank inside. The man, too, smelt of the sea, and of Mr Morcillo's mother's tobacco.

'I must phone her,' he said. 'Oh Christ.'

'Well, there's telephones – '

'I must phone my mother. Now.'

'You sit down,' said the man. 'You look done in. Do you understand me when I talk?'

Mr Morcillo replied that he had to phone his mother.

'*Escucha,*' said the man. 'I know where there's telephones. You rest a while. You look done in. You got money?'

'Money?'

'I'll need money if I'm going to call your mother for you, won't I? Where do you keep it? In here?' The man slipped a hand into Mr Morcillo's jacket pocket and deftly removed his wallet and a map.

'Oh,' said Mr Morcillo. 'Not the map, if you don't mind.'

'Any particular message?'

'What?'

'For your mother. Any particular message?'

'Mmm?' said Mr Morcillo weakly. 'Tell her I arrived.'

After ten minutes, he realized the man did not have the

number. Then he realized that it didn't matter, that it was in the wallet. The man would find it.

Then Mr Morcillo realized he had been robbed. He sought to remember the man's appearance, but could recall only the odour of his mother's tobacco.

He felt he deserved it, anyway.

Well, he couldn't sleep here. Too many angles. Too much light. Mr Morcillo decided to leave his suitcase on the docks and go in search of an evening meal. The case was heavy: no one would wish to steal that.

He wandered back up the hill into the town. With no map in his hand, he felt naked and overfree. The sadness came, and this time it told him that no matter how many times he walked these streets, over and over, still he would not recognize them, still not understand how they connected up one with the next. He looked up and saw faces, and was amazed that their owners showed no fear that they might not be able to return to where they were, or that they might never reach their destination.

In a narrow cobbled street, yellow light and the sounds of merriment issued from a door. Mr Morcillo hovered and allowed his head to fill with the aroma of cooked fish, which rolled out at him like fog. A woman carrying a bucket of water limped out and emptied it on to the cobblestones. Mr Morcillo listened to the slap it made, watched the shapes as the water chased itself down the gutter.

'*Qué tal?*' wondered the woman absently.

'I'm hungry.'

'*Se ve.*' She looked at him now, beating the bucket against her calf. She had a round, reddened face and grey-black hair and a flourishing moustache. 'Where you from?'

'Madrid.' It occurred to Mr Morcillo that the woman was debating whether or not to give him food. 'I'm a cartographer,' he said, thinking this might help. 'I'm lost.'

The woman's face creased up into a grin. There were gaps in her mouth where teeth should have been. Hers was not a well-designed face. 'Xavier!' she shouted hoarsely, drawing out the word. 'Xavieeer!'

Xavier appeared, rubbing his hands up and down his apron.

'*Es madrileño*,' said the woman, nodding at Mr Morcillo. The grin had not left her face. Indeed, it seemed to be building into something bigger. 'He's a cartographer. He's lost.' She exploded into laughter and Xavier joined in. Each fed off the amusement of the other until they were holding one another up. Mr Morcillo, smiling, nodded in agreement. 'He's hungry,' wheezed the woman.

'He'll not go hungry if he tells people that,' said Xavier, bringing his apron to his eyes. 'Oh, God.'

The restaurant was empty: a oddly shaped, dull little room with ancient, worn-out tables and chairs and a stone floor. Xavier gathered his family round to introduce them to the lost cartographer. Shortly, food was brought in on a steel tray: cockles, prawns, shrimps, clams, a lobster, far more than Mr Morcillo could tackle, a dish of *pimientos de Padrón* and a bottle of white wine. At Xavier's command, the family dispersed to complete their tasks, but when this was done, they returned one by one to the table – eight or nine people, from an elderly, shivering woman, evidently Vigo's finest flan-maker, to a timid little boy. A flow of laughter and chatter was kept up which was quite different from home, or from the office. The wine was strong, and three glasses of it were sufficient to transport Mr Morcillo to a region several centimetres above the norm.

'I am a murderer,' he declared jovially.

The chatter ceased. Glasses of wine, on their way to mouths, halted. A cat padded past on its way to the kitchen.

'Perhaps you had better leave,' said Xavier quietly. Mr Morcillo listened again to what he had said.

'In a manner of speaking, of course,' he muttered, and sucked a mussel.

'You should explain,' said the ugly woman.

'You will know,' said Mr Morcillo in the manner of one getting down to business, 'about the murders on the Islas Cíes.'

'*Por Dios*,' said the ugly woman. 'Purita, get the others to bed.'

'They can stay,' said Xavier, relief written all over his face. 'That was no murder.' He refilled his glass. 'We get a lot of tourist trade here. That was no murder. It was an accident, thank God.'

'It was a bad map,' said the ugly woman. 'I was only saying, the other night, how I'd hate to be –' She was looking at Mr Morcillo, and Mr Morcillo was shaking his head.

Silence.

'The lost cartographer,' said her husband.

'It wasn't a murder, then?' Mr Morcillo, who had been peeling a shrimp, let the pieces drop from his fingers and onto his plate. He pushed it from him. From his jacket pocket he took the map and unfolded it.

'Is this *the* map?' said the ugly woman. Mr Morcillo, however, addressed her husband.

'Do you know the Islas?' he said.

'I do, sir,' declared Xavier, as though on trial. 'Bring my spectacles,' he instructed Purita. 'Get out of the light.'

Mr Morcillo shuffled his seat round next to Xavier's.

'Here is where they walked off the cliff,' said Mr Morcillo. His finger traced a footpath along to where the sea started. Then it turned east to follow the contour of the cliffs. 'It was here, wasn't it?'

'It was, sir.' Xavier reached and took his spectacles from the waiting Purita, who wasn't going to come too close. 'Oh,' he murmured. 'Please don't do that. Have a glass of wine.' He had seen Mr Morcillo's shoulders twitch, and the makings of a tear. The first tear ever at Happy Xavier's.

His wife had seen it, too.

'Imbecile,' she said fondly, and came behind the two men. 'You are going blind. It wasn't there. It was here.' Her finger descended and landed on a point to the north-west of Mr Morcillo's footpath. Here there was nothing, only cliff and sea.

Xavier spotted the brightening of Mr Morcillo's features and wished to encourage it. He jammed his spectacles firmly on his nose and leant forward to examine the area.

'You're right!' he shouted. And then, more quietly, 'My wife is right, sir.'

'Are you sure?' asked Mr Morcillo. 'My path does look so much nicer, doesn't it?'

'It is important to be happy in this unhappy world,' said the ugly woman. 'It's a lovely path, that.'

'You didn't need a map to find us here, did you?' asked Xavier, and held the bottle over Mr Morcillo's glass.

That night, the goodness and decency of things flowed in Mr Morcillo's blood. He slept well, with the cat, on a campbed by the ovens. He scarcely thought about his mother. But it wasn't enough only to be sure. You had a responsibility to be doubly sure.

The journey from Vigo to the island took about half an hour through choppy water, and Mr Morcillo returned most of the previous evening's food, in altered form, to its rightful owner. On arrival, he sat pale and drained on a bollard on the quayside, staring at the ground. Several of the people who passed commented on the unsuitability of corduroy for a Spanish September.

Again he took out the map. After Mr Morcillo's pocket and Xavier's table, it was now less than pristine.

The route to the spot carried him over a quarter of a kilometre of dunes. The going was hard, what with the sun and the flour-like consistency of the sand, and very soon Mr Morcillo's heart was beating as quickly as it ever had. He removed his jacket and left it on the beach. Naked bathers, glistening on their stomachs, followed him past with their eyes. The sand gave under his tread, the Atlantic crashed, but such mutability troubled Mr Morcillo no longer. These things were not his responsibility.

A small boy went to explore the jacket, but was called back by his mother.

Mr Morcillo left the beach and scrambled fifty metres up the fire-break of a pine forest. Here there was a wide footpath of packed sand, along which Mr Morcillo turned right. As he was finishing off the job begun on the boat, a man in a blue shirt wished him good morning.

'I do hope so,' said Mr Morcillo, and wiped his mouth.

The path continued for another kilometre before coming out of the blessedly cool forest and into the climbing sun. It grew steeper. While in the campbed, Mr Morcillo had marked two X's on his map: one for the turn of his footpath, the other for where the couple had in fact died. It was there that he would go first. Because he had to *know*. He passed the turning for the crucial footpath and shortly found himself standing on the grease mark left by the ugly woman's finger.

Mr Morcillo gasped and looked up, feeling deceived.

Above him, there rose to a jagged peak a small mountain of loose scree. It was inconceivable, beyond all understanding, that a couple, however young, should wish to climb up there, at night. Even were there not barbed-wire fencing and a 'Danger' sign.

In desperation Mr Morcillo looked at his map and up at the mountain again. This was definitely the ugly woman's finger.

Perhaps they were night mountaineers. Perhaps they had a suicide pact.

No. Not really, no.

Mr Morcillo wished, then, that he had not come. In fact he wished he had never been born.

He turned and ran. When he came to the turn-off, he ran for a hundred metres up his path. At a certain point, he knew, it would veer off to the west. At a certain point, everything would be just as it had been, nothing would have changed, and he would be able to return to the Calle Dos Hermanas and take up his pens again. He halted only when the path became indistinct. Brambles tugged at his trousers and he edged his way forward, to the point beyond which the young couple had gone.

'No,' muttered Mr Morcillo, and squeezed shut his eyes.

'No,' he said again, and a seagull cried.

*

Mr Morcillo rapidly stripped down to his vest and underpants and began to do what had to be done. He scurried back to the pine forest and found a sturdy branch, which he carried over his shoulder to the edge of the cliff. Then he attacked the ground with the branch, wishing to clear the brambles and scrub, wishing to scrape through the mess of fertility to the barren earth beneath.

He would forge a path to match his map. He would work night and day until there was a footpath there. It would follow the cliff-edge to the top of the forest, where it would join another footpath. It would be a beautiful path, all Mr Morcillo's own. He would bring people here, to show them. His mother. The Director. The newspapers. Everything would be restored.

Several people passed him by. One or two backed away from the fevered, lean figure as uselessly it hacked and chopped: some laughed, others took photographs. Towards nightfall, the man in the blue shirt tapped Mr Morcillo on the shoulder and asked him what he thought he was doing.

Three days in the prison at Vigo and still Mr Morcillo had not withdrawn his confession of murder. He seemed happiest with that belief. Yes, he said eagerly, that's it exactly, I was covering my tracks to hide my sin.

Even when the letters arrived, first from the Director and then from his mother, Mr Morcillo continued to insist: he struck an officer on the cheek to demonstrate what a nasty, murderous sort of person he was. I ought to be locked up, he declared, for having done a thing like that: yes, locked up, in a still, dark room, for ever, with only my paper and pens for company.

The newspapers ignored this development.

Exmoor

———

in and around cities photochemical smog is yet another negative consequence of modern life.

Me and Columba, lying in the huge greenhouse far from any city. Columba's face glowing with health like an advert, her colour up full, her ankles fat from walking, Columba spitting on her hands and rubbing it into her tight calves. The muscles on her neck grown large from the Life Pack. When we came she smelt of perfume: now she smells of herself, strongly, and the hair is thick under her arms, untameable on her head.

It is her voice that is broken.

– I want the feeling to return.

– We're the only ones left now, la-la.

– They'll remember us one day.

– Shake out of it, Columba.

Her name is Columba: that's a mystery to me.

She told me her story when we met. How she came to be here. It was strange to hear it. I remember thinking as she spoke, This story could only happen now: it could not have happened before, perhaps it's already too late for it to happen again. And it's mine too.

She prefaced the story with a poem for the new century.

> 'Mary, Mary, it's all too scary
> How does your garden die?'
> 'With CFC's and acid rain
> And X-rays from the sky.'

157

Boom. Boom.

– Do you remember when the fear changed, said Columba, from
Ming to Fare? The eighties?
  – What the hell does that mean?
  – Global War. Ming or Fare? Take your pick, Sunny Jim.
  – I love you, Columba.

Her story emerged, jerks and starts, huge leaps as Columba
followed herself, didn't follow time. We thought the age of
experimentation on human beings was well past, didn't we: but
the government grew unsettled, spotted the population becoming restless with words, words, more words, as the world
around them changed. The Warming (a chilling word) took
place, as predicted a long while back: the average surface
temperature of the globe rose one degree in ten years, to $15\frac{1}{2}$
degrees, as not predicted. With all that entailed. The hoped-for
harmony did not materialize: the international scientific
community went to war with the international political community. Global warfare conducted in minds and hearts. Crisis fathers
tyranny. The civil servant who jokingly related that he would be
the first of his kind for years to present evidence that what
they're saying *is* true: that we *can* survive the subcontinents of
scorched earth that are to be upon us.
  We would be the evidence. Me and Columba.
  – But it's *not* an experiment, he added. It's a contribution. A
challenge, on behalf of humankind.
  I was so, so out of it after the wires they clamped to my
temples. Boy. I'd forgotten how much damage words can do to
things.
  – It has its roots in a Christian tale. Forty days in the desert.
  – And nights.
  – Logically.
  – But that was Christ, who did that.
  – The time is with us to all make that leap.
  Whatever that meant.

At first, we'd cycle out to the glass in the daytime to see what was there. Nothing. One day, Columba thought she could see barbed-wire fencing through the heat-haze, a soldier, a military truck. I told her that was just wishful thinking.

And at first, Columba made angry comments about the pandas in Regent's Park Zoo. She stopped making these comments soon after: me, I can still face my memory, that is to say, I don't break down just before sleeping, like Columba.

our projections for the future are discouraging if one assumes

The worst is the Life Pack. It weighs heavy: moody Columba is always threatening to take it off, but never will, not while I'm here. It's large, flesh-coloured, like a slim, ergonomic rucksack: it pulses with us, releasing vital minerals, proteins and vitamins into our blood at regular intervals through pinpricks in our backs. I thought it was a metaphor for something at first, but that was before I became dependent on it. We can't take them off: they respond to us as individuals, our bodies are continuously supplying them with the designer information required. Well: you get attached to a thing and you have to see it for what it is. Like myself and Columba, with each other.

Some things are 'normal' here. The 'house'. I'd never had a house before. I wouldn't have chosen a house like this. I suppose this is the kind of construction built by expatriates in the tropical colonies: white, fans whirring, run off a generator which hungrily feeds off the sun. We have a living-room, what a joke. A toilet with an artificially produced chemical which used to dematerialize our faeces. (It's not necessary any longer.) The pressure of the taps is controlled, so only a dribble comes out: water is the one thing they had to concede.

But they're working on it. Artificial, recyclable water.

With irony I said, Let's have a housewarming.

Columba said, Let's go all the way. Let's have a global one.

We're good together.

The kitchen is a tap. After all, what's a kitchen for?

*

They clamped wires to our temples in an underground office in Westminster. I have had a fear of having wires clamped to my temples ever since I saw *One Flew Over the Cuckoo's Nest*, but you can get used to all sorts of ideas. You can. The wires were linked to computers which checked us over for tolerance, resistance, truthfulness, etc., qualities they thought we'd need. Just like the astronauts in *The Right Stuff*. We watched that again some time ago.

It's all like films, now. Forgive my old man's tone: I'm only twenty-nine. It's, first they write books, they make films: then the world catches up. The metaphor prior to the event.

The wires weren't only asking us things, though. I'm sure of that. They were telling us things, too. Two-way traffic. We've spoken to Charles three times a week since we've been here, and often I've wanted to tell him:

– That's it, I want to come home.

But something in me goes. Every time. And I can't say those words. I checked this with Columba. She has the same thing.

They supplied us with those items which they think will survive. They gave us entertainment: a video, a camera, bicycles. They gave us a compact disc player, and a choice of ten discs each. Really. But who will make the music? And a copy of the Bible: I don't think they understood their own joke.

– Columba, if you'd asked me to name one person who wouldn't have occurred to me in this place, it would have been Roy Plomley.

There were other things they didn't supply us with. Cigarettes. Where does the tobacco come from? Or a car. Obviously. Or newspapers.

Or birds. A tree.

My favourite play at college was *Godot*. Of course. That's us, now. Really. That's the only thing Beckett got wrong, the tree. It makes you wish you'd learned more of their names.

Me and Columba have stopped watching these videos. We realized. We realized that almost every damn one of them was set in the twenty-first century, or at some 'unspecified time in the future'. *Bladerunner*, *Exterminator*: vile. None of those French countryside films, all green and hillsides and animals and people covered in dung. Well, we decided to fight that, by not watching them. I mean, if they're going to leave us alone, why can't they leave us alone?

a great geophysical experiment, not in a laboratory, and not in a computer, but on our own planet

The telephone rings.

We used to say, Who can that be? Oh, hello, Charles.

– How's tricks? says Charles.

– Not so good, Charles. I'm having serious problems with time.

I find myself saying these big things without the merest hint of irony.

– Look at your watch then, suggests Charles. Any problems with the heat?

– No.

– It's rising. You know that. Veeerry slowly.

– Air-conditioning, Charles?

– I try to keep you informed, Mark. I'd appreciate it if you listened.

– Time and memory, Charles. I think a small degree of paranoia is justified.

– Your air is conditioned already. You could keep a Masai tribe alive for seven generations on the money it's costing. And it is humidity-controlled and temperature-controlled, but in an opposite way to what you're used to. Air-conditioning does two things. A, it destroys air on one place to clean it in another. B, it consumes an excess of electrical power. We know now that we can't avoid it. All we know is that when it comes, we will have to ration the current to limits which are currently inconceivable. To buy time.

– You could ask people to start now. Cutting back.

– People won't. Not until we make them. They'll only learn from experience, or at worst demonstration. (That's you.)

From words, from rhetoric, never. The government encouraged the wrong sort of economic climate at the wrong time, Mark. We freely admit that. I might also add that you have suggested air conditioning three times now. I suggest you try to be strong.

– I was always told that words and rhetoric were different things.

– Point taken. Such is life.

– Charles. Look out of the window. What can you see?

– Nothing. A wall.

– And when you go home tonight, what will you see?

– Mrs Charles. I'd rather be with you. Life Pack feeling any lighter?

do not promote feelings of nostalgia in the subject

– You're well trained, Charles.

– This is my job. May I speak to Columba?

CE Subject 00002

– Columba's unhappy. She doesn't want to speak today.

– Get me Columba, Mark.

– Columba has not had her period for I don't know how long. Columba's Life Pack is killing her. Columba is feeling anti-social, and she's justified. She feels she's not a woman.

It is a horror to have to rebel against the only other human you speak to.

CE Subjects 00001/00002: both lost parents early. Both 'drifters' since early teens. Both have unusually high Independence Levels

– Talk her out of it, Mark. We'll speak on Tuesday.

Tuesday: day of week, following Monday. Week: period of seven days reckoned usu. from and to midnight on Saturday–Sunday (what day of the — is it?)

They supplied us with dictionaries. Words! The fun you can have!

how long does it take, once a habitat is reduced or destroyed, for the species that live in it to become extinct

– I didn't have it today, Columba. The wanting to get out. She sits on the sofa, looking at her hands, clenching them till the knuckles show white through her tan. No doubt she's wondering what they're for. Who put them there.

– I feel stupid, she says. That's how I feel. I know that if I think, I'll be happy. So I don't think. So I feel stupid.

– They told us not to look too hard at ourselves. You remember that. Be strong. Natural resources, Columba.

She's stopped laughing at that.

She says, We're going to be so famous. So rich. We'll be mythical. The stuff of myth.

– Like the astronauts. We're somewhere where nobody has ever been. Unlike the astronauts, we're somewhere where a lot of people will go.

– I was *joking*, though, she says. That was *their* metaphor, like the astronauts. We feel sorry for a monkey with cancer, we feel respect for an astronaut. Anyway, it sounds like rat-tat-tat when you speak. One word follows the next. You weren't like that before.

– That's my way.

– We sleep too much, Mark. Twelve hours. Plus siestas.

– It's our natural condition, I say. Towards lethargy. The confusion of dreams. Entropy. It's the Second Law of Thermodynamics.

– Is it balls.

– That's the Third Law.

– Well, if they keep us all alive, it's going to be a very sleepy world. That's all I can say.

I am not internally empowered to criticize. Only to state. Well, that's how I feel. The history of this project, what went on behind closed doors round oak tables, they have kept from us, save from the untantalizing glimpses I had of information files, open on official desks.

Columba is right about the way I speak: the only problem with their 'Don't watch yourself' routine is all the time you have to do just that. You make patterns: you impose order. I wish they'd dreamed up a job for us to do. 'Gainful employment'. But evidently the times ahead will not permit such luxuries, such gain. Natural resources will be exhausted. Because all employment has its roots in the land. Money grows on trees.

urban heat island

It took us a while to understand fully the humiliation of our descent. From sleeping uncomfortably in the echoing halls of European railway stations to the occasional spell in jail for dealing drugs, both Columba and I, separately, had long nurtured a romantic streak, long played the rebel. I was a Green only until the image-makers declared it ridiculous. This made us ideal for their purpose. We lacked qualities. We took pride in being our ideas of ourselves. And I admit that the idea of being a non-violent hero had long appealed to me. When we are out of here, it will be like Columba says: it'll be press conferences, flash-bulbs popping: it'll be analysts poring over our every utterance, from Tokyo to New York to Brussels.

With the Life Pack, and all this uncorrupted air, we look so damn healthy that they just won't *believe* us if we tell them we've suffered.

burning of vegetation releases soot and gases particularly carbon dioxide (CO_2) carbon monoxide (CO) hydrocarbons nitric acid (NO) and nitrogen dioxide (NO_2)

– Mark? And have you talked Columba out of her mood?

– No. I can't.

– You know your responsibilities, Mark. You must be feeling a little urgency down there. You have the power.

– I *love* her, Charles. I do.

– Well, that's good.

– But you have to understand that when your bowels are probably all shrivelled, and you don't have your period, and your beard has stopped growing –

– Keep a grip, Mark.

– Yeah, yeah. You have to feel human to love, Charles. It becomes hard to cancel these things. That's all I'm saying.

– Well, think about how you *look*, then. You great big hunk of man, you.

the developed world – hundreds of billions of dollars every year – achieve a stabilized and sustainable planet

At night, we lie in our separate beds and stare up into the night. The night is still here: it's one thing we've still got, the mood the night brings on. The stars, the thickening, protective clouds. And sometimes I think of the people standing on mountains in Scotland, or in the Pyrenees, and of the sun catching the glass of our greenhouse, marvelling, wondering what sort of power can build a edifice which runs up as high as those clouds, and of the people in aeroplanes leaning over to try to get a glimpse of us, down there on what used to be a part of Exmoor, asking themselves what it must be *like* in there.

m) recommended that tolerable sacrifice be made of the more abundant species in order to facilitate construction of the Greenhouse
n) recommended that project commence with minimum quota of subjects. This number to be increased only when efficiency of Life Pack in sustaining human life has been demonstrated

I awake in the night and murmur her name. My voice echoes back at me off the white walls. I can hear the rasp of my own breathing, deafening in my ears.

I run downstairs. Columba is in the kitchen, smiling at me. Sort of crazily, as though she's been smoking.

– I just wanted to see what it would be like, she says.

She's knocked off the ASIM. The aural simulation. She's cut out the endless tape loop which runs off, at a subliminal level, those reassuring sounds of traffic, of industrial hum and of rivers, of forests creaking in the wind.

I hit the switch. The difference it makes.

– Columba, we're far enough out of it as it is, don't you think?

– Too fucking hot in this place. I don't want to be reassured.

She kicks off her shoes and slumps to the floor.

I go to her, put my arm around her shoulders. I have been afraid of doing this. Afraid of the touch of breathing flesh. Fearful of the things it sparks off.

– We could sleep in the same bed, I say quietly. I think that would be a good thing for both of us.

– It's not love, she says. You only think it is. Sooner or later, one of us was bound to think that. It's natural. They knew it, too. They want us to reproduce. Not to be in love.

For Columba of late, this is coherent.

– It's love, Columba. If I believe it's love, then it's love. The rest follows.

– Why protect yourself? She wonders. These neat phrases, these tidy feelings. They're lies, Mark. Why not just suffer?

– It's all the nature we have left. Inside ourselves. We should be celebrating. Suffer I do not want to do.

Columba stands up and takes one deep lungful of air.

– This air, she says, is clean. It's too clean. An abundance of super-clean, triple-filtered air in here. This air is what the air will be like when they turn off the industries, when the wood-burning stops, when the cars are gone, when the new balance is restored. This is the air of Paradise, Mark. That's why I turned off the machine. To know the pre-Paradise world. It was hell. I don't want to have to share this with you.

– And?

– And when we step outside, our first breath of the old air is going to kill us. Instantly, I should imagine. No grief, no pain. Has that not occurred to you?

It must be clear from my expression that the answer to her question is no.

– We're not innocent people, says Columba. We aren't. They've made us innocent, is what's happened. They've made us stupid.

tolerance

– But it doesn't matter to me, I say. It really doesn't matter to me.

– Welcome home, Sunny Jim.

Rich lands and poor lands alike, all of which share the one big mobile pool of air

– How's tricks?

– Charles? We have a problem here, which is that me and Columba think you have taken us for a big ride. So me and Columba want –

– What?

– Want –

– Go on, Mark.

aaah

– A little paranoia is justified. Me and Columba –

– I'll call again on Tuesday, Mark, OK?

Me and Columba, in her bed. The ASIM machine is off. The Life Packs on the floor. We're in pre-Paradise.

Columba's sighs my groans fill the house my face her hair my fingers going as deep into Columba as they will eat me Columba writhing curling both of us fighting dig deep as we can into ourselves into each other the skin on Columba's back on mine itching punctured dry refusing to sweat like the rest of us I may be some time struggle for a feeling that our bodies can't supply eat me and Columba temples wires – oh

Controlled Experiment 01: Failed (psychospiritual)

PHILIP MACCANN

—————

Grey Area

There was colour, I could not argue with that. Even though we languished in a Catholic ghetto in Belfast, even though what soon proved to lie beyond it was nothing but the same burnt concrete, scrapmetal sky and sooty rain, and even though we failed throughout to get more than a distant glimpse of sex, it is true that at the end there was uniquely one delinquent wee splash – if I can refer in this way, without downplaying it, to an act of killing. Yet, to be frank, it was a matter of no great significance on that dirty white evening as it began to drizzle and Vomit's khaki jacket was flailing back at the bleached breeze and the light was going down over identical chimneys and cable lines of birds, indeed, it was at that last moment with even more than our usual stolidness that the three of us conceded that yes, as things stood, we might as well murder. Since I ought to recount all the background facts from the beginning, I should make it clear that, apart from this brief more colourful, more favourable spell, all things were invariably one or another shade of grey. I must begin by evoking the smoke-greyness of burning buses on our wet way to school while the depressed sun slept in. One such morning I shouted up ahead of me: 'Bleep!'

The streets were thronging with our charcoal grey uniforms and I thought I could recognize a schoolmate of mine standing in an untidy gang, each member of which stared pop-eyed and flummoxed down the road. 'Duffies!' It was purely by shape or size that I could tell a person from a distance, or very occasionally by the particular slogan on a canvas bag, each one vicious but none original. And while gender was a factor which played a part in differentiating us from girls, by far their most remarkable feature, I was about to observe, stood out on the greywash like a bright hope, a wish, a temptation, but it was – for more than myself, it seemed – a struggle to define it.

'Look at that!' Bleep, who was occasionally known as Duffy and whose figure and dark complexion had to all appearances been squashed at some stage from above, spoke to me without turning as I drew up. Distantly, a sluggish cortège was dissolving into the curves of the cemetery wall. I stood for a moment thinking. The girls became the morning mist. Quite suddenly, he let out a wolf whistle and the others started up with agitated, idiotic signals to the air. 'Look at her white socks,' they yelled and, 'Hey, umbrella!' In contrast to the life around me now, down there – even with umbrellas – a graceful, unabashed quality expressed itself. I could tell that this recognition was causing me some concern by the sparkling in my lower torso. It was rough down the road; there it was ultimate ghettoland, a no-go zone, and I had never been there before, yet the distance seemed to throw back from long ago a delicate whirl of confusions. Bleep rummaged on the ground for missiles and tossed them forward in sheer bewilderment. I tried to concentrate despite him. Down there was the forgotten pleasure of carefree movement; I seemed to be remembering that rare encounter with the human body I had had on one or two occasions – I felt I was getting close as the gang now brayed and quacked like certified tubeheads – an encounter which had, right in front of me, swept or twitched back into the world its fugitive colours. There was a full-bloodedness now, even amidst the mist. Yes – I was almost there – at last I could acknowledge how much it was troubling me – my embarrassing peers were on their toes flapping their arms and chanting, 'Wee girl with the ankles!' – that these girls' uniforms (if they were indeed female) were distinctly, daringly reddish.

Admittedly they were a dull red, you might say a grey-red, a red as near to redlessness and black while still maintaining some hope of red, but all the same, here was a lightness sufficient to transform, to inflame what, after all, were merely swaying haunches and swinging pigtails. The passionate colour had to explain my perplexity because – and here I must stress the need to cover all significant aspects of my story – it was not as though girls themselves were unfamiliar to us. They played out on the streets like us in denim suits. Very often girls stood as men beside us boys. It was their toughness which we tried to emulate. Karen Burns, to name only one, once beat up my best friend's dad. They were physically intense like butchers or pylons. We were jealous of their biceps. But now as we stood delaying, unwilling for school, captivated by those cloud-red images of grace – no matter how reluctant – you could say that a new, unformed knowledge stirred of possibilities somewhere in the world which could somehow shine forth, be somehow quite distinct, which could, finally, though it seemed fantastic, simply be, in their natural colours. Be. 'It's five to nine, fuck it,' Bleep shrieked, shocking each of us out of our personal reveries. We turned and bolted up the road, arriving at the school gates as the siren died away.

The hydra-headed vigilance of gate duty ensured this morning that we would retain the right to boast of the most dislocated ears. It was, as I hope will be recognized, no small wonder that thoughts of murder came to us so young. 'Christ,' Bleep sighed in despair, pressing on his ear as we made for the school building.

'What?' I snapped.

'It's fucking Tuesday.'

Some bureau-loving midnight malefactor was no doubt the cause of our having to endure first thing on a Tuesday morning most unlucky, nefarious double Latin. We were a tiny, rancorous, smarting protest for The Embryo – Mr Turner, Latin teacher, so-called because of his formidable age (he was so old he *looked* like an embryo).

'Oh Maguire-us! Wretche maxime!' The class sniggered damply.

'And . . . with the death most heroic,' I struggled, 'so shall the law,' – in my pauses I could hear pages rustling – 'do nothing otherwise than,' – a few hissers were not waiting for me to finish – '. . . climb.' He let out a loud squeak. I risked a glance up. He was fluttering his watery eyes. I made another guess: 'Wander?' As he cleared his lean throat tendons sat out. 'Be?'

'Having been found treacherous to his class,' that thin voice began to quaver, 'Maguire-us The Untrue shall now be sacrificed.' I gazed through the page. I had very little to give Latin. Each single one of my thoughts recognized that their first duty was to render powerless the tormenting mystery, psychology or aesthetics of girls' skirts. 'Maguire-us, altar – now!' Raising myself up, I clodhopped through the schoolbags to the front of the class. 'When are you likely to learn, small dog,' he said, his fine white eyebrows trembling high above me, 'that Latin is not random like your mind?' He was working himself into a passion. 'We have rules, Maguire-us, logical and predictable rules.' The parts of his body wobbled. Everybody was eager to hear what the logical consequences for me would be. 'Dog . . .' he began. There was full attentiveness. '. . . bucket!' A single honk sounded from the class. So, I took stock, it was the head-in-the-bucket routine, there was nothing more predictable. I advanced to the wastepaper bin and knelt on one knee. He looked expectant.

'All the way in, sir?'

'Utmost speed, canine.' I lowered my head into the bin to the applause of my peers. Banana skin, crisp packet, Fanta tin and a nostril-crumpling whiff was the godforsaken world into which I now descended. I cursed him darkly: *One day, Embryo, I'll pickle your swollen head, have you aborted, give you hell, etc.* At length, 'Maguire-us, sit,' tinnily reverberated and, retrieving my head from the rubbish, I grinned all the way back to my seat and the luxury of fresh classroom perspiration. 'At the neglect of home-works there will be weeping and wailing and ululation of mothers,' the crooning continued. 'Duffius, next.'

'I haven't done it either, sir.'
'Duffius – bucket!'

I sometimes saw myself cast as Aeneas, escaping with great
fortitude from the Cyclops in some vague old Technicolor film.
But most of the time it was impossible to work up any respect for
that incredible lot who, when personally instructed by gods,
would storm forward in swollen obedience and restore all
properness with magic spears. Few of us listened to the ageless
Embryo wail about that world he remembered before Christ. We
passed notes in class: 'Up the Ra' and 'I'll get you tarred and
feathered, wee lad, right?' One lunchtime at last our disrespect
burst forth. Bleep and I were up on the football pitch exchanging
girlie fantasies and damning the very invention of all-boys
schools. Roaming about like two oversexed male beasts was half
exasperation but half luxury, so it peeved me to see, of all people
from hated Latin, hesitantly stalking forward with an apologetic
wave, Vomit. He was the third permanent idler, dubbed so on
account of the severe condition of dry peeling skin he had which
made everyone want to throw up at first sight of him. He had a
suggestion to offer.

'Get him seen to.' He looked down at us, suspending a grin.
'Beamer has this secret phone number.'

Bleep broadly swept Coke out of a bottle and gave it an
underhand bowl on to the grass bank. 'What are you talking
about?' He peered up fatly as Vomit, who was roughly twice his
size, explained.

'You know the way The Embryo's really Irish and all?'

'Is he?' I asked.

'Yeah?' Bleep hurried him.

'Well, look, Beamer has this number.' Vomit winked and
nodded as though he had proved himself at long last. As far as I
was concerned, this was shameful and painfully simple behaviour which it was discreet and charitable to pretend not to notice,
so I was taken by surprise when Bleep answered.

'Yeah?'

'It's foolproof,' Vomit added with a gloating face. Bleep smiled. Obviously this was not his usual backfiring, overly elaborate effort to be accepted. I tensed my brain for any drip of inspiration. There was a confidential phone number which everyone knew about and could use, or then again, more sneaky and ingenious pranksters – though everyone knew this too – could ring up the Brits with far-fetched stories about their noisy neighbours or sullen grandmothers. But my imagination extended no further.

'What number?' I asked. 'Is he into the IRA or something?' They gave no answer. Down at the school building the siren started up, as droning and meaningless as The Embyro himself.

'How did Beamer get the number?' Bleep now wanted to know as we turned down the steps from the pitch to the playground.

'Probably where he lives,' Vomit answered squarely before we cut along to the school building, hastening slowly to another crazy double bill of our least favourite superhuman characters.

I wasn't at all clear what they had been saying, but it amazed me to think that we could possibly bring about the real live death of The Embryo, by some intricate deceit involving telephone calls, to slap the jowls of the farcical law and have our own justice *in personam* as it were. Over the next few days at lunchtimes Bleep and Vomit came up with further suggestions. Although these were idle at first, it was not long before we were all plotting in a spirit of hilarious self-discipline. A momentum developed, we goaded each other on, producing ever finer points, choosing the best day to strike; we even dreamed about the scheme and came in the next morning with divinely ministered details. And finally, and at last, when we held under our gaze a strategy, perfect and monstrous and unwanted, a baffled and ugly thing independent now with its own life and unlovable demands, there was one point of embarrassment when we each agreed silently, without saying a word more, to ignore it. As for myself, the truth was that I had only sworn in dead earnest the whole time to prove to Dryface and Action Man Duffy in what depths of cynicism I could still thrive. But to actually do this deed, for me, would have been a brand-new concept entirely. So, as before, typically, predictably, nothing happened; the status quo was endured. Until one Thursday at break Bleep came up to me by the lockers. We had just enjoyed his protracted and stammering distinction between *therefore* and *because of* from the waste bin.

'I wanna kill The Embryo,' he hissed. His eyes vitrified.

'Do you?' I said.

'Yeah.' He was serious.

'Well . . .'

Calmly, rationally, we arranged to meet after school to discuss all the alternatives to stoicism.

'The half lamp-post?'

'Aye.'

The half lamp-post was our meeting-place according to custom. Consistently, diminutive boys made thwarted efforts to ignite the half lamp-post – though the term was used less to describe than to designate a broad geographical area. As I came up the road from my house that evening I spotted by it a stumpy individual in brown cords and a gangly idiot in a camouflage jacket.

'Hiya.'

'Hiya.'

'Well?'

'Well?' Vomit leaned back against the sad, limp post. A low sky flowed over our heads.

'Will we do it?'

'Do you want to?'

I yawned and let them talk. It never ceased to amaze me, and it amazed me once again as I looked about, that our area lacked true girls. True girls only lived elsewhere, elusively. A woman was watching us while chamoising her window.

'We get the number of the UDA off Beamer, right?' Vomit explained. A car passed us with a screech.

'Is Beamer a Prod?'

'Don't be a binlid! At our school?'

Once again they went over the details, but I was preoccupied by lower things. I stared dreamily back at the woman, trying to unzip her dress without her feeling it and peel off the strappy contraption of a bra. She jiggled her breasts for me as she waved her chamois. To me it seemed preposterous and wonderful that she would want her windows to be pristine while the façade of her house was almost graffitied over with 'IRA' and 'GET OUT'. 'Ring up on Saturday morning, right?' Vomit was verifying. 'Say Turner's recruiting for the Ra.'

'Do you want to?'

'Suppose so.'

I sat up on a low wall and leered provocatively at a soldier leading a foot patrol. The woman tried blatantly to peer up and down the road with an anxious frown. She was what we referred to as a 'snob'. The graffiti on her house came undoubtedly in response to the fact that it was painted an ostentatious blue.

'Write it on a piece of paper. One of us'll read it out.'

'In a different accent.'

'Good idea.'

'Will we?'

'Suppose.'

A Pepsi bottle smashed beside Vomit's foot. 'What else is there to do?' he said. It looked as though a riot was imminent. We decided to shift.

'Let's go to our house,' said Bleep. He proposed, having come across seasickness tablets in the medicine cabinet in his house and having noted that they contained codeine, that we try to get high in celebration of our brand-new concept. So we scuffed up the hill to his house and bald bedroom to go over the details again carefully and eat Quells. It was a bleak evening of 'I think I can feel something', 'Can you?', 'Maybe not', and much time devoted to worrying about the perils of overdosing on four tablets. Bleep tried to retch in a panic at the last minute and failed while I, supine on the bed, awaited a visit by sensation. It was a patient and sober wait ending in self-contempt, with rain at the window, Bleep's mother shouting downstairs, Bleep's ashamed eyes, doors banging and agreement that Vomit and I had overstayed our welcome. My image of us as fated to the glamour of vice and abandon was not sustaining. But we were, I can affirm as I reflect on it, anything that evening but *compos mentis*. We fixed a time and a place to meet to begin the execution of our plot: ten o'clock, Saturday, my house.

Using a domestic phone for our purposes was out of the question. Our area was the centre of a magnificent telecommunications network of tracing, tapping, bugging, snooping on party lines, cross-wiring Tarzan-fashion up telegraph poles, do-it-yourself extensions that put kitchen gossip on army radios. We had to set out, therefore, on the chosen, the dreaded day, from my front door with our secret number and our scrawled message, at nearer to noon than ten, for the closest kiosk. At the bottom of my narrow terraced street there was a bombed-out shell – we knew about it – implausible container of human excrement and contraceptives, its royal red slopped over with the obligatory green (for Eire) and concluded with a paint bomb (to white). Heading out of my estate, we walked together up the street towards the main road. An amplified voice scratched the air unintelligibly. 'Right, where is there one?' Vomit said as we came out into the heavy traffic. We scanned the road. The clouds were splashed with muddy water. Bleep and I glanced at each other uneasily. Vomit dug into his hair. Across the road a man was bawling at a microphone. 'But,' Bleep offered unsurely, 'won't they all be smashed?'

I perched on a random metal pole and smirked. Bleep's eyes darted, promising a blush. But Vomit glowered with the effort to keep his countenance. Vomit was entirely bent on holding all together now as chaos threatened. It was Vomit who kept us at that moment, though only by an eyebrow, from spinning off back into the void, the domain of sleepwalkers and all the aimless ones from which we had only just emerged triumphant and hooting with a purpose. Vomit would not let the admission be made that if we had been relying on finding a telephone in our area *in working order* then all our preparations, what we were glad to think of as our master tactics, were truly no better than, no different from any odious schoolboy sniggerings over an ink pellet. And even though greensick pillar-boxes had their scalps ripped off, zebra crossings were skinned of their stripes, elongated 'DEAD SLOW' markings rendered 'YOU'RE DEAD', traffic lights swiped, Belisha beacons pocketed and even the very footpaths in places rendered inoperative, Vomit, by his hot frown and peeling impatience, was forbidding us outright to betray any doubt in our search for order. 'I can't see one near,' he faked.

Some people were delaying near the man with the microphone. He was shouting at them, 'What's fuckin' wrong with youse!' Bleep watched uneasily. I had no political conscience and, provided I could keep my kneecaps, I had only sneers for our revolutionary brothers, so I felt no pang of guilt in recognizing now that our aim for services as normal reversed all expectation of us. Still, it was wise to get off the scene. I peered gingerly down the road in the direction of the cemetery.

'Down there,' I suggested. Some of the passing cars sounded their horns in support of the man. 'What about down there?' We stared for a moment. I was hoping, though I felt it best not to mention, that we might come upon females in this direction naturally straying in their kinky uniforms, even though today was Saturday.

'Right,' said Bleep eagerly. Vomit let out a worried 'Mmh' and said, 'It's tough.'

'Not really,' I said. 'We'd get a kiosk down there.'

'There's a chance,' said Bleep. Vomit nodded, so with a certain faith that down there a solution lay, we set off towards the cemetery.

It began to brighten. Vomit did most of the talking in isolated sentences, invariably along the lines of 'This'll teach him a lesson'. As we skirted the cemetery, clouds lodged between the chimneys of an old factory. The traffic was pulling out round a burning car. 'This is mad,' he continued to mumble. He was nervous. There were white handkerchiefs drooping from most of the lamp-posts. In spite of my ignorance, which was impressive enough to inspire pride, I was aware that these had been strung up the summer before during more hunger striking and that, though the rain had now washed the dye out of them, they had been meant to serve as tiny mourning flags. Clearly, I concluded, we were still safe in a Catholic area. I decided that this detail of the handkerchiefs was, to cynics like Bleep and me, probably worth a grunt of recognition, so I sighed, 'Ah, look,' nudging him, 'white flags.' He shrugged his shoulders – from him a strong sign of approval.

'This is useless,' Vomit mumbled. There weren't any kiosks about. But Bleep spoke over his words.

'Is that a phone?' We squinted. It was difficult to see if it was or not without the conspicuous, eye-catching cherry red to go by. A whitish, greenish daub on the far footpath did almost resemble in shape at least one side of a kiosk. And, in effect, that is what it proved to be: a solitary door to nowhere, standing clean in a concrete base, one part green, nine parts white. I gave an exasperated smack through my lips.

'Jesus, this is fucking a load of fucking . . .'

'Let's get off this crappy road,' Bleep said, so at the next turning on the right we diverted our course down a dilapidated tree-lined hill. The light was clotting.

'Let's go over the plan again,' Vomit said, being mature. I felt a tear of rain.

'I ring up,' Bleep sighed, with a dubious glance at me.

'Remember the accent.'

'And what do you say?'

'I've it written down, haven't I!'

'What do you say anyway?' We broke into a children's game of football. Somewhere a fire was burning. I ran an eye over the side streets and, as Bleep went through his exhausted performance of booming into a mimed telephone with any authority that he could muster that Gregg Turner of whatever the street was regularly coerced kids to join the IRA and that he, a leading citizen who shall remain nameless if that's OK, was just about sick of it, and that his whole loyalist community expected that Turner character to be no less than shot for it, and while Vomit directed this unedifying drama, my attention was everywhere else: between dustbins, in the hedges, up the driveways, through gardens of rubble, panning round at a pitch of readiness hoping to identify by the unforgettable reddish imprinted on my deprived senses, girls. But by the time we had come up to a busy roundabout the only femininity I had seen was a naked doll being chewed by a dog, a boy who resembled a girl from behind and who bawled, 'Why're you fuckin' smilin' for!' and an obese lonely woman leaning over her garden gate cursing everything, including, it seemed, the very air. A man's voice called after us, 'Whata youse want!' and then, 'Hey, White Socks!' Vomit glanced at his socks. If we could think of our wanderings as a miniature Aenead, this was surely a visit to the Underworld. Separately, we dashed through the traffic to the far footpath. Bleep made it across at last, bouncing up to us on his short legs, and we resumed.

'And then you hang up.'

'Mmm.'

'OK.'

'Do you think he'll get shot?'

'Hope so.'

'Kneecapped anyway.'

I tutted. 'Jammy bastard.'

We joined another road off the roundabout. Up ahead there were some soldiers standing about laughing. Together they formed a shrub of camouflage that broke the monotony of paving. Vomit dropped his voice:

'Where're we going?' But before he could get an answer, and rather more swiftly than can be recounted, we were spreadeagled against one side of a jeep. Normally this was a safe enough routine provided you were polite. But Bleep started up too polite.

'Empty your pockets,' a mustachioed soldier silenced him. Everything went on to the bonnet of the jeep: nibbled biro top, locker keys, ball of fluff and that slip of paper from which Bleep was going to read. My heart started to thud. If they read that, my mind was racing, we won't just be lifted, it'll be actually real-life internment maybe! As his subordinate frisked us I kept my eyes on it, sitting apart from the other things, folded in a half-open, twitching, inviting V. It was begging to be explored. The soldier was stroking his treasure. The V was irresistible, tantalizing, I thought, a note, it was obvious he would read it. Any normal red-blooded fingers would be itching to undo it and smooth it out pale and prostrate. 'Turn round,' he shouted suddenly. 'What's this?' His English accent pierced through the smoke.

It was then, all at once, as I wobbled under his godlike authority, that I recognized my naked self. Until then I had only been passing by in a cloud of vagueness. This voice instantly dispersed it and what remained were bare facts. That slip of paper was proof of a murder plot, it was as good as a plea of guilty to malice aforethought. Before it had seemed natural to ignore mere details like these. But not any longer. Now for the first time I was goggling at the unsightly truth. There would be no dozing on the fat border between yes and no beneath these discipline fanatics. Their certainty had muscles which bruised the air. With them, there was no neutral zone reserved for childish fickleness. 'What's this?' he repeated. I sickened. I saw my meek little parents suddenly involved and me puling with feigned astonishment, 'It was a joke.' How had this all happened in a moment, I puzzled: here was the army of Great Britain being literal about a blur and a daydream. I was about to pipe up. 'That's his note,' I was about to say and point to Bleep. The soldier spoke again. 'They're car keys.' He was holding up our locker keys.

'They're my locker keys,' Vomit was saying. My heart was boxing on the wall of my chest. 'They're locker keys.'

'Where d'you live?'

'Well, we live, you see, in West . . .' That note was shifting in the breeze.

'What are you doing round 'ere? You're doing cars, ain't ya?'

'They're locker keys.' Vomit gesticulated like a reasonable revolutionary. 'We've lockers in school. They're locker keys.'

The soldier jabbed his finger forward. 'I'll put you inside that fucking jeep in a minute.' Vomit dropped his hands. Behind, another soldier sang our addresses into a radio. 'What are you doing round 'ere?' he resumed. 'You shouldn't be out of your area.'

Bleep volunteered: 'We're going for a walk.' The radio cackled. The soldier wrung his face in disbelief.

'A *walk*!' We looked at each other with innocent surprise. He frowned. 'OK, take your things,' he said. We clutched for everything. 'Don't go out of your area in future,' he bawled as we sidled off. He climbed into the jeep. We had their camouflage on the backs of our necks.

The road was leading up into the city centre. Whatever bitterness Bleep and Vomit were thinking, my regrets were possibly quite particular. Now that the cloud around me had been blasted away, everything was clear: it wasn't a telephone kiosk that I had been in the least concerned to find. Indeed, it was a statement of just what imbeciles I hung around with that these two had allowed me to coax them into the epicentre of Catholic deprivation, the heart of the ghetto, in search of a functioning telephone – unless they too had each been privately seeking the same as myself, or something else. My regret was that no girls were running up to comfort us. I had been in search of gentleness. As we came into the centre we didn't feel like talking. We found a vinegary hamburger joint.

'What did they want to know all that for anyway?' said Vomit when we were sitting round a table. But neither he nor Bleep were as stung as I was by the episode. Perhaps we weren't in a position to be righteous, I thought to myself, but, all the same, no one should tell us that we should not go outside our area. There was nothing to keep us there except Quells and cough bottles on Saturday evenings. Both of them munched away. I didn't order. I simply sat staring out at two policemen with their bullet-proof vests and plastic-bullet guns. There were no shoppers on the street. It was turning to evening, peaceful apart from, somewhere, the clicking of a metal turnstile. Eventually Bleep said, 'What'll we do?' Vomit was scratching his flaky arm over the table. I looked out of the window again instead of answering. A newspaper blew against a policeman.

'This is good, isn't it,' I said. Bleep looked straight at me with his long stupid eyelashes.

'Yeah,' he said.

Exasperated, I stood up and the three of us straggled out into the dirty pallor. It had got windy. We walked round to queue for a black taxi into our area. A dog piddled against a telephone kiosk. We stopped.

'That's a phone.'

'So what?'

'What do you mean, "So what"?' Vomit laughed.

'That's a false laugh,' said Bleep.

'You're a false person.'

I opened the door with my weight and lifted the receiver. 'It's working,' I said.

'Well?'

'Well?' said Bleep.

It was beginning to rain. I tried to be amusing. 'Duffius,' I croaked, 'The answer – utmost speed.'

'*This* isn't fucking logical, anyway.' He tried a superior sigh.

Vomit shook his head and said with all the Apollonian dryness he could concentrate: 'What's the point!' The breeze was blowing him to flakes. But something was reassuring me; it was our destiny, perhaps. Here, after all, was what we had been searching for, a genuine working telephone, unignorably, indeed, proudly, royally red.

'We might as well,' I suggested. I wedged myself in the door.

'What do you think?' Vomit asked. Bleep thought for a moment. A tin thrashed past his foot.

'It's murder,' he answered.

'So fuck!' I said loudly.

He looked at Vomit. 'Might as well,' he said.

'We might as well,' Vomit repeated.

We all got into the kiosk. Bleep ferreted for the slip of paper. A piece of one of the windows was lying on the shelf inside like a big set square. 'What's the number?' We sniggered. I dialled it as Bleep pressed the receiver hard against his ear. We all heard the ringing tone. It kept ringing. Suddenly he slammed his hand on the rest. He and I burst out laughing. 'I'm not ready.' I started to dial again. 'No, I wanna rehearse,' he said. Vomit's face was hard as wood. I squeezed round and squinted out through the smoky plastic while Bleep attempted a convincing adult voice. 'Gregg Turner of twenty-seven. . .' he hummed. A police jeep crawled past the semi-detacheds. '. . . and we want him wiped out for good.'

'Look,' I said, 'perfect, do it and we'll get out of here.' I angled the slip of paper in his hand towards me and dialled the number again.

'Jesus.' He crossed his legs. We heard the ringing tone again. It rang and rang. And then, strangely, Bleep turned away from us. The drone faltered. He put a finger in his ear, frowning. Vomit smiled. The slip of paper was quivering. His voice was loud. I turned away with a grin. Suddenly he wrenched an arm up through the squash of our bodies and, with a karate chop, cut himself off. He looked at us, breathless, expectant. We looked back at him so he said, 'It was a woman answered.' We didn't say anything for a moment. Then Vomit mumbled, 'We've actually done it.'

'I know,' I said.

'We shouldn't have. It was really banal.' We looked at each other.

'I know,' said Bleep.

On the way round to the black taxis and in the queue we didn't speak. It was raining invisibly. When our turn came we squeezed in with three women who nattered all the way up the road. Until we got out of the taxi to part at the corner we hadn't exchanged a word since the kiosk. 'See you,' I said, breaking the silence.

'See you.'

We made off in different directions. Well, I admitted to myself on the walk to my street, it was a selfish thing to do. The whole long day lay behind me like my disgrace. But so what, I thought, so what if it was banal, it was no worse than anything else. Some skinheads were lolling against our wall. Birds were dotting a wire. To me, if to no one else, the adventure had been barren. But at the same time there was an assurance that at last we had acted. We had done something which was better than our shadowy, brooding, morose, wait to be older before we would start to live. I walked stiffly past the skinheads. Today we chose clearly, it was black and white. For the first time, probably, I thought, we were really ourselves, distinctly unwise and ungentle, that was how I saw it. I would stew in selfishness and banality and badness and anything else before I would let a scruple stop me from kicking out this time. At anything. Now I was perfectly clear. That unloved, skimpy excuse for a man, our teacher, he did not spare a blind wank for our pains and fears. All he could do when he stood at the front of the class was ridicule. Well now, I said to myself, yes, now as I glided through the little gate into my house, it was we who were laughing. There would be fuck all beauty, wailing and ululation of women at his last pretty hour. So what if we had actually done it? So what if we punctured the fatuous hot air out of his one clapped-out lung? I could see him wheeze as the gunshot reverberated, a trickle of blood down his quivering chin, his spindle legs would buckle and he'd be down, red eyes blinking for mercy. Beautiful!

Real Difference

So when she came Mother christened her Albertine and smiled it all through the house in nap time, googled it at bath time. Mother's finger lingered now on the mock Victoriana tallboy, head well back for the three syllables contralto and on the sustained eeeen a warble.

'Alberteeeen!'

The very first good dress was not so long ago posted up from Paige of London. How that missie had quite looked, said all, the proper doll in her calf-length organdy Perkin's mauve and Mother tying eggshell ribbons to her plait. Albertine had wept and kicked: Oh, Mother! Everyone noticed the pertinacity Mother had with plaits. Those were hard times, appearances were everything. As she had tied she enjoyed slow blinks. Frowning was a delight to Mother. Please Mother, oh please don't make me. And just so she was persisting still today: 'Tiney!' with one broad shake of the head, knowing her, so indulgent. And for the ninth birthday Dad had had a hand-carved naughty figurine sent on from Sierra Leone, he repeated, Sierra Leone in a zebrawood box to Manchester, and local lasses were invited round at four o'clock to see it in their party frocks and each with a present all looking so (ah!) beautiful. And Crystal came and she was nice, but right stand-offish, but nice. And how much fun Mother had had that birthday morning dressing up her young daughter as a toy lady. But, of course, she, the ostensible girl knew all along that little plain Albertine should in fact really have been properly, *was* in all truth, deep down, a little boy.

Even before Varsha she knew it. Oh Varsha, my death would be natural, oh love.

'Albertine!' Mother called again, less now of a warble on that third syllable.

At first it could have been customary, harmless, boys at the front door asking for, of all diminutives, Bert, and the young girl felt quite happy in a gang, short-haired and – Mother watched bemused – swarming up the knotty oak to their secret den hidden in the leaves at the back of One One One terraced Ashton Old Road, didn't she, strangely. 'Shall we go paddle, Bert?' 'What? In our scuddy knickers, lad?' And where was her modesty as she would race with the lads over the black ooze by the riverside down to the old mill. Splashes. A giggling flash for Bert. Oh that's the way I should have looked, handsome with that crucial jiggly bit to hang on to and flaunt. But it were girls were magical. She would lock an elbow under Frankie Morrison's daft chin. 'Go on, do a moony, Bert.' 'No I won't.' And maybe she could have gone on being Bert the tomboy coming home muddy and Mother and Dad thinking, of course, she'll grow out of it once the time comes, we'll buy her a new spring smock and puff sleeves and trimmed with lace, and nothing at the back of their minds whispering, 'No, she's a monster,' – indeed maybe it could have gone along smoothly if it only hadn't been for loving in just the way she fell in love that day with dear dear Varsha. Oh love. No. Something was wrong.

'Dooooo make an effort, dear!' Mother called on the fateful Sunday, this early beginning, her ring finger along the walnut veneer and doubtless her mind already on a dark thought. The grandmother clock, queer old thing, chimed impatiently on lanky-legged eleven twenty-seven. Beneath its golden globes Dad stood tall, suited, sad column of too much himself. Often would Dad have a smooth distance: 'Ready, Ceci?' And gathering suddenly her scattered thoughts, Mother would wobble her bum in slacks to the kitchen. 'No hurry, my princess,' to the front window, his eyes creased, wondering out of the window.

She fussed now over a carrier bag, cheeping to herself,

'Blanket, yes, now, have we . . . Oh hell's bells!' patting her more salt than pepper hairdo. 'Now where *is* Albertine?' with her saggy jaw. 'Ready, yet my sweeeeeeet?' she called.

Dad smiled, his eyes of Sheffield Steel. 'No hurry, queenie,' he nodded, she: 'Daddy's coming up, pet.' No answer. 'Albertine! Now listen girl!' Her garneted fingers, knobbed, spread out over her breast, starfish carbuncled. 'Daddy's getting angry, love!'

The bedroom door cracked open and, well oh here we are, there on the first stair stood the blocky presentable wee doll, scampish but kissable in daffodil check. But those tiny eyes were, oh for God's sake, downright turbulent pools. 'No, Mother, please. . .' Mother might lose her patience. 'Don't weep, dear. Why weep?' The grandmother chimed again. 'You look a picture.' Dad's hand reached for the newspaper. Wide-eyed and bushy-tailed, his lips were thinking. Oh terrible Dad.

'Ready, Ceci?' he said.

'Ready, Daddy,' Mother said with intimacy. 'We're off,' hand trembling her perm.

So off they set into the outside, down the garden and up the pleasantish, tolerable old road, a steady walk to the train, Albertine behind. 'Don't lag, pet.' A baby and a cat gaped. Eyes watched from a Venetian blind.

On the train Albertine sat surly. Mother watched her. Does my daughter not enjoy, she showed she was thinking, an enviable dress, costly slip-on buckled shoes, a matching ribbon of no slight price. 'Does Tiney appreciate,' she asked Dad, 'that children ran barefoot once? Dad nodded, yes it is true, Dad remembers, his eyes closed tightly. 'Manchester Victoria!' declared a portly voice. They descended. They changed. A new string of carriages bumped them off among tumble-down red-brick, between mill walls, until, gentle slopes, leafy air, there was it, destination, park, vast carpet, ice-cream vendors, girls in whites and gay colours.

So the threesome straightened belongings, all-sorts on a private corner of grass to play Donkey. But always Albertine was staring, then catching, then staring. 'Don't stare, sweet. Catch.'

But who were those lasses chasing each other around a shrub? Tiney was curious. Why couldn't I play with, go over to, that's all, get to be with, talk to only, chat, play? But it were wrong, I knew. So I'd look and look away and look and look away and look. 'Silly Billy, Albertine, you're nearly Donkey.' But wasn't that Varsha What's-her-name? Oh, but wasn't Varsha pretty! 'Donkey, Albertine,' Mother flapped. 'Oh I mustn't laugh so much,' holding her side but her heart wasn't in it. Dad set down his newspaper on the grass and crumpled it up with a patronizing arse. Varsha was walking away now with friends faraway on to a road trafficless and silent. 'Sandwiches now.' A cool breeze promised twilight. Blue now hung where laughter had. Mother and Dad chewed quietly. A hooligan shouted. They ate bread and daydreamed till home time.

When they trailed back to the tired platform they were just in time to scramble aboard. But at empty Victoria Mother shivered. A call preoccupied the dome roof. A man with a cap leaned. At last the train sissed followed by a whistle's peep and Mother swept aboard her frustrated and worn-out girl. 'Ghastly!'

That night in the cosy safety of One One One Mother sat on the edge of Albertine's bed. 'What's wrong, my precious?' she asked, glassy fingers in the girl's hair. Albertine had been crying. 'Oh, Mother, Varsha. Varsha is so bonny.'

Albertine was Mother's sensitive girl.

And when the time eventually came for the plain young thing to blossom, to metamorphose, all eyes were on her. The first mere dribble on the child's sheet one late summer troubled with fragrance and Mother sang out through the house. Upstairs Albertine lay belly down on her counterpane, kicking it with bare feet beneath her poster of Marie Osmond, tearing her hair: 'Oh why? Oh no!' to drown out Mother. Now it was horrible, she was deforming, it was happening, growing monstrous, and she riffled through the big family dictionary for herself: sex, boy, growing up, she searched, different. That evening Dad returned from work, Mother broke to him the good news, Albertine heard it in whispers, craning from the landing. Then one week before September and a new school, Mother took the bold reluctant missie for her first brassière.

She backed herself now against a mirrored pillar adjacent to the underwear, arms folded so that Mother could not pull her, face dark like a bruise, pout more unequivocal than her 'I won't! I won't!' Mother glanced nervously about, 'Will you come *on,*' through her teeth. But Albertine's fold tightened, you can't make me, and she knocked the back of her head against the pillar to signify conviction masculine to her core. 'I'm not going to!' she snarled, but her words, like her outward signs, were a dead script. To Mother's relief, she at last caught the eye of an assistant and, 'Ahem,' over a bodice rack, 'excuse me, eh . . .' she asked, 'her first, em . . . bra.'

'Would she like to . . . come this way?' said the assistant, wasp-waisted, grace at her step. So Albertine followed her confusion. 'This is what's called . . . it's just a training . . .' The assistant was ransacking a box. Finally she smiled and held up the bespoke elastic machine, white with miniature dangling leafs. Albertine flinched. 'Would she like to . . . try . . .' But, all of an instant, Albertine had taken to her pink heels. Mother's head swung right, then left. 'Oh my God!' she flustered and, 'I'm awfully sorry,' breaking away now towards the entrance doors.

Mother found the girl against a lamp-post with sterile eyes, one unique dead drop to her candy-striped dress. She was staring unfocused and far, unlistening, dud. Mother skimmed the passers-by. A crane swung high over the road. Workmen called out. She crunched her voice: 'Albertine, I'm not a well woman, you know!' They walked back in together.

Strangely enough, it later seemed to Albertine, she learned to love in one way those soft machines. Who, oh, who, she thought, out of all the sweet electric, face-pulling variety of eyes, lips, twinkles, frowns, who was in Form 1Cb but Varsha What's-her-name! The joy of it, the pain of it. During gymnastics then, in the changing room, Albertine would fake fiddling with her clothes, would force indifferent faces, a yawn, while strategically, her nervous eyes aimed to burn into that beauty's tan striptease. She would make as if to examine a stubborn blotch on her tunic until those shorts of Varsha's were bound to be down, then she'd stare. And gauging how long a stare can feasibly last in a changing room before one suspicious eyebrow will spoil all for ever, Albertine got in those lessons as close to that tender brownish, that baby ebony as ever she might. And she became too by a subtle acrobatics almost on pally terms with her as each week they carried in the horse together. 'Will we put it there?' 'What about there?' 'Here's a good place.' 'Yeah.' In gym she lost herself, she was good at it, bounding and furiously running. And at the softest contact her bulky form receded, was serene. There was applause, sometimes a hug and then, once more, the thrilling discomfort of the changing room. But it was right here among the wet, pink and steam one spiteful day she learned to hate that Varsha as much as, oh, she adored her.

Weary after a dreary afternoon of rusty irony and wooden pardox they all went to gym. Now unzipping watchfully, now lowering her skirt bashfully, Albertine heard from behind her a horrible 'whoop' and a 'yaaalook!' No, it can't be happening! She was dizzied. She was now seeing up the legs of so many half-bare girls of all shapes while at her beating ankles her skirt was clutched. Only one voice was needed now to howl at the unnatural, the unimaginable, Varsha's freakish discovery, oh, the shame:

'Y-fronts! Aaaah!'

'Wearing boy's Y-fronts! Yaaagh!'

What has she on underneath, became the issue shrieked along corridors from this day forward as Albertine would swagger past determined. What's the truth about Albertine underneath her uniform surface? So every day she spurned from a distance that cruel self-centred bitch Varsha, every night dreamed of her. Until finally one afternoon in detention she found herself with mixing feelings alone with the *fillette fatale*.

She held her hand. Varsha by the hand. What recklessness was it raging in her own clutch? It was warm, a boy holding a bird. Oh love! The blood heats inside Varsha. It comes out hot on her face when she smiles, through her cheeky cheeks. 'Can't we be chums?' she said to Varsha's svelte inquisitive eyes. Still she held the hand, still played with the fingers, those mad fingery things of hers, spellbinding. Varsha had peachy breasts by now. Albertine could see down to the end of her tan on tan. Later at half past four when school ended she went home, she sat on her bedroom ottoman and she felt her own breasts like Varsha's. She could look in the mirror with her bra off. It is a girl I see. If I cover up my head I could fantasize. But oh no, she had these, oh how hideous udders, she was weighed down with big hips, she loathed it. Later that evening she was stroking her own hand thinking of Varsha. She. Varsha, my girl. Fingering her own strange bloody sex and crying, she took that hot hand to her lips and surged into a teary ocean, the warmnesses, the shorelessness. Mother came in that moment.

'What is it, my chick? Tell me what it is, Tiney. Tell me.'

She quickly dried her eyes. Mother put a finger on those tears. 'You can tell me. What is it?' she asked. 'You're my flesh and blood, Tiney. There's nothing you can't tell me.' But never would Mother admit, let herself admit it. She and Dad would keep smiling at the plain girl unblooming, their little flower, a dead dandelion, cold as a moon, a weed that fouled indoors, choking for air. No, she would not admit. She glided through the house touching ornaments, paused at the kitchen table vacantly, recapturing someone else who had passed her by. She stood behind her own ear chattering that her marriage was normal, that her house was approvable, her figure was admirable. But this thing Albertine had always known. What was the name for it, if only I had told, maybe, maybe they could have fixed me up. 'Tell me, my lamb, there's nothing you can't tell me.' Should she tell her, Albertine was thinking, 'I'm your mother, your troubles are mine,' that she was one of those, what's the word? she couldn't remember, bilingual, ambidextrous. . .

'I can't tell you,' Albertine said rubbing her eyes. Mother put an arm around her further. 'I can never tell you, Mother.'

Mother lowered her look.

'You'll not fail me, Tiney,' she said and patted her elbow. 'We're in this together.' Tiney nodded. 'I'm counting on you.' They both dried their eyes.

A few days later after school she was tidying her locker and Varsha, decent weakling, shallow conservative girl, confused person, hung back and chatted. 'Are you tidying your locker?' 'Mmmm.' 'I'll have to tidy mine one day.' They tee-heed, they chatted and they walked out of the school and home together. 'Do you forgive me?' 'Mmm.' The next day they walked home again together discussing drama. Now Albertine found herself on a brand-new world. Suddenly, this was the inverse life, the big bright one, that had hidden always behind the opaque air. Had, she wondered, immensities, heavens rearranged themselves for her? She trod with startled frailness, not wanting to alert the universe of its lapse. Meanwhile Mother began to worry.

Dad now being away doing business, Mother's brother came to talk. Lank Uncle Pete, worked for the coal board, jet black blink, his lump of nose a triangle. Somehow, deceiving her wits, one evening shuffled her with him into the dark park, dusty, black railings, they sat together under the convent, leprous statues among the shrubs the eye, one evening juggled him and Tiney into the dark park together, they sat together, she was safe with him, he protected her. 'Listen now, Tiney, let me tell you a fact. Let me stroke your hair and tell you a plain outright friend-to-friend fact.' Uncle Pete squeezed up all lovey-dovey beside his soft boyish niece for a nice whisper between themselves, strictly hush-hush between niecie and Petey. 'Tiney will brush her hair and look the beauty, like this, with her hair back,' and he explained how normal it is to have bad thoughts of men, good thoughts, lovely thoughts. He was warm beside her and strong. 'Those thoughts are natural, but only for men . . .' Peter was lost in his niece's moonlit hair. 'But I wonder has?' He coughed. 'Has Tiney ever heard of . . .' he coughed, ' "warped love"?' She said she was tired now. 'Now, now, Petey knows everything.' Oh

Varsha, love that Varsha, hold you by the waist, hug around the dance floor for all swirling eternity. In a disco. 'Will Petey show Tiney?' Oh Varsha, you and I. 'I'd rather not, Pete.' Concentrate. Together one day. Please don't. Varsha, my life. Darling. I love you. Deep as the firmament. Will always.

Uncle was sparkling the cutlery as Mother fussed between hot oven door and sticky whisking bowl, and even with all that she still found room for the odd breathless trill. Brother added an *umpah*! or a *dah-dah*! 'Yo-ho!' She leaned away now from the crackling hump of turkey. 'Is Tiney downstairs?' No answer. 'Alberteeeen!' No answer.

Mother strode the stairs. There was a sound of frantic rummaging, she walked in, 'Yes, I'm coming . . .' to Albertine's room: 'But, oh what's this? Hey hey, what's this supposed to . . . in the name of . . . ?' Scent of aftershave, brilliantined hair bent low. 'Well, I don't know!' Albertine sat on the edge of her bed wearing, can you believe it, Mother told her brother now, 'her father's jacket and tie and oh, trousers and shoes and, oh my God . . .'

'This day and age.'

Albertine heard it all from the landing.

Some time later, 'Tiney! Dinner!' was called. Nothing more was said of it. They munched through dinner. 'Albertine, you've hardly touched your breast. Well, now ahem . . . dessert of the day.'

'Can I be excused?'

'You may.'

Up in her room Albertine stood in a horror. Why did it happen? Couldn't she just go back in time, in such an emergency after all, not make that trivial mistake, hear Mother's call. Her heart pounded with solitude, the room was acting strangely, it showed her a thousand cold glittering shoulders. She sat down. Poor Bertie, poor little lad putting on trousers, poor little girl she is, a boy like me, to attract Varsha. When she closed her eyes she was stinking black afraid. This bad bad mistake, it were gruesome. Why did she not hear? That name, that chocky sound *Al-ber-tine!*, it clotted in flight and dropped to the carpet. Mother's words were the husks of meanings. 'Perrr-soh-naaah!' she could have been calling. 'Ambig-yooo-iteeee!' Oh this life, her face hung heavy, there were no tears now, she was earthbound, blank, imprisoned in the dead word Albertine. Maybe one day I shall wake up and not be one in a million, everything back to normal the way it never was. Then I could take my girl out in a startling world, to the shore, in starlight harmony, whisper of waves. Kiss. Maybe one day I can have the operation.

But as days passed the incident was opening up to mild interpretations, theatrical, educational. The perplexing week wouldn't make up its mind to be either cruel or kind, for out of a smiling blue now Varsha invited her to come one day to her house to discuss Eng. Lit. in her attic bedroom. The morning before she accompanied Mother to the antiques shop. They giggled together at odd objects, suggested for them preposterous uses. 'I believe,' twittered the experimental girl, and pointing to her thespian reputation with Victorian nail-clippers or thinguma-bobs, 'my nails are a trifle long.' 'They're fine,' said Mother. On the street they walked arm-in-arm to the bus. 'You know, Tiney,' said Mother, 'we believe in you'. Albertine swallowed, smiled back and as she stopped to tie her shoe Mother noticed ahead of them, by surprise, Uncle Pete again and Auntie Bee. She called out and they all went, lugging their heavy shopping, for chips and tea.

When Pete nipped up Back Piccadilly, desperate to powder, Bee joshed with hilarious eyes, she was tipsy, that stumpy nose – Albertine made an examination of the sugar – Mother com-mented, 'Albertine would make a good friend for Edward.' When Pete returned scratching his moustache the suggestion was aired and all agreed how smashing it would be to drive out for the afternoon to their house in the pleasant part of wherever it was.

Mother sat in the front seat of Pete's Sunbeam chattering with a quivering Black Magic she is partial to, tends to have a preference for, she meant she liked them. 'Albertine, what's your preference?' asked Auntie. A silence. 'Fudge,' she mumbled. Pete kept his eye on the road as is necessary at all times, highway code, he said to Albertine in the mirror especially to cheer her up, and Albertine sat right up beside her aunt in the back seat. How Tiney was richly dressed in red corduroy, flocculent jersey, a turquoise slide in her hair.

'Tiney's turning into a proper young lady.'

The car pulled into the driveway of Pete and Bee's. They all got out and stretched their legs. The grown-ups had more tea and more tea in the parlour. Albertine's cousin Edward was a straight up and down, a most well-mannered lad. And shy Edward actually took Albertine for a short pace on the patio. And around the back garden. And up the laburnum ginnel. And out to the allotment. Edward spoke with a strong lisp, 'going to shit my A-levelsh,' he told her, nodding with a quick chuckle, picking steps on the muddy narrow crazy paving, 'anshioush to read Enshineering. At Cambridgsh.' Oh Varsha, tomorrow, tomorrow. 'What do you study?' he asked her, nodding. 'English,' she said and he chuckled. When they returned, radish-cheeked and mud on their shoes, Auntie Bee got an idea. Let him show Albertine his radio which he had built himself from various spare bits and which received transmissions from Luxembourg and even Rabat. She watched him with gentle tedium in the spare bits room finger and drop and chuckle. The exasperating boy knew nothing about radios. She had to snatch the unfunny nonsense from him and show him. 'You're a right chump,' she told him.

They were getting on so well together that, 'Perhaps,' it was ventured, 'Albertine would like to stay. . . ?'

'Oh thank you, Auntie, she would love that,' said Mother. And Mother really had to be going now.

'Stay for a short holiday,' they chatted on her way to the door. She could have the guest room, all made up and ready, as it happened, to just suit the fancies of a young lady, stylish with what you call that *trompe l'oeil* wooden wallpaper, expensive too, Bee was thrilled. 'She's the picture of surprise,' said Uncle Pete, 'and she won't take too much notice of Edward, and Edward knows not to impose on a girl's privacy at all during the evenings.

Edward nodded.

Mother bade goodbye to Tiney, have a nice time, 'T'ra now, T'ra Albertine,' and Pete drove her down the driveway, the engine powerful and foreign now on the gravel, exhaust fumes in the hushed evening. Distantly a tin can rattled. Tiney excused herself one moment and tore upstairs into that scented bathroom. Oh Varsha, so far away now, when can I see you? She smudged her tears on a Posy bravely, and her eyes lowered through the open window to the still road through the peeling petals of a cherry blossom at evening.

One night, then, when Edward and Auntie Bee were out, Albertine found herself alone in the house with the one who understands her, the man.

She sat in the kitchen pouting over a sandwich. Pete sat and smiled at her. She wiped her mouth. 'What's wrong, Tiney?' She took a sip of tea. He sat in beside her. 'What age are you now? Fifteen? Fourteen? Too old for pouting.' He smiled warmly. She looked at her piece of sandwich. 'We're friends. Won't you call me Petey?' She shrugged her shoulders. 'Do you like that?' He rubbed them.

'Mmm.'

'It's OK,' he whispered. She took a bite. 'I know your secret.' He patted her arm. 'Let's go upstairs and talk.' Pete's petting was firm. 'What you need, my girl, is – is that nice? – to learn.' Albertine stood up to get the teapot. He laughed and took her arm.

'Look, I just want . . .' she grinned.

'Come on,' he smiled.

'Look . . .' He led her. 'Look, eh . . . Uncle Pete,' she kidded, 'you know, eh . . .' She grabbed her sandwich.

Up the stairs he pretended to tug her. 'Good girl, it's just a joke.'

But I am a boy. She gulped the crust. 'No, I don't really . . .' Oh God. Lumps, tiny, of coal for eyes. 'Uncle Pete!' He was a blur now of her tears.

'Mother will understand,' he swallowed, 'if Tiney was,' he swallowed. She took a strip of lettuce from her lip, 'curious.' He coughed. 'Lie back.'

'Look, that's enough!'

'Watch this,' he said, 'Mother won't blame you.' She lay. It would be over soon, she knew. Oh Mother! It would be over soon, she nodded to herself, and found an interest in the wallpaper. Terrible, no, it was all right, an experience, so this was sex, and she stroked the wallpaper, interesting, it was, how it formed, she hadn't noticed it, the shape of the wallpaper, yes, imagine this happening, no it was all right, yes, it was all right, no, it was mmh. 'What time is it Pete?' it was mmh, well, terrible.

Oh Varsha, if I should live now. Who could I find to snatch away my child?

Off White

I could hear kids on the waste ground behind me. The voices were muffled in the pale calm. My uncle was polishing the back lights of our car. I heard him mumble from where I was standing at the boot at the front, 'Dear dear.' People passed by us on the road, an old woman with a trolley, some black kids. I found a good place in the boot for my frisbee. 'Dear dear dear,' he mumbled. He was peering up at my trousers. Inside my head I shouted, Fucking shut up! I went back in through the front door to get the big thermos flask. My uncle had got this car only recently and he had been going mad taking me on trips in it. I had been living with him since I was a tiny baby and for as long as I can remember we had always gone places together, like the country or the beach. When I came out again the first thing I noticed was his eyes rolled upwards as if he was jealous of the black cloud floating above. The footpath was sharpening and dirtying. He looked at me.

'Where are you going?' he said in an inquisitive way. I had to think for a minute. He was standing tall. His hands were oily.

'On a trip,' I said.

He said, 'Oh?' raising his eyebrows. 'Off you go then.' I clashed the boot shut and said,

'What?'

'Bye bye then.' He looked at me. He was waiting for me to walk away. I looked up and down. I started off down the street. When I was down the street a bit he called after me, 'Hey!' I looked back. 'What about our trip?' he said. I stood for a few seconds before walking up again. I climbed into the passenger seat.

Inside had a faraway smell of milk. He walked along the side of the car and turned in to our garden.

'Denims,' he said to himself.

The window was stiff to roll down. I knocked the seat back a notch. The kids' calls were sleepy and warm in the distance.

It was usually my friends who played down on the waste ground. Our area had mainly black families living in it. My uncle didn't like that and he often compared it to other better parts of London. Nowadays he planned our trips in the car even more carefully than before. A few minutes later I saw him come towards the car. I expected him to say on every trip we went on that it would deepen my knowledge of my country. When he squashed up into the car he grinned and let his breath out. He twiddled the gear stick before trying the engine. It wouldn't start at first, but after a few twists it revved up. As he took the car carefully off the kerb he grimaced at me and said, 'Looks like thunder.' I shrugged and looked out through the window. The car stuttered as it gathered speed. It was dull and bright at once. 'I suppose you've never been inside an art gallery.' I hated questions like that because he always already knew the answers. I didn't want to go anywhere. We drove out by the big poster of the kid sucking an iced lolly. 'I don't like that waste ground,' he said. I knew he would start on about my playing down there. 'Only strange people hang around there,' he said. There was some cheerful Scottish music coming from a bar. We passed the derelict shop. 'This was once a great country,' he said. A big cardboard box took a leap on to the road. 'That used to be all Rupert Street and Henrietta Street.' On the corner I caught sight of some of my friends in a gang. Delmar swept his arm high. I turned to see them through the back window. I smiled and throttled my neck in a jokey way. My uncle took his eyes off the road to look at me. I stopped and watched them shrinking as we jiggled up the broad road out of our area.

We drove for about an hour without really speaking much. I knew something was getting at him again. My uncle made a big deal out of everything. I looked out of the window mostly. High buildings revolved, grey and wet. We crawled in a lot of traffic, there were lines of dusty taxis. A cream ambulance sat parked. Soon there were fat buildings everywhere, stubborn-looking in the dry rain. Our left and right became packed with pillars and frills and umbrellas, some see-through, others like black tulips. It was my first sight of the West End. We slowed to a halt again. Then I heard him breathe in deeply. It was warm in the car. Smoothly, he wound the window down all the way. He spoke suddenly. I had my lips against my window.

'Just tell me.'

'What,' I said dreamily. I sat back.

'Will you just tell me?'

I mumbled, 'Yeah.'

'I just want to know,' he said. 'Have you only denims?' He knew better than me how many pairs of trousers I had since he bought them. I said, 'No,' and looked out of the window again. 'I'll say nothing,' he said in a sarcastic way.

We drove on. I thought he must have wanted me to dress up, but I hadn't known where we were going until I recognized the West End just now from the telly. A short time after he pulled into a back street and parked on a corner. We closed up the windows and he strained round and ruffled about in the back seats. I wrestled with my anorak.

'Did we remember the flask?' he asked, taking an umbrella on to his lap. He was in a cheerful mood again.

'I put it in the boot.'

'Right.' He opened the door and patted his pockets. 'Money. Sweets.' He unfolded from the car. We got out into the sharp dullness. It had a silky feel of drizzle. We were crammed in by tall streets. 'You'll see what an art gallery's like now.' He handed me my wellingtons from the boot. 'Just round the corner, right? There's the biggest one in all England. Flask, yes.' I took my shoes off. 'Jotter?' he said. 'Pencil?' I gave a grunt. I thought he was probably going to make me take notes. I put on my wellingtons. I carried the flask and some things in a plastic bag along the streets beside him and up the steps of the gallery.

Inside it was clammy and quiet. We walked among the paintings. Everywhere I looked there were people in old-fashioned robes. There were boys my age with wings and strong men. I felt mixed up because they were making me think of something.

'What do you make of it?' he said.

'They're nice,' I mumbled. I was beginning to get tired.

'Dear dear,' he said to himself. When I heard that I trailed behind him in a bit of a huff. I felt heavy from thinking about the paintings. As we passed through another room he screwed his face up. My wellingtons were too loose for me. The robes too were half falling off the people in the paintings. It was like a church. We kept on walking into another room. 'Dear dear dear,' I heard. His face was chalky. I hung further behind him. When he looked at me I gazed at the floor. He ran his fingers through his hair. 'Who do they think they're pleasing?' I was grinning. 'It's all bums in here!' he said.

Soon we left the gallery. We went and sat in Trafalgar Square. I felt a weight in my body. He poured us out tea from the flask. The wind was dry now and chirpy with pigeons. He scanned the square before speaking. 'Is that the sort of thing *you* want to see?' I looked at him. His eyes were squeezed thinner and watching me.

'No,' I said.

He looked away. 'Who wants to see it?' he said. He took a sip from his tea. 'People's bare bums!'

When I finished my tea he tightened the cups on to the flask and we walked back to the car. We drove to a small park in the north of London and we fed birds. I was thinking inside my head most of the time. I knew I was unhappy seeing people with no clothes on.

'They're tame,' he told me during the drive home. 'London sparrows, they'll almost come and eat out of your hand.' I didn't say anything so there was a silence. He looked at me. 'It's time you did something about your bloody appearance,' he shouted. I

just jerked my shoulders to annoy him. As we cut into our area
the rain began drumming on the roof of the car.

The next afternoon my uncle worked at the engine. He had
pieces of it sitting all over the footpath and the car was cranked
up. There was a blotch of oil on his face. My eyes kept avoiding
it.

'See those sparkplugs?' he said. I said, 'Those?' but I was really
watching Delmar up ahead. He had climbed into a skip that sat
on our side of the road. He began to trampoline and wave his tee-
shirt in the air. Another boy was with him. Their calls got
drowned in the washed light. 'Never mind them,' my uncle said
quietly. I looked down at the engine again. 'Always keep your
sparkplugs well filed.' He unscrewed one slowly. He took it out.
He began filling the tip. 'It tells people that you know better.' The
two boys started down the footpath with long languid movements towards us. 'You do it,' he offered. Delmar flashed his
teeth. 'Take it,' said my uncle.

'What's happening man?' Delmar butted his head rhythmi-
cally.

'Dunno,' I said.

I sneaked a glance at my uncle. He was filing again. His elbow
was jerking tinily. 'Now why am I doing this?' he asked me,
ignoring them.

'You coming down the dump?' Delmar wanted to know.

'I can't,' I told him, 'I have to do this.' My uncle didn't stop
filing.

'Don't worry, mister, we won't get in no trouble.'

'Are you watching me do this?' was all he said. I could hear
him breathe angrily. I answered, 'Yeah.' The two of them
sauntered away. Delmar shouted back,

'Is that your brain you're fixing, chief?' I looked at the
sparkplug being filed.

'Is that . . . filed down?' I said. He twisted it back into the
engine. When he spoke his voice was tight.

'I seriously wonder about this country.' He wiped his fingers over the file. There was a small bubble between his lips.

Since we had come back from the West End my eyes were stuffed with muscles and boys with wings and muddy feet. They appeared more clearly when I shut them. I went to find Delmar one day after school to tell him about my trip. The bland sky came right down on to the street. My pictures floated on it, limpid, as I took myself up the terrace to the waste ground. He lived on a road at the far side of it and we always crossed part of it on our way to each other's houses. I turned in behind the hoarding poster of the kid with the lolly. I could make out two figures far away on the flat land, tugging at a rubber belt or something. I recognized Delmar's cries so when I got closer I hauled up some plasterboard.

'Watch out,' I called and slugged it a small distance into a ditch of brown water in front of me. It splashed softly in the quiet.

'Oi! That was nearly my head!' his friend called across. He mimed the weight of a brick and lobbed it full at me. I drew up. 'My head, right, weren't meant for lumps of rock man.'

We kicked through the rubble and cans. There was never anyone down here except us. The other boy's name was Ancel. 'What, pencil?' I said.

'Shuttup!'

I told them about the paintings. 'We went to a museum and all. And see angels, right? They're real.'

'What? With your uncle? Nutter?'

'Shuttup, look, they're just regular kids and all, without any clothes on.'

'In the nude?' We had drawn up to the top of a wild slope.

'Yeah, with all these extra wings and, you know, out their backs.'

'I wish I had wings.'

'Yeah, a pair of wings man, ea*zee*, just fly down! Waaaaah!' We chased down through brambles to the bottom.

The grass was long. The slope went down on to ground which

stretched a few yards to the rear of some old shops that looked disused. We lay on our backs panting with the moist clumps round us. I knew that since they hadn't seen those paintings they didn't have the pictures of angels in their heads. Invisibly, a dull aeroplane passed. Delmar sat up.

'Hey,' he whispered. 'Ssh!' We peered over the brambles. A man had stepped out from behind a greeny grey electricity box. We could see him clearly, moving through the clean breeze. He was tall and black.

'It's a geezah!'

The man scanned the slope on his way along the wall. 'What's he at?' Delmar said. When the shop corner eclipsed him we raced over the loose stones to the electricity box. We examined the narrow space between the railing around the box and the back wall of the shop. There were jaggy half bottles on the ground and a crap.

'Shit man!' We recoiled. Ancel clanged pebbles off the metal sides.

'What he come down here to crap for?'

'He's a weirdo,' I said.

Ancel looked at us with glee. 'Yeah,' he said quietly, 'he's a pervert.' We laughed together. Then Delmar suggested that we look for clues. We started idling along the wall. We had never been as far as these shops before. As we explored the outline of the building there were interesting things to prod at. A shadow appeared beneath us and faded. It came into my mind that Delmar had once found a magazine on the waste ground. I said casually, 'Let's look for dirty pictures.' Ancel picked up a rusty battery.

'Yeah,' he said.

Delmar was walking ahead of us. He seemed not to hear my suggestion. I picked up a stone. I tried to think how naked pictures could be taken. It amazed me that a man and a woman would take off their clothes in front of each other, never mind in front of a man with a camera. I imagined them standing side by side like in a family photo, only with no clothes on. I said a little louder so that Delmar would hear, 'What do they look like, those pictures?'

'Just people,' he shouted back. 'They're in the nude on beds.'

'They're having sex,' Ancel said. His toe was digging up a buried bottle. 'Aren't they?' I wanted to know more about the magazine but I didn't want to seem too interested. In the distance factory chimneys were standing.

'How would they get them photographs?' I said. Delmar had bent down. He didn't answer. Instead he turned round and shouted out,

'Hey, have a look at this!'

We beat along the stones and hugged round him.

'Is it dirty pictures?'

'You know it!' His hand was inside his denim jacket. 'D'you want it?' he said. We pulled at his arm and he crouched over. Then he skipped ahead of us and slung his hand high in the air. A sweet-wrapper blew down on to the rubble.

'Shit,' I said. 'We never believed you.'

'Will we get him?' said Ancel.

'C'mon!' Delmar ran so we gave him chase along by a nettle-bank and up over grass on to the waste ground.

On our way back we didn't talk about naked people again. Half-way across I broke into a diagonal. There was a factory siren far away. 'I gotta get home,' I said. 'See you!' I walked off in the direction of the hoarding over the waste ground on my own.

At the end of that week I was sitting on my bike supported by the garden hedge when our car rattled up in front. Every day my uncle came home shortly after I got back from school. Today he was jaunty on his way up the path. He was wearing his postman's uniform and grinning. He stopped in front of me. I didn't feel like smiling at all. I was thinking about the waste ground and how peaceful and empty it was. I had wanted to go down there but Delmar was away visiting his father. 'How did you get on at school today?' he asked me. He was still beaming. Somebody was loading the skip on the road. I had to think for a minute for an answer. He had one hand on his neck. He kept his smile. I said, 'Well', though I wasn't really sure what I meant. Then he said, 'Have you been good today?' I turned my head in the direction of the skip to get away from his smile.

'I don't know,' I said. I knew that he was talking strangely.

'Well,' he said, 'I might take you to a wax museum tomorrow. Don't get your hopes up though.' I didn't say anything. I made out I was examining something over at the skip. I knew he had his eyes on my face. 'Well?' he said. I looked at him.

'OK,' I said. He stopped smiling. I wasn't sure what to do. I sighed quietly.

'OK?' he repeated. 'OK? I don't have to take you anywhere at all.' He let his words hang in the air. It was my turn to speak so I mumbled, 'Oh.' I didn't look at him. 'Oh,' he said. There was a ladybird on his knee. 'I've shown you this whole bloody country up and down and he says, Oh!' I back-pedalled a few times. 'Dear dear, you need to smarten up altogether.' He marched up the path. He jabbed his key into the latch and opened the door. I kept on the bike. From up the path he exclaimed, 'Listen to me.' Then he walked back down again and stood close to me. He pointed his finger at me. 'You're a disgrace to me.' His eyes were wide and round and he was blinking. There were loud smashes from the skip. We were breathing the dust. 'You'd better keep away from that waste ground,' he said.

'Why?' I said. I wanted to tell him to fuck off and that he wasn't my real father. He hooked his thumbs inside his belt. He was blinking more now.

'Do you know what I'm trying to teach you, Sonny Jim? About your environment?' I felt uncomfortable with way he was looking at me. There was spit on his lips. 'Do you understand what that means?' His face came closer. 'Environment!' he shouted.

'I don't care!' I yelled. 'I like it down there, right?'

Instantly he clasped the handlebars. I slid quickly back off the saddle and stood looking up at him. The bike flew across the path. He started to breathe through his teeth. He looked down.

Silently his lips moved. He looked at the ground. 'You,' he gasped. 'You will obey me!' Then he passed me and went into the house. The door clicked shut. I walked over to the bike and lifted it upright. I took it down the path. There were birds in the air. I rode up past the skip towards the waste ground.

I thought I heard Delmar laughing out on the street the following morning. When I opened the front door to have a look I saw him and Ancel perched on the rim of the skip. They were looking up at my bedroom window. I went straight out, dragging the door closed behind me. On the street my uncle was polishing the car with an old handkerchief. He was wearing his bright cardigan with the sleeves rucked up. He followed me with his eyes as I approached. 'Hi,' I mumbled as I walked past him. When I was a few yards down the street he called after me.

'Tomorrow.' I stopped and turned round. 'Wax Museum. You and me.' He said it firmly, pointing the handkerchief. 'Think on.' I said, 'Right,' and walked up to my friends. Once round the hoarding we decided to look for dirty pictures round by the shops. The way I had said 'Right' was making me feel awkward. It was as though I was working with my uncle, polishing the car with him, doing my duty. We trekked on past the dry whitewash of the day. There was no air. Delmar asked where we had got our car. I gave a mumble.

'It should be in a museum,' he said. 'I just don't wanna see nothing that lame when I am on the street.' He was grooving over the rubble with a white smile. Distantly a miniature church was chinking like a musical box. I upturned a heavy stone with my heel. There was a cloud like the tip of an angel's wing in one of the paintings. 'It just gets on my nerves man, know whata mean?'

'It's not,' I told him, 'it's well safe. It only looks bad.' Ancel stamped on a can. Delmar started to describe his big brother's car, so I walked along daydreaming. Ancel showed me a crescent of teeth. He knocked the can forward gamely so I kicked it back over to him.

'Rare man!' We passed it to each other lazily over the dust and rubble. The clouds were making faint shadows on the ground. When we reached the top of the slope we looked down. The man was there.

He was crouching by the side of the electricity box. We ducked low. 'He's having another crap,' Delmar rasped, peering over.

'Let's sneak down,' I said. Ancel threw out spit in a giggle. 'We'll flick things at him.' They laughed.

'In the middle of a shit.'

I edged down behind a clump. 'Spread out,' I said. I lay on my back and let myself bump quietly down the slope. When I was close to the bottom I knelt forward into some thistles. I peeped through the dry grass tops. When I saw the man I started to giggle. I groped about to get a stone. My fingers dug for a marble sunk in the mud. To get the best time to throw I watched the man carefully. I saw that as he crouched his trousers were open. I imagined Delmar and Ancel sniggering. Just then he stood up straight with a toilet roll tube in his hand. I blocked my mouth with the side of my hand to stop myself giggling out loud. He was standing holding the tube up in the air. I wanted to look closer. He was a young man with very black skin. He had a good smile. I thought that my friends would be bursting their sides. I leaned forward on my fingertips to toss the marble. Then I thought I recognized what the tube really was. I went cold.

My eyes darted over the grass for Delmar or Ancel. They must have had their heads down. I peered closer at the man. My heart was pumping. I couldn't understand the size of it. His face swept over the slope. He looked happy. I couldn't believe that he was doing this. Suddenly my hand slipped.

'Ah,' I heard. I fell forward on my face into the grass. A thistle was beside my cheek. When I looked up the man was bounding away along the wall. He slipped round the side of the shops.

Ancel hurried across the slope. I sat back. I put on a grin. 'Hey, did you see that man?' His words splashed on the warm smell. He came and knelt beside me. Delmar joined us from behind. He caught sight of me as my eyes were fluttering. Ancel imitated the man standing. 'He's a rapist.'

'He shouldn't ought to do that,' said Delmar. 'That's wrong man.' I still wasn't sure about what he had been doing. I was trying to grasp how anyone could do that in the open air.

'Yeah,' I said. My voice was dry. 'That was a laugh.'

We got to our feet and climbed back up the slope. I didn't want to be with them any more. I wanted to think about the man. The clouds sat low in the sky. There was no sound, not even a bird. We walked together across the waste ground. I still had a picture of him in front of me.

'What'll we do now?' said Delmar. Ancel scooped up a shard of dark glass. He swung it. There wasn't anything to do. We walked over the waste ground throwing stones up into the paleness for a while.

'You didn't know about that,' said my uncle. I was lying back in the passenger seat. 'That's something you can tell your friends about.' The car halted so I sat forward. We were coming close to home. It looked about six o'clock. Three skinheads loped across in front of us. I adjusted the seat and sat properly. 'Do you fancy a Coca Cola?' he said. 'Would that stop you huffing?'

'OK,' I answered. A few seconds later he slewed round into a side street. The brake made a squirting sound.

'Right,' he said and opened his door. I opened mine and stood out. My legs were stiff. Although it was still early the buildings were like night, brooding and dilapidated. We were only up the road from our street. 'Button up,' he said and stepped towards a bar. I buttoned my shirt and followed him.

It was almost empty inside. There was only a woman at the counter. He asked for a half pint of beer. 'And a Coke,' he said and winked, 'for him.' I stood beside him. The woman took a glass and rubbed it slowly with a rag. We watched her fill it with Coke. She was dreamy. She set it on the counter in front of me before pulling his half pint for him. He started a conversation with her.

'I took him to a wax museum,' he said. 'It's good for him to see around, learn a bit about life, know whata mean?' The woman had lots of wrinkles. I took a sip from my Coke. I had hated the museum. It was the most dreary place he had ever taken me to. He was talking about the car. 'A beauty, the best,' he said. 'Haven't we?' The woman had big sad eyelids. She closed them for a moment like she was praying. 'I mean you should feel it on the motorway, girl. He loves it.' She looked at me. 'Didn't come cheap,' he added. She lifted my glass and wiped under it, smiling at me. I tried to imagine the woman and my uncle naked under their clothes. I didn't like the idea. I could never believe that my uncle might have a trunk that would stick up in the air. I passed the time imagining them naked on a bed until he said to me, 'Tell her.' I looked up at him and across at the woman. 'He can't get over it. He'll tell you.' She was wiping the counter again. I didn't know what I would say. My uncle's head was squeezed and smiling. His eyes were all over the woman's face. 'One hell of a girl,' he said.

The woman said, 'Where is she?' in a jumpy way.

'Waiting outside,' he told her. He blinked. There was a silence. It surprised me to hear him talk about the car like this. I thought that if I had to say anything I would say that the car was just OK.

'A car's good,' she said. 'Get away in it.'

He looked at me widely. 'Tell her,' he urged me. 'Tell her what a car it is.' He asked me with his eyebrows. 'Go ahead.' He was leading up to something. I decided that I would ask, What car? The woman was looking at me. I shrugged.

'Are you not going to tell me?' she asked, winking. I smiled back at her.

'What car!' I said.

She glanced at my uncle. Then she gave a laugh, 'Oh,' and wiped the counter swiftly. I didn't know why I had said that. From the side of my face I could tell that he was blinking and smiling. The woman's neck was jumping in and out. 'That's an answer. That was a good answer, son.'

'Well,' he said, 'now . . . well, I wasn't expecting that.' He took his glass.

'He doesn't know much about cars, does he?' she said.

'Him? He couldn't change a bloody screw.' Quickly he finished his beer. He paid the woman.

'Do you not want the rest of your Coke?' she asked me. I shook my head and she smiled at me. He went into the toilet. I went outside and made for the car at the corner. I stood by the passenger door waiting for him. I wished I hadn't said that. I looked off into the distance where a lorry was approaching. A tall black man was walking along on the footpath. Eventually my uncle came round his side of the car and unlocked it. It was just then that I recognized the tall man.

My insides tightened. It was the man from the waste ground. From inside the car my uncle had opened the passenger door. I looked down to see if he had noticed the man. I glanced quickly at him walking off. Then I climbed into the car. I pulled the door shut. My uncle hadn't noticed him. I wanted to see his face. I flattened my hands on my legs. They were trembling. We sat in the milky smell of the car for a few moments. He wouldn't look at me. The man was disappearing.

'What did you mean, "What car"?' he said. I lowered my head. I still had in front of me a picture of the huge tube sticking out of the man and his smile. 'It's just the car that took you all over England. I can't believe you said that.' I glanced at him. His eyes blinked. I wasn't sure if I had got it wrong about what the man had been doing. My uncle said, 'Dear dear', with a shrug and twisted the key tiredly. Then leaned back. 'Why did you say "What car"?' he asked me, shaking his head. I shrugged my shoulders. I was trying to think who the man might be and where he might live. 'Dear dear.' The light around us was grey like the concrete. It glinted in my uncle's eyes. He tried the engine again. 'Just tell me this,' he said. He lifted his face forward and looked ahead where the man had walked. But he didn't say anything.

After a minute he started the car and pulled it out on to the road. I was floating above the seat. All the way back he had his chin out. 'Why did you say "What car"?' he said. I just raised my eyebrows. There was a black drape over the tops of the houses. His lips moved. We came to our street. He parked the car. We got out and went inside.

The next day I didn't go down to the waste ground. I didn't tell Delmar or Ancel that I had seen the man on the street. Instead we talked about the magazine Delmar had once found. Ancel and I asked him to describe the pictures. We sat behind the hoarding poster of the kid while Delmar described them most of the afternoon in detail.

ANTHONY MCCARTEN

A Modest Apocalypse

When Roscoe Stillwater opened his doors that first week, he did so with his fingers crossed. The previous owners had let the business run down. The interest rate on his forty-five-grand loan, he knew, wanted his life. And the first week would be only slightly more difficult than the second or fourth or tenth . . .

Bella Watson loafed at the counter, depressing the new microchip-empowered scales with the pinnacle of her pinkie. She was thinking of doom. 'Do you know what Nostradamus has said, Rossy?'

'No,' said Ross, heating up the fat for the chips.

'There shall be a crack in the earth as wide as the sky and we shall each have an individual number. One each. On our foreheads. Do you believe that?'

'Do you?'

'Yes.'

'Why?'

'Because he was right about the Kennedys.'

The heat was coming up in the fat. Ross watched it for a while, then asked, 'What did he say about the Kennedys?'

'He said they would die.'

'You mean eventually?'

'No. They would be killed.'

'And they were.'

'Yes.'

Ross turned to look at Bella, but her back was to him. 'So when do I get my number?'

Bella pushed the scales up to a reading of twenty kilos. 'I

s'pose on the eve of the end of everything as we know it,' she said, turning to look at him. Significantly, she did not smile.

Ross had a plan, and the plan, which he hoped would bring prosperity, took the shape, size, smell and cultural significance of a hamburger.

He didn't know much about the fish-and-chip business and he was taking a risk. He would prefer to be without the risk, but he needed an ace in the hole. That was how times were, or so he'd been told. You needed an ace in the hole to make your shop stand out from the rest of the hotchpotch. You needed to stand out if you ever wanted to get enough customers to stop you going broke, and plenty of shops had gone broke. Ross wanted to give his customers a better hamburger than they could get anywhere and he had a plan.

He'd worked out the plan in the back of his shop during the weeks before he'd opened. Sitting on a stack of empty fish trays with a piece of paper, working it out, he'd been conscious of two things that could go against him: his inexperience and the letter from the bank about the repayments, which he'd nailed to the wall by the back door – a white sheet with a few markings on it, a funeral shroud.

He'd worked out all the phases of this plan, and then he'd swallowed and decided.

When Ross told Bella about it, lying beside her, skew-whiff after that certain temporary excitement that goes by many names, she said something as final as, 'A hamburger will not save you now – don't you see that?'

'I won't be making much on each one', Ross said, 'at least for a while – maybe only twenty cents or thirty – but it'll build goodwill and I can adjust the price later. Then, with a slight margin on the normal orders, I should make it through the first quarter and roll on out of the year. So, tell me honestly, what do you think? And please, if you're up to it, can we try not to mention a plague of locusts.'

'In that case, I have no opinion.'

'For God's sake say something, Bella. It's important to me.'

'I s'pose in a way you're lucky really.'

'What do you mean by that?'

'As all the ignorant are lucky.'

Bella was lying on her back with her head at the foot of the bed. She was playing with her belly button, pushing her index finger into it and rotating clockwise. Ross wondered what he was doing with this woman.

Ross phoned his mother for the first time in six months to tell her he'd bought her a mixer, a big red electric mixer, and to ask her whether, if she didn't have anything immediately planned for it, she'd mind preparing the special home-made meat mixture he'd needed for the shop. She asked him what the meat would be for, and he carefully explained the complexities of his plan. 'It's amazing what young people will eat, isn't it?' she said.

Still, she agreed to do it, and a week before Roscoe opened she began to mix the beef mince and onion and breadcrumbs and tomato sauce and seasoning and eggs. She added garlic, Worcester sauce, salt and pepper and threw in whatever herbs she could find. Then she moulded the mixture into thick round patties and laid them in a box with flour and grease-proof paper between each one. Ross phoned for the second time in six months to find out how she was going.

'It's a shit of a job,' she said.

'I didn't know you swore, Mum.'

'I don't.'

'How many have you done?'

'About four hundred. The mixer is overheating.'

'Don't worry about the mixer. How are you?'

Roscoe's mother, a big-busted war bride, wasn't interested in her own health. 'Are you sure this will work, son? I prayed to your father last night. The kitchen is a pigsty. Oh no! Look, I've got to go, the carrots are boiling over!'

'Carrots?'

'I thought a bit of colour.'

She was right. The patties looked good with a bit of colour – bright casinos studding dark islands, an archipelago of meat.

Sure, Bella helped out a bit, but it was mostly up to Roscoe to get the shop ready. He wouldn't double-cook the orders; that was also part of the plan. He would batter everything himself as the orders came in. It would take longer, but the batter was lighter and crispier that way, and he'd put a hired colour TV above the counter so the customers wouldn't get bored waiting. The two couches he'd bought were cleaned and moved in. He flicked paint up into the corners of a shop and removed cowebs. He bought in the fish, the buns, the chips and everything else. He changed the name of the shop from 'Blydon Fish and Chips' to 'The Burgerlary', despite warnings from his mother that it would attract dubious custom and drive away the traditionalists. He thought the name was forward-looking, go-getting. When he had more time, he'd paint a hand stealing a burger on the window. You had to bring in the kids. They were the stomach of the nation. 'Look at McDonald's,' Ross would say to his mother. 'McDonald's, McDonald's, McDonald's,' she would reply, foiling further discussion.

Soon the big day came and Ross opened up his shop. He hooked the doors back, went out the back, put one of the vats on medium heat, adjusted a tower of picked lettuce leaves ready for implantation, combed his hair in a little cracked mirror above the sink, and resolved that if no one bought anything within the first hour he'd lower himself, Baptist-like and battered into the smoking fat – but the bell out the front did ring, clearing his nerves, and he was in business. Two Hawaiian burgers, four potato fritters and sauce. He would never forget this order. It made the world OK. Two Hawaiian burgers, four potato fritters, and sauce.

Three days later, Bella's buttocks apportioned themselves on Ross's primary serving bench like a neat double order. She had dark rings under her eyes and a blue vein had become visible transecting her smile lines. Yet she was illuminated. 'I've been reading Revelations.'

'Could you pass me the scoop?'

Bella looked around, spotted the implement, and passed it to Ross. He was sieving off the residue batter from the oil, throwing it into a bucket. A crab-stick was bobbing amid bubbles and going golden. The TV out front was playing lead-in music to a customer. Ross looked up as he took the scoop.

'You look awful.'

'I'm having visions, Ross.'

Bella pushed some of her blonde hair behind her left ear. Ross had heard this sort of thing from her before. The last time ended with her running off to Coromandel for three weeks, with only a pile of country records and a portable turntable, and working as a hostess at a Lions Club jubilee while anticipating the end of everything. He'd found her at a motor inn off the state highway where the beds had rubber sheets, which said much for its exclusiveness. She was pretty down and out. The room was bare except for a bed, a table and a John Denver poster. She'd been living off leftover butterfly cakes for the last week. The Lions had not treated her well. She refused to return at once, and for two days she and Roscoe sat in the room largely silent. Eventually she gathered up her records and said, 'Let's get out of here.'

So Roscoe's mind was not too far away from rubber sheets now, and noticing the amplitude of his eyebrows Bella guessed as much.

'I misread . . . I misread the signs, that's all!' She was getting fired up.

'That doesn't matter. I still think you're crazy.'

'But you always say that I'm not when I ask you if I am!'

'I lie.'

Roscoe heard the door closing.

At the end of the first week Ross took home his accounts book. On Saturday morning he did a lot of adding up and taking away.

He made a few mistakes and started again a few times. Sometimes he arrived at a final figure and didn't know whether it meant a profit or a loss, so he went over it once more with a fine-toothed comb. Around lunchtime he put the book under his arm, got into his car, and drove across town.

Bella's place was a low-rent two-bedroom affair with a view of nothing on the left and a street leading to nothing on the right. But a house that holds a lover is irrelevant, like a wrapper that can be thrown away. Ross half-ran up the path to the porch. The front door was open, as was the door to the bedroom, and he looked in, eyes all puppy-dog wide. Bella was sitting naked on the floor, and behind her a strange guy, equally bare, was doing things to her. Confusion. A moment to confirm. Yes . . . Ross took two or three steps backwards and slipped out on to the porch. This was a new one. His heart was racing. He really should have phoned before he called. That was his mistake. He told himself off for being so rude; it was something to occupy his mind, which was floating terribly. He even opened his accounts book, looking over a few figures but taking nothing in. It seemed to have hit him hard.

Bella had caught sight of Roscoe's head as it withdrew from her doorway.

She whispered something to her partner, put on a dressing-gown, and went to the front door. Ross had his back to her. He was looking through his book.

'Ross?'

He turned and smiled pathetically, as if he'd come to read the meter. 'Oh hi.'

'What are you doing?'

Ross wondered what he was doing. He couldn't stop it coming out. 'Who's he?'

'A friend. He does massage.'

'Massage?'

'Yes.'

'Oh.'

'Why?'

'You were naked in there.'

'Ross, I'm often naked in there.'

'Not with a stranger.'

'He's not a stranger. He's a friend. He does massage.'

Ross considered the options and concluded he didn't know what to do. He started down the drive towards his car. then stopped to say something, anticipating that she would be running after him. He turned. She was still on the porch looking down at him. Her red dressing-gown. The one he'd always disliked. It did not console him to think he'd never have to see it again. Nor did the slick feel of his car's steering wheel console him, once he'd slammed the door.

Beyond the window, a conciliatory sunlight filtered through Venetian blinds to spread fan-like on the kitchen table. Roscoe was at breakfast. He clutched a ballpoint, however, and his head overhung a degenerating exercise book. The fact is, he was losing thirty-five cents on every burger. He'd learnt, with a fervour approaching the religious, how to manipulate the figures to show that he was actually making fourteen cents on each one, but he couldn't forget the figures were manipulated, and if the truth were to be told he had to admit the burgers were breaking his back.

The straight fish-and-chip orders were making sixty to eighty per cent profit, but with overheads deducted from that there was hardly anything in it. Then to have the burgers making a loss meant he was in trouble. He had some savings left after buying the stock and the couches and paying the TV rental, and he would be OK for another couple of weeks, but after that he had to start making a profit, a clean one (which meant money in his pocket), or he would crash before he had even begun. He couldn't imagine what he would do if the shop failed. The finance company would force a sale, and he would be left with peanuts. Fortunately, there were no wife and children. He wouldn't be taking them down too.

He picked up the pen and manipulated the figures again to

show he was making fourteen cents on each burger. Life is, as
Bella had once said (and he remembered it because it had
touched him), 'a spunky illusion with boxing gloves on'.

The telephone at the back of Roscoe's shop wobbled as it rang.
   'Hello,' said a voice, and you could imagine from the tone that
the face behind the voice was jettisoning a smile.
   'Who is this?'
   'You don't know me but . . . well, I'm a lawyer friend of your
mother's.'
   'Yes?'
   'Yes. She ah . . . asked me if I would mind giving you a call to
check on how you are doing. I said I'd be delighted.'
   'Oh.'
   'So, here I am.'
   'Yeah.'
   'So, Ross . . . so, how are things going?'
   'Good.'
   'Oh that's good, then, isn't it.'
   'Thanks.'
   'Yes. That's lovely.'
The conversation found, all by itself, a natural pause, broken
by the lawyer friend. 'Of course, it's none of my business, but it
was just your mother's wish, y'know, that I enquire. I knew your
father.'
   'Well, I won't know for a few days. I need to do some more
book-keeping.'
   'Oh! Fine! Perhaps I'll ring back at some later date?'
   'Yes, do that.'
   'Right, yes, and thank you, Ross, for your time.'
   'No, thank you,' said Ross.
   'Goodbye.'
   'Yes.'
Ross put down the phone. Bella was standing behind him.
   'Who was that?' she asked.
Ross jumped and turned. She looked good.

'A friend of my mother's.'

'I just came to look at you.'

A trifle stunned, Ross managed, '. . . fine.' Bella took a good long look at him, gentle and sustained and sad, then left the shop, quickly, through the front.

Ross didn't move for a minute after that, then he went over to the number one vat and looked at his reflection in the oil. It didn't ride on the surface but hung midway down, the way a reflection does in oil.

On a small tear-shaped table beside Bella's slat-bottomed bed lay an exercise book that contained numerous pages of what could be called 'apocalyptic verse' – not bad, but depressing. In it she plagiarized and, on occasion, meditated originally upon the rueful condition of her soul. She saw the fear of death as rooted in an overemphasis on temporal security; she disagreed violently with the communists that material poverty made people quarrelsome and unhappy; and she agreed with Freud that love and death were bonded – all this written in a simple but effective metric form that usually followed the rhyme pattern *a b a b a*. Also she was convinced that the world was about to end. 'Not with a bang but a whimper' was the phrase she often used, without crediting the poet. She feared only that she wouldn't be ready.

No one knew she had a plan. She'd been working on it for some time and was now involved in making fine adjustments. She'd thought about telling Ross, but things had not been good between them, and unless she was absolutely sure about him she wouldn't tell. His was a struggle with the material world. If the material world were going to last for ever, she could have understood it better, but deep down she knew fish-and-chip shops would come and go. However, she was fond of him and knew that he loved her. Somehow, she felt, this should matter.

She worked on her plan during the long days, paper laid out on the kitchen table. Drinking coffee, she would stare out her front window over roofs, bulwarks, bridges and altering cloud shapes. Then she would pace about the house, counting her steps, return, and note the number. She would test the capacity of suitcases and satchels and shoulder bags by emptying the contents of her fridge. The results would be recorded. The growing volume of her notes, interspersed between the pages of her exercise book, meant the book would no longer close flatly but sat, wedge-like, beside her bed.

Bella's talk of Armageddon made Ross nervous but, what the hell, she was *his* girl. At the moment, he had to concentrate on making the shop work. You had to live somehow, and he tried to shut the latest incident with Bella out of his mind. He'd never had a nervous breakdown in his life and wasn't about to start now. But he had never seen Bella's exercise book.

That second week Ross did what he knew he couldn't put off any longer. He phoned his mother.

'You'd better turn the mixer off. It's no good. It's . . . well, I can't afford the home-made patties any more. I'm going to change to production line. That's it.'

'What happened? Are they not right?'

'They were right.'

'Weren't they good?'

'Yeah, they were too good. I was selling hundreds of them and they were driving me out of business. I've tried.'

'What're you talking about?'

'They just cost too much to make. I can buy them from the works, already made up, and save nearly fifty per cent.'

'But what about the ace in the hole, son? You were going to stand out with your home-made burgers.'

'What good is standing out if you go bust? I'm going to go with production line. I haven't got any choice. The home-mades are breaking my back.'

'I'm worried, Roscoe. Your father . . .'

'My father? My father what?'

'He would be worried too.'

Roscoe had more than enough pressure without getting this from her.

'Listen, I know what I'm doing here. And you can call off your lawyer friend too. Tell him to mind his own business.'

'I asked him to phone you, Roscoe.'

'I don't need him.'

'Roscoe?'

'I don't need him.'

Roscoe put down the phone. He expected her to ring back, but she didn't.

There was no doubt that The Burgerlary's original burgers had attracted customers. In the first week word had got around on the burgervine, a little-publicized network of fast-food connoisseurs who can discriminate in a munch between pure stodge and a truly excellent feed.

Roscoe's product had been more than mere novelty; it was a favourable fluke of ingredients that his vanity allowed him to believe might never be repeated in his lifetime. He was thirty-two, and remembering all the chicanery he had witnessed in that time, he figured that his burger was the luckiest he'd got. Now he had shelved it. Two weeks earlier it had been in his top three: himself, the world attending that self, and his ace in the hole.

When Roscoe opened his shop Tuesday afternoon to start the second week, he was nervous about his decision. He'd bought in two large cardboard boxes full of production-line patties with the intention of beginning to use them. He really had.

But when the first customer entered his shop that day and ordered an egg burger, a young woman who was familiar, Ross found himself going to the fridge, taking out a handful of the old pattie mixture, moulding it, and throwing it on the hotplate. Thus, he learnt the extent of his own guilt.

Later on in the day he did begin to use the new patties. They were slimmer by half and had little more in them than pulverized beef gristle and a binding gelatin. When handing the new burgers over the counter to the customer, wrapped in the same white bag, he prayed they wouldn't open them until well clear of the shop. He was ashamed of them. He had no faith in them whatsoever. Yet they would make him money.

The second week Ross sold as many burgers as the previous week. In fact, business was even better. The normal fish-and-chip sales had been going well, and a demoralized rugby side stopped one night in their van to buy a $250 order. He was not having to turn the vat on to low so often either, which he did to save electricity during the slow times. Things really seemed to be getting better at the end of the second week. Accordingly, he was shocked to find, as he added up his figures that second Sunday morning in the front room of his flat, that his balance was still surrounded by more red than Leningrad.

It was the interest on the loan. Simple. Three thousand every quarter. Two hundred and fifty every week. How could he keep up with that after he had taken out overheads? If his vat was cooking full-time, he'd still be behind, behind even what someone on the rigs could earn in a week. So what good was all this worry?

He wished he could stand the thought of working for someone else again.

But he couldn't stand that. He couldn't stand it because when he was working for someone else he felt his life was wasting, dissolving, and for no concrete benefit except money – that stuff. Also he'd be thinking how much better it was to work for yourself, which spoilt things.

But now, *now*, he *was* working for himself, Roscoe John Stillwater of Taranaki money, Roscoe Play-It-Straight Stillwater, and it was breaking his back.

When railing against adversity, Roscoe could respond as single-mindedly as the next man.

Lying on his back in the centre of his living-room, his eyes closed, his hands joined over his chest corpse-fashion, he decided not to move until the day out there no longer sustained a sun.

It was true, he had seldom felt so alone or picked on. As he lay there he thought about not opening for the night shift and going to a movie or something. Then he thought about himself in a more general sense. Then he thought about the world attending that self. It got him up off the floor.

Later he opened the shop for business.

There was a reasonable flow of people – fat ones, ugly ones, beautiful ones, ones with not enough hair, ones with too much hair, ones that smelt, ones that didn't smell, big spenders, middle-sized spenders, ones in a hurry, ones with nothing on their minds, happy ones, hopeless ones, ones with wax in their hair. They came and went. Roscoe served them.

Still, no one delivered the question he feared to hear. It gave him peace, which allowed him to concentrate on despair.

He served them all.

The phone rang. He picked it up. There was silence. 'It's you,' he said, precognitive.

'Yes.' More silence. 'Do you want to talk, Ross?' came the voice.

'Yes,' said Ross.

'Well, what's the matter?'

Ross thought for a moment. 'Grief,' he said.

'Over a massage?'

'I s'pose so.'

'You're being pathetic over this, Ross.'

'I'm sorry.'

'Do you want to talk?'

Ross wanted to talk. 'The shop isn't doing so well,' he said. His forehead and nose were pressed up against the wall. His eyes were closed. 'I don't know if I'm going to make the first loan repayment. So far, I haven't banked anything. I feel like I'm going to blow it. But I can't do anything about it. You know how that feels?'

'How?'

'Like I'm going to lose it. Like I'm going to lose everything, Bell. Like, Christ, I'm going to lose it!'

'You know what I've been writing, Rossy?'

'. . . What?'

'Listen . . .' Ross could hear the flapping of pages through the phone. It was her exercise book. She would read to him. Through a phone the flapping of pages is like slow applause. He stood with his eyes closed listening to the slow applause.

'Are you still there?' she asked.

'Yes.'

'Well . . . here goes. It's not very good . . .

> 'Bella's Poem (Number 56)
>
> Not with a bang but with a whimper.
> I'm talking to you and you and you.
> Please, it's all much simpler
> Than you think. Just be ready, soon too,
> And not for a bang but a whimper.'

Hearing this, Ross had the urge to entwine this woman in his arms, lower her over the shiny Formica counter, and enter her from behind. Love.

'What do you think?' she asked. 'It was hard to rhyme with whimper.'

'It's good.'

'You see, we don't have long now, Ross. Let the shop go. Save yourself. I'm going to. And the town. We must be away from the towns, Ross. We will be forced to wear numbers on our foreheads, and that'll be just the start.'

'Can I see you?'

'When?'

'Whenever you like. Hell, I don't care, whenever you like.' The line fell silent.

'I'll call you.'

'When?' Ross said.

'I'll just call you. I've got to go now.'

'Come on, Bella.'

'I've got to go. See ya.' Across town Bella hung up. She could feel Ross holding on to the receiver for quite a while. He was like that. But she wasn't. There wasn't time for that. She dropped on to the floor midway across her living-room and started doing press-ups. *One, two, three.*

She was now capable of twenty, but hoped, one day soon, to top twenty-five. Her teeth were bared over her bottom lip as she passed through *ten, eleven, twelve,* her back just starting to cheat, her eyes to bulge, and even making little sex grunts as she moved into the late teens, blood flooding her head. *Number twenty* was very shaky indeed, like a colt finding its first legs, and *number twenty-one* was pure mad guts. She collapsed with an explosion of emotion, not exactly a bang or a whimper – perhaps ecstasy.

Across town Ross still held a dead receiver in his hands.

All that week Ross waited for Bella to ring. He kept one ear open as he worked in the shop, or watched TV alone at home, or sat hunched in the bath. Every now and again it did ring, but it wasn't her. It was someone else.

Word had started to go around that Ross had changed his patties. He read the contempt on his customer's faces. They knew all right; he could tell from the way they spat their money down on his counter. He tried not to look up at them at all, gathering up the money as if he were a beggar. And then someone asked him.

It was the big-arsed guy in the Swanndri who often carried an export six-pack and was good for a half-dozen oysters. He still bought the burger this time and was almost out of the shop when he turned at the flyscreen door and blurted it out as if he'd been suppressing it for some time: 'SAY, HOW COME YOU DON'T MAKE THE BURGERS LIKE YOU FIRST DID?'

Ross went white. He felt he wasn't up to eye contact and looked at the till. There were a lot of one-cent pieces today. Oh look! A five-cent has found its way into the twos . . .

'HEY MATE!'

'Yeah?' said Ross, trying to pick out the five-cent piece.

'How come you've changed your burgers?'

'Oh, there were too many . . . complaints.'

'What?'

'That's right.'

'But they were the *best*, man!'

'I was getting threatening telephone calls.' Ross put the five-cent piece where it belonged. He wished the man were gone.

'Yeah?' said the big-arsed guy as he approached the counter. he looked devastated. 'I don't get it. They were the best, eh. Onion. Even a bit of carrot one day.'

'Oh. That was to add some colour.'

'It worked.'

'Thanks. I'll tell my mother.'

'Your mother?'

'The carrot was her idea.'

'Yeah? It was beautiful that carrot. I'm not kidding, they were good burgers, eh. I just don't understand you getting complaints.'

'Oh well.'

'No. It's sort of terrifying.'

Ross looked up into the face of the stranger. Here was a very sensitive man. His eyes were downcast. A big thumb rubbed the edge of the counter.

Seemingly, he was going deeper.

'It's things like this that really make you wonder, y'know. They get me. Make me think it's all a giant cock-up. You're doing something good with those patties and wammo, y'know? Complaints. Bullshit! They . . . I'm telling you, bullshit! They were *good* burgers. Take that from me. Don't let them crucify you, man. Because they will if they can. Remember Jesus? They crucified him. Just like that. Wammo. And they'll do it to you if they can. You're like Jesus, man . . . with those patties . . .'

Ross groped, unequipped, for a reply: '. . . Thanks.'

The stranger maintained his vigil a moment longer, cuddling his fish and chips, then turned, his big arse diminishing into a point out in the darkness.

Ross left the counter to sit down out the back. He felt bad.

Beside him, on a bench, a fly vainly struggled for a clean wing-beat in a giant pot of tartar sauce. Ross noticed it but let it struggle. It had a right to know the truth.

'Good afternoon. You won't recognize me but I'm your mother's lawyer friend.' Two eyes swam through thick lenses above a scything nose and lips like limp earthworms. It was several days later.

Ross had been continuing to open. He knew when to expect the busy times now and when to turn off the vat and try to read a book or sweep the shop or even watch some TV out the front. He had also continued to work on his figures and each week was falling behind on his target for the first loan repayment. There was no chance of refinancing. He knew what it meant but would not talk about it. What good did it do to talk? He would just go on opening the shop, buying in supplies with cheques, skimping on nothing, and wait for a miracle.

'Well, well, you've got the place set up nicely,' said the lawyer friend. 'TV, couches, mmmmm, good serving space. Nice little business. Oh . . . sorry, the name's Den. Den McGaskill. Your mother asked me if I would drop in to see you on a social basis, and I said I'd be delighted.'

Ross watched the lawyer friend closely. He operated with the overt confidence of someone far better-looking. His eyes swam out of his head and wandered all over the shop. Physically he was strictly Phantom of the Opera, but optically we're talking Mark Spitz. And also a touch of the odious.

His protective instincts aroused, Roscoe reacted to this scanning with feelings not unlike violent distaste.

'What can I do for you, Den?' however, was all he said.

'Well nothing in particular. Just a little visit. Say hello. You know. That sort of thing. On your mother's behalf. I knew your father.'

'Did you?'

'Oh my goodness yes. For years. Since we were kids. You know. And your mother too. In fact, Ross, if things had worked out just a little differently, I could have been, well . . . your father, just between me and you. Ha!'

'And who knows,' replied a red-faced Roscoe, 'then it might have been my father who was dropping in here this afternoon for a gawk and claiming that years ago he knew *you*, and my mother too . . . and that if things had worked out differently he could have been my father, just between me and you. Ha!'

The lawyer friend obviously had an appetite for that sort of impromptu humour, which Roscoe could turn on when cornered by someone claiming, among other things, potential progenitorship, because he laughed. Heartily.

'But really, Ross, how about a look out the back?' he asked after recovering.

'Go ahead.'

The lawyer friend went behind the counter and out the back. Ross stayed by the till.

A customer came in but only wanted change for five dollars. Ross got a lot of that. There was a bus stop outside. And a telephone box across the road. It was two-thirty in the afternoon. In half an hour school would be out and he would sell a few bags of chips. The door closed as the customer left. The lawyer showed his face once more.

'Well, Ross. A tidy little business. I see you don't make your own chips. You buy them in, I noticed.'

'That's right.'

'Isn't that a mistake?'

'You know about fish and chips?'

'A bit, yes. You've got to in my field.'

'I wouldn't have thought so.'

'So you don't make your own?'

'I can't afford the machine.'

'I've heard it said you'll never make any money in this business unless you make your own chips.'

'Is that right? I can't afford the machine.'

'Isn't that interesting. You should perhaps look into it.'

'Is that right?'

'Yes.' The lawyer friend's eyes were swimming again. 'You know, I think I could be of some help. Yes, I think I could. Just . . . possibly.'

'You could buy me a machine?' Roscoe brightened by a quarter-turn.

'Well, no. Not exactly . . . I could buy your business. I've been talking to your mother, Ross, and she's told me that, quite frankly, the odds are you'll go bust any time now – "sooner or later," I think, were her actual words – and she asked me, as a friend, if I might be able to be of any help, and I said I'd be delighted. Of course the decision is yours, Ross. But if you allow this business to go bust before you sell, you won't get anything for it afterwards. Nothing at all. Perhaps enough to taxi home from the mortgage sale, but that's it, Ross. Now I understand from your mother that you paid forty-eight thousand all up for the business. Right? For the licence, good will and capital stock. OK. Now, I'm prepared . . . and I'm going somewhat out on a limb on this one . . . I'm prepared to go to forty thousand – that's right – to help you . . . to help you, Ross, *you* . . . to allow *you to get out of this one without losing your arse.*'

Until this point the lawyer friend had been looking out the window. Now he turned, glowing.

Listen to him, thought Roscoe. But where would I hide the body? What a nuisance.

'Now I'm prepared to go that far because I'm an old friend of your mother's and she has asked me to help you. Also I knew your father, as I've said. Believe me, this is not easy for any of us. I have no personal interest in making this business work. In fact, I intend only to possess it temporarily, as I have a potential buyer in the process of a title search on another property, a fruiterer eager to expand, and I've told him about the shop and he came in and bought an order of chips and was reasonably happy. Now he won't wait for ever on this, Ross, and unfortunately despite my commitment to your mother, neither can I wait for ever. The worst thing you could do is be indecisive. Honestly – and this is horse's mouth now, Ross – forty thousand is more than this place is worth. Declining sales figures are like the black plague to a buyer. The black plague. Your mother is in agreement. It's the best of a bad situation. Listen . . . of course . . . if you have some idea of how to turn . . . and I'm saying *turn*, this business around, into a winner, in the very near future, I'd be glad to hear it . . . I'd be the first to want to . . . but I'm sure you see that turnarounds like that are unlikely without *significant* capital injections, which your mother tells me you don't have, Ross, and do not, I'm afraid, seem likely to have in the foreseeable future. These, Ross, appear to me to be the facts before us.'

Ross had moved to the front window and was looking morosely out, his early defiance now something of a daze. He thought about Bella. If he could get back with her, things might change. Who knows, strange men might even stop coming into his shop and making him feel like he was dead.

'What do you say?' said the lawyer friend, smiling, post-coital.

'I'll get back to you,' Ross replied, turning on a heel and retreating to the back. And then the dream broke. All this was a chimera he could be woken from. No it wasn't. No fear.

Two days short of a month since Ross first opened his doors with hopeful fingers crossed, Bella finally phoned. Ross knew it was her and snatched up the receiver. On the other end she almost instantaneously hung up, but two words survived: *come now*.

He could have cried.

He had been scraping the fat off the walls of the cold vat. He cleaned his hands with soap and took off his apron. He wasn't due to open for the afternoon for another three hours. Perhaps, however, he wouldn't open today. He combed his hair and messed up the side parting. A supplier was meant to be calling some time to deliver a load of crab-sticks and frozen fish, but to hell with him.

He locked the back door and went into the front, taking a moment to catch his breath. Above him the electronic fly-killer hummed, and cars passed outside, but it was still very peaceful. For a few quiet moments Roscoe comtemplated the difficulty of succumbing to genuine despair over a modest apocalypse when coupling with the woman of one's choice. He thought of Bella and missed her desperately – a combination that finally managed to get him out the door, into his car, and heading, just above the legal speed, towards a number of disappointments.

Five miles to the north of Roscoe, a phantom picked up a telephone receiver – a phantom, because it is hardly conceivable that anything feeling *that* guilty could actually be fully alive.

Betrayal is a bleak word and Roscoe's mother felt bleak enough.

Tears fell out of her brown Scottish eyes, two trails curving down both cheeks, following the jaw lines, meeting again at the chin and falling directly onto the chequered linoleum below; miraculously, combined with the collapsed parentheses of her eyebrows, they formed a streaming heart. She loved her son. Her fingers dialled. She did. Didn't she? Certainly. Nothing else could provoke her into a betrayal of this magnitude.

Bella's quadriceps were splendid.

In the sunshine on the back lawn, where she was putting down a pile of blankets wrapped in plastic bags, they twitched sunlight heliographically down the drive as Roscoe's car turned into it.

Bella rose to her full height of five feet two and waited for Roscoe. She had three reasons for all this. The time had come for goodbye, she wanted to put the fear of God into him for old times' sake, and she also needed a hand in executing the final phase of her plan.

Roscoe got out of his car and started up the drive towards her. She noticed a slight bow in his legs. She deduced, quite correctly, that he had some sort of showdown in mind. But it was more serious than that. He had come to work things out. He would say it meant everything to him to work things out. And she wouldn't believe him; she would think it didn't mean enough.

'Hi,' said Ross. The smile was very broad.

'I want you to close your shop, Ross, and come with me this afternoon to save yourself from destruction.'

'I . . . I came as quickly . . . as I could,' he replied. The smile still shone on his face. Bella looked at the smile. It was a most unusual one, joyous and yet pathetic. A clown's smile. 'How are you, Bell?' he added. Bella considered the question honestly, but there was only one possible answer.

'Peak condition,' she said.

'Good,' he said.

'I'm leaving today, Ross.'

'Yeah?'

'Today is the day.'

'Today?'

'Do you want to come?'

'No. I sort of . . . can't today.'

'OK.'

Ross wondered if everything was over then. Perhaps it could be like that. A few words. He waited and looked at her. She didn't say anything. It felt like everything *was* over. He turned to go back to his car.

'Ross?'

He stopped. 'Yeah?'

'Can you give me a hand to get away? Quarter of an hour? You can say no.'

'All right.' He didn't look at her.

She led Ross to the garden shed, her spirits unreasonably high, and, taking out a steel pin from the doors, threw them wide open. Ross was speechless. Bella ginned with the pride of a new mother.

Well, it wasn't an ark exactly, this vessel of deliverance, just a three-metre Indian-style canoe with tarpaulin coverings fore and aft, and two little double-finned oars lying across it. It was a flat-bottomed fibreglass job, a slow-river craft, with wooden-plank seats set two feet apart and six inches above the hull so the bum could settle well back and the knees hug the bodyline. It looked like it could really move through the water.

'What do you think, Ross? This is what I'm going bush in.'

Ross moved closer. Supplies were stowed in either end and tied down with straps in case of a roll. Specifically, he could make out a first-aid box, a gross of tampons and a bottle of Samovar Dry. There was no doubting her conviction that the world was in peril. He stepped back, a little dizzied by the last ten minutes. She awaited an answer.

'Nice canoe,' he said. He actually felt like smashing his head through its hull and walking back down the drive, perhaps to cleanly impale himself on his new AM/FM bonnet aerial.

'I've bought a hut way up the river. That's what I've been planning, Ross. All this time. And today is the day.'

'What happens tomorrow?'

'You don't understand, Ross. It's not going to be a bang, you see . . .'

'No, I know.'

'And not tomorrow either, but the hour isn't far away, Ross, and if I don't get out now I never will, because it'll get harder and harder. You don't believe me, but it will.'

'I believe you, Bell.' Maybe he did.

'You've never taken me seriously about this, but I'm telling you. IT'S HAPPENING!'

'I know.'

Bella's face was glowing.

'You'll help me get my boat to the river? We'll have to carry it.'

'Through town?'

'We could take the back streets.'

They didn't take the back streets. They went right up Central Parade, Ross in front, Bella following, and not up the footpath either – it was too crowded – but up the middle of the road.

On the footpaths the kids pointed, giggling, convinced it must be a maverick Christmas float. And through the hairdresser's

window puzzled faces looked over their *Woman's Own* maga-
zines. Likewise, Ron Monroe cut short his insurance spiel, the
bare-shouldered staff of the Velvet Touch sauna drew back their
heavy curtains to gape, and lotioned shop assistants lying on
upper-storey balconies lifted their sunglasses off their gleaming
noses.

Ross was in a haze of his own making, no longer concerned
with the unsupportable weight of his thoughts. A new image:
Atlas bearing canoe. He was somewhere else. Bella, however,
was motivated by a far more simple force: *determination* to reach
the river. Between them they formed an almost reverential
procession up Central Parade.

They reached the corner, ran a red light amid a cacophony of
car horns, and turned north towards the river. Easily maddened
drivers shouted obscenities from the left and right. One
businessman pulled over, jumped out, and chased them, shouting: 'HEY! WHO THE FUCK YA THINK Y'ARE? ARSEHOLES!
TRY THAT AGAIN! JUSS TRY IT! FUCKAARS!'

Bella was looking at the back of Ross's head, seldom noticing
anything else. She was fairly impressed by her partner. Yes,
there would be things she would miss about the normal
world.

A bus slammed on its brakes and stopped inches from the rear
tip of the canoe. Bella thought, 'You see how hard they are
making it already to get away.'

They marched steadily up Langlorn Avenue towards the
bridge, past the base hospital, the Presbyterian church, and kids
on bicycles ringing their bells, then veered into Blydon. As they
passed the laundromat on the right and the BP all-nighter, Ross
found his head starting to turn. There, in clinical white ahead,
was the fish shop – small, unvisited. Coming abreast of it, he saw
in the window and through the passage to the back. His name
was painted on the awning: 'Manager – Roscoe Stillwater'. Then
he turned his head suddenly away. The shop was looking out at
him. It was confused, like all those others, and calling out to him:
'What the hell are you doing, Roscoe? What's this all about?

What *is it* that you want?' He was unsure, but he had one answer. It had to do with just saving himself.

The canoe sat in the water well, not too deep in the stern, despite the load, and it wouldn't be too hard to control. In any case, the river was mostly deep and slow for twenty miles up to the headwaters.

'What'll you do, Bell, when this stuff runs out?' He was looking at the supplies in the plastic bags.

'Whadaya think? I'll buy some more.'

So, thought Roscoe, she would be coming back from time to time. She couldn't get away entirely. No one could do that. She would go bush, but she would still be around. He wondered why he hadn't thought about this earlier, as it consoled him somewhat and he needed as much of that as he could get. It was because she'd never mentioned it. He said it to himself once more: from time to time she will have to come back.

'Oh well . . .' she said, 'the day's getting on, Ross.' Nervous for the first time, she put her arms around Roscoe's neck and held him tight. Roscoe felt her tremble, so lightly, and he trembled too. This crest of emotion was awful. Roscoe's heart wavered and the crest broke and his heart went down with it. The question of what he should do with his life was leaking out into a simple desire to hold on to her, just that, until the sky quaked and fell apart. He began to cry, a slow pent-up release, but she pushed him away, got into the canoe, took up the paddle, and dug in for midstream.

Let's call it the lesson for the day.

Roscoe opened, ran and closed his shop without a hiccup for two days after Bella's departure. Business was all right. He didn't look at his books.

He took to sitting on an old apple box out the back and closing his eyes a lot. He didn't sleep, just closed them and listened to the shop. Someone would come in, he'd get up, do their order, maybe wipe down a bench, then go back to the apple box. He didn't wait for someone to come in any more. They came in, he got up. They didn't, he stayed on the apple box. Simple as that. It was better with his eyes closed.

There was no telling how long Ross could have gone on this way – maybe weeks, years, who knows? – if his mother's betrayal had not interceded.

The man from the Health Department burst in one afternoon, surprising Ross on his box, flashing his jurisdiction into every corner of the shop, and finally zeroing in on the giant jar of tartar sauce, which now had two flies mortally stuck to its whipped surface. He fished out the two flies snapped them into a white envelope and departed. Ross hardly moved from his box. His eyes were heavy. He closed them against the caustic hum of the world.

The phone rang. His mother.

'It was me, Ross. I told them. But it'll be all right, son. This way they can't call you a bankrupt, and you'll be able to sell. You'll be able to get a good price instead of nothing. The best price, Ross. Believe me. It'll all work out. Maybe you can try again in a better place. This country is full of fish-and-chip shops like yours. We're lucky it's worked out like this. We're lucky, Ross. You hear me, Ross? We're lucky.'

The next day the Health Department suspended Roscoe's licence to open his shop. The actual date is unimportant. It was the end of the world.

The Kid

———————

Throughout his reading of the official statement the Prime Minister's voice had once again become high and thin. At its worst it had been a whine. As the gallery journalists crossed the press room to retake their seats he berated himself, jolting his collar loose on his neck. What in civilian life had been a pleasant but gentle speaking voice was now – if he believed his advisers – a major part of his 'image problem'. He couldn't deny that he was not a popular leader. He'd lost at least eight pounds off his gut, and the cartoonists were flaying the flesh off his back. Was it any wonder that his vocal chords betrayed him, making his voice sound emasculated – like 'an aroused marsupial' as one newspaper described it.

He discreetly mopped his brow. Monroe, his press secretary, was now gesturing to the journalists from the doorway, calling for silence. 'Gentlemen, thank you.'

Water. The Prime Minister filled his mouth, almost gargling, eyeing his tormentors. He was the fourth Prime Minister in four years, his leadership the legacy of a dead man. Every day this old razzmatazz, wooing a population hardened against him.

But now, the question-and-answer session. Death. He arranged his notes alphabetically, by topic headings, for quick referral. What was the delay? The Australian film crew were still setting up their lights. This would lead tomorrow morning, coast to coast in Australia, making page five in London and New York. At home, it would fill the entire front page, with backgrounders on three and five. The party hoped for a reprieve at the polls from this.

The TV lights finally came on, illuminating the back of the Prime Minister's brain. He blinked and grappled with the microphone, pulling it towards him. 'Very well, gentle—' But the end of his opening sentence soared into a raking shriek of feedback. He gazed hopelessly about for assistance. A cry came from his press secretary. 'Don't *touch* the microphone!' He was being told off. It was true – told off like a child. He let go of the microphone, and the electronic crackling died down. Where else on earth was the head of state spoken to in this manner? And in front of TV cameras? He tapped the microphone with his finger – *thug thug*. Clearing his throat, he looked up into the supernova of lights and . . . smiled. That smile. The most lampooned smile in parliamentary history. Cartoonists had given him the front teeth of a beaver and the mouth of a drag queen. He tried again. 'All right, thank you, one at a time please, ladies and gentlemen . . .'

'David Altmore, *Sydney Morning Herald*.'

Where was he? The Prime Minister couldn't see him. He nodded generally towards the voice behind the glare, his expression serious now.

'You have expelled the Soviet Ambassador, Mr Solokov, as of this evening. Have you personally spoken to him yet?'

'Ah . . . Mr Solokov will be meeting with the Minister of Foreign Affairs this afternoon. The expulsion will' – he glanced down at his notes – 'take effect immediately. That will be that. He knows we mean business and' – *finish it* – 'he . . . ah . . . he ought to have known that's what we intended to do.' Too clumsy – he'd ballsed it. Coast to coast. His head pointed aggressively elsewhere for another question. For a moment there was silence, that awful live-TV silence, broken only by the delicate whirring of a dozen cassette tapes recording under his nose.

A new voice: 'Sir, how do you respond to Mr Solokov's claim tonight that the expulsion is merely an election strategy, and that you are an incompetent politician who doesn't know what he is talking about?'

Chuckles. The question was clearly out of line. He must corral it instantly. 'Mr Solokov' – *voice, voice, voice!* – 'has a lot to learn.'

Better. Speak from the diaphragm. 'He can perhaps learn some of it in the Gulag, if he has the time.'

He expected a laugh, but didn't get it. Still, his true audience was further out, and he must remember that his performance was for *their* profit. Not for these leeches, quenching their thirsts right now on his sap.

Another voice: 'To what extent has the leaking of the intelligence service memo on Mr Solokov two days ago affected the timing of his expulsion?'

'It hasn't.'

Someone else: 'Mr Solokov's statement tonight suggests that the security organizations of other countries are involved.'

'Mr Solokov will say anything that comes into his head.'

'But . . .'

Another voice: 'Sir, you said in your statement that you have obtained evidence that proves the Ambassador has personally been involved in activities inconsistent with his diplomatic position. Can you be more explicit?'

'Mr Mondrigan' – he recognized the voice – 'you do your job, and let us do ours.' It was going well. Considering. Two days ago he'd had no intention of acting this quickly on the Security Intelligence Service report, but after the memo had been leaked to the press he couldn't afford to be seen soft-optioning those Russians. Whitehall's obscure warning not to proceeed with the expulsion – which they had twice refused to clarify over the past forty-eight hours – had to be overlooked given the public reaction here. He had acted strongly, decisively. The general election was, after all, breathing down his neck. Whitehall would learn what sort of man they were dealing with. And the cartoon in yesterday morning's *Herald* was still on his mind: the Prime Minister being dined by a Russian Valentino, his full lips wrapped around a hideous sausage inscribed with the words 'The Kremlin'.

'There has been speculation . . .'

But through the glare came Monroe, holding up his big hand and cutting the question down. 'Thank you, turn those lights down. That's all for now.' He signalled to the Prime Minister, who quickly understood and leaned forward to the microphone. 'Ladies and gentlemen, thank you.' There were a few protests, but most of the journalists rose without argument to their feet. A surprisingly abrupt end. The Prime Minister pushed his microphone gratefully away, rocked back in his chair, and released the bellows of air he'd been trying to keep in his chest, a public-speaking trick he'd picked up from a Covent Garden opera singer who had persued him years earlier.

Monroe was swiftly crossing the room towards him. His bald head was creased with anxiety. Mounting the stage, he approached the Prime Minister, holding a piece of paper.

'It went well, don't you think?' said the Prime Minister.

Monroe slammed the paper down on the desk. 'There's been a cock-up. It's from Whitehall.'

'A cock-up? What do you mean? What's the matter?'

The lights went out.

New Zealand Press Association

Departing Soviet Ambassador Andrei Solokov yesterday fired his last salvos, declaring the big losers in this affair to be the New Zealand Government.

'I know these accusations are false; the Prime Minister knows these accusations are false. He and his government have been deceived by dishonest people,' he said at Wellington Airport a few minutes before his departure.

'The New Zealand Government and the SIS must take full responsibility.'

He and Mrs Solokov took their leave of Wellington in a flurry of embraces, kisses and red-and-white carnations.

The Ambassador's expulsion comes after the Prime Minister's announcement on Monday and a week of claims by the opposition that the British government has some links with Mr Solokov extending back to his term as Soviet cultural attaché to Britain during the 1960s.

Opposition defence spoksesman Terry McMahon

announced on Wednesday that he possessed documents from Whitehall suggesting that Mr Solokov had been in New Zealand 'under terms more favourable to MI6 than the Politburo', and that British intelligence heads were presently 'fuming' over the sudden expulsion, which was made without international consultation.

The Prime Minister has since dismissed these claims as 'ridiculous'.

At 9.20 last night a black embassy Mercedes drew up outside the domestic terminal at Wellington Airport, where Mr Solokov and his wife were to board a flight forty-five minutes later.

Flanked by fifty embassy staff and well-wishers, they attracted curious stares from other travellers as they were led towards the VIP lounge.

Questioned at this point about the likely consequences of his expulsion, Mr Solokov said, 'Tonight your Prime Minister will be a very lonely man.' Asked to explain what he meant by this, Mr Solokov declined to comment further, shaking his head gravely as he entered the lounge with his staff.

New Zealand's ties with the Soviet Union seemed to have been given elevated status with the appointment of Mr Solokov ten months ago.

He is a senior diplomat and is said to have access to the highest levels of the Politburo.

Outside Parliament were a dozen or so Maoris and half a dozen white women holding placards reading 'Sellout' and 'Leaderless Left'. Emerging on to the steps, the Prime Minister saw them before they saw him and retreated back into the building. They were shouting angrily, dressed in white clothes – windcheaters, sneakers, gloves and scarves. The wind had driven them together in a huddle for warmth at the bottom of the steps. The Prime Minister decided to go out the back way. As he walked past the guard with his head down, the Prime Minister snapped his fingers, as if to suggest he had forgotten something inside and that the demonstration was unworthy of his attention. But the guard had obviously seen how he had backed away at the sight of a few protestors as if confronted by his own demons. So why the finger-snapping routine? Reflex. Bad acting had become habit. Every moment counted politically. This was the new super-sensitivity of the TV politician.

Inside Parliament he walked quickly across the building from east to west. Encountering nobody, he emerged into the official car park, which contained twenty or thirty white Ford Cortinas. He strode through them, raised his hand to the guard at the gate, received a salute, and then, unusually, headed on foot down Bowen Street, falling in with the flow of pedestrians.

He had decided on a pie.

As a backbencher in the late 1950s – he was thirty-nine when he won his first seat in Parliament – the Prime Minister had always enjoyed travelling by bus and mingling with the crowds. It had kept alive his connection with the people. And that was when he'd eaten pies – steak or mince – between sessions. Now he walked through the downtown throng towards the old cafeteria he'd once frequented, in the hope that it still existed, because he hadn't tasted that meat and pastry in his mouth for ten years.

Anonymous! He looked up every now and again into the faces of home-bound pedestrians and remained unrecognized. He had his collar up and was squinting heavily, which he imagined altered his face. He felt like he'd become an imposter.

The gloomy, stoically suffering faces of the people – *his* people! The Prime Minister was sailing unknown through his constituency. Tall men, skinny women, fat bureaucrats, young office girls – all fought their way up Bowen Street against the wind, their thick coats drawn up to their throats, chins on their chests, clinging to cases, handbags, umbrellas. The wind was strong. Rain seemed imminent. Why, he wondered, did everyone look so behind the times? They carried themselves like people of the land who have evolved strong bodies but suddenly find them irrelevant and burdensome in their new urban surroundings.

The Prime Minister himself had been taught to discard such attitudes by his advisers; his image had been minutely tailored, and he was now working on what they called his 'new sensuality'. For sex and power merged in the age of satellite politics. The Prime Minister's upright High Church demeanour – as his advisers described it – was developing, on the eve of the election, a 'come hither' and 'trust me' component. His grey suits were now shot with red and his hair was swept up every morning.

Did he find all this disagreeable? Not at first. He had cooperated totally, having no particular affection for his current appearance and no concept of what his style might or might not be. But then it had become humiliating. When? Perhaps the day his eyelashes had been curled. *Curled*! A party TV ad was being produced. An advertising man by the name of Sloane had given instructions to the make-up woman, and his lashes were curled before he knew it. The pain he suffered watching the video had been unbearable. His lashes stood out like those of a barmaid. He felt like a closet queen! But he was told he looked excellent, so he remained silent and it went on.

What could he do, spiritually weakened by public scrutiny and universal criticism? The campaign was at a tenuous stage. It was a close two-party contest, and the outcome would be determined by swinging voters, which meant that women would decide it. The Prime Minister passed the gates to the grounds of Parliament and glanced back at the bunch of protesters. The Maoris would go with him on the day. But the women? He scurried across the street unseen, making a mental note to bone up on the abortion and equal pay issues.

He was near the old cafeteria now. Only one woman at the bus depot magazine stand, looking up over her copy of the *New Zealand Woman's Weekly*, seemed to have recognized him. Her mouth had dropped open. As well it might. After all, it was not every day that the Prime Minister roamed abroad and could almost be touched in the flesh.

So why was he doing this? Because the flame of his private life – his individuality – had gone out. When one's public life is all that's left, he thought, one needs to retrieve something tangible from the past, something inexplicable. A pie. A piece of filled pastry, to be eaten among ordinary people at a rundown cafeteria.

Miraculously, the cafeteria had survived. Grubby labourers between shifts filled the smoky alley-shaped interior. He inhaled the sweet odours and took in the sight: ten tables with chequered plastic clothes and thirty rowdy patrons. Approaching the counter, his spine tingling, he smiled at the big-eyed girl in her plaid smock and slid open the door of the pie-warmer. The continued existence of the cafeteria caused an unreasonable rejoicing within him. His party's roots lay in places such as this.

The Prime Minster sat alone with his pie at the only available table. Although he was by himself, he felt united with these people around him. Keeping his head low, he remained unrecognized; his collar was still up and his hair was lank on his head. Did he look different? What a fabulous idea this was. He had instinctively found what he most needed. Brotherhood. The spirit of his forty-year-old party was right here, and he had just drawn closer to it.

Only one ingredient was absent. Tomato sauce. Risking everything, he turned, smiling, towards the six workmen at the next table. 'Do you mind if I borrow the sauce?'

The men's eyes widened. He was recognized. At last. Yes, he had secretly hoped for this. Come hither, for I am your Prime Minister.

'Eh?' one man said.

'The sauce. Thank you.' The Prime Minister, smiling still, reached out his hand to receive the bottle.

After a silence, their spokesman replied, briefly and finally. 'Stuff off!'

The Prime Minister turned away, stunned. He hoped that he had not in fact been recognized at all and that – perhaps because of his new coat, an expensive Aquascutum – he had been mistaken for a poisonous businessman. But how was this possible? The most famous face in the land? Returning to his pie, he forced himself to enjoy it without the tomato sauce. He bit off a huge mouthful and chewed it, wondering how he could hope to win an election when face to face with his own constituency in a workman's cafeteria he had been refused the use of a red plastic tomato.

By nine o'clock the Government's seats had begun to fall. A silence descended on the dance hall in the Prime Minister's electorate. Supporters in straw boaters and red ribbons held their glasses of punch to their chests, expressionless, staring at the TV as results appeared on the screen. The victory band had gone outside for a smoke. 'You see there, it's a swing against us,' whispered Marjorie Donahauser to her husband. 'No it's not,' Wally Donahauser replied. 'We'll make that up. You'll see.' Another voice nearby said, 'Wait till we take New Plymouth. We're bound to take New Plymouth.' At this a dozen heads nodded in agreement, trying to shake off the idea of losing, turning their eyes back to the set and saying 'Shhh!' as a new result came up.

But despite the gaiety of all the banners and streamers, the heart had gone out of the campaign. The swinging voters appeared to have jumped ship, and the rally had not happened. By half past nine the supporters had stopped drinking and become subdued, gathering morosely around the TV mounted over the canteen at the end of the hall. Any moment now the rout would begin. This was the moment the TV crew in the corner were waiting for. Chewing gum and leaning on their cameras, they were under strict instructions. Their task was to follow the Prime Minister back to his own electorate and to photograph his face upon the fall of his government. They wanted his expression as close to the critical moment as possible the moment of knowledge, when the bilge split open and the sea rushed in, the moment he realized his country had disinherited him.

The Prime Minister and his wife were somewhere in the middle of the huddle around the TV set. None of his advisers or cabinet ministers had returned with him to share the election results. There were only forty or so members of the local party branch with their families. Rumour had it that none of his colleagues wanted to be stained with the mark of defeat alongside him. It was felt that this loss – should it eventuate – ought to be handled as a personal one. Many of the Prime Minister's colleagues expected him to take the blame, as this would take some heat off the party. And, after all, the writing had been on the wall: they had failed to sell this man to the country. The nation had resisted him from the start and now this was their verdict. Seats were dropping like flies.

The Prime Minister had been rejected. The country had turned on him. Even his own party. The people from the TV network were trying to set up an interview. A journalist had been sent into the crowd to weed him out from his supporters. And now he was emerging, straightening his tie, tightening it, touching his hair with his open palm, looking around the room for the cameras and for whoever was in charge. The lights came on.

'Sir?' a journalist called out.

The Prime Minister walked right in on the camera, somewhat surprised. They were rolling already. He smiled, his eyes darting between the journalist and the camera.

'There's been a three per cent swing against you at this stage, and it looks like this could reach five or six as the rural seats come in.'

'Well,' said the Prime Minister, fixing on the reporter now, 'yes, we would like to have picked up Auckland Central – we did a lot of work there – but I guess it just went against us on the day. That's politics.'

'And how about Avon? You lost by a big margin there. In Wellington, five seats went to National – even a couple of your safe seats . . . We understand you're about to lose Otara for the first time in twenty-four years.'

'I don't know where you get your figures from. We haven't lost Otara yet and we've got high hopes with Doug Angus in New Plymouth. We think he might steal one back for us there. That's been a National seat for thirty-six years, and if my memory serves me correctly it would upset a majority of 2,400.'

'Can you come back from a three per cent swing, Prime Minister?'

'We can come back.'

'Prime Minister, thank you.'

The lights flicked off, and with a nod the Prime Minister returned to his group. Arms clapped him on the back and old supporters pumped his hand. Another final result was coming in. The crowd hushed. New Plymouth. 'It's gone to National', called someone at the front. The Prime Minister's wife leaned towards her husband and whispered, 'Did we need New Plymouth?' The sighs of disappointment were almost audible above the noise of the TV. The Prime Minister took her hand. 'Dance with me,' he said.

The band, back from their cigarettes, struck up a tune after a signal from the campaign manager. The Prime Minister's wife smiled and rose to her feet. 'Come on then, Nijinsky,' she said. They were the first couple on to the floor, but taking their cue several other couples turned away from the TV and joined them.

'You gotta get this!' said the TV producer into the telephone. 'He's *dancing*. That's what I said. Yes, with his wife. It's a waltz or something, I dunno. Look, I'm going with this. Counting down . . . four, three, two . . . *cameras* . . . we're live!' The cameras floated towards the couple. The Prime Minister danced well. He held his wife closely, intimately. The TV producer was excited. He had found the image he wanted. A failed Prime Minister dancing out of office with his loyal wife. Such an image would shame the public. Many voters would wish they could withdraw their eager ballot papers and shred them. In the last analysis, the cameras didn't want a crucifixion. They wanted a tear-jerker. The condemned man singing a surprising tune as the rifles slipped their catches. They wanted nobility.

More and more couples were now taking to the floor, responding to the imperative of the moment. Some TV viewers might smirk at the scene, but no other moment in the campaign had been quite so vivid: the Prime Minister's palm open gently, his wife's fingertips pressed delicately upon it. *Tenderness*. What no one had expected from him – something good and simple and free of madness at the fatal hour. Something they could recognize. At last.

'Move in on him!' said the TV producer. 'Go in tight on his face. I want his *face*. The expression! That's it. That's better. That's good.'

The Trouble with Elliot

The travel agent smoked in the empty church. It wasn't permitted, of course, but he had the knack of getting away with it. Unknown to anybody, he would often stop in for a cigarette. And today he was thinking, somewhat laterally, of the trouble he was having being himself.

The smoke twisted up into the massive empty space above his head; he watched it rise over the altar towards the bright windowed apex of the roof, where it gathered unable to go any higher, like a sinner's prayer.

Above the altar cross, in mid-launch, was a cheerful blue-gowned angel with the podgy body of a two-year-old boy. Well, there is room for everything, thought the travel agent. After all, the world is essentially ludicrous, so why not angels? For a moment, he imagined he could hear wings beating.

The touch on the shoulder startled him. 'God!' he blurted, with unconsidered irony. She was somehow sitting behind him – young, with long dark hair, big glasses, and her round eyes troubled, far too easy to look at, as he would learn, for anybody's good.

'You are Mr Leo Elliot,' she said.

'That's right.' He was quickly grinding out his cigarette on the seat.

'You must help me. I was told you could help me. You are a religious man. I am a Catholic also. I am Italian. I was born in a small town in the north where the Virgin has four times appeared. My name is Carmina Maria Liolla. I run the amusement maze down at the beach. Hello.'

She held out her small hand. Elliot, without further encouragement, took hold of it. She was his idea, as he looked at her now, of a truly erotic beauty, and this masked the suspicion that the handshake was his first major mistake of the day. She smiled and retrieved her hand. Even then she must have known that this unimpressively balding travel agent staring at her with rapt eyes was already throwing his heart in the air for her personal target practice, because she acknowledged it by saying suddenly, 'Thank you.'

'That's all right,' he said. He even managed a smile.

She asked if they could talk somewhere else. He finally suggested his car, a this-year's Corona, and they walked out to it from the church. There, in halting English, she could elucidate without fear of being overheard.

Elliot imagined himself recounting this meeting by the agency coffee machine: 'I swear she just appeared. I thought all my prayers had been answered. What did I do? I'll tell you what I did . . .' This was a way of distancing himself, of turning real life into reportage, so that if things got scary he could convince himself it was all happening to someone else. One needs a strategy, Elliot thought, to deal with people like Carmina Maria Liolla who, as she talked in the passenger seat of his car, gripped and regripped her hands in her lap as if forming shadow-pupped shapes.

'. . . and when I told him that I was going to leave him, that I was going back to Valese forever, he got mad and beat me. Here, you see the mark he gave me?' She turned her head to look at him, and the light caught a faint broken line above her far eyebrow. It seemed to have had stitches in it at one time.

'If he knew I was talking to you now, he would probably try and kill you. He is crazy. I'm sorry.'

Elliot's self-protective heart leapt.

'But I have been very careful. Don't worry. I am used to him following me and I have a way of getting away from him.'

Those Eyetie men, thought Elliot – only their daughters save the whole race from being a complete washout.

Beyond the car park a priest pulled the blinds in the presbytery window. Both the occupants of the Corona had just been watching the man doing exercises in his front room. Elliot pushed back in his seat and stole a sideways look at Carmina Maria Liolla. She was biting her thumbnail and looking away. He surreptitiously ran his eyes up and down her body; there was much to excite him. But she was out of his league. Perhaps when he'd been at his best, some years earlier, and if they'd met under favourable conditions (favouring him), he might have got somewhere with a looker such as her. Sure, she was an immigrant on her back foot, and he might impress her with his status, but he'd never appropriate her desires, her horniness. So, subduing his lust, he tightened his tie around his neck and consoled himself with his own moral stamina.

Carmina Maria Liolla began to talk. She opened up to Elliot, placing a hand over the swelling V-neck of her cardigan. Her small face became animated as she confided her secrets. She talked of her homeland, of Italy's northern provinces where she was born, of the Valle D'Aosta and its fertile wheat fields, her English faltering now and then and lapsing into Italian. '*Però il clima del settentrione, è più simile a quello del* North Island! *Signor d'inverno*, the winter! Brrrr,' she said. 'It is colder than anything.' She talked of her town, Valese, in the shadow of the Gran Paradiso (Great Paradise) mountain, her relatives who still farmed there, the colour of the soil, 'which is as dark as this', she said, 'no darker', pulling at her skirt. She described her poor but strong-spirited family, and how her father, a big man with crutches, had died standing upright in a field and was dead for two days before the crutches toppled and people realized what had happened. And how they buried him standing up as a sign of respect. And how, when her mother came to New Zealand on the invitation of an uncle, she found him already in his grave and so had to work in orchards in the summer and clean churches in the winter.

Elliot, once or twice, had gone to church on a Sunday. But Carmina never missed. And not only on Sundays: benedictions, funerals, holy days, rosaries and recently several baptisms, though it was not the same as back in Italy. 'In this country you have no religion,' she said, shaking her head.

'Of course we have religion.'

'You have churches and you have priests and you have prayers, but you don't have religion. I would rather live in America than here.'

'America has religion?'

'No, America does not have religion, but at least in America there is *colpa*. Guilt, Mr Eliot, guilt! That is second best.' Carmina Maria Liolla looked beyond the misty windscreen, deeply serious. 'You see, Mr Elliot, every country, every country in the world, feels guilty for something. In my country it is many things – for the war, for what we have done to ourselves. We were once *gran' impéro, Signore, gran' impéro*! Now we are too poor to go to sleep. But in New Zealand, you do not feel guilty. You feel guilty for nothing.' She paused before continuing, turning to look at Elliot. 'Here, everyone thinks they are holy saints. They think that they are nice and fair and good but, *signore*, you cannot *be* those things, because you cannot be holy saints unless you have religion. Everyone thinks they are nice, but to have true religion you have got to see that you are not so nice.' Carmina Maria Liolla stopped talking.

She is trying to hypnotize me, thought Elliot, wrenching his eyes away from hers. He guessed she was a dangerous woman, which meant he could not understand her, though something other than her good looks and *décolletage* was holding him, and causing his present output of sweat. Moreover, his dicky bladder, gibbous, called for relief. At least all this would have some payoff, in that corner of the Econotravel office where the coffee machine shot steam up over a poster of Pompeii. Intrigue, though tiring, was good copy there. It was desirable to have a secret life.

'So,' said Elliot, 'how did you know I would be in the church, and what's this about your Italian boyfriend, and why are you talking to me in the first place anyway?'

'I rang up your work, Mr Elliot. They said you would most likely be smoking in the church. And he isn't Italian, my boyfriend, he is Kiwi like you. He is mechanic.'

'They told you I would be smoking in the church?'

'Yes.'

'They knew?'

'Yes, Mr Elliot. They told me.'

'Shit,' said Elliot, who had been under the illusion that his lunchtime activities went unobserved. His daily cigarette in church, he'd believed, was a well-kept secret.

Across the street, pretending to post a pile of letters (though it was actually the same letter over and over again), the second grandson of an Italian merchant seaman turned sausage-maker, now a genuine Kiwi with axle grease on his hands, peered over the red box towards the church car park. He'd successfully followed his woman around the aisles of two supermarkets, and now he had cornered her. 'Shit,' he said.

Elliot's daughter Bridgit had a girlfriend to stay overnight. They played cassettes behind closed doors, and the music was transmitted through the house as a bassy thud-thud. Every now and again a peel of laughter broke through to the living-room, where Elliot watched *Hawaii Five O*, sipping Milo.

His wife was already sleeping in a bed nailed to the wall to stop it creaking when they made love. His son's bedroom door was open. Simon Elliot could be anywhere in the range of a 50cc scooter and was often out after twelve. A T Rex poster flapped unfashionably on his noticeboard. Another screech of laughter and a bang on the wall came through to Elliot, who was losing interest in McGarret's problems with ammo and Dano's non-rendezvous with a Chinese sexpot who stashed a dagger in her undies, so he got up and slammed the set off.

On the bookshelf, which had long since developed a his-and-hers division, he pulled out a book club edition of *Great Rivers of the World*, switched off the light, and walked down the hall to his bedroom. Stopping outside Bridgit's room, he tapped on the door and called her name in a half-whisper. There was no answer, so he tapped more heavily: 'Bridgit?' There was a sound of scrambling bodies, then the music went off and there was silence. Finally, Bridgit said, 'What?'

'How's things in there?' Pause.

'All right.'

'How about shutting it down for the night, eh?' More giggling.

'Yeah. In a minute,' came back her voice.

'It's late.' Elliot turned and walked to his bedroom. The music came back on, with more noises indicating choreography. At the end of the hall he stopped at a row of wooden pegs holding an umbrella, a denim jacket and a fan-belt. He put down his book and started to undress. Thud, thud, thud.

Elliot had taken to disrobing in the hall years before when he'd realized his legs were ugly. He would remove his clothes in the dark, duck into the bedroom, and turn on the lamp once he was horizontal, all legs looking better that way.

His wife was awake. 'What's the smell?' she mumbled.

'Well, it could be a number of things.' Once upon a time she would not have reacted this way to him, he thought standing naked at the end of the bed.

'Something smells,' she said.

'I can't smell anything.'

She sat up and switched on the light. She saw her husband, wide-eyed and blinking, clutching an oversized book.

'My my,' she said. And she laughed.

He was getting tired of nudity. 'I can't smell anything,' he said again. Then he turned. Perhaps the girls were smoking. He stepped into the hall, put on his underpants, and knocked on Bridgit's door. 'Bridgit? Hey Bridgit, you smoking in there?' Elliot could smell smoke. Knock, knock. 'Bridgit?' A touch on his shoulder startled him. He turned to see his son, obviously half-cut, smiling at him inanely.

'Hey Dad.'

'What?'

'The letterbox is on fire.'

'Is it?'

'Uh. Yeah, it is.'

A scream came from the bedroom. Elliot flew to the door. His wife was looking out the window. It was true. The letterbox, boasting dual pigeonhole, milk rack and 'No circulars' notice, was ablaze, a flaming torch at the end of the driveway. The neighbours' fox terrier stood next to it, barking. Elliot was on his way outside, heading for the hose. He would fight to save it, though this was probably useless as letterboxes burn so quickly. But even so, he wanted to be remembered as not having just stood by and observed its demise – call it his St Bernard complex. However, by the time he got there with his running hose, the letterbox had almost burnt itself out. He fired water at the blackened frame, eliciting white streams of smoke followed by the collapse of half the letterbox on to the ground.

'How is it?' came a call from behind him.

'It's out,' he called black, and it *was* out, though Elliot's heart throbbed in its calcium cage as if the fireworks were only just beginning. Which they were.

Across town, a mechanic re-entered his bedroom, looked at the clock, and saw that it was already one a.m.

At the sink he dipped his hands into a jumbo jar of Swarfega, rubbed them together until they slid easily against each other, and flushed the muck free from his pores with cold water. Then he undressed and got into bed beside a sleeping female figure. She stirred, and he put a heavy arm over her. He whispered, 'Hey . . . *amante* . . . you awake?' She was awake but she wouldn't answer him. 'You awake, *amante mio*?' She had her eyes closed, not tightly but convincingly. He lay on his back and breathed out. Then he breathed out heavily again. She wasn't listening to him breathe. She was thinking about a complete Italian countryside afternoon: hay, piglets, hens and rabbits. The quiet simplicity of a world only a valley wide. She'd once had her own secret grotto in the foothills of Gran Paradiso where she would bathe. She loved to sunbathe, and also to pray. She was very religious. The Valle D'Aosta could glow, as if lit from within. In her village a blind man had made honey. As he made a mess, the flies would stick to his clothes, and her job, as a girl, was to free them from his sleeves. No, she wasn't listening to him breathe.

Leo Elliot knew exactly what he thought of Gisborne. It was a pisshole. Thus, as a travel agent, helping people to escape from the town, he saw himself as having the benevolence of a Florence Nightingale. He could lift someone from Disraeli Street and set them down in Vienna, with little more than a few taps on a computer keyboard. This came from years in the business, working his way up through the ranks, a process he approved of.

Nowadays, he could have a pensioner out of her Honda Civic and banking over Abu Dhabi within hours, gazing out of the window through a gauze of cloud at a yellow desert dotted with oil wells like rearing ants, wondering if the stove was still on from the pikelets while an airline lolly melted briliantly in her lap. This he could do, and people loved him for it. They would seek him out, in his check suit, solidly plump like a hotel manager but with thin disappointing legs. They would find him at the agency, surrounded by brochures, maps and model aeroplanes. They would discover that he had supreme confidence in his product, which was all those *elsewheres*. Despite the Pacific Ocean rolling in down the road, and all that sun every day, he believed Gisborne to be a pisshole. He was a travel agent.

Specifically, though, Elliot was terribly shallow, had fallen arches, and was badly afflicted by a spate of slow racehorses. In his favour, though, he was liked by sparrows. When he went for a walk, as he sometimes did to remedy his heart murmur, they flew around him. This was a very good sign, though Elliot hated it, batting at them and telling them to fuck off. The sparrows, however, were undeterred and seemed to be waiting for him whenever he went outdoors. There was no doubt about it. They sensed, dozing inside him, his St Bernard complex. There was nothing else worth hanging around for.

'. . . so what did you do then?'
'What do you think I did? I turned the hose on the fucker.'
'It went out?'
'Eventually, yeah. I had to battle with it.'
'Bloody funny thing. A bloody funny thing.'

It was Clarke McConachie, Elliot's right-hand man at the agency, head of European bookings and direct descendant of *the* Clark McConachie, World Billiards Champion of 1951, who said 'bloody funny thing' twice. He was leaning, with hunched shoulder, up against the Magicmaster Two-Cup-A-Go coffee machine and scraping plaque from his teeth with a toothpick. Clark was seven years older than Elliot and had been at the agency twice as long. His lowly position in the firm was based on consistent long-term evidence of ineptitude, and there was no grudge between them.

'So, didja get the cops in or what?'
'Yeah. We got the cops in. Course we got the cops in. You have to, don't ya? But what could they do? They had a poke in the ashes, salvaged our letterbox number, and told us to keep our eyes open. To think we pay those bastards. I dunno why we bother.'
'Probably kids.'
'We're not safe in our homes, Clark. What's the point of living in a country the size of an ant's arse, totally isolated by several oceans, if at night your letterbox is in jeopardy. It might as well be New York or Tokyo or Berlin, or bloody Belfast.'
'Maybe it was . . . y'know . . . a natural phenomenon.'
'Spontaneous combustion? Come on, Clark.'
'No. Lightening?'
'What are you leading up to?'
'I'm just running through the possibilities. I wouldn't want you to think someone was out to get you.'
'Which is, in fact, what you're thinking?'

'Yep.'

The automatic doors at the front of the office parted. A young dark-haired woman with glasses approached the counter. She wore jeans with a scarf around them instead of a belt. Clark McConachie turned his conical head and looked at her.

'Mr Leo Elliot, please,' she said.

Elliott pushed McConachie aside and stood before her. She spoke quietly. '*Buongiorno*, Mr Elliot.'

Elliot blushed. 'What do you want here?'

'I wish to talk to you, please.'

'We talked yesterday.'

'I know. I wish to talk to you. Once more. Please.'

'I have nothing more to say than I did yesterday.'

'I have something more.'

'All right, say it.'

Clark McConachie found something he wanted to do by Elliot's shoulder. Carmina Maria Liolla flashed her dark eyes at him. 'Not here,' she said. McConachie got the message and retired to the coffee machine. 'Our special place. We can talk there. Twelve o'clock. OK? Please?'

'We talked yesterday. I haven't changed my mind. I don't have anything else I want to say.' Elliot summoned an impressive amount of conviction for this delivery, but what Carmina Maria Liolla said next demolished his firm resolve.

'Mr Elliot. You are my last chance in the world. I believe . . . you are a nice man.'

Ah, she must know him better than anyone. His eyes locked on hers, unblinking, until they began to water. His breathing seemed to have ceased. Then she reached across the counter, squeezed his hand lightly, and whispered, '*Lei è un uomo molto simpático, Signor Elliot, molto . . . simpático.*' His heart jumped. Her breath was on him, warm. And not understanding her words excited him. He let her hold her hand over his. She was very exciting, even her smell, which was simply that of a young woman. Then she released his hand and turned. Her trailing black hair untied. Her jeans. He watched her walk away. *Molto simpático.*

That lunchtime Elliot went to look for her again.

Jeanie Elliot, Leo's wife, was upside down against the lounge wall in the pelican position and had been there for some time. Before her, on the carpet, was a copy of *Yoga for Yoga's Sake.* In this position the body balances on the head, legs bent at the knees, bringing oxygenated clarity of mind and lasting serenity. But, Jeanie Elliot, inverted, would be satisfied with nothing less than ecstasy.

However, after twenty minutes, the predicted state of well-being had still not arrived. She could only feel a slightly compressed mudulla oblongata and a quickening of breath, but nothing remotely exciting. It was depressing, she thought, that despite the increased opportunities, thrills were increasingly difficult to find with age – her breasts and midriff flopping the wrong way and, the scent of trodden peanut brittle and moth-balls in her nostrils, she noticed how all her furniture had legs, watched the birds flying upside down in the garden, and thought about Leo, the cause of her problem.

It was not easy for Jeanie to explain to any of her friends the particular trouble she was having with her travel agent. He was neither brutal nor gentle, neither malicious or dumb, nor particularly compassionate. To complain about him sounded like complaining about normality.

The front door opened, and Bridgit's silhouette appeared in the frame, home for lunch, her skinny legs sticking out of a black gymslip.

'The pelican position,' observed Bridgit.

'Yup,' said Jeanie.

'Is it Dad again?'

'Yup.'

The streets of Gisborne are not unusual; the lazy filigrees and awnings of pre-war shops, the box shapes of the 1920s and the glass and chrome and gratuitous Roman columns of modern office blocks. Elliot was born in 1946 to a WAAF from Morrinsville during that era of reconstruction, and he had always preferred 'the new'. He could just as easily watch something being destroyed as something being created. In fact, as he walked down Fitzherbert Street towards the bridge, he stopped to watch a giant bulldozer climbing hills of collapsed brick and rubble behind the façade of an almost demolished building. It was a doll's house opened up, the interior of upper offices exposed and crumbling as the bulldozer pushed, until a wall finally caved in. Dust showered up in the air, and a dull rumble sounded deep underground. Some of the dust got in Elliot's lungs and settled on his suit. He coughed and walked on, disturbed by this sensation and other things.

Although Elliot was shallow, he could be relied upon to put two and two together when it mattered, and he had long since seen a connection between Carmina Maria Liolla's boyfriend and his incinerated letterbox. However, he was not a brave man, so he needed time to consider his options carefully.

A smooth wind blew him south down Palmerston Street as the afternoon sun soaked into his safari suit. Carmina Maria Liolla was dangerously desirable. He would have to reject her before he became hooked. Elliot could feel himself slipping into reverie, beyond even the popular fiction of the Magicmaster Two-Cup-A-Go. A sparrow flew in front of his nose, making him pull up in mid-stride. It climbed to a telephone wire and landed. He'd have to think about it. Sometime. This other-possibilities stuff.

There was no sign of anyone outside the church. Elliot went around the back and through the sacristy door. He peeped inside from the vestibule; it was dark and empty, the air cool. The altar was bare of finery – just a white cloth and two unlit candles. A red tabernacle light flickered beneath a life-size crucified Christ. To the right of the altar, in an alcove, stood an effigy of the Virgin, and a brass terraced bench carried innumerable prayer candles, only a few of which were lit. Carmina Maria Liolla was nowhere to be seen. He put his hands in the pockets of his safari suit, his fingers circulating coins, and moved to the prayer candles to watch the wax burn, the wax of old women's wishes, going up in a thin thread of black smoke. Watching the candles burn, he thought of the likelihood of sex with Carmina Maria Liolla.

A creaking door broke the silence. It was her all right. She was in the entrance to the confessional across the altar.

'Psst! Mr Elliot. Come quickly. I've been waiting for you!'

She gave a sad smile, sad because it faded too quickly. Her hair was down, and she looked changed. The impression of her scar was stronger. She motioned to him, then slipped into one of the confessionals and shut the door. He stood for a moment outside it, considering his own teetering state of mind, then crossed himself out of pure nostalgia and entered the other chamber.

Elliot coughed, as if to test the darkness. He found the expected wooden kneeler and knelt down. He had no fondness for places like this. It wasn't the darkness, or the odour of varnish, or the church-inspired guilt. It had to do with chambers in general and his fragile sense of security, which depended on many things, including money, friends, a logical universe, and the need for enough space around his body to swing a cat. So he was sweating it. He was sweating for the space and he was sweating for Carmina Maria Liolla.

Elliot could hear the pulse of her breathing near him. Her face must be close to the grille. She was in the priest's box, and he in the confessor's. He leaned forward, and the tip of his nose touched the cold grille, flattening ever so slightly. Through his cage he looked for her in the darkness, but only the sound and warmth of her breath came to him.

'We can talk here,' she said. 'It's safe. We can say anything we want.' It was a whisper, suitable for a genuine confession.

'Listen, Carmina, do we have to be so damn – ' he searched for the word – 'devious about all this? I really don't go in for this sort of thing. OK, you want me to help you. Possibly I can. Possibly, also, I can't. But do we have to act out this *Mission Impossible* stuff?'

Carmina Maria Liolla was unfamiliar with a TV reference and only concluded from his tone that he was annoyed with her.

'Please do not be angry with me, Mr Elliot. You are a very nice man. That's why I came to you, of course. I don't want you to be angry. Please, *mi perdoni*, please!'

'For God's sake put on a light or something.' The darkness was too exhausting. Carmina turned on a small bulb above her head to one side, revealing her profile, eyes downcast. She faked this humble peasant routine terribly, thought Elliot. Yet it appealed to him. 'So,' he said, 'What is it?'

'I am very sad, Mr Elliot. As I've said, I wish to go home to Italy, but I cannot. I have asked people here to help me, and they will not. Also, I have something to confess to you. It is very hard for me to say this, Mr Elliot, but it was my Ricky who burned down your letterbox. There, I have said it! Now you will never want to speak to me again.'

'Who's Ricky?'

'He is my boyfriend.' She covered her face, looking convincingly ashamed.

'I've seen the police, you know. Tell him that. They could bust him just like that. You tell him.'

'I knew he had done something. He was very quiet this morning, and I knew he had done something bad to you. I made him tell me. He is big and jealous, but I can make him tell me things. *Signore* forgive me. He saw us talk yesterday.'

As Elliot watched, a tear slid into view. Her hand appeared and smeared it away, leaving a shiny patch. This moved him. He was not implacable.

'You all right?'

'Yes.'

'What do you want?'

The prospect of unburdening herself had a restorative effect. She sniffed and straightened her hair. Here was a man, thought Carmina Maria Liolla, with the power over *things*, and he had come of his own free will to listen to her. She would reach out to him gradually, make him feel her problems, embrace them, carry them away. She had a right to do this. Even if it dragged him down. It was her idea of human responsibility.

'There is no reason, Mr Elliot, why you should help me. I know it. I am nobody to you. You owe me nothing. You hardly know Carmina Maria Liolla enough to smile at her in the street. If you give to me, you do not know how much more I will ask of you. I could ask and ask until you are ruined. This can happen, even between strangers.'

Elliot knew it. She didn't need to tell him about the dangers of involvement. Shit, he could feel it in his bones.

'What I am is of my own making,' said Carmina Maria Liolla.

'Your family was poor,' said Elliot. 'That's not easy for anyone. I know. My family was working class.' For some reason he was feeling tender towards her.

'I am fit and young, but I have got tied down. I am twenty-eight, Mr Elliot, but I feel tired. I see myself in the mirror and I look like someone else. I could have done much. This makes me feel guilty. I have wronged myself, Mr Elliot. Do you see?'

'Sure, it's very common,' said Elliot, almost inaudibly.

'I have wronged myself. I have been too long here, wasting. Ricky wants to marry me. He even has a ring, but I will not put it on. He can be nice, but sometimes he is very bad, and anyway I am too much tied down. I want to get free so badly, but I need help, and nobody will help me. Nobody.'

The proximity of a specific request was slowly dissolving Elliot's mood of tenderness. He watched her through the trellis and waited for her to spit it out.

'Have you heard of the grey market?' she asked.

'I understand the term.'

'I have $500 saved. I want you to buy me a ticket to Italy for $500 on the grey market. I have no more money. I have no other chance to leave. If I do not go . . . I will be ruined.'

She waited for his reply, banking on it.

It didn't take Elliot long. 'I can't do that,' he said.

Her complexion paled significantly. Elliot could see white throb visibly across the cheek. Her fingers were at the grille.

'You will not help me?'

'I can't.'

'You won't.'

'If you like. What you're asking me to do is illegal. The grey market is only a fashionable term for company fraud. It's a crime, Carmina. If I was caught, I could go to jail. That's *jail*. Do you want me to go to jail?'

'No, Mr Elliot, no, but you wouldn't go to jail. You could do it so no one ever caught you. With your computer. I know you could.' She was getting excited again. 'There are empty seats on all the planes. Who will care if one more seat is filled? And if the airline loses the cost of a seat, they can cope. Mr Elliot, I have nothing! It is two years since my *mamma* died. It was the end for me. I loved this country when we came here. I no longer love this country. I just want to go home to Valese. That is all, for me and my little Carla.'

'Who is Carla?'

'She is Carla Maria Liolla. My daughter, my baby.'

'Oh.'

'It is for her too. For Carla. Do you have children, Mr Elliot?'

'Yes.'

'Then you will know what it is to fight for the life of a child. And Ricky. He is the father. Mr Elliot, sometimes . . . sometimes I think he is a bit mad. You know? Not right in the head. He hits me. I have not told this to a soul, but I will tell you.' Elliot was beginning to tire of all these disclosures. She was going too far. 'He hits me, like this!' And she actually made a fierce face and demonstrated, hitting the air.

'Please,' Elliot said. He was finished with this.

'And not only that. When it comes to the bed . . . he can be bad. He makes me do things to him. Dirty things. I would not talk of them, but this is what I put up with, Mr Elliot. He hits me, and I am always praying for help, but . . . nothing. Nothing! You don't know! You don't . . .'

'Stop it!' shouted Elliot.

'Mercy! Please! Mercy!'

'Stop it! Leave him if he hits you. Leave him. Help yourself. God!' Elliot hated these sorts of stories. They disgusted him.

'Where can I go? I have no skills, just like my *mamma*. I am buried alive, Mr Elliot. I taste the dirt in my mouth. And Carla. It is the same for her.'

'I can't do what you want,' said Elliot. 'Someone would find out, then we would all be in trouble. That way nobody wins. It's crazy to even suggest it. And anyway – God! – we don't even know each other! We're complete strangers. But you want me to risk my job – everything. I can't . . . I can't do that. Let me give you some advice, Carmina. Don't ask people to do these sorts of things. Just don't!'

For a moment there was silence, then Carmina Maria Liolla broke from the confessional and ran across the altar towards the door. Elliot jumped out to see her running. He called after her. She was shaking her head in grief, as if saying 'No! No! No!'

Clark McConachie had several things to say. 'Get this – the cue ball sitting on the back cush, OK, the red over the middle pocket, a possible straight pot, and the spot ball down the other end. What's he gonna do now? Just looking at it, what's he gonna do now? Leo? You tell me.'

'What?'

'Tell me, what's he gonna do now?'

'Who?' Elliot was clutching coffee and writing, on a flight sheet, ECONOTRAVEL backwards.

'The champ! The champ, Leo!' The champ was McConachie's term of endearment for that ancestral figure who had given his line credence.

'Shoot?' offered a listless Elliot.

'Shoot what? Will he take the straight pot or what?

'Never the straight pot, Clark.'

'Damn right. He never took a straight pot in his life. Get this, he chalked up, sighted that deadeye, bent low, *real* low with the cleft of his chin running above the cue like it did, and belted one down. Boy oh boy, there was a terrific side on it. The ball was heading south, but it was spinning west all the way – just skidding, y'know – until it touched the spot ball, then cut left, off two walls, took the cannon, and sank the red. Pow! The spot ball came back up the table, met the cue ball for the *second* time, then rolled into the top corner as easy as you like. That put him in the finals. He won it. Within the year he was national champion.' McConachie took a swallow of coffee, then went for a leak. When he came back, he sat on the corner of Elliot's desk.

'How's Jeanie?'

'No change.'

'How long is it since she's talked to you now?'

'Uh, two weeks, not counting the odd thing.'

'Like what?'

'*My my*, stuff like that.'

'Is that right? So . . . how long since you talked to her?'

Elliot didn't raise his head from the flight sheet.

'You gotta be careful about this sort of situation,' said Clark, brushing lint off his corduroy. 'I went through something like it with Ruth. *Non communicado*, y'know. It got so bad we weren't saying anything at all to each other. Ruth got in a guidance counsellor. She reckoned that, although we seemed so quiet, inside, *inside*, we were really crying out for help.'

'It's nothing like that.'

'Oh we still had, y'know, affections for each other, but boy oh boy . . .'

'Right. What have you got on TWA's Christmas runs? I . . . can't find them . . . Clark?' Elliot looked up from his search, and McConachie saw for the first time the strain on his colleague's face.

'Yeah, OK,' said McConachie. 'I've got them.'

'Good. Can I have them. Confirmations. All of them.'

'OK, Leo,' McConachie rose from Elliot's desk, perturbed, his eye caught by Elliot's doodlings: LEVARTONOCE.

*

There was another woman with a part to play. Her name was Maureen Hogan. She was a full-time antisocial busybody, and a good one.

The view from her front-room window took in a street, other houses facing hers, several lamp-posts, distant hills rising from orchard land, a sky traversed by planes, birds, clouds, frisbees and other projectiles, and a church car park. Through this wonderful window she saw things.

Maureen Hogan knew everybody. She was married to a champion potholer and was a martyr to varicose veins.

'Maureen!' It was her husband calling. 'I'm stuck, love!'

She turned from her permanent post at the window and hurried distractedly towards the loo, from whence the voice had echoed.

Ricky Stagazzo. Unshaved. Five feet nine inches. Stocky. Built like . . . well, just built. Seated in an armchair beneath the concertina pattern of a row of *The Outdoorsman*. If not blind with hurt and jealousy, then at least severely short-sighted.

She had been due home for two hours, and yet the sun had set, he'd eaten beans out of a can, the milk truck had just gone past, which meant it was after 8.30 p.m., he'd fed the child semolina and put her down for the night, and still she wasn't home.

But the time would come. He'd hear her shoes clip on the landing, the pause as she looked for a key. He'd jump up and hit off the light. The door would open, he'd throw on the light and she would be blinded for a moment, he'd walk towards her, she would drop her bag and step backwards one or two steps, knowing what was coming, he would probably catch her in the region of her jaw or the side of her face, hard enough so that his big hand hurt the following day, she would go down on her knees, then fall to her side, he'd want to hit her again, but the remorse that always arose would take hold and stop him from doing so. . . . She would lie that way for a while, silent, and he'd go into the bathroom, lock the door, and punch the tiled wall until he was worn out. Not a word would be said again for couple of days.

He loved her like crazy.

He sat in his armchair wondering if there was any other way of handling things. There wasn't any other way.

When Carmina Maria Liolla arrived home at 10 p.m. (after going to see *Dr Zhivago*) she paused on the landing to find her key. Then she opened the door. It was dark. The lights were off. This made her nervous. She called, 'Ricky?' The lights came on with terrible quickness. She didn't see it coming. She was suddenly on the floor and then she stopped remembering.

Elliot waited at the lights for a green, the Corona humming evenly. Idiot, he thought. Nitwit. He'd always known he wasn't designed for involvement. His own life had enough hassles. Hadn't he often averted certain disaster with a practised side-step? What about the time Clark had wanted Elliot to join him in a ludicrous deal importing South American mohair. He'd refused, and the exchange rate had soared the next day. And then there was his impartiality during the Springbok saga, when he had been an eye in the storm. Millie Delahunty at the agency had wandered around with her eye swollen shut and hated the world for two weeks, so that's where *stance* got you. Some people were only too keen to destroy themselves. Elliot? Well, he loved life.

The pedestrian buzzer went. A terrifically big woman whom he knew supported Social Credit, because he'd heard her saying so somewhere, set off across the long diagonal, wobbling in the void between arrested engines. Elliot was glad at least for the weekend. It would take him, however, until Saturday night, which was still six hours away, to truly come down. This was the usual pattern. Until then he would be victim to the flashbacks, previews and interruptions that were the habits of a brain shot through, forty times, by the working hour. Elliot pinched his groin. He was hurting to relieve himself. The lights changed and he buried his foot, heading, perhaps unconsciously, towards the sea.

His bladder had been problematic for years now – since his twenties, in fact, when he'd been stamped on during a social game of ten-a-side that had turned vicious. He'd been trapped in the maul, first man down, and as the forwards crashed in he felt a tremendous blow and lost consciousness. His 'waterworks', as the doctor called them, were to this day 'erratic'. The result was that he always had to be conscious to a fantastic degree, of where the toilets where. In a strange building he compulsively noted their whereabouts, and at the movies he sat near the back. His awareness was gradually perfected. McConachie, never lacking, called him a piss artist. It scared Elliot, however, to think he might one day be caught out in public. He pinched his groin once more.

His particular mission this Saturday afternoon, clear but not cloudless, was to pick up Bridgit from netball. She would be flushed and talkative after her game. A friend would be with her. 'Can you give Janice a lift home, Dad?' she would ask. Elliot was not clairvoyant, merely well rehearsed. He took full hold of his crutch, squeezing penis between thumb and forefinger, and observed the flashing scenery, just as assured with one hand on the wheel. He knew he was not free to piss himself this day. Grown men put one foot in the madhouse when they allowed that to happen.

Having reached the Parade, he parked the car on the Mercury Bay weed skirting the foreshore, and strode into the surf club toilets. His slash was almost a spiritual experience after the long minutes of retention. He emerged cheerfully, doing up his flies. Little had pleased him at all over the last couple of days, but he was happy when he was pissing.

Pausing to watch a freestyler far out punch the living daylights out of a calm ocean, his attention was caught by a big sign advertising 'The Maze'. Just the sight of it deflated his improved humour. He remembered that Carmina Maria Liolla worked at the maze.

The maze was just for fun. It had once been the beach's changing sheds, but someone with enterprise had ripped off the roof, kept the external walls, and developed a movable system of internal passageways no-exits, false starts, and fruitless journeys. For a dollar you could enter at one end and, depending on your luck, eventually emerge. Elliot had been through it once shortly after it opened a couple of years earlier. He'd taken the children in with him. It was their last year of being happy to do things with him. They were lost for a long time, became separated, joined up again in different combinations, and then panicked after someone screamed. It was fun. There was a platform high up in one corner. From time to time a controller would appear there to direct a stranded soul, turn by turn, out of the baffling labyrinth. It was a reasonable form of punishment, that maze, and the kids loved it.

There were two doors into the place. One led to the controller's tower, and the other led to the ticket-seller and the maze itself. The door to the maze was open, and Elliot could just see a young girl going in, stopping at the ticket counter, and digging into a satchel. He walked to his car, started it, and edged forward to the entrance of the maze. The young girl handed over a note, and in reply a forearm swiftly appeared from the ticket counter presenting ticket and change. Elliot, leaning over the passenger seat, immediately identified the forearm as female, joined the dots, and could virtually see Carmina Maria Liolla through the wall of the ticket booth. It seemed unjust that with all the universe's infinite variety one aspect of it should be so prevalent. She was so entrenched in his mind that everyday reality felt unnecessary, even wrong. He kept watching, wanting to see more of her and not wanting to. But it would involve waiting for another customer, and then he'd only get a second glimpse of forearm. Ambivalently, he put the car in gear. He needed to get out of here. He needed a clean conscience. He needed *more* than this. He spun the car around and headed back downtown, determined not to look into the rear-view mirror and failing twice.

His daughter needed a lift. Idiot, he thought.

*

After dropping off Janice, a withdrawn Elliot and a yackety Bridgit drove for home. Bridgit had ripped some skin off her knee. She was holding some gauze on it and re-enacting the game, using the word 'bitch' a lot, with no objection from Elliot.

'She's a good player, all right, but if that bitch crosses me next week I'll flounce her.' This *flounce* thing was new with her. Bridgit was fourteen.

Elliot was gazing across the river at the Cook Memorial, site of the Captain's first landing. The three-cornered hat, the wig, the britches, that English nose for trouble.

'She doesn't even keep to her zone! Her zone!'

It was people like Cook who really opened up the travel business, really blew it wide open, thought Elliot.

'If she puts one foot in the circle, she's *dead*!'

Arriving home, Elliot found his wife out on the back lawn, sitting in a deck chair, clutching what seemed to be a tall gin and tonic. She looked like she had been crying for some time, which in fact she had.

'Jeanie?'

She turned her eyes toward him, red bands underneath, creases filled with moisture.

'I wanted to talk to you first. I wanted to give you a chance, before . . . before . . .' Her voice was slurred.

'Before what, Jeanie?'

'Before I took you apart with my bare hands,' she said brokenly. Elliot paused in his confusion to consider how violent his family was becoming. Jeanie took a pull on the gin and tonic, choking back her tears.

'What is it? What are you talking about? What?'

'CARMINA MARIA LIOLLA! THAT'S WHAT! THAT'S WHAT, LEO! THAT . . . THAT WOP SLUT!'

Elliot turned and headed indoors. He was looking for a room with a stout lock on it. Jeanie was behind him, gin in hand, ferocious and hurt, a dangerous combination.

'I don't care that you screwed her! TWICE! I don't care about

279

that! It's the fact you couldn't tell me about it! Leo? We never talk! Come back here!'

Elliot rushed down the hall and into the bathroom. Bridgit was sitting on the bath daubing her wounded knee with Mercurachrome. Elliot slammed the door shut and locked it, breathing heavily. There was a crash of fists against the door and Jeanie's muted voice pleading, 'Leo! Don't do this! Leo?'

Bridgit looked up at her father. 'What's going on?' Elliot shrugged. The sound of fists on the door was repeated.

'Hadn't you better let her in?'

Elliot shook his head. 'No.'

'Why not?' asked Bridgit.

'Your mother wants to flounce me,' said Elliot.

'LEO!'

There were times, weren't there, when it was OK just to cry?

Twenty minutes later, Jeanie's determined voice could still be heard.

'I can wait here all day if I have to, Leo'.

Elliot had let his daughter out the tiny bathroom window high up on the wall. She had stood on his shoulders and wriggled through. A touch of blood from her knee spotted the white ledge. He was under siege, alone.

'Anyway, I know most of the details, Leo. And I don't see how you could have done it. I just don't see. My God, you did it in a confessional. Don't you realize? Don't you realize what you've done? That is the house of God. God, Leo. Maureen Hogan saw you both go in. She cried over the telephone when she had to tell me, Leo. At first I wouldn't believe such . . . such an *evil* thing could happen. I wanted to wait until I could talk to you. But then, when I saw your face . . . when I saw it, I knew it *was* true. God. You must hate me so much.'

Elliot could hear the clink of ice in a glass, evidence of her determination to get smashed. There would be no reasoning with her when she was like this, and the vast amount of explaining he was overdue for would be too humiliating just now. He sat in silence, his back against the door, like her, in strange symmetry.

'Once we could talk, Leo,' said Jeanie, and soon she began to snore.

Elliot eased the door open. Jeanie's weight was against it. He lowered her smoothly until her head dropped the last few inches on to the floor with a thump. The few remaining ice cubes slid from the glass she was clutching to her chest and glissaded into the chink of her breastbone. She looked hopelessly beautiful then. Her mouth hung open, and her neck stretched out like that of dead swan. She was more serene, thought Elliot, than he could ever remember. He bent over and tried to lift his wife. They say a corpse is twice as heavy as a living body, he remembered. Struggling to get her upright, he used the doorway, the wall, his thighs and the muscles in the small of his back, as well as a set of principles concerning leverage that he was only just discovering. Then, once she was unnaturally up, he let her go, and she fell smack-dab on his waiting back. He reached behind, grabbed her thighs, stood up, and headed for the bedroom.

'Hey, what's wrong with Mum?' It was Simon, standing behind him, eating an apple. Elliot stopped.

'Your mother is under the weather.'

'She pissed?'

'In a manner of speaking.'

'Oh. She gonna be all right, Dad?' Simon's tone indicated genuine concern Elliot sensed it. He paused to look at his son. A spitting image. Skinny legs too. He remembered he loved him.

'She's gonna be fine.'

'That's good,' Simon smiled. He had bad teeth. Awkward about this unusual contact with his father, he averted his face to bite his apple.

Elliot returned to his primary task, which was putting a drunk wife to bed. And when he had achieved this, and she slept the sleep of the truly blottoed, he went out to look for the woman who was the real epicentre of his troubles.

*

Leo Elliot, travel agent, was panicking.

The normal components of his life, which he'd always taken for granted simply refused to *hang in there*. He realized that his old covenants with the world were in need of renegotiation. Someone he'd lost that certain sense of himself that made him Leo Elliot and also made him reliable but shallow. In other words, he was gradually getting the picture.

He was presently heading, at over sixty kilometres per hour, towards the twenty-four hour cash machine downtown, rattling his car into the corners and darting over the centre line.

When he reached the bank, after several near accidents, he emerged from his car, clutching his Anytime Card and smelling rubber.

He punched out five hundred dollars from the machine. Five scarlet bills. And this might have been a moment when the old Elliot could have reasserted himself, feeling something so 'real' in his hand, but, no, he put the money in his pocket and walked back to his car.

Jeanie, lying pinkly on her face, surfaced through fathoms of dreams to find she was still drunk, but not too drunk to realize she was a desperate woman. Desperate. And lonely. And angry. And wronged somehow. How? The details slowly returned.

But deep down that wasn't all. There was more. As a girl, she'd always set her sights high, but she'd gradually lowered them over the last decade, without even acknowledging it. So things had rolled on artificially, and because no one had seen the damage, the repairs were waived. Instead of action there was silence. Other couples were busy hanging out their dirty washing, but all she and Elliot managed to hang out was their clean stuff. And when the cracks in the walls she had built around herself really began to open, she discovered that all the yoga manuals in the world couldn't paper over them.

She went to the cupboard and pulled down a vanity case and a soft leather bag from the top shelf.

'You off somewhere, Mum?' It was Simon, standing at the door, eating a Chesdale triangle.

'Yes,' replied Jeanie. 'I'm leaving your father.'

'Oh,' said Simon, noticing that his mother was still unstable on her feet. 'Can I come too?'

'If you want to.'

Simon watched his mother bunch up some pantihose and attempt to throw them into the bag, missing by a wide margin. Then he watched her unpin the Balinese wall-hanging suspended above the bed.

'What about Bridgit?' he asked.

'Will you ask her for me, please?'

'OK.'

Simon went and asked Bridgit. She was cutting out some new pictures from *Vogue* for her wall. He returned.

'She said she might as well come too.'

Jeanie was by then going through her handbag.

'How will we go to school?' asked Simon. He was trying to sound older than fifteen, perhaps eighteen.

'I don't know, Simon,' Jeanie replied. 'I only just thought of this a few minutes ago.'

'Maybe we could take Monday off, Bridgit and me?'

Jeanie couldn't get her compact open. She worked on it, tried levering it open with the corner of the bed, and then started to cry.

'Maybe we won't though,' said Simon. 'It doesn't matter. Hell, what's a day? It doesn't matter, does it Mum?' He tried not to look at his mother; he didn't like to see adults when they were like this.

The ancient passage into Italy from the north, over the snowy Pennine Alps via the Great St Bernard Pass, has always been a tricky one. Crevices, chasms, holes masked by carpet snow . . . and that's where the dogs came in. Named after the pass, they have been big and fluffy and irrepressible since the seventeenth century, bounding over the white wastes to rescue the lost traveller. So what motivates these creatures? Is it bred into them, this canine altruism that sends them burrowing through the freezing snow towards the muffled beat of a pulsing heart? It can't be the paltry rewards of din-dins or a warm kennel to sleep in, as these are every dog's dues, and in any case, no one is cynical about St Bernards. The only other conclusion is that it's purely a matter of self-image, that the St Bernard considers itself, at the end of the day, basically a *nice dog*, a decent beast, which means more to it than anything else. And refusing to perform its duties would mean submitting to a new image – becoming a *bad dog*. A St Bernard could never bear this.

Elliot was bad-dogging it down to the maze.

Jumbled images flashed through his mind: confessionals, scars, skinny legs, sparrows, aircraft, Bridgit's heels disappearing through the window, Jeanie's mouth, angels, Clark McConachie's comical head turning to intone, 'Boy oh boy!', a good portion of his recent life.

The traffic was thin. A siren from a fire engine rose and faded as it shot the other way, making Elliot briefly wonder whose letterbox was burning down now.

He reached the maze and parallel-parked in an angle-parking zone. Two adolescents in a car, up to hanky-panky, noticed and then ignored him. There was no activity around the maze. Carmina was not in her ticket box. Before he knew it, Elliot was walking into it.

Not too far away, the bang-bang-bang of hammer on wood could be heard. Behind the hammer was undoubtedly Carmina Maria Liolla. Elliot was bent on finding her. It had to do with the absolution she owed him. He moved down the first passageway, dedicated to his task, clutching his money. If he could get this over with efficiently, there was still a chance that his life could be kept intact.

Elliot's heart fluttered. 'Down boy.' He turned the corner aisle of another long passage, his fingers running along the walls. If he could get back before Jeanie came to, what a smile he'd give her! If he could subdue his guilt over this Italian affair – for it was guilt that was afflicting him most – things would soon improve. And a winning smile would only be the start. Good dog. Pant, pant.

The second passageway was heading slightly away from the hammer's banging, but so long as it turned left at its end it should take him to Carmina.

It did turn left, and reaching a fork, Elliot didn't hesitate in turning left again and walking straight past further turns on both sides. But somehow the banging was now behind him. He stopped, listened. *Bang-bang-bang*. 'Carmina!' he called out. The hammering stopped. The maze was open to the sky, and Elliot looked into a faultless blue rectangle. 'Carmina!' But nothing. 'It's Leo Elliot! Carmina!' His shouts, echoing a little, bounced back at him, '. . . iotiotiot . . . inainaina . . .' Still no reply. Best do something quick. He backtracked, or attempted to backtrack, taking two consecutive rights, using the only visible landmark – the observation platform up high, which, he recalled, was somewhere near the entrance. He then started to run down the passageways, an action that if he'd been more himself, would have seemed a hopeless way to try to beat a maze; but he wasn't himself, and he ran this way and that way, coming close to the platform several times but never reaching it – the passageway would either be cut short in a dead end or swing away at the last minute when he was sure he was there. So then he slowed to a walk to catch his breath, hoping not to repeat passageways, and tried taking a route that was against his better judgement. And for a time he did seem to be reaching one side of the platform, but then the passageway turned towards the centre and then to the right, and as Elliot turned the corner he couldn't let himself see the dead end that faced him. He turned his back on it – panic – and was taking his second step away when he stopped, rived with surprise, and grabbed at his chest to still the sparrows that were oddly flying out of his heart. 'Uh-oh,' said Elliot. He smiled. His head grew light. The pain in his chest was severe. He didn't want this. Death would make him miserable. The pain held. It neither increased nor went away; sharp and deep, it held on and refused to release him. And then he heard his name, perhaps his last straggling echo coming back to him. He turned his head, and above, on the observation platform, he saw two distant faces, a bright Madonna and child. It was Carmina. The pain held, then began to ease, releasing him slowly.

Her hair, unhitched, billowed in the breeze. The child extended one arm towards Carmina's neck and gazed at him. Elliot started to breathe again, elevated by the sight of her, his old heart settling back into its task. In this new life, he felt, there was light at the end of the tunnel.

Although twenty or so metres away, Carmina could clearly read the multiple anxieties on Elliot's face. He seemed very small – tiny in fact. His small face shone, and one hand was on the collar of that silly safari suit. He stood, slightly hunched, one thin partition separating him from the entrance.

'Are you all right, Mr Elliot?' she called.

'Carmina! Carmina! where have you been?'

'Here, *Signore*. I have been here.'

'Why didn't you answer me? When I called?'

'I was afraid.'

'What?'

'I was afraid, *Signore*!'

'Afraid? Why?'

'I don't know.'

'Carmina. I've got something for you.'

'What, Mr Elliot?'

Elliot pulled the notes from his pocket. Scarlet. She could see them. 'Five hundred dollars!' he called, 'For you. For your ticket home. To Italy.'

'Oh Mr Elliot. Oh *Signore*,' Carmina Maria Liolla said.

'Five hundred. It will be enough. With what you have already.'

'Please,' she said, bowing her head.

'What is it?' Elliot wanted her to have the money. No, not quite. He *needed* her to. It was in his mind to throw it towards her. For, ironically, it had boiled down to this.

'Oh Mr Elliot. No,' she said.

'What?'

Carmina Maria Liolla raised her hand in the air, and there – a symbol of fate's sneakiness – was a silver ring twinkling on her third finger.

'He has asked me to marry him. I gave up on you, Mr Elliot. I did. Now it is too late. It is too late, *Signore*. Oh Mr Elliot!'

She was crying. Elliot was thinking rapidly.

'All right,' he said. 'I'll get you a ticket. No, leave it to me now. I'll get you a ticket. You and the baby. All right? Do you hear me? How could you marry him? You can't. He hits you. Think, Carmina. Think. Please. OK? I'll get the ticket. Please,' he said, and finally, 'Please, Carmina.'

'It is too late.'

Then it came out. 'Think of me!'

'Oh Mr Elliot. Why are you like this? First you will not help, and now *you* come to *me*. But you are not good to Carmina Maria Liolla either way. I must look after myself. My daughter shall have a father. And if he is a hard man, then at least I will have my ticket to heaven. You must go away, Mr Elliot. You bring me suffering. I am sorry. You can bring me no good. Please leave us alone.'

She was gone before Elliot realized, disappearing like a figment. She didn't even give him directions.

A little girl skipped cheerily down one passageway after another, content, it would seem, to be lost for ever. When she stumbled upon a wasted-looking travel agent standing before a dead end, she stopped and smiled at him. When he did not return the smile, and she realized his face was a bit scary, she hurriedly spun around and skipped away.

For Elliot, not smiling was the result of a profound failure of Plans A to Z. After standing for a bit longer, he slid down a wall until he was sitting down, his legs splayed. The notes he'd held unfolded from his hand in the breeze, tumbling in the sunlight.

Filling his lungs ambivalently, he looked up into a sparrowless sky. It was a pretty picture, yet he felt nothing. He wanted rest. Later, if there was time, he might sit up on his haunches and perhaps even slaver a bit – he'd enjoy that, submitting to an old doggie urge he'd never understood. And then, if it was dark enough, maybe he'd bay at the moon too. He would play it by ear. When you are deeper in a maze than life is deep in *troubles*, you can play it by ear. Elliot thought this as his pants warmed around his crotch and through the darkening fabric a small puddle spread like silver foil across the ground.

DENISE NEUHAUS

———

The Crispens

'The number to the theatre is by the telephone,' said Mother, glancing at me in the mirror. I was lying on my stomach on the bed, feet in the air. She put on more lipstick, her mouth spread wide. Then she pressed her lips onto a folded Kleenex, leaving behind a dark pink kiss. I knew this was the way to put on lipstick. I had read about it in *Seventeen Magazine*. '*Learning to put on lipstick takes patience and practice.*'

My young womanhood with its endless evenings of practice loomed far away. I was only twelve; I could not wear lipstick.

I jiggled my feet. What did people think about my mother when they saw her dressed up? Was she charming and cultivated? Did men admire her? Did they think that my father had a lovely wife? Maybe they could tell that she usually didn't wear make-up, that she went around in faded green cotton slacks and thong sandals. Maybe they thought, *Just somebody's wife. Somebody's old housewife. Somebody's old worn-out housewife trying to dress up and look good.*

My mother had once been young and beautiful; I had seen photographs of her, with a full skirt and three-quarter-length gloves and a hat like a plate. Her hair was golden brown. That was before she married my father and had us.

She had told my sister and me, in the casual and significant tone she used for such announcements, 'The Crispens have invited me to the theatre next Saturday,' and I knew she did not mean the movies. When she went out with the Crispens, it was always somewhere out of the ordinary. She was sitting on our orange vinyl sofa, crocheting. She crocheted endlessly, blankets which she called 'Afghans' and pillow covers, all of ugly colours, and all of which quickly turned dingy and stretched out of shape.

Her usual tone was threatening. *I am going to play bridge at Mrs Ashland's this Saturday and if you kids smoke in this house or do ANYTHING I swear to God.*

She had never talked about the theatre before, but I knew that I was supposed to pretend that this was something she did all the time. I always tried to fulfil these silent demands. I could not bear to see her diminished, to suffer her haughty stare, her determined nonchalance, her raised eyebrows that would say, *And what is so remarkable about my going to the theatre?* Her affectations embrassed me; I wanted to protect her from the poverty of her life.

I said, 'Oh,' trying to sound slightly bored, but my sister was only six and, as usual, didn't pick up the hint. 'You mean to see a movie?'

I snorted contemptuously. 'Dummy. The *theatre*. Not the movies. *God*, Leslie.' She immediately started to sulk. Mother didn't look up from her crocheting and I pressed my advantage. 'God,' I said, disgusted by her hopeless ignorance, 'don't you know anything?'

'Now, now,' said Mother softly, as if appealing to my mature self who was compassionate toward the handicapped, the deficient, the backward of this world. She glanced at me conspiratorially: she and I knew what the theatre was; Leslie was just an ignorant kid. I shouldn't tease Leslie; she was just a stupid, ignorant kid.

Leslie began automatically to whine. Poor Leslie. She would always be literal-minded, obtuse, arrested in childhood. She would never learn the pretension of adults. She would never learn to drink coffee or alcohol or eat with her knife in her left hand or drop names without appearing to. She would never grow out of saying 'brung' instead of 'brought'. She would stay happily in the phases others outgrew, keeping her toy animals into high school, only to replace them with a collection of turtles, a tank of guppies, stray kittens. Her twenties she would spend working in a pet shop, cleaning animal cages. She would be offered promotions to the front part of the shop, and she would always refuse; she would be happy only when spared from having to talk to human beings.

She was still whining in the way we knew meant, *Tell me what I didn't understand. How am I supposed to know what you're talking about?* Mother interrupted her. She was going to have to rely on us kids to behave ourselves, she said. With our father overseas, and the theatre downtown, she would need to know that we could handle anything that came up. *Anything that came up.* What could possibly come up? Once Leslie had swallowed a penny. My mother called the doctor, but he said she didn't have to go to the hospital. In the summer, I sometimes stepped on a rusty nail or pulled an arm hastily through the barbed wire fence behind our house, and would run home, squeezing the split flesh until the beads of blood swelled and broke. I would have to get a tetanus shot at the doctor's.

These things could not happen so late at night. Leslie would go to bed, my brother and I would watch TV. Of course there were other, unspecified, possibilities: a fire, an obscene phone call, knocks on the door, burglars, *accidents*. These weren't, however, what she meant.

'I'm counting on you kids,' she said. This was her generic warning, but I knew she was talking to me. I was always the one in trouble, and paradoxically, the one she assumed would be responsible if something happened, an accident, a fire. Already she had given up on my brother, who was too passive to get in trouble, except with me, or to do anything about it when it arose.

Leslie was still mad, her eyes small and hard, her breathing rapid and tense, her mouth opening and closing. She clinched her fists, ready to throw a tantrum. She hated being the stupid one, the one who never understood. She always would, too. At sixteen, at twenty-five, at thirty, Leslie was still the same. During my visits home, we – Mother and I – would shake our heads and roll our eyes over Leslie's howlers and it would drive her mad. *God, Leslie!*

It was only much later that I felt ashamed and angry thinking of this, the damage my collaboration wrought.

We lived in the very last suburb. Behind our fence was a creek and then the barbed wire, and a field larger than our entire neighbourhood with hundreds of cows grazing on it. Down the highway, past the houses, there were woods, and a lake; the kids in the suburb built tree-forts there to hang out in and drink beer and smoke pot after school. We lived about an hour's drive from downtown and I had been there maybe three or four times in my entire life.

I spent the week trying to imagine what the theatre would be like. I had been to the ballet once, in elementary school, on a field trip. We went downtown in a school bus. The boys wore clip-on bow ties and the girls lace socks and patent leather shoes. On the end of each row sat a teacher or somebody's mother to chaperone us. They wouldn't let us get up at intermission. The stage was far away. One girl had a little pair of binoculars and showed off so much that everybody was whispering and trying to ask her for a turn and the teacher took them away.

I thought that the theatre would be small, chairs crowded intimately around the stage. Everything would be black. The set would be sparse. The play would be intellectual – something about ideas – with allusions to books that only cultured people would understand. My theatre was a sort of garret out of *La Bohème*, which my mother had seen with the Crispens, combined with the dark mystery of a night club. Because I thought of the Crispens as European, I elevated them from being merely rich and sophisticated; I made them bohemian.

Mrs Crispen was not European but I would forget that. Getting married to Mr Crispen had transformed her. I knew I was not supposed to mention anything about Mrs Crispen's former life, and this was not difficult. She was a new being.

Mrs Crispen's name used to be Mrs Jackson; she had been our neighbour and she had had three children. She was divorced and a secretary, the only working woman anybody knew. All the neighbours talked about her and the children, who were never called in at dark, and were allowed to eat anything they wanted and stay up as late as they liked. She wore gold sandals and velour jumpsuits when she was at home. She both fascinated and frightened me. The word *divorcee* suggested a series of men, excessive drinking, parties; things as far from my mother's life as could be imagined.

Yet, my mother liked Mrs Crispen and defended her to anyone who gossiped about her. When she married Mr Crispen, Mrs Crispen quit her job and sent her children to live with their father in Arizona.

Later, Mother would tell me that the children were sent to boarding school. This made me wildly envious; I imagined boarding school to be where girls learn to speak French and waltz and arrange flowers and give dinner parties. But Mother said it wasn't like that; it was a school for 'problem' children.

Mother only went out with the Crispens when my father was away. This seemed perfectly natural. My mother's other, stifled self belonged to the Crispens. Their charmed life was the one Mother would have led had she not married my father. I pictured her with some other man, who remained dim but generally resembled Mr Crispen, driving around in the Crispens' Jaguar, to one art gallery after another, from a French restaurant to the opera.

Nobody drove foreign cars then, and I thought it daring. Foreign cars were considered slightly eccentric, almost effeminate, like soccer, imported beer, a man carrying a bag.

Why did I assume that my mother's true life was this? As she put perfume behind her ears and on her wrist, I rolled over on my back and read the instructions on the package of ultra-sheer stockings she had bought. They were supposed to be rolled on, not pulled.

She came over and held out her hand for the package. She was wearing a new bra with no straps and her old beige slip. Under the slip she had a girdle on. Even though she was as skinny as a rail, her stomach stuck out like a shelf from having children.

She sat down next to me and I watched her roll a stocking up each leg. As the stocking unrolled, the millions of tiny holes on her calves became invisible and her knees, which were really bony like mine, were pressed into smoothness. I knew her legs by heart: the needle-thin varicose veins behind one knee, which she got when she was pregnant, her faint birth mark, the pale mole on the back of her right thigh. She had dry skin and let me put lotion on her sometimes after her bath. I particularly liked to slather it all over the cracks in her heels, and watch it soak in, like dry, cracked ground filling with sudden rain.

She stepped into her dress and let me zip her. Then she picked up the black beaded bag she had had ever since I could remember and an embroidered shawl she had borrowed for the evening. She looked into the mirror a last time. She pulled on the curled tendrils of hair in front of each ear and patted the teased-up part on top.

I had watched her make her dress. I came home from school the day after she told us she was going to the theatre, and on the bed was a Vogue Original Design pattern and a folded square of black crêpe de chine. I flung the material open, wrapped it around me and examined the pattern. I thought I would die if I did not someday have that dress. I was already taller than Mother, and larger-boned, but just as thin and I knew it would make me look perfect.

It had no shoulders, but fell from the neck by a strip of rhinestones. It wrapped and twisted and had a slit in the back. It was a mini-dress and had cost $7.50 instead of the usual $1.95 because it was an original design.

I stared at the pattern envelope. I couldn't bring myself to open it and look at the instructions. I couldn't believe that dress could be cut out and sewn like a regular dress on my mother's Singer. It was a dress from a Paris boutique. English words could not describe that dress. I almost didn't want my mother to make it; I

was afraid that she would ruin it, I couldn't bear the disappointment.

I was taking Home Economics and Mother took me material-
shopping when I was to start a new project. I always left her at
the broadcloth table and walked among the bolts of silk and
satin. I loved the shiniest and brightest; the sheer, the swirling;
taffeta, chiffon with sequins, dyed fur. Mother would come fetch
me. *That's not very practical, dear. You can't machine-wash silk. Don't
you think that's an awfully large print for a skirt? Wouldn't you rather
have dotted Swiss?*

I didn't want dotted Swiss. Or corduroy or broadcloth. Or a
machine-washable skirt with a small flowered print. I wanted
black and glitter and hot pink and a fake tiger-skin cape.

She would pull me over to the pattern counter. *I am NOT
paying $5 a yard for something you can't even put in the washing
machine for you to learn how to sew.* We would sit on the high stools,
Mother flipping summarily through the pattern books. I would
hardly be through the first section before she would be through
every book they had.

She would urge me on. *You don't really want that Empire waist,
do you? I am NOT going to set those sleeves in for you.* But, I wouldn't
be looking at the dress. I was looking at the way the whole
picture made me feel: the way the model looked, and her hair
and jewellery, the way she tossed her skirt and glanced over
one shoulder. How did they look like that? Were they born that
way? Mother would interrupt. *That is not appropriate for your age.
Where on earth would you wear such a thing? Why are you looking in
the designer section? Why are you looking at Vogue? You should be
looking at Simplicity.* But I didn't want a pattern if I didn't like the
picture.

Of course, Mother ruined the dress. First, she replaced the
rhinestones with a strip of the material. Then, she lengthened it
and closed the slit in the back. I hated it. I didn't know which
alteration made me the angriest, but the dress was now a sickly
relation of its cousin in the Paris boutique; it looked like
something from the shopping mall.

And I was angry that Mother was all wrong for it, with her drooping arms and pointed elbows, her sloping shoulders. She hunched slightly, and the material that was supposed to flow down fell out from her body, making her look even more flat-chested than usual. Anybody could tell that she never knew what to wear, didn't know how to 'make the most of herself'. I hated her for thinking that she was being so daring to wear this dress, and for knowing and yet ignoring that it was all wrong, for trying without hope to be sexy and fashionable.

'You look pretty, Mom,' I said.

'Thank you, dear,' she said flatly. She was too used to being disappointed for it to bother her much.

We went out to the living-room and she called my brother. His door opened and the whole hall was flooded with a smell like the boys' gym at school. He shuffled towards us and stood in the doorway to the living-room, his head hanging, his hands in his pockets. He always looked as if he were waiting for somebody to step on him. His hair was long and greasy and over his mouth were some patchy dark hairs he thought was a moustache. He was going to have to shave and get a haircut before our father got back if he didn't want to catch hell.

Mother looked at him a few seconds and then sighed, deciding not to say anything about his appearance. When our father wasn't around, she didn't like to disturb the peace. She said mechanically, 'You can eat anything you want but clean up your mess. The number to the theatre is by the telephone. The Ashlands are at home if you need them. Leslie is to go to bed at nine. Yes, Leslie, at nine. Read her a story. One story. No, you may not stay up and watch television. I do not care if it is Saturday. Nine o'clock means nine o'clock.'

She sighed again and opened the door. 'Nancy, if you let any kids into this house –'

'We *won't*,' I said, exasperated. I had been through that with her about a million times that day.

She draped the shawl over one arm and took her car keys out

of her bag. My brother was looking at the floor. I kept my eyes level with her thin shoulders.

We stood there for a minute. I could tell she wanted to say something else but couldn't think of anything to say. Finally, she said, 'And no fighting.'

I didn't bother to answer. My brother and I hadn't fought for over a year.

She stepped out on to the porch. I wished she would hurry up and go, but she stared at us as if she was trying to decipher through our blank faces what mischief we were plotting. She sighed, and finally, in the weary, slightly pleading voice she used when she was tired of being a parent and didn't really care any more what we did, said, 'And *don't* burn the house down.'

Now, this was an extraordinary statement. It was the first time she had admitted frankly that she could do nothing about our smoking; that however much she carped, and however much my father beat us, she knew the minute we were alone, we would light up. It meant, I know you're doing it; just don't let me find out.

My brother and I kept our faces completely expressionless at this new cynicism. As she closed the door, we both raised our eyebrows in amazement. We watched her start the car and pull out of the driveway. Leslie ran off to the kitchen, but we waited, listening to the car drive down the street, and turn at the end of the block. We could just hear it continue towards the highway that would lead Mother to the city.

'*Alright!*' I yelled, going to the kitchen.

'Do you have a joint?' my brother called.

'Yeah, sure,' I said sarcastically. 'I have a whole pound.'

Leslie was sitting at the kitchen counter, devouring a box of Oreos in the fashion she liked, which was to break them apart, and first lick the white middles out. I looked at her with disgust, ready to berate her for her childishness and the mess she was making, but she gave me such a fearful glance that I did not bother. I heard my brother putting on a record in his room, and I yelled, 'The Stones!' I mixed myself a glass of chocolate milk. We no longer pilfered the liquor cabinet; my parents marked the levels on the bottles. After a moment, I heard Led Zeppelin at top volume.

My brother came back to the living-room with the cigarettes and ashtray. We opened all the windows. I took one of his cigarettes and we both lit up.

Leslie said from the kitchen, 'I'm going to tell.'

'You do,' I said, 'and you're going to bed at nine.' She resumed eating her Oreos calmly. 'Is Mother's door closed?' I asked my brother. He was sitting on the back of the sofa next to the open window. He nodded.

I turned on the television with the sound down and then sat on the other end of the sofa and read the TV Guide while I smoked. '*Some Like it Hot*,' I read between puffs. 'With Marilyn Monroe, Tony Curtis and Jack Lemmon. 1959. Directed by Billy Wilder –' My brother ignored me, playing an invisible guitar to Led Zeppelin, with his cigarette hanging out of his mouth.

'Marilyn Monroe!' I said. 'Don't you want to see Marilyn Monroe?'

'Who's Marilyn whatever?' said Leslie.

'God, Leslie,' I said.

'Well, who is Mara-whatever?'

'Forget it. You're too little to understand.'

'I am not.'

'You are too. At eight o'clock. Don't you want to see Marilyn Monroe?'

My brother shrugged. 'Sure.'

'I am not too little.'

'You are too. Shut up or you're going to bed at nine. I'm not even sure if you're old enough to see this movie.'

Leslie started to whine, so I told her she could to shut her up. My brother still pretended that he didn't care whether he saw Marilyn Monroe or not, and I decided not to tease him about it.

It had been around my twelfth birthday that our cruel taunts, fist fights, and nasty tricks quite simply ceased, without fanfare or discussion. I had, in a few months, shot up nearly three inches, and was suddenly almost as tall as he; no longer was he so clearly my superior in a fight. I was about to go into the sixth grade and he, the seventh, junior high.

He had always been big for his age, and a bully; the kids at his elementary school were terrified of him. But in junior high, he wasn't the biggest around. There were older kids. And, it wasn't enough any more to be just big. Strength was less important than the ability to run, to manoeuvre, to talk the right way, to carry yourself the right way, the way that said, *Don't fuck with me.*

My poor brother. He was lazy and actually a weakling. He could beat me Indian wrestling, but only just. He was flabby, uncoordinated and a slow runner.

The kids from sixth grade who went to junior high with my brother all seemed to spurt up and fill out that year. They spent the first part of seventh grade getting him back for all that they'd taken in elementary school. Then, they left him alone. He kept on eating and getting bigger and flabbier. He had acne. He never brushed his teeth, which were yellow and looked like a lab experiment. He took showers, but somehow always smelled, and his hair looked like it hadn't been washed in years. He had only one friend, a boy who avoided him, and girls ran from him in the hall at school.

My first year in junior high, kids would ask me, 'Hey, is that weird guy in eighth grade *your* brother?'

He would marry a timid, neurotic and miserly girl who was terrified of strange inevitabilities, hoarding food, hiding money. She would keep him in a steady job and off drugs. My mother would be grateful, never say a word against the girl, count her blessings. My brother would be large and silent, moving crated washing machines and refrigerators from a factory floor into waiting trucks day after day, going home for lunch. He would lurch about, an enormous cripple; the men would leave him alone, not testing the strength of his bulk, speculating on the cause of his limp.

The news came on the television. While the anchorman mouthed in silence, Led Zeppelin shrieked in the background.

Then a reporter in front of the White House appeared and talked into a mike, his hair blowing in the wind. After a minute the camera cut to a man talking from a podium with the President's seal on it. We watched, smoking.

Some film clips were shown of soldiers in the jungle and then a map with arrows. I wondered idly how many planes crashed in Vietnam. A few a week? A day? I wondered what the chances were of getting shot down. I imagined a plane spiralling, then disappearing into velvety green, and a parachute bursting open, then floating down. How long would it take to notify the family? It might take weeks because of the jungle. Maybe they didn't tell the family right off, hoping they'd find the guy. Maybe they didn't even send out search parties for crashed planes. At least, they wouldn't if it crashed in enemy territory; it would be too dangerous. I wondered how much money the family got if the pilot was shot down and never found. Would it be enough to live on?

'How much money does the family get if your plane crashes and you're killed?'

My brother took a long drag. 'Nothing that lucky ever happens to us.' After a minute, he added, 'Anyway, he doesn't fly a fighter plane. He wouldn't get shot down. He flies transport planes.'

I knew my brother was right, but I still paused for a moment to imagine all of us in black, being photographed by the newspapers. I would be standing out in front, tragic and beautiful with a black veil and somebody would discover me and I would go to New York and become a model and make so much money that I could buy Mother anything she wanted and take her to the theatre and to French restaurants and go to Europe, just like the Crispens.

I had babysat for the Crispens once. Mother drove with me to their house, which was downtown and had an electronic iron gate. Inside, my first impression was that everything was in shades of white: the marbled hall, the two sofas, the numerous, stuffed chairs, the carpet. After a few minutes, I saw small,

delicate wooden tables, Persian rugs. On the walls were paintings, of pink and blue nudes with enormous rears climbing into
bathtubs. I held my mortified gaze stiffly from these, knowing I
would blush if I looked at them.

Mrs Crispen and my mother went upstairs, and her daughter,
a girl of four or five called Anna Maria, came down shortly
afterwards. She was wearing a pink pinafore. She had exquisite
features, large eyes, white skin, glossy hair. We looked at one
another, and our ages melted into insignificance; I saw us
stripped to some fundamental sum of what we each had and did
not have, of privilege, money, choices; the purity of *having*.
Instinctively, I looked away until she had descended the stairs; I
knew already that my defences against females like her were
small, essential, and had to be guarded closely, like a talisman.

Mr Crispen followed his daughter down the stairs. He was not
handsome, but he was elegant, and his face was sharply angled.
He was so unlike any American man I had ever seen, he could
have been of a different race. He was putting on gloves. I had
never seen a man wear gloves before. He thanked me for staying
with Anna Maria, as if I were doing him a great favour. Then he
said, with a vague wave, in his strange, wonderful accent,
'Please make yourself at home.'

I never found out where he was from. When I could have
asked, later, I did not. Swiss, Belgian, French? He had come over
after the war. He had been orphaned. He was a DP, a Displaced
Person, Mother had told me. I pictured a war-torn little boy with
a Dutch haircut, in ripped *Lederhosen* wandering past heaps of
rubble, eating out of garbage cans, making his way to a port,
stowing away on a ship, emerging on to the deck after days in the
hull, the Statue of Liberty on the horizon.

He made his money in the construction boom, Mother had
said.

They left, Anna Maria and I still facing one another. She
examined me with a sort of benign curiosity, sensing inferiority
and intimidation. Then, without a word, she went over to one of
the white sofas and, with proprietary nonchalance, sat down and

began to bounce up and down. I watched this and saw that she was at once establishing her right to do as she liked, and putting me at ease, telling me that the marvels she lived around were, after all, merely *things*. Things she used every day. Things I could use, too, for the moment. I watched her.

After a minute, she stopped bouncing and said, 'We're not alone.' I did not reply. 'Cook's downstairs. She lives there.' Then I saw that she was not only telling me that I was not in authority here, but also that I had been brought along merely to keep her company.

'Do you want me to read you a story?' I asked with icy politeness.

'No, thank you,' she returned. 'I will show you my room though if you like.'

It was as large as our living-room. In the middle was an enormous creamy lace canopy bed, and against one wall, a polished, heavy dressing table, covered with a lace ruffle. In her closet were rows of starched dresses with Peter Pan collars, bows, lace cuffs and below, dozens of shoes, each pair in a box.

But the best thing in the room was the mural, which covered one entire wall. It was of a little girl on a swing which was attached to the overhanging branch of a tree by ropes of woven flowers. Behind the girl was an enchanted forest with trees and birds and animals. The little girl was swinging out, her legs straight, toes pointed, hair streaming long behind her, dress billowing in the wind. I looked at it for several minutes before I realized that the painting was of her, Anna Maria.

That was when I knew that I would never be precious, to anybody.

Some Like it Hot started, so we turned off the music and turned up the television. Marilyn Monroe looked drunk throughout the whole movie and slurred when she talked, but in a sexy way. It was hard to believe that she was, after all, only a female, of the same stuff as I. I thought she looked like an alien, or something that had been made up by special effects, like the idea of the perfect movie star.

The movie was very confusing. The men in the movie leered at her, as if they desired her and yet wanted to harm her. She was supposed to be the epitome of femininity, and yet she existed in opposition to every virtue women were supposed to have – modesty, chastity. Her near-nudity embarrassed me, not only because I knew it was immoral in the way *Playboy* was immoral, but because it was so acceptable. There seemed to be some special rule for Marilyn Monroe, which made it all right for her, but not for a normal woman, to flaunt herself indecently.

We had a photograph of a woman who looked a lot like Marilyn Monroe. My brother had found it in a box in my parents' closet. When I was ten, I thought she *was* Marilyn Monroe. In the photograph, my father had his arm around her. They were at a party, somewhere overseas. (Europe, Asia; I never thought about it; he was just 'overseas'.) The woman wore a long dress, very low-cut, and trimmed around the top with fur. Her shoulders and breasts looked as if they were perched on this bed of fur. Some people were standing around them in the photograph, holding drinks and laughing. My father was looking down the woman's cleavage, with a stupid grin on his face.

During the commercials, we raided the refrigerator and made popcorn. Leslie fell asleep about nine o'clock, but when we tried to move her to bed, she woke up and made such a fuss that we left her on the floor in front of the television. At the end of the movie was the 'public service announcement', a voice which demanded reproachfully, 'It is ten o'clock. Where are *your* children?' We always replied to this, 'Out smoking and drinking and screwing around!'

I checked the TV Guide but the late movie did not interest me. I didn't feel like staying up, so I went to bed, leaving Leslie asleep on the floor and my brother smoking in front of the television.

This was the night my brother had the accident that gave him his limp.

Because of the accident, he would miss some school. He would begin to fail and eventually drop out. Then, he would start taking drugs in a serious way. One night, he would lurch down the middle of a major highway, against traffic, his pockets filled with pot, speed, LSD, waving his arms and shouting at the cars.

There would be a way to get a first offender's reprieve, which was to enlist. But the army would refuse to take my brother because of his leg, and he would go to jail for nine months. After jail, he would get married.

The accident happened like this:

From the middle of nowhere, I am jolted awake. The ceiling light jerks me up and then, immediately, my sister leaps screaming on to the bed. She jumps up and down on the bed and on me. I almost slap her, but then hear her disordered words: bathroom, shower door, glass, cut, blood. I push her aside and run out.

My brother lies on the tiled floor, propping himself up on an elbow. He is dressed. He looks up, calm, a little dazed, embarrassed, as if he knows something has happened, but he is not sure what. He is ineffectually wrapping a dirty bathtowel around his leg. Blood is spreading through the towel with steady progress.

The shower door is gone. Everywhere is glass, shattered into large and small pieces. Bright blood trickles down the cabinets and walls and on the toilet, and is all over the floor, mixed in with the glass. In the toilet is piss, my brother's urine.

My brother is wedged between the shower stall and the cabinet under the sink. The toilet is inches from his head. I have never realized before how small the bathroom is. He is wrapping the towel closer around his leg, looking at me confusedly. He seems to be waiting for me to do something.

'Let me see,' I say, kneeling carefully in the glass. He smells and I blanch slightly. Then I lift the towel. The calf is sliced open to the bone in two bloody trenches, each about ten inches long. One starts near the knee, the other lower down, ending at the ankle. All around are more cuts, glittering with glass dust, the blood clotting and matting the hair on his legs.

Pure panic seizes me. I know I have gone pale and cannot

move. I look at him to see if he understands how serious this really is, and he stares back at me dumbly. Then I realize, he is stoned. He would have to be stoned to have fallen back with such force through the shower door. I ask him what he has taken; he denies that he has taken anything. I think, *I will never get through this. I will not cope. He will bleed to death.* Here is the crisis Mother has always warned about. Here it is: an emergency. The middle of the night. Nobody at home. Nobody but me, and I have to do something. I freeze.

A moment passes. My brother watches me. 'I'll get someone,' I finally say, backing out of the bathroom. I see the bleeding again, swelling, engorging the towel and am afraid he will die while I am gone. I find some clean towels and make a kind of tourniquet. Then I run out.

I run out of the house in my nightgown and across the next door neighbours' wet lawn and driveway to the Ashland's house. I ring the doorbell over and over again, without stopping, and bang on the door at the same time.

Mrs Ashland, in her dressing-gown, her head wrapped in toilet paper, comes to the door, listens, tells me to go back and wait, and calls to her husband as she shuts the door. I obey, relieved to have directions to follow, to have an adult taking over, to have done what I should.

As I run back across the grass, I collide with my sister right in front of the next door neighbours' house. I shake her by the shoulders. 'What the hell are you doing here?'

She begins to cry. 'I was getting the neighbours.'

I am livid with anger at her insubordination. 'What do you think I was doing?' I shake her harder.

'I don't know,' she cries pathetically. I slap her. 'You stupid idiot! Did you wake them up?'

'No!' She holds her face.

I push her down on to the grass and then yank her up by one arm. 'Get in that house. You know Mother says they're trash. How dare you go to them? Don't you think I know what I'm doing?' I half-pull, half-drag her to the house. 'Get in there and shut up. Do you want to wake up the whole neighbourhood?'

I send her to bed and go back to my brother. He is holding the tourniquet, and now looking scared, like a wounded animal. I flush the toilet, replace the blood-soaked towels, help him sit up. We are both embarrassed now, by this intimacy, this touching; our indifference to one another has become our bond since we have quit fighting; we have passed from the fierce love and hate of childhood and into the mutual contempt of adolescents. We know this closeness is thrust upon us by sheer chance, as much as our sharing of the same parents. We know that we actually share nothing, except the desire to shed this present life; we know that we are already strangers who meet, touch, care only because of this present moment.

Mother has left her cotton housedress on her bed and her sandals on the floor, and I put these on. I glance at myself in the mirror. My face is white and my lips red. My hair is a mess and I pull Mother's brush through it a few times. I feel strangely excited.

Mr Ashland comes and we carry my brother to the car and put him in the back seat. Then Mrs Ashland comes and takes Leslie back to their house. I am afraid that she will try to make me stay behind as well, and am prepared to defend my right to go to the hospital, but neither object when I climb into the car.

I tell Mr Ashland in an efficient voice the name of the nearest hospital and the theatre where my mother is. He nods without comment. When he turns in a different direction than the hospital, I say, 'Hey, you're going the wrong way.'

He says, 'That hospital doesn't have an emergency room.'

'Oh,' I say. It dawns on me how limited my role actually is in this. After a minute, I add conversationally, 'Well, wouldn't you just know. An accident just had to happen with my father overseas and my mother at the theatre.' Mr Ashland smiles a little at me but doesn't answer.

Mrs Ashland has called the hospital to tell them we are coming, and when we drive up, there are two nurses waiting with a hospital bed on rollers. They don't seem very concerned, which shocks me. Even when they lift the bloody towels from my brother's leg and see the cuts, they chat cheerfully, like the school nurse used to when we would fall on the asphalt. I get madder and madder at this indifference, and am about to tell them that they'd better do something fast before my brother starts to bleed to death, but then, he is gone, rolled away through some swinging doors. I follow and am left in the bright, dirty waiting-room.

There are some children there, one with an ear-ache and one with a burn, not very bad, and some old people. After a few minutes, some policemen come in with a man who is drunk, bleeding all over his head and yelling about his wife, calling her a bitch and saying he is going to kill her. The nurses, who march around like military sergeants, warn him that he will go straight to jail if he doesn't shut up. He tries to grab one of them, and she twists his arm so hard that he cries out and begins to whimpers like a dog.

A Mexican comes in holding a cloth around his hand and he can't speak English and all the nurses are yelling at him at the top of their voices, trying to make him understand. The lady next to me asks me what is wrong with me and I tell her about my brother. She tells me that her husband had convulsions and she doesn't know whether it is epilepsy or a stroke.

Then I remember: what if he has taken some drugs? Should I tell them? Such a betrayal is nearly equal in import to the risk of his death. I stare at a nurse sitting behind the desk, writing. Then my mother walks in. She looks stiff and white. Her make-up lays on her face like a transparent mask. I can see the bags under her eyes that she had covered with a special make-up and her skin hangs down as if she is very tired. I try to say something to her, but she walks right past me and to the nurses' desk. I am dismayed. She isn't happy that I've done something right for a change, that I have handled an emergency. She has grimly assumed responsibility for this; I am now of no importance.

I watch her go through the swinging doors.

After a long time, she comes out again with Mr Ashland. She stares at me for a minute as if she does not recognize me. She looks very small in her dress, as if I am looking at her at the end of a telescope. Her dress and make-up and teased-up hair stand out like a costume; underneath, she looks like she usually looks: tired and fed up.

She continues to stare at me and I wonder if it is that I am wearing her dress – she hates me to touch her things. Or, maybe it is that I have come to the hospital when I should have stayed at home. Or maybe she knows that my brother is stoned. Then I wonder, can she be in shock? That would have been the way a mother in the movies would act.

I briefly imagine Mother being paged at the theatre and then dramatically rushing into the hospital, her black dress in a swirl. Two gentle nurses would guide her to where her handsome son lays bleeding to death, and she would take his hand and gaze tenderly into his eyes.

She sighs, deciding not to mention whatever it is she is mad about. And, I know she has rushed over because that's what mothers have to do, even when their sons are smelly, have yellow teeth, take drugs. She is not in shock; she will take care of everything now.

She says, wearily, 'Mr Ashland will take you home.'

When we drove up, the front door was open and all the lights were on. Standing inside were Mr and Mrs Crispen in their evening clothes. We walked in, and the Crispens and Mr Ashland spent about ten minutes politely disagreeing about who should stay and clean up and wait for my mother. Finally, The Crispens won and Mr Ashland left.

Mrs Crispen said, taking off her gloves finger by finger, 'Let's just see if we can't clean this up a little for your mother.' Mr Crispen followed her down the hall and I came last.

'Well!' said Mrs Crispen, 'When you kids have an accident you certainly know how to do it!' I laughed a little to be polite, and watched her. She was wearing a green taffeta dress, gathered at the waist and with a neckline like a heart. I wanted to see if she was really going to start cleaning up all that glass and blood in that dress.

Mr Crispen surveyed the bathroom. He did not appear embarrassed; he seemed to be considering things.

'What we need is a bucket and some rags,' said Mrs Crispen with forced heartiness. I stood there, entranced. I had never been around the Crispens alone before. I wanted to study them.

Mrs Crispen had changed from the days when she was Mrs Jackson. She was blonder and thinner. I had heard Mother tell Mrs Ashland that she had had a boob-job and I tried to see if I could tell the difference. She had done it, Mother said, because they went to the South of France on vacation and the women there go topless on the beach. Mother had said this in a odd way, as though it were funny but kind of embarrassing and not very surprising. After all, she seemed to say, that's the Crispens.

The telephone rang and I went to answer it. Mother asked me where Leslie was, and I told her. Then I said, 'The Crispens are here.'

She groaned. 'What are they doing?'

'We're cleaning up the glass,' I said, even though nothing had been done yet.

'Oh God,' groaned Mother. 'Tell them to stop immediately.'

'Mother says to stop immediately,' I called to the hall.

Mrs Crispen came and took the phone from me.

She said, 'Virginia . . . Don't be silly . . . How is he? Well, thank heavens . . . No, no, don't worry . . . We won't . . . Of course not . . . You just do what you have to and . . . All right . . . Yes . . . Bye-bye . . .' She put the telephone down. 'Your poor mother.'

Mr Crispen had left the room and now returned with a bucket and some rags. He began to pick up the larger shards of glass and put them in the bucket. Mrs Crispen bent down to help him.

Then she turned a little towards me, still bending over, to pick up a piece of glass that had flown out of the bathroom and on to the hall carpet. Her hair had fallen forward and across the side of her face, a perfect blonde curve coming to a point on her cheek. Her neckline gaped open a little, and I could see the edges of her bra.

She said, 'Well, at least your brother waited till the end of the last act to have his accident!'

I didn't say anything.

'Your mother,' she went on, 'certainly enjoyed the show.' She looked up at me as she shook out the contents of the rag into the bucket. I suddenly felt very tired and wanted them to go. I knew that Mrs Crispen felt sorry for my mother for being married to my father and saddled with us while she was married to rich, European Mr Crispen. And I knew that there was nothing I could do about that. I wanted to tell them that they didn't have to clean up my brother's blood and the glass, that I could take care of it myself, that I didn't need their help. But, my part in all this was not to decide; I knew I would have to wait until, eventually, they would leave.

When I was in high school, the Crispens got divorced. Mrs Crispen, my mother said, 'came out of it very well'. But a year later, she found out that Mr Crispen had hidden a lot of money from her in Switzerland. When she tried to sue him for some of it, the judge ruled against her.

When my mother warned me about the perils, the awful responsibility, of adulthood, I knew already that the risks I would undertake, and the damage I would live with, not only from childhood, but collected at every stop ahead, would discourage me, but not for long. I had already seen the women I would never be.

The memory of Mrs Crispen faded with her divorce, as though she had again transformed. Into what? I never found out. What I remember best from that night is not Mrs Crispen, nor her daughter, nor even my mother, who, like us children, were only appendages, who could be discarded, ruined, protected as others saw fit. It is Mr Crispen, the displaced child who made dreams come true, who I remember best.

In Milwaukee

———————

Mrs Wolcheski, a widow twice over, stood at her kitchen sink, staring out the window. It was early afternoon in the autumn. Across the street people were pouring out of the side door of Christ King Church. The swap-meet was drawing to a close.

As she watched, Mrs Wolcheski drew on her cigarette in regular, short puffs, and, without inhaling, ejected little clouds which she waved out of her field of vision with her free hand. The cigarette ash grew longer with every puff. Transfixed by the sight at Christ King, she did not notice.

Another puff, cloud, wave of the hand: the ash curled and fractured. Then two little boys broke away from their parents and ran across the church's newly mowed lawn to the sidewalk. Mrs Wolcheski snorted with irritation. She had known that something like this was bound to happen. Then she looked down and saw the long ash splattered in the porcelain sink.

Mrs Wolcheski couldn't understand why all these people suddenly wanted to come to Christ King. Why they didn't stay in their own parish and make it as nice was beyond her. If they had to go drive around town and look for nice swap-meets she wished they would do it somewhere else. Her Saturdays were now spent watching complete strangers walk away with armfuls of parishioners' once-loved possessions, who let their children run wild across the lawn and who parked their shabby cars up and down the block.

She was raised attending Christ King and still attended Mass there every morning. She preferred going to the old father for confession although there was now a young priest helping him:

she didn't appreciate all the new rules, the changes, what she considered to be a slackening of standards. It was he who had encouraged her to take her vows as a girl. But her parents had refused her their permission. They believed that this Catholic girl should marry and have children. Of course she loved her son Billy – she adored him! – but she still felt the distaste of marital relations and the bitterness of having to abandon her true calling.

She put her cigarette out carefully, stamping the butt nearly in the centre of the ashtray. Then she lifted it to wipe the counter and put it on the edge of the sink; she would not wash it until she was sure the fire was completely out. She turned on the water and rinsed out the sink. The ashes whirled down the drain.

She turned away from the sink. 'Did I tell you I couldn't sleep a wink last night thinking about that oven?'

'Yes,' said Mary Agnes, Mrs Wolcheski's stepdaughter. She was removing a tray of Mrs Wolcheski's date-nut cookies. 'Do you want me to put another tray in?' Mary Agnes was thirty-two and had her own kitchen but when she was at Mrs Wolcheski's she was as unassuming as a child. She was so used to doing exactly as Mrs Wolcheski asked that part of her brain seemed to turn off whenever she stepped foot in the house.

'You might as well,' said Mrs Wolcheski, adding to herself, *Since Jim'll eat a whole tray himself.* Jim was Mary Agnes's husband.

Mary Agnes filled an empty tray with rows of cookie dough, scraped from two spoons and dropped from above so that they plopped on to the tray into round, slightly flat shapes. Then she pressed each cookie lightly with the back of a fork.

Mrs Wolcheski watched her until the cookie tray was in the oven. Then she resumed looking out of the window. 'I'm going to finish all my baking on Monday except for the cake.' She watched the crowd. 'I don't understand why all these people have to come to Christ King's swap-meets.'

Mary Agnes began to remove the still warm cookies from the other tray with a spatula. She wore a paisley apron of Mrs

Wolcheski's which covered the length of her dress front and back and was tied at the sides.

Mrs Wolcheski said, without turning, 'You should let them cool first. You'll break them if you take them off right away.'

'OK,' said Mary Agnes, putting the spatula down. She looked at the bowl of dough. 'I guess you'll want to bake up the rest of this batch now? Or do you want to freeze it?' She spoke without expression, removing from her voice any hint of interest in this problem.

'I like to have all my baking done well ahead of time, except for the cake. I get so nervous when Gertrude comes.'

'I know,' said Mary Agnes. She was tall and big-boned like her father. She wore her brownish hair short. Once it had been long and blonde, nearly white in the summers as a child, and still blonde on her wedding day. She had been an athletic girl but was now broad. She cut her hair after her first child, when it began to darken. When she met her brother's girlfriend, who had long blonde hair, she advised her. 'After you get married, cut it off. It's so much more practical.'

'So I guess we'll just bake up the rest of this batch now? Or do you want to freeze it and cook it later?'

'Gertrude taught me everything I know about housekeeping,' said Mrs Wolcheski. 'I'll just never get over being nervous when she comes over. I can't help it. She'll always feel like my mother-in-law.'

'Mother, Gertrude is eighty-six. She can't even see.'

Mrs Wolcheski turned from the window to look at her stepdaughter. 'Her kitchen cabinets are spotless. *Spotless.*' She picked up the ashtray and threw the butt away and wiped it out with a paper towel. Then she reached inside her pocket and drew out a fresh cigarette, which she lit with a gold lighter. 'Spotless.' She blew out a little cloud and waved it away. 'I scrubbed every single cabinet in here yesterday.' She looked around. 'And, I ironed every single one of my tea towels. Just in case Gertrude decides to look in my linen closet.' The thought of tea towels made her turn back to the church. She was not going to donate her worn tea towels to this season's swap-meets. 'I don't see why all these people come to Christ King's swap-meets. They can go to their own swap-meets.'

Mrs Wolcheski had lived in this house for thirty-five years. Her parents had bought it for her after it became clear to them that her husband would never be able to buy her a house. He died about ten years later, when Billy was in his first semester of community college. Mrs Wolcheski insisted that he drop out when his father died. 'I just pulled him right out of there,' she told her friends, although Billy had been flunking all his courses.

Mrs Wolcheski's neighbourhood had changed little through the years; it had only grown older. She was not grateful for this since it had never occurred to her that it might change. The stone houses and neat sidewalks and brick church and corner florist looked as if they had always been there. Mrs Wolcheski could not have imagined a better place to live than Milwaukee. The Italians had always lived in the south part of town, and the Jews in White Fish Bay. In her neighbourhood were only Poles, Germans and Irish people.

Mary Agnes said, 'Mother, do you want to freeze this dough?'

'What? Oh, no, no,' she said irritably. 'Bake it all if you want to.' She snorted again. 'Take whatever's left home.' She thought about how much she did for her stepchildren. Too much, really; it wasn't fair to Billy. And they didn't appreciate her generosity. She touched her pearls with her free hand. It was funny to be dressed up on a Saturday. Who ever heard of a *Saturday* family dinner?

The children used to come on Sunday. Mary Agnes and Jim and the kids went to Mass at their own church and then joined Mrs Wolcheski and Billy and his wife. Sometimes Dennis, Mary Agnes's brother and Mrs Wolcheski's other stepchild, drove down from Madison. Then he said he couldn't come on Sundays anymore. Mrs Wolcheski hoped that this was because he was going to Mass, but it wasn't. It was because he had joined a rowing club. 'A rowing club, Mother,' he said. 'You know, in a boat. We are out on the lake at eight and rowing till midday.' He was too tired to drive down afterwards, he said. She listened to this in silence. He must have read her mind, because he added, 'And I'm not getting up and going to six o'clock Mass beforehand.'

Now Mrs Wolcheski had to do her Saturday chores during the week. She knew this would cause her no end of problems and it did. What was worse Dennis didn't come every Saturday, but only when it suited him. But she had learned over the years that she had to accommodate Dennis. Nobody could change his mind about anything. Mary Agnes had gone to St Margaret's, the Catholic college down the street, and lived at home until she married. But as soon as he graduated from Christ King, Dennis had gone off to the University of Wisconsin in Madison. Mrs Wolcheski couldn't believe this, with Dennis's father ill at the time, and certain to die; but what exasperated her beyond imagination was that when he did graduate he didn't get a job. He went to Europe. And when he got back from Europe he still didn't get a job. He went back to school.

Mrs Wolcheski had let Dennis know exactly what she thought of his going to law school. He had had a very good summer job while he was in college building swimming-pools in Milwaukee. He made good money. She could not understand why he would not go into business with the man who owned the swimming-pool company. When he said, 'Mother, I am not going to spend the rest of my life building swimming-pools,' she had wanted to reply, *And what is wrong with building swimming-pools?* But she did not try to argue. If that was all college had taught him, to put himself above honest work, then she was thankful that she had pulled Billy right out when she did.

Sometimes she thought about all the good money Dennis had made building swimming-pools, and how he had spent it all on Europe and law school, and she felt ill. She would never forget how Dennis came home from Europe with a dirty beard and hair down to his shoulders and not one dime. Now that he was a lawyer he didn't make any more money than he had building swimming-pools.

She had seen Dennis flout everyone and everything and always get what he wanted. Well, now Dennis wasn't going to get everything. She had changed her will. Now her Chippendale and her china and crystal were going to Billy. Billy was already getting nearly everything else, but she had hesitated over the Chippendale and china and crystal because everything she had ever given him was destroyed in weeks. But, she told herself, that was not his fault. It was a wife's job to look after things. It was Shirley's fault that the dogs had reduced the Bierdermeier settee and chairs to shreds and that there remained of Mrs Wolcheski's second-best china only a platter and four partial place settings out of the original twelve.

She had promised her silver to Mary Agnes, who already had china and crystal from her wedding, and a few pieces of jewellery. The rest of her personal effects were going to the church: every ring, chain, dress and coat. The thought of her daughter-in-law wearing her fur or her jewellery was enough to make Mrs Wolcheski nauseated.

And she was prepared to go straight to eternal damnation before leaving anything to Dennis if he didn't change his ways.

The back door slammed and a man walked in. His eyes were puffy from sleep, his tousled hair glistened with grease, and he had not shaved in a few days. He wore brown trousers and a plaid shirt which, as it was missing the bottom three buttons, parted at the crest of his paunch. Mrs Wolcheski turned, ready to scold him for slamming the door, but when she saw how cute he looked she laughed. 'Poor Billy!' she cooed. 'Sleepy boy!' Billy and Shirley lived next door in the house Mrs Wolcheski had bought for him when he married.

'Hi, kid,' said Mary Agnes, as Billy presented his face to Mrs Wolcheski for a kiss. Mary Agnes was filling another cookie tray with rows of dough.

Billy stretched and said, 'Lemme have a cookie, Ma.'

'You know you shouldn't eat before dinner.'

'Please, Mommy! Gimme cookie, Mommy!' said Billy in the way he knew Mrs Wolcheski could not resist. She smiled and gave him a cookie which he stuffed into his mouth. When she had turned back to the window he winked conspiratorially at Mary Agnes and grabbed several more from the plate on the counter. He put these in his pocket.

'Is Grandmommy coming to my party?' he said.

'She wouldn't miss your birthday!' said Mrs Wolcheski.

'My party! My party!' sang Billy. 'It's my birthday! My birthday! And it isn't yours! It isn't yours!' He suddenly stopped; a car pulled into the driveway. Mrs Wolcheski walked abruptly out of the kitchen and Mary Agnes looked up.

'Dennis is here!' cried Billy. He dashed out the back door, letting it slam. As Mary Agnes watched, a tall man and a young woman emerged from either side of the car.

They have been driving down every third or fourth Saturday for about a year, since they bought the house. Barbara had met his stepmother before they bought the house, of course. They have been together for nearly four years, since Dennis's last year in law school.

Barbara always enjoys the drive down. Today, as usual, they took a thermos of coffee with them, made on the hotplate in their still unrenovated kitchen. They took some tapes to play in the car, and sweaters, as it is starting to get cool now. They left Madison, passing the university, quiet except for a few joggers, and the lake, still and steaming.

Leaving Madison the countryside starts abruptly. Barbara loves driving past the small farms. She tells Dennis what is growing in their fields as he is a city kid and can't tell oats from alfalfa. They talk about the house (a wall to be torn down, the plumbing in the second bathroom, the kitchen cabinets). They tell each other about their week and gossip about friends and sing along with the tape. They drive for nearly two hours.

As they leave the interstate everything changes. Barbara's face turns dull and settled and she becomes quiet and neutral as she remembers where they are going. She sees Dennis shift, too. He becomes too cheerful, too indifferent, even more easy-going than usual. She feels separated from him, as if she can only be a part of him in Madison.

Today she tried to remember how they began the every third or fourth Saturday visits. Dennis had stopped going on Sundays because he was rowing. Then they bought the house, and the first Saturday he was to go she went with him. They seemed to agree tacitly that Mrs Wolcheski was going to have to be told about the house, that she was going to have to get used to the situation, that she was going to have to accept Barbara living with Dennis.

Up to then Mrs Wolcheski had pretended to ignore their living together; when they told her about the house she had to face it. She listened, turned away, saying nothing.

Barbara now knows that Mrs Wolcheski will never accept the situation, but she also knows that now that they visit together they must continue to do so. For her not to come would provide Mrs Wolcheski with a chance to talk about her to Dennis. He would come home and she would want to know everything that was said. Eventually there would be a quarrel. She would be the loser. She refuses to give this woman any more power than she already has. She will not try to pry this man away from his family, but she will be there when he is ready to break away.

Barbara is a silk-screen artist. They met at a party nearly five years ago. She was doing her MFA then. She was lounging in an armchair, wearing tight jeans and her hair in a French twist. He told her later that he wanted to come to her and unpin her hair. He still loves it when she pins her hair up and puts on tight jeans. She does this for him from time to time, but it worries her. She is not sure whether Dennis will love her without tight jeans and long hair; when she is older, or sick, or pregnant.

They slammed the car doors shut as Billy ran up to Dennis. Barbara walked slowly up the drive.

'How's it up in sin city?' said Billy breathlessly.

'Madison's the same as always,' said Dennis. 'How's everything in Milwaukee?'

'Dullsville.' He pointed this thumb over his shoulder toward the house. 'With the old biddy around. Ought to send her cathedral-hunting again. Her and Shirley together.' This idea struck him suddenly as extremely funny, and he giggled uncontrollably. Dennis tried to pass him but Billy put his hand out. 'Did I tell you I was up there last week?'

'In Madison? No.'

'Yeah, Shirl's in the hospital.'

'Oh, I'm sor—'

'Got me two of 'em,' he went on with relish. 'At the same time! Weren't no older than fifteen neither.'

Barbara was standing at the top of the drive near the back door. She watched the two men further down. The front lawn was wide, green and trimmed. The trees were turning but only a few leaves lay on the grass; they had been raked that day. The street was quiet except for a few people coming out of the side door of the red brick church across the street.

She assumed a completely neutral expression. She knew exactly what would now happen, what she had to do, what she had to say. They would go in, say certain things, eat certain foods, make certain gestures. Then they would go home.

Dennis gently manoeuvred around Billy and they walked up together, Dennis with his confident strides, the shorter, older man skipping alongside like a friendly mongrel.

'Hello, Billy,' said Barbara. 'How are you?'

'Oh fine,' said Billy, grinning at Dennis. 'Just fine.'

Denis went in the back door first, Barbara following, and Billy close behind. Mary Agnes was alone, dropping cookie dough with two spoons onto a tray.

'Hello, Mary Agnes,' said Dennis.

'Hi, you guys.'

Barbara stood between the back door and the kitchen table with Billy behind her. She would not sit down yet. She would wait until Mrs Wolcheski returned with her drink. Then she would ask if she could help with the washing or chopping or peeling. Mrs Wolcheski would ignore her. Dennis would nod at her to sit down. Mrs Wolcheski would finish her drink and begin another. Then she might answer. Well, Barbara could chop if she wanted to.

That was how it always went.

Mrs Wolcheski walked in holding a whisky Manhattan. She said, 'Is your car going to leak all on my driveway?'

'No, Mother,' said Dennis mildly. 'How are you?'

'It did before. And I had to scrub it myself with bleach.'

'That was five years ago, Mother, and a different car. Where's Jim and the kids?'

'Coming,' said Mary Agnes. She was washing out the mixing bowl in the sink. 'He took them to the Super Slide.' She dried the bowl and put it away. Mrs Wolcheski was sipping her drink. Dennis sat down at the kitchen table.

There was a pause and Barbara said, 'Can I do anything to help?'

Mrs Wolcheski was silent and after a moment Mary Agnes said, 'Not for the moment. Have a cookie.' She held out the plate.

'Those cookies are for dessert,' said Mrs Wolcheski.

Barbara froze, cookie in hand. She looked at Mary Agnes, who hesitated. She put the cookie back.

'Well, you might as well eat it since you've touched it,' said Mrs Wolcheski.

Barbara looked at Dennis, who was frowning. She left the cookie on the plate and went back to her place near the door. The neutral, indifferent expression returned to her face. Mrs Wolcheski picked up the cookie and threw it in the garbage. Then she washed her hands and lit a cigarette. 'I just couldn't sleep a wink last night thinking about the oven,' she said.

Billy was still behind Barbara, absently inserting cookies from his pocket into his mouth. He nudged her and tried to slip a slightly smashed cookie into her hand. She smiled and shook her head. He shrugged, opened the door. He was humming a little tune.

'Why were you worried, Mother?' The back door slammed.

'Well, it's only Billy's birthday!' Mrs Wolcheski drank from her glass.

'What was the problem?'

'The problem! The problem was that I'd never have forgiven myself if I couldn't have made him a cake, that's all!' She snorted. 'What a time to get a new oven!'

'The new oven is wider than the old one,' explained Mary Agnes.

'Didn't you measure it?'

'Of course! So many times! Do you think I would buy a new oven without measuring it? There was an inch to spare, thank heavens. But I just couldn't sleep a wink thinking about it. Not having an oven and it being Billy's birthday!' She drank from her glass. 'And of course we all know that Shirley doesn't bake.'

'And how is Shirley?' said Dennis. 'Billy says she's in hospital again.'

Mrs Wolcheski put her drink down and looked out the window.

'Better,' said Mary Agnes. 'The treatment seems to do some good.'

'I don't see,' said Mrs Wolcheski, 'that she needs anything except a good day's work. She should be at home taking care of Billy. He can't go to work and do her work around the house too! I suppose she'll expect him to take care of her ladyship when she comes home!' She sipped and then added woefully, 'And after he's been in the hospital!' She stubbed out her cigarette.

'And how is he?' said Dennis, pushing his chair back and putting his right foot on his left knee. He gazed around the room calmly, without appearing to be looking at anyone or anything.

His step mother turned to him, her face reddening. 'You know what they did to him? They went and made him a janitor! A janitor! Why he's got a high school diploma! He has almost a whole semester of community college! And they're making him clean toilets!' Her voice broke and she pulled a tissue from her pocket. She blew her nose and took a large sip from her glass.

'Just because he was in the hospital!' She wailed, tears forming and then streaming down.

Mary Agnes took out the final tray of cookies from the oven and set them down to cool. Dennis continued to look around the room at nothing. Mrs Wolcheski wiped her face, crumpled up her tissue and felt in her pocket for another. Barbara leaned against the back door wishing Mrs Wolcheski would stop crying as she really would have liked to sit down.

Mrs Wolcheski has never seen their house, a four-bedroom Victorian with a large front porch.

They have finished renovating the living-room, one bathroom, and one bedroom. They will soon start on the second bathroom and the kitchen. They split all the work and the costs. They are, in fact, co-owners. They had a contract drawn up so that they could own the house together without being married. They did this so that if they break up there won't by any messy community property.

Barbara is almost always broke since she doesn't make much money in her job teaching art at the community college, and the little she has left after renovation costs she spends on silk-screen supplies. Dennis makes a lot of money compared to Barbara but they still split everything. Dennis realizes this, however, and whenever they go out to dinner or to see a movie he pays.

In the days when Barbara thought that Mrs Wolcheski might get used to her stepson living with a woman she also believed that Mrs Wolcheski might come visit them. She thought the house and their hard work would impress Mrs Wolcheski. (Why shouldn't she have thought so? Her own parents were impressed.)

Now Barbara realizes that the insides of that house matter not one iota to Mrs Wolcheski and that Mrs Wolcheski would probably walk through the streets of Milwaukee naked before she would step foot in a house in which nightly sins, unexpiated by confession, are committed.

However.

Mrs Wolcheski somehow got the notion that Dennis and Barbara are engaged to be married. This is not true, but Barbara realizes that this is a convenient lie that allows Mrs Wolcheski to tolerate her presence every third or fourth Saturday. A house of sin is still a house of sin, but as an engaged couple they are yet suspended between eternal damnation and salvation. The thread, however thin, is still there.

In fact, Dennis is overtly hostile to marriage. He does not hide this from his stepmother or from Barbara. He is also hostile to children. He calls them 'rug-rats'.

Mrs Wolcheski believes so much in this engagement that she has since moved on to more important matters. She has taken to leaving church pamphlets on conversion around the house. She has cut out from the human interest section of the *Catholic Herald* articles on the problems of inter-marriage and pinned them on the bulletin board. She often brings up the son of one of her friends whose fiancée converted so that he could marry her.

Barbara realizes that Mrs Wolcheski is not particularly supporting Barbara's candidacy; she understands that Dennis's stepmother would simply rather see her son married to Barbara than in hell for ever and ever. There is another reason why Mrs Wolcheski would like Dennis to get married, although she would never admit it, and that is that she loves weddings. Mrs Wolcheski hasn't been involved with a wedding since Mary Agnes's and she wouldn't mind at all being involved with another. Even if the bride were Protestant.

Mrs Wolcheski can talk about weddings any time, day or night, without hesitation. She reads the wedding announcements in the Milwaukee paper even before the obituaries. She can describe every wedding she has been to in elaborate detail, as though she had witnessed it the day before. In fact, whenever Barbara finds herself feeling uncomfortable with Mrs Wolcheski, as she always does when Dennis leaves the room, she simply brings up the subject of weddings.

Mrs Wolcheski's favourite wedding is the one Barbara calls the swimming-pool wedding. Barbara used to enjoy hearing about this wedding. In fact, their discussions of this wedding constitute the majority of words that Mrs Wolcheski and Barbara have exchanged.

The swimming-pool wedding was Dennis's third cousin's, whose family swimming-pool Dennis helped to build during college. The bride's father and brothers spent weeks building a runway on scaffolding the length of the pool – and it is a very long pool – for the girl to walk down.

The runway was decorated on the sides with looped chains of blue and white flowers, and where each was attached, a little Polish flag. In the water floated more blue and white flowers, and at the end of the runway was an enormous canopy of blue and white flowers and streaming white ribbons where the bride and groom were married.

Mrs Wolcheski was still weeping a little over Billy's demotion from stock-boy to janitor. She blew her nose a final time, gathered up her tissues and then, cleaning out the ashtray with one, threw them in the garbage. She took another sip from her glass and drew out a cigarette. She lit it.

Mary Agnes said, 'I guess I'll make the salad now and it'll be out of the way.' She paused, waiting.

Mrs Wolcheski drained her glass. Mary Agnes took out the salad bowl and walked over to the refrigerator near Dennis. She leaned over the vegetable bin and said in a low voice, 'I don't see why they don't install an electro-shock machine in the house so that they both can use it whenever they want.'

Dennis laughed and winked at Barbara, who smiled slightly. He nodded at the chair nearest her and she sat down.

The back door slammed and Billy walked in. He said, 'Did you tell 'em, Ma? Did you tell 'em? About the oven?'

Mrs Wolcheski brightened. 'Why it just clean slipped my mind! You just don't know what a clever boy my Billy is!'

Billy grinned and rocked on his feet.

'When those workmen came to deliver the oven yesterday they just walked all over my floor with their dirty boots on. I'd just mopped and waxed, too, on account of Gertrude coming. You know how nervous I get when Gertrude comes. I'll just never get over –'

'So what happened, Mother?' said Dennis. He was looking out the window. The sun was setting.

'Well, you know how I'm always waiting to clean behind that oven and the refrigerator. And every time you're here you never remember to move it for me. Well, Billy came in to make sure they were putting in the oven right, and I was cleaning there behind it before they put it in and Billy says, he says, 'Why don't you boys move that refrigerator out for my Ma and she can clean behind it? And they did! It was such a relief! Billy made them wait right there while I got the mop and cleaned everything right up. I'd been thinking about cleaning behind there since I don't know when. And every time you're here you never –'

'That was very smart of you, Billy,' said Dennis.

'Billy,' said Mrs Wolcheski, 'can you make your Ma another drink?'

'Sure, Ma!' he yelled, and ran out with the glass.

'Mother,' said Mary Agnes, 'should I go ahead and start the meatloaf?' She was putting plastic over the salad bowl. 'Jim and the kids should be here soon.'

Mrs Wolcheski agreed and said she would go down to the basement to fetch the potatoes. Dennis offered to go down for her but she said that he wouldn't know which ones she wanted. She opened the basement door and as she descended they could hear her mutter, 'A janitor! With his education!'

Barbara is from a small town in the northern part of the state. She is of pure Norwegian extraction, born in the house in which her father was born, the house her immigrant grandparents built. In her town there has never been a non-Lutheran mayor elected. The Catholic minority in the town are almost exclusively German. They drive to a nearby town Sunday mornings to attend church.

But Barbara is not Lutheran. She is the youngest of six

children of converted Quakers. Her parents met during the war, matched up by friends who discovered that they were from the same town. They had known each other slightly as children. They married, returned home, and became pacifists.

Barbara's parents raised her without religious or racial prejudice. They believe, and she used to believe, in what they call the 'community of man'. When Dennis told Barbara that he was a Polish Catholic Barbara thought that meeting his family would be fun. She thought it would involve eating new kinds of food and listening to different stories from the old world than those she grew up with. The Catholics at home were indistinguishable from the Lutherans, except that they ate German food. There was never a 'problem'.

Now Barbara sees something deeply irrational connected to the word 'Catholic'. It was the swimming-pool wedding that made her see this.

One Saturday Dennis left the room and Barbara, in desperation, asked Mrs Wolcheski if she still had the photographs from the swimming-pool wedding. Mrs Wolcheski immediately fetched them. She held the photographs to her chest, passing them singly to Barbara, explaining each before moving on to the next. First came the pictures of the runway in progress. In these the pool was drained and the father and brothers were standing next to and in it, taking a break, each holding a beer, lumber and tools scattered around.

Then came the wedding itself: the bride and bridesmaids, the priest, the cake, the presents. Barbara asked all the questions she had asked on previous visits about the wedding, which Mrs Wolcheski was happy to answer again. Barbara listened avidly, for she actually loved hearing about the swimming-pool wedding and all its details. She found it wildly funny and kitschy.

Then Dennis came back to the kitchen. She thought that Dennis found the swimming-pool wedding as funny as she did, although he never commented on it. That day, however, he began to make sarcastic remarks. Mrs Wolcheski ignored him and began to speak to Barbara in a tone that implied that they shared some particularly feminine understanding, that a man could not be expected to appreciate the marvels of this wedding. And Barbara realized that Dennis was in fact very offended by this wedding. Then she saw why. It was because Dennis saw this use of his swimming-pool as an encroachment on his life by his stepmother and her fanatical Catholicism.

Now Barbara no longer asks Mrs Wolcheski about the swimming-pool wedding.

Barbara doesn't want Dennis to confuse her in some dark, irrational, Catholic way with his stepmother. She wants him to see that she represents an alternative. She believes that Dennis is slowly extracting himself from the grip of his stepmother and the Catholic church. She believes that one day these visits will cease and that she and Dennis will get married and have children. She sees these two issues as linked: Dennis's disconnection from his stepmother and his wanting to have a family.

Barbara believes in the ultimate dissolution of Dennis's bond to Mrs Wolcheski because she is not his real mother. Her influence began late, when Dennis was twelve. More importantly, the woman doesn't love Dennis; all she understands is emotional blackmail, guilt, and retribution.

Besides, Barbara secretly thinks the woman is evil.

It was the summer before they bought the house. They drove to Milwaukee to fetch some things Dennis had stored in Mrs Wolcheski's basement. Dennis searched and packed while Barbara sat around looking at old photo albums. She saw pictures of Dennis as a child, of his mother, a sad, over-worked and unhealthy-looking woman, of his father when he was young and of the family hardware store which Dennis's father sold upon his wife's death.

She came upon another album of people she could not identify. There were pictures of a little girl, about four or five, in a smocked dress and Mary Jane shoes. She had long blonde curls falling to her shoulders.

'Who is this child?' she asked, showing Dennis. A daughter, she wondered sadly, now dead?

Dennis frowned. 'That's Billy,' he said.

Mary Agnes sat down at the table between Dennis and Barbara. 'I guess he told you about his latest trip to Madison.'

Barbara shook her head.

Dennis said, 'Oh, he goes up to the massage parlours whenever Mother is away.' After a minute he added, 'The DA says he's going to start cracking down on the johns now when they raid the parlours. That should be good!'

'Poor kid,' said Mary Agnes. 'She'd disown him. Then he'd really be up a creek.'

Billy walked in, holding a whisky Manhattan in one hand; the other hand he held behind his back. He sniffed the glass and said, 'Can't touch the stuff myself.'

'On the wagon, Billy?' said Dennis.

'Can't drink, says the doc. 'Count of my medicine.' He put the drink down and drew from behind his back a wooden plaque, lacquered, cut in an oval, with a picture hook on the back. He handed it to Barbara and said. 'Look what my Pa put on the bar. It sure is funny.'

It said, 'To our guests: If we get to drinking on Sunday and insist you stay till Tuesday, just remember, We don't mean it!'

Then Mrs Wolcheski came out of the basement with the potatoes and picked up her drink. Outside another car pulled into the driveway and Mary Agnes's children jumped out of the car, waving. Mrs Wolcheski waved back. Jim got out of the other side of the car as the children burst into the kitchen.

The girl, who was about four, squealed and dived into Dennis's lap. The boy, a few years older, remained shyly by the door until Dennis called him over. Mary Agnes said, 'Hi, kids. Have a good time?'

Jim walked in. 'Hi, hon. Hi, Mom. Dennis. How's the crime business?' He nodded toward Billy and glanced at Barbara.

'Not too bad,' said Dennis.

'You kids better play outside till dinner,' said Mary Agnes. 'It's a little crowded in here.'

The little girl protested and clung to her uncle's neck, and the boy remained behind him, one hand on Dennis's shoulder. Jim told them to obey their mother and they left out the back door.

Mary Agnes was mixing ground meat with onions and eggs and bread crumbs in a bowl. Jim said, 'What a day! Those two never get tired! I need a drink.' He left the kitchen. Mrs Wolcheski muttered. 'Thinks he lives here!'

Barbara watched the children go, wishing she could join them. She suddenly wanted to be busy and said, 'Can I do anything?'

Mrs Wolcheski looked at her as if she noticed her now for the first time. She seemed slightly offended by the question. She looked at Mary Agnes's preparations and said, 'Well, I guess you could peel potatoes. If you want to.'

'I'll just wash my hands,' said Barbara, standing up. Mrs Wolcheski at that moment picked up her ashtray, walked over to the sink, and began to wash it out. Barbara looked at Dennis who was staring off at nothing, frowning.

'Go ahead and use the bathroom,' said Mary Agnes, looking at Mrs Wolcheski.

Barbara went down the hall towards the bathroom. Suddenly in front of her Jim appeared from the living-room, holding a drink. She stopped a few feet from him, waiting for him to let her pass. He stood, letting his eyes move slowly up and down, examining her. He said. 'I'll bet you're a good teacher.'

'Get out of my way.' He shifted slightly; she had to brush him as she went by.

When she returned to the kitchen she whispered in Dennis's ear, 'I want to leave.'

He frowned. 'I want to leave!' she repeated.

'After we've had dinner.' He looked away and Barbara turned to Mary Agnes, who was holding out a potato peeler to her.

Mrs Wolcheski lit a cigarette and said, 'You wouldn't believe how many people were at the swap-meet today.'

'Really,' said Dennis.

'I don't know where they come from. I've never seen such crowds.'

'Oh?' said Dennis.

'I don't understand why they have to come to Christ King. They can go to their own parish. Of course, Christ King is one of the nicest. But they can still go to their own.' Nobody replied to this, and she sipped her drink. 'Did you know that Billy's a server at Christ King now?'

'No,' said Dennis.

Mary Agnes looked up. 'Where's Billy?'

'At home, I expect,' said Jim, who had come in and was leaning against the refrigerator. 'Or outside, maybe.'

'Go check, Jim.' Jim said nothing.

'Jim, go check.'

'They're fine.'

'Jim,' said Mary Agnes.

'Cool it, baby,' said Jim.

Mary Agnes put her spoon down. 'Jim, bring the kids in. I mean it.'

'OK, OK,' He went out the kitchen door.

'What's the matter?' said Mrs Wolcheski.

'Nothing, Mother,' said Mary Agnes. 'I just think it's a little late for the kids to be outside.' It was nearly dark now.

Jim walked in with the little girl in his arms. The boy was behind him. He set the girl down and said. 'Go watch television, you little Polacks.' Then he whispered to Mary Agnes, 'He wasn't even outside.'

'Don't mess anything up,' yelled Mrs Wolcheski as the children ran out. 'Jim, can you get me another drink?'

'Sure enough, Dolly Pop,' said Jim. Mrs Wolcheski grimaced. She hated it when Jim used her first name that way.

She said to Dennis, 'I don't see why you can't drive down Sundays any more. You could come in the mornings and go to Mass here.'

'I don't want to drive down on Sundays and go to Mass.'

'You drive down on Saturdays.'

'Sundays I row.'

'I wouldn't mind if you went to Mass in Madison.'

'I don't go to Mass, Mother.'

Mrs Wolcheski stubbed out her cigarette. She walked over to Barbara and said, 'I've never seen anybody peel potatoes like that. That's no way to peel potatoes.' Barbara put the potato peeler down and returned to her seat at the kitchen table.

Mrs Wolcheski began to peel violently. 'I don't understand how you've fallen from the church so suddenly.'

'Mother, I haven't gone to church since I left home.'

Jim returned and handed Mrs Wolcheski another whisky Manhattan. She wiped her hands on her apron and took a sip. 'I just can't see what goes wrong with a child after a good Catholic education.'

'Mother, let's not get into this.'

'Mother,' said Mary Agnes, 'do you want carrots or broccoli with the meatloaf?'

'Christ King is a beautiful church. And the school was excellent. Excellent.'

Dennis did not reply. His niece was peeking around the corner into the kitchen and caught his eye. He waved to her to come to him and she ran over and jumped into his lap. He bounced her up and down.

'Didn't you like Christ King?'

'Not particularly.'

'Didn't you get anything out of your education?'

'Mother,' said Mary Agnes, 'would you help me peel the carrots?'

'Heaven knows I tried my best with you two.'

'*Mother*,' said Mary Agnes.

'When I married your father I promised to try my best to do right by you children.' She took a large sip. 'And he was grateful. Grateful. Grateful that I took an interest in you. Grateful that I wanted to give you a decent education. Grateful that I taught both of you, or at least I thought I taught you, what a lady was.'

'Jim,' said Mary Agnes, 'would you take Cecilia into the other room?'

Jim picked up the little girl from Dennis's lap. 'Now, Dolly Pop, you just calm down here and we'll have a nice dinner.'

'I was just as thankful as a woman could be to meet a wonderful man like your father. He was lonely and I was lonely.' Her eyes filled with tears. 'The least I could do was to see to your education.'

'Mother,' said Mary Agnes, 'let's talk about something else.'

'Things weren't like this in my day. A good Catholic education meant something.'

'Mother,' pleaded Mary Agnes.

'Oh, I know what it's like to have a boyfriend. I had a boyfriend once. Yes, before I was married. But I waited, like a lady.'

Barbara opened the back door quietly. Mrs Wolcheski said, 'I waited. Yes. I wore white on my wedding day.' Her voice rose. 'I didn't go around like some fancy woman.' The door closed softly and Mrs Wolcheski turned around and yelled at it, 'And I sure didn't live in sin with anybody!'

Dennis rose and took the drink from his stepmother's hand. 'Mother, you didn't have to say that.' He poured the drink down the sink.

'Why do you have to live together?' wailed Mrs Wolcheski painfully. 'How did this happen to you? What has that girl done to you?'

'Mother,' said Mary Agnes. 'Just stop it now. You're going to get all worked up.'

'Just knowing you're damned,' she wailed louder. 'Damned for eternity!' She sobbed for a few minutes. Dennis and Mary Agnes looked at one another.

Mrs Wolcheski stopped crying suddenly. She glared at Dennis. 'I've made an appointment with my lawyer. About my will.'

'Mother, you should do with your will what you think best,' said Dennis.

'Well, if I die and you haven't come to your senses you won't see a penny. It's in a covenant.'

'Mother, that's your decision. Maybe you should lie down a little bit,' he added.

Mary Agnes glanced out the window and saw Barbara walking down the driveway. After a moment she saw Billy come out of his house and walk down his driveway. The next time she looked out he was crossing the yard toward Barbara.

Barbara is walking up and down the sidewalk in front of Mrs Wolcheski's house. She considered walking to the bus station but she isn't sure where it is. So she walks, waiting.

She expected Dennis to come out fairly quickly after her. She understands that he has to stay and calm the woman down, but she's been walking up and down on this sidewalk for at least ten minutes. He is still in the kitchen. She can see him through the window in the lighted kitchen. He is standing there talking to the woman.

She is cold. She left her sweater in the car and Dennis has the keys. She feels trapped and angry. How did she get into this?

She looks at the church across the street. Behind it is the high school. She tries to imagine adolescent Dennis, sweaty and pimply in his Catholic uniform, walking across the street to school every day.

Before Dennis's father married Mrs Wolcheski Dennis went to a regular public school. It now occurs to Barbara that a Jesuit education was probably not a bad foundation on which to build a career in law, and that Dennis's life might have been very different without Mrs Wolcheski's money. She would rather not believe this; she would rather believe that Dennis would have gone to university and been a lawyer anyway, even though his father did not have much money and worked in a factory, after he sold the hardware store, until he died.

She sees Billy come out of his house and walk down his drive. The house is smaller than Mrs Wolcheski's and in need of repair. The rain gutters are rotting, the shutters need painting, and the yard trimming. Mrs Wolcheski thinks Dennis should do the work but Dennis always refuses.

Billy walks down his driveway casually, humming a little tune. He pretends he has not noticed Barbara but is merely out for an evening stroll. Then he circles back towards his house and surreptitiously glances at her. He stops, goes back down the driveway, watches her for a moment, then crosses. He approaches carefully, as if she is a wild animal and he is not sure how she will react.

Barbara knows that Billy does not know how to classify her. She exists outside his orbit of mother, wife, prostitute. He is mystified that she sleeps with Dennis and does not appear ashamed. He knows that many women who are not prostitutes have slept with Dennis and this amazes him.

Barbara now thinks of Billy's reaction were he to be told something of the true number of Dennis's lovers; Billy is only aware of a small percentage. Billy would be bowled over.

Barbara sighs. She should be thankful that this seems to be less of a problem now. Since they bought the house he hasn't slept with anybody else. He would tell her if he had. He always does. He makes a point of being honest and fair.

'Hello, Billy.'

He comes closer. 'Trouble?'

She smiles at this. Billy has more on the ball than people give him credit for. 'A little bit.'

'Yeah,' he says with understanding. 'That's the way she is.'

Barbara is touched. There was a time, Dennis told Barbara once, when Billy had it pretty well together. At least he had a job, in a factory, and he could drive. Shirley, too, wasn't the basketcase she is now. She worked, cooked dinner every night. Barbara has met her, a nervous, giggly woman.

Barbara remembers seeing the pictures of Billy as a child and how she hugged her unborn children inside her. She swore never to let the woman touch them.

Billy is standing there with his friendly mongrel look. 'Don't pay any attention to her,' he advises. Then, 'I got some Oreos in the house. Want some?'

She smiles. 'No thanks.' She wonders again how she got into a relationship with a man with family like this. People like this do not exist in Madison. 'But thanks anyway.'

Mary Agnes comes out of the house. She says, 'I guess we'll have dinner in a little while, Billy. You'll have to wait.'

'Yeah,' says Billy resignedly. He walks back to his house, glancing over his shoulder twice to look at Barbara.

Mary Agnes sighs. 'Don't mind, Barbara. She's an old lady.'

Barbara tries to think of some reply, fails.

'If you two don't want to drive back tonight you can certainly stay at our house. We can put you in the kids' playroom. The sofa folds out.'

'Thanks, Mary Agnes, that's very kind. But I'm sure we'll be heading back.'

'Sure?'

'Well, here comes Dennis. I guess we'll have to discuss it.'

'Well,' says Dennis, 'she's lying down. She'll be all right in a minute.'

Mary Agnes walks away, saying, 'Let me know what you want to do.'

'What's this about?' says Dennis.

'Oh, she offered to put us up. I told her we'd be driving back.'

'Of course. I'm rowing in the morning. We'll head back as soon as we've had dinner.'

'Sorry,' she says carefully. 'I'm not having dinner.'

'What? Oh, come on. We came for dinner. She's calmed down now. Let's just have dinner.'

She waits. Anger builds. She controls it. It will get her nowhere with him. He shuts up like a clam when she's angry. She wants to say, *To hell with her! Do you think I'm going to go back in that house like nothing happened and eat her food? Are you out of your mind? And why aren't you standing up for me? I was the one who was insulted!*

'I'm not staying. If you don't want to drive home I'll take the bus.' She has never said anything like this before; she has never forced a show-down.

'Don't be obstinate, Barbara. She's lying down. She'll be all right now.'

She is enraged. 'No! Do you understand?'

He sighs. 'Oh, all right. But she's not going to like this. You'll have to come in and say good-bye.'

'I don't give a damn whether she likes it or not. I'm not going back in there.'

Another sigh. 'OK. Wait here. I'll tell her we're leaving.' He walks back up the drive as Mary Agnes comes out. Barbara forgot to ask him for the car keys; she's cold.

'Driving back?' says Mary Agnes.

'Yes.'

'I'm sorry about this, Barbara.'

'Thanks, Mary Agnes.'

Dennis comes back, and they get into the car. Mary Agnes is leaning in the car window. They all wait a moment. Then she says, 'Thank heavens we're not related to them!' They all laugh.

Dennis starts the car. Mary Agnes says, 'Come and see us sometime. The kids love you both.'

'Well,' says Dennis, putting the car into reverse, 'back to sin city!' They drive away, and Mary Agnes stands on the driveway, waving.

They are silent until they get on the interstate.

'Look, I'm sorry.'

By now she is furious. 'That's not the half of it. Your horny brother-in-law accosted me again.'

'Oh.'

This pushes her beyond belief. *Oh?* Is that all he has to say? *Oh?* She puts up patiently with this insane family and that's all he can say? 'It doesn't seem to bother you much,' she says bitterly. Then, she watches misery grow on his face and her rage passes. He is trapped. He is trying to get out the best he can. If she is patient he will eventually extract himself from them.

They drive.

'Well,' he says fatuously, 'we showed her we won't take it any more.' She decides to let this pass. She looks out the window at the black fields and silos against the sky. The city light is behind them; ahead, darkness, except for the road of headlights.

She says idly, 'I can't understand how she can stand being married to him.'

He shrugs. 'Oh, I don't think they're unhappy.'

'How can you say that? He's horrible.'

He shrugs again. 'There are worse marriages.'

She looks at him incredulously. Barbara doesn't know it yet but she will remember this drive back to Madison more clearly than any other. It is their last drive. She will remember looking over at Dennis staring out past the headlights to the road. And, later, in about a year, she will remember how he looked when she also remembers the way he would frown when he was angry and shrug when he didn't want to confront, admit, discuss things.

She will remember the swimming-pool wedding, and how all weddings to Dennis were swimming-pool weddings. How she wanted him to see that there was another way, but he refused to see that. How he had stated at the outset with lawyer-like precision the conditions of their relationship: no marriage, no children, no monogamy. How he grew so irritable whenever she brought up marriage and children. How he refused to see that their house was something they were building together. How much she ignored because she hated his stepmother so much.

Dennis will marry, of course. He will marry and move to the east coast where he will get a job with a big law firm. Barbara will hear about it through friends. She will not be surprised. She will feel vindicated, but that will not make it hurt any less.

But now they are suspended in the car between Madison and Milwaukee. Madison will soon light up the sky, but they are not there yet. Milwaukee and Mrs Wolcheski will recede and fade, but for the moment they are still here, in the car, and Dennis is still part of them.

Easter Break

We packed the bus with our sleeping bags and stove and the rest of the stuff and made the two-hour drive without a hitch. I sat on the engine, on a cushion, between Carolyn and Robert. She drove the whole way and I played with her long black hair until she got tired of it and said, 'Don't.'

Robert is our roommate. We've rented an old house together – it must have been built around 1900 – not far from campus. In the oldest section of town, with a lot of trees. My parents nearly had a fit when they found out I was moving out of the dorm after fall semester. Robert lived in the same dorm, although he is older than us and getting a PhD, and he hated it as much as we did. Robert is gay too and everybody knew it and gave him a hard time about it.

Ever since we moved in together, we've been talking about going down to Mexico in Carolyn's Volkswagen bus. (Her parents are loaded.) But, I absolutely have to go home to see my parents in suburbia land down the interstate at every vacation or I get guilt trips like nobody would believe. So we decided to stop for one night and split the next day to the border.

I worried a little about what they would say about Carolyn, but not too much: my parents are really into pretending that we're this nice, normal family. They never ask me why I don't have any boyfriends. And, they pretend this business when I was sixteen never happened. That was when my girlfriend's parents caught us red-handed in bed and gave us this incredible lecture on how we were going to turn into butch dykes.

It was the middle of the night. They called my parents and my father drove over. I sat in an armchair and stared at the wall while they told my father what they had found us doing. He didn't look at me. He stood, listening, with his hands in his pockets, playing with his keys. He didn't say anything to me on the way home. When we got there, my mother was furious. Standing in the hall, in her nightgown, her hair all messed up, she said, 'Get to bed. You'll never step foot out of this house again. How could you do this to your father?'

I couldn't believe he didn't hit me. He just pretended that it hadn't happened.

As soon as you get a little ways south on the interstate, past these historical monuments about the French and Spanish and all, it starts getting ugly. No more hills or trees, or anything green. It's flat as a pancake and there's nothing but scrub growing along the side of the road and Dairy Queens and Denny's restaurants. When you get close to my parents' suburb, the sleaze begins. My parents will bend your ear telling you what a great place they live in, but it's really a pit: freeways with insane people tailgating you doing eighty, strip joints, big sign boards. Everything new and cheap. Miles and miles of tracts of identical houses.

We get to my house. My parents' house, I mean. It looks like every third house on the street.

We go in and I barely get Robert's and Carolyn's names out before my mother starts trying to stuff our faces. 'You kids must be starving!' she says, waving her arms around, as we drop our backpacks in the hall. She's trying to act like what she thinks mothers are supposed to act like when their daughter comes home from college. Usually, if it's just me, she starts bitching. *What took you so long. You're too late to go to the store for me. If you think I'm doing that laundry you've got another thing coming. How much time are you honouring us with this trip?*

'It's only a two-hour drive, Mom. We'll just have a sandwich.'

She is shaking all over. Our being here is a big deal. I've never brought many friends, much less a guy, home before. She runs into the kitchen, going on about how she can make some enchiladas or an omelette or anything we want.

'It's OK, Mom,' I say, going over to the pantry.

She is smiling at Robert. Then she turns to me and says, 'Sandwiches! I can't let you feed your friends sandwiches!'

'It's no big deal, Mom,' I say, taking out bread and mustard. She looks at me and then suddenly seems to deflate and she sinks into a chair at the kitchen table. She's like that. She gets really worked up and then kind of collapses.

Robert and Carolyn are standing around, looking embarrassed, and I say, 'Sit down, you guys.' My mother jumps up, pulling out chairs and shouting at Robert to sit and would he like anything to drink? Water, Coke, Sprite, orange juice, beer? Or tea, coffee? Or . . . Or . . .? She ignores Carolyn.

Carolyn is Jewish and incredibly beautiful. I was drunk the first time we slept together. I was nervous, like you always are. It's the first kiss that's hard. The first time, girls don't know how to kiss. They don't know what to do when they can't count on somebody else taking all the initiative.

Carolyn's much tougher than me. She thinks I'm weak and gutless for feeling like I have to go home, for feeling guilty. Carolyn doesn't care if people don't like her. She doesn't worry about being accepted. More than anything I admire her indifference, her freedom.

I look at my mother in the chair, breathing like she's been running. I can't believe she is capable of embarrassing me this quickly, and I spend a few minutes looking in the refrigerator. It is crammed full of stuff that my mother usually never buys. It's because I called and told her I was bringing my two roommates with me. It's kind of pathetic. Poor Mom trying to do everything right so that we can be like a normal family. 'Oh! Your friends!' she cried. 'Yes, come home with your friends from college.'

Robert starts telling Mother about the trip and she calms down. Robert can be Mr Manners when he wants; he's especially good with old ladies. My mother keeps repeating things over and over, like she does when she gets nervous. She says, 'You three must be tired after such a long drive,' three times, 'Are you sure you don't want a shower?' twice, and 'Robert, you won't mind it if I put you in Louise's brother's room? He has twin beds,' so many times I lose count.

I find some ham and cheese and stuff and start making sandwiches. I know I have to start preparing her about our going to Mexico, so I start right in on it. It always takes time to ease her in gently to whatever it is I want to do. 'Mom, you know we're going on from here to Mexico.'

She ignores me. She keeps this frozen smile on her face, blinking at Robert across the table. Carolyn looks out the window with a bored expression.

'Mother,' I say. 'We're going to Mexico.'

'Oh?' she says vaguely.

'Mother, I told you we were. I told you two weeks ago.' I try to keep my voice steady.

'Yes, I recall your saying something about maybe going down there.'

Robert is looking at his hands, and Carolyn stares out the window, smirking. 'So, we're really only passing through to say hello.'

'Well, it's dangerous down there right now,' she says. 'I don't think it's a good time to go. There've been attacks on white people.'

'We've been planning to go for a long time and we'll stick together.'

She sighs, as if she is considering whether she will let me go or not, which really pisses me off. I feel like saying, 'I'm eighteen now, and you can't tell me what to do anymore so just shove it.' But I don't. Once we start fighting, it just turns into one big guilt trip, and I am hoping that for once I can get out of here without that.

I sit down and we start eating our sandwiches. Mother says, 'While you're here you should take Carolyn and Robert down to the waterfront. It's so picturesque. Mrs Allen says it looks just like the South of France.' The waterfront is this scummy port where the fishing boats – all of which are filthy – come in. It smells and there's dead fish everywhere, and you can see the oil platforms out in the Gulf.

'We don't want to go to the South of France. We want to go to Mexico.'

She ignores that. 'And you should stop by your aunt's. She asks about you all the time.' I have just seen my aunt at Christmas. There is no way in hell I am going to sit around and drink coffee and listen to her talk about her trip to Florida on the Greyhound bus for the hundredth time. 'Mother, I don't think we'll have much time for visiting. We want to get going soon.'

Robert says, 'Louise, you can go visit your aunt if you want to and we'll do some sightseeing. We can put off starting one day.'

Count on Robert to be Mr Reasonable. I give him the dirtiest look I can manage, and he blushes. Mother smiles her gracious-hostess smile at him and says, 'How long have you been down here, Robert?' Robert's from Boston; he has this park-your-car-in-Harvard-yard accent.

'Mother, Robert is wrong. We don't have a day to spare. We want to try to reach the Yucatan.'

'How do you like studying here, Robert? It's a fine school, isn't it?'

It always amazes me how every time my parents meet somebody from somewhere else, they have to make him admit how great it is here. Robert begins telling her a pack of lies about how much he enjoys living in this crummy state, where rednecks go out on Saturday night to beat up queers. 'Mother,' I interrupt, 'we are going to leave tomorrow.'

'I heard you, Louise,' she says in her most patronizing voice, as if I am a small child interrupting her very adult conversation. 'Perhaps you'd like another beer, Robert?'

After we eat, Robert and Carolyn go out to the bus to get the maps and I do the dishes. 'You must be tired, Louise,' says Mother, and I know what is coming. 'I don't know when I've been so embarrassed. Your behaviour in front of your friends was most – '

'I'm not tired,' I say stubbornly, but I suddenly feel like crying; she is going to do everything she can to keep me from going.

'Louise, we've hardly seen you. Your father thought you would be spending Easter with us.' This really pisses me off. I had made it clear on the phone that I wasn't going to stay more than one night. My parents can't stand it that I'm going to college. They never got over my graduating a year early – they even called the principal and tried to get him to make me do my senior year again – and they think I did something really sneaky by getting a scholarship. My father wouldn't give me a penny if I was starving to death.

I am afraid that I am going to start crying but fortunately my creepy brother walks in. He takes one look at me and says, 'Oh, it's you,' and opens the refrigerator.

'Thanks for the warm welcome,' I say sarcastically, which restores me.

'You're welcome.' His eyes are bloodshot and he smells like the inside of a bong. My brother has probably taken more drugs than Timothy Leary but my mother has convinced herself that he is a 'late bloomer', and my father, that he is just lazy.

Robert and Carolyn come back and I show Robert my brother's room. He says he will take a shower, so I find some towels. Carolyn and I go to my room and look at maps.

She sits on the bed, figuring out how many hours it will take to get as far as Vera Cruz. She didn't want to come here at all. I went through days agonizing over whether I should go and for how long. She kept saying, 'If they give you shit, don't go. Why put yourself through their head trips?'

Now she says, 'Your brother's weird. What's his trip?' Carolyn can be very insulting. Just because she has this nice, loaded family that's so cool, they're always glad to see her, and never ask her too many questions, and buy her anything she wants, she thinks everybody else that isn't that way too is completely abnormal.

'Hell if I know. Too much acid.' I don't want to talk about my stupid brother.

345

'And your mother's a nervous wreck.' She's capable of going on like this until I get angry. It's the only way to get her to stop.

'Lay off,' I say. 'We're getting the hell out of here. If Robert can shut up about my goddamn aunt.'

'Jesus Chree-ist, you're touchy.' She takes off her clothes, and puts on her bathrobe. She's standing by the door. We can hear the shower on in the bathroom and my mother in the kitchen.

'Oh, come on, Carolyn,' I say. We lay down on the bed. She is so beautiful. I love her skin, her hair. When I touch her, I want to know everything about her. Sometimes I wish I could be part of her, live in her. But I can't relax here: I am very nervous and besides, my door doesn't lock and my mother makes a habit of barging in whenever she wants. But, Carolyn wants to do it, and so do I and in a way, it's exciting when there's a chance you might get caught.

Carolyn never slept with a girl before me. She had boyfriends and all that. But, the minute I put the idea in her head, she didn't hesitate one minute. After we moved into the house, she turned into this wild woman, and started bringing girls home. We have our own rooms, even though we usually sleep together, and those nights I lay in bed, listening to them on the other side of the wall. And I fantasize about us being together, and that being enough for her.

I think she thinks of us as a kind of game, not a real relationship. She always acts like I'm trying to get her to, like, marry me, say we'll stay together for ever. Once, after a fight, she went out and brought a guy home just to remind me that I can't make her into what I want, I can't own her.

I don't want to make her into anything. I just want her to love me. But maybe what you are isn't ever enough for somebody. I remember going to Sunday school when I was a kid and being told that God loves you no matter what you were like. I don't believe this. I don't believe that God will love me if I keep on being gay, if I keep on hurting my parents. I believe that when I die, I'll be alone.

I barely get my clothes on again when sure enough my mother

comes barging in. She takes one look at Carolyn, who's got my robe on now and says, 'What have you been doing?'

'We're just talking. Carolyn's going to take a shower when Robert gets out.'

She frowns. 'Your father's home. I think you should come down and see him. Dinner will be ready in a little bit.'

'Right, Mom.' She closes the door. I can hear my father downstairs droning on. 'What a pompous ass,' I think. I got 'pompous ass' from Carolyn. It really fits my father. I listen to him, and then I realize he must be talking to Robert.

Carolyn goes into the bathroom, and I go downstairs. There he is, holding a drink and waving his other hand around, trying to look intelligent. He ignores me, which is what he usually does. I figure that Mother has told him that Robert is getting a Ph.D. and now he is trying to impress him. My stupid father thinks I don't have any business at a university, but the minute he hears the word 'Ph.D.', he fawns like a groupie.

He goes on about this stupid city like it's some kind of cultural centre of the universe, with concerts and theatre and all and how Robert would appreciate living in a city like this. Not that my father ever put a foot in the theatre. He starts boasting about the story we heard three million times growing up about how he had to study at night school and how it took him so long to get his degree. A lot of good it did him. Still works in the same stupid job, still lives in the same crummy house in the kind of neighbourhood I have nightmares about. I think I am going to die of embarrassment. But Robert just smiles and nods. He could be an actor.

Then my father gets on his favourite subject: kids these days. He can't understand why my brother doesn't take advantage of the wonderful education opportunities this wonderful country of ours has to offer. My father is very big on how this country is the best place in the world.

'He just can't understand the importance of getting good training. Getting a foot in the door. I told him I'd pay for his tuition at the community college.' Like hell you would, I thought. 'But, no. Kids don't have to work these days. That's the problem with them. They get through college without working and they don't have to pay for it. We didn't have all this financial aid when I was in college. No sir. No scholarships for me. I did it the hard way. And they didn't just pass us like they do now. Hell no.'

'Well, Robert,' says my mother, 'we know how hard you've worked for your degree.' But my stupid father hasn't even realized that he's insulted Robert.

Robert just smiles and smiles. Carolyn comes down. My parents ignore me and Carolyn all through dinner and fawn all over Robert. I can tell the strain is getting to him. I want to ask him if he doesn't want to stay a few more days after all.

The next day is Saturday. We eat breakfast and load the bus. Mother gets up just as we finish and comes into the kitchen, where we are making some coffee for our thermos. She says with fake surprise, 'You've already made breakfast?' I know then we are in for a rough time.

'We wanted to pack the bus,' I say.

'Pack the bus?'

'We can't thank you enough. You've been such a wonderful hostess,' Robert says.

'Well, you're welcome, Robert. It's been a pleasure to have you. You'll have to come back the next time you're down this way.'

'We've decided,' Robert goes on because I made him promise to say this last night, 'to head out early and beat the holiday traffic.'

'What's this?' Mother says, turning to me as if this is the first time she's ever heard anything about it.

'We're leaving, Mom.'

'But you just got here.'

'Mother, I told you we were just going to pass through on our way to Mexico.'

'I would have thought you would want to spend Easter with your family.'

Robert and Carolyn start to back out of the kitchen. *Goddamn you*, I think. 'We'll finish packing,' Carolyn says and they split, the traitors. 'Just tell them it's your goddamn life,' she told me on the way downstairs this morning. Like it's that easy.

'I don't see why you can't go some other time with your friends.'

'I can't skip classes. This is my only vacation until the summer.'

'Well, you could go then.'

'It's too hot.'

'Well, that's not my fault. Besides, you see your friends all the time.'

'Mother, it's my vacation. I want to go with them.' My voice cracks, and she pounces right on it.

'You just think the world of yourself since you got that scholarship. You think we just live here for your convenience. You'll never believe, will you, that you broke your father's heart when you left home.'

'Is that why he hasn't said two words to me since I got here?'

'Did it ever occur to you, young lady, that maybe he is just too upset? Your moving out of that dorm, and just coming in and out of this house when it pleases you? How do you think we feel having our daughter behave like this?' She starts to cry.

I can never win. I can't fight them. I know I am going to start crying now too, and I suddenly just don't feel like fighting: no matter what I do, they turn it into some kind of cruel thing I am doing just to hurt them.

I walk out of the kitchen and towards the door to go out and tell Carolyn and Robert I won't be going with them. She's going to kill me. 'What's the worst they can do?' she said before we left. 'Disinherit you?' This idea wouldn't bother her. I reach the door and then my father comes out of the bedroom and sees my mother. He says, 'What's going on here?'

'Louise is leaving,' she sniffs.

'What do you mean, leaving?'

'We had planned on going to Mexico,' I say.

'When the hell do you think you can just pop in and out of here when it suits you?'

'I told Mother two weeks ago that we were just stopping through on our way.'

'Well, you didn't clear it with me.'

I sigh. I know there is going to have to be a big fight, and suddenly, I feel better. If we fight, I can leave. I say, 'I don't live here anymore.'

'Oh, you don't, well, you think you're so smart with your scholarship, let me tell you young lady if I wanted to I could make you move home and take you out of that college. I can make you work and pay us for your room and board.' This isn't true – I am eighteen – but he thinks it is. 'You live up there only because I say you can.'

I close my eyes, waiting for the blow. I wish he would just get it over with and then I can walk out. But, it doesn't come. I hear the door open and Robert say, 'Sorry to disturb you. I just wondered if – ?' I open my eyes; my parents' faces are frozen; Robert closes the door.

My father watches the door close, and says, 'Why can't you learn something from that fine young man?'

I say, without thinking, 'For your information, Robert's a fag.' I can't believe I say this; I have never said anything like this before to him.

My father's face stops like a switch was thrown and then dissolves into fragments. 'What?' All the air seems to rush out of him, like an old balloon. I have never seen him so stunned.

'A fag. A queer. A fairy. Your fine young man. The one you tried to impress so much because he's getting a stupid Ph.D.' I want to laugh, and at the same time I am horrified. I can't believe I am doing this, flaunting this, gloating. 'Spending the night in the same room with your precious son.'

My mother comes up then. 'How dare you talk to your father that way?'

We stand there a minute, all of us afraid of what I might say next. I know I have torn something, exposed us irreparably.

I say, 'Well, I think I'd better get going. They're waiting for me.'

'Well, I'm so-o glad we had the honour of your presence,' my mother says.

I walk towards the door. 'Please drop in again at your convenience,' she goes on.

I walk out the door and they follow. Carolyn is in the driver's seat, tapping her hand on the steering wheel, and Robert is standing outside, looking at a map. Carolyn sees me and starts the engine.

I turn around and look at my parents standing in the doorway. 'Look, I'm sorry –' And I am. I'm sorry that we can't just be normal together. I'm sorry I'm not what they want.

Mother starts to cry. 'Why don't you come home? Come home and go to the community college and meet a nice boy?'

My father puts his hands in his pockets. He looks so pathetic. I take a step backwards, wishing we were already gone and feeling this creeping fear that I can't leave them, that I will go to the bus, take out my backpack and sleeping bag, stay home, make up for everything – going to college, girls, making them suffer, leaving, staying, being.

But then they look at me with that begging look. Like I'm supposed to forgive them for giving me a hard time. Like I'm supposed to feel responsible for their misery. Then I know that from somewhere I will yet again find the anger to leave them, like this, at the front door, suffering, pleading.

We look at each other for a moment, and then I hate them. I really hate them. They make me hate them; it's the only way I have of getting away from them again. Until the next time. I turn and run towards the bus.

I get in next to Carolyn and Robert climbs in, slamming the door. We drive off. Nobody waves. In a few minutes we are on the interstate headed south.